ROGUE ONE

A STAR WARS STORY

ROGUE ONE
A *STAR WARS* STORY™

ALEXANDER FREED

BASED ON A STORY BY
JOHN KNOLL AND GARY WHITTA

SCREENPLAY WRITTEN BY
CHRIS WEITZ AND TONY GILROY

DEL REY
NEW YORK

Copyright © 2016 by Lucasfilm Ltd. & ® or ™ where indicated.
All rights reserved.

Published in the United States by Del Rey, an imprint of Random House,
a division of Penguin Random House LLC, New York.

DEL REY and the HOUSE colophon are registered trademarks of
Penguin Random House LLC.

ISBN 978-0-399-17845-0
Ebook ISBN 978-0-399-17846-7

Printed in the United States of America on acid-free paper

randomhousebooks.com

2 4 6 8 9 7 5 3 1

First Edition

Book design by Elizabeth A. D. Eno

THE DEL REY
STAR WARS
TIMELINE

A long time ago in a galaxy far, far away. . . .

ROGUE ONE

A *STAR WARS* STORY

PROLOGUE

GALEN ERSO WAS NOT A good farmer. That was only one of his many flaws, but it was the reason he was still alive.

A man of more diverse talents—a different Galen, a Galen who could intuit what colonial crops would thrive in an alien world's soil, or who could check a withered tree for rot without peeling away its bark—would have grown bored. His mind, left idle in the fields, would have returned to subjects he had forsworn. That Galen, consciously or by habit, would have sought out the very work that had driven him to exile. He would have stared into the hearts of stars and formulated theorems of cosmic significance.

In time, he would have *drawn attention*. His obsessions would surely have killed him.

Yet an unskilled farmer was anything but idle; so the true Galen, the one who inhabited the realm of reality instead of idle fantasy, had no trouble filling his days on Lah'mu without succumbing to temptation. He took bacterial samples off boulders left by prehistoric volcanoes and looked in awe at the evergreen moss and grass and weeds that seemed to sprout from every surface. He surveyed the endless crooked hills of his domain, and he was grateful that he had yet to master his new profession.

He constructed these thoughts like an equation as he looked out the window, past his orderly rows of budding skycorn and toward the black soil of the beach. A tiny girl played near the rows, sending her toy soldier on adventures in the dirt.

"Is she digging again? I swear she didn't learn the words *strip-mining* from me, but we're going hungry next year if she keeps this up."

The words breached Galen's concentration slowly. When he heard them, understood them, he smiled and shook his head. "The agricultural droids will repair the damage. Leave her be."

"Oh, I never planned to do anything. That girl is all yours."

Galen turned. Lyra's lips curled until she smiled. She'd started smiling again the day they'd left Coruscant.

He began to reply when the sky rumbled with a boom unlike thunder. One portion of Galen's mind narrowed its focus and was aware of only his wife before him, his daughter on the beach. The other portion processed the situation with mechanical precision. He was walking without conscious intent, striding past Lyra and the cluttered kitchen table and the worn couch that reeked of clove aftershave. He passed through a doorway and reached a device that might have evolved in the junkyard of a machine civilization—all cracked screens and loose wires, apt to shatter at a touch. He adjusted a dial and studied the video image on the screen.

A shuttlecraft was landing on his farm.

Specifically, a *Delta*-class T-3c, all sharp angles and bare metal. It busily broadcast active scans of the landscape as its broad wings folded in for landing and its sublight engines tapered their thrust. Galen studied the associated readouts and let the specifications settle into his memory—not because they might be useful, but because he wanted to procrastinate for just a moment. To shut away the implications of what he was seeing.

He squeezed his eyes shut and gave himself *three* seconds, *two, one.*

Then it was time to accept that his family's life on Lah'mu was over.

"Lyra," he said. He assumed she was near, but didn't turn to look.

"Is it him?" she asked. She sounded unafraid, which frightened Galen more than anything.

"I don't know. But we have to—"

"I'll get started," she said.

Galen nodded without looking from the console.

Galen was not prone to panic. He knew what needed doing, had rehearsed it on those rare days when the farm tended to itself or on those less rare nights when sleep eluded him. Such preparations were the only obsessions he permitted himself. He turned to another machine, tapped in a code, and tore a series of cords from the wall with swift jerks. He began another countdown in his head; if the data purge did not complete in five minutes, he would begin physically destroying components.

He heard footsteps at the front door, quick and light. He turned to see Jyn dash inside, brown hair matted and face touched with dirt. She'd left her toy in the fields. Galen felt an unexpected pang and feared—absurdly, he knew—that the loss of Stormy would distress her once she was far from the farm.

"Mama—"

Lyra stepped away from the bundle of clothes and datapads and portable meals she'd piled on one chair and knelt before the girl whose pale, slender features mirrored hers. "We know. It's all right."

Galen approached the pair, waited until his daughter had seen him. He spoke softly but somberly. "Gather your things, Jyn. It's time."

She understood, of course. She always did, when it mattered. But Galen had no time to be proud.

He turned back to his machines as Jyn sprinted to her room. The data purge had not completed. There were other files he had to handle as well, files he should have erased on Coruscant but which he'd brought to Lah'mu instead. (Why had he done that? Was it nostalgia?

Misplaced pride?) He opened a drawer stuffed with spare droid parts and removed the arm of an agricultural unit. He flipped open a small panel, dug his fingertips between wires, and extracted a datachip.

"The scrambler, please?" he said.

Lyra passed him a metal orb the size of his palm. He inserted the datachip and—before he could doubt himself—pressed the toggle. The orb heated and produced a smell like burning hair. He tossed it in the junk drawer and felt a tightness in his stomach.

"If there's anything else, make it quick." Lyra's tone was clipped. A light blinked faster on the sensor console.

"Set the rendezvous and take Jyn," he said. "I'll finish here."

Lyra abruptly stopped double-checking her bundle of provisions. "That wasn't the plan, Galen."

"I'll meet you there."

"You have to come with us."

Her eyes were hard. *Please smile,* he thought.

"I have to buy you time," he said.

The sensor light went dark. A fault seemed unlikely.

Lyra just watched him.

"Only I can," he said.

It was an argument impossible to refute. Lyra didn't try. She stalked into the kitchen and tapped at the comm unit as Galen made for Jyn's room. He caught just a snippet of Lyra's words: *"Saw—it's happened. He's come for us."*

Jyn stood with her bulging satchel at her feet. Galen surveyed the tiny chamber's remaining contents: a few toys, the cot. Easy enough to hide. Enough to buy a few more minutes. He pushed a doll out of sight before returning to the doorway.

"Jyn. Come here."

He considered what he might say; considered what impression he wanted to leave Jyn if everything ended in disaster.

"Remember—" He spoke with deliberate care, hoping to etch the words in her bones. "Whatever I do, I do it to protect you. Say you understand."

"I understand," Jyn said.

And this time, of course, she *didn't* understand. What eight-year-old could? Galen heard his own foolishness, his ego echoed by her voice. He wrapped her in his arms, felt her slender, warm body against him, and knew a better memory to leave her with.

"I love you, Stardust."

"I love you, too, Papa."

That would be enough.

He looked to his wife, who stood waiting. "Galen," she began, all the harshness gone.

"Go," he said.

She did, coaxing Jyn with her. Galen allowed himself the luxury of watching, heard his daughter offer a last confused, "Papa?" Then they were gone from the house, and he resumed his work.

He collected objects out of place—more toys, Lyra's clothes, unwashed dishes from the kitchen—and stashed them in niches he and Lyra had prepared long ago. He checked the unfinished data purge, returned his mind's eye to his mental countdown. A few seconds past the five-minute deadline. That meant he could keep busy while he awaited his visitors.

By the time Galen heard muffled voices approaching the farmhouse, two of his homemade data processing units billowed acrid smoke as their circuits melted. He stepped out the front door to greet the new arrivals under the cloudy sky.

A company in bleached white and gleaming black advanced toward the doorstep. The leader was a narrow man of Galen's own age in a spotless ivory officer's uniform, head high and movements stiff. The breeze failed to disturb the sandy hair beneath his cap. His cohorts wore armor like a scarab's shell, bore pistols and rifles as if ready for war. The troopers stepped when their leader stepped, matched his pace; to Galen, they seemed to exist only as extensions of their superior.

The man in white halted less than three meters away. "You're a hard man to find, Galen," he said, not quite smiling.

"That was the idea." Galen did not quite smile, either, though he could have. He could have let the farm and sky fade, let the troopers become shadows, and conjured an office on Coruscant around him; allowed himself to believe he was sparring again with his friend and colleague Orson Krennic.

There was no point in nostalgia, however. Orson surely knew that as well as he.

Orson was tugging at his gloves as he studied the fields with an exaggerated crane of his neck. "But farming? A man of your talents?"

"It's a peaceful life," Galen returned.

"Lonely, I'd imagine."

With those words, Orson had declared his game and his stakes. It did not surprise Galen.

"Since Lyra died, yes," Galen said.

The corner of Orson's mouth twitched, as if he were taken aback. "My sincerest condolences," he said, then gestured to the troopers and spoke more sternly. "Search the house. Shut down any machines— we'll want them examined by the technicians."

Four of the troopers obediently, rapidly, made for the doorway. Galen stepped aside to allow them past.

"I don't imagine," Orson said, "you've laid any traps? Nothing that would harm a patriot doing his duty?"

"No."

"No," Orson agreed. "I've always found your constancy refreshing. Galen Erso is an *honest* man, unaltered by stress or circumstance."

Troopers called to one another in the house behind Galen, and he stifled the impulse to turn. "Honest, perhaps. Still just a man."

Orson spread his hands, conceding the point. He moved as if to join the troopers in the house, then stopped. "When did she die?" he asked.

"Two, three years, I think. It's a bit of a blur."

"She was a wonderful woman. Strong. I know you loved her very much."

"What is it you want?"

The words were a mistake. Galen barely hid his wince as he heard himself, recognized the edge to his voice. The longer he played, the longer Lyra and Jyn had to escape. Instead he'd grown impatient.

Orson was replying carelessly, feigning the blunt honesty of a man too worn to lie. "The work has stalled, Galen. I need you to come back."

"I have the utmost confidence in you. In your people."

"You don't," Orson snapped. "You were never that humble."

"And you have too little faith in your own skills," Galen said easily. "I told you that when we were practically children. You could have done everything I did, but you preferred to dabble; to shepherd people instead of nurture theory. I always respected your decision, but don't let it narrow your world."

All of it was true. All of it was also designed to hurt Orson, to pry at his insecurities. Galen kept his tone measured, casual. Infuriatingly so, perhaps, but Orson's fury did not frighten him. He feared focus, efficiency, speed; not wild rage.

Orson only grimaced—a forced smile that didn't take. "You *will* come back."

So much for that sidetrack. Galen straightened his back. They were coming to the end. "I won't do it. This is where I belong now."

"Scratching the dirt with a shovel? We were on the verge of greatness, Galen. We were *this* close to providing peace, security for the galaxy."

Behind Galen came the sound of ceramics shattering as the troopers continued their search. He mentally cataloged dishes and ornamental vases, then dismissed the list. Nothing in the house mattered.

"You're confusing peace with terror. You lied about what we were building."

"Only because you were willing to believe."

"You wanted to kill people."

Orson shrugged, unmoved by the argument. "We have to start somewhere."

Galen almost laughed. He remembered when he could laugh with Orson, instead of feeling nothing but hollow defiance.

Snapping sounds from the house. Furniture being broken apart, hiding places revealed. Orson would have his proof momentarily.

"I'd be of no help, Krennic." *Needle him. Deny all familiarity.* "My mind just isn't what it was." And now he could only talk, not try to persuade or to enrage or do anything more than buy a few more seconds, a few precious moments for Lyra and Jyn. "I thought at first it was only the work—I would sit some nights and remember equations and theorems, but I couldn't hold them in my head anymore. I chalked it up to exhaustion, to forgoing the habits of a focused intellect . . ." He shook his head. "But it's more than that. Now I have trouble remembering the simplest things."

Orson wove gloved fingers together, eyes glittering with cruel amusement. "Your child, for example? Galen, you're an inspired scientist, but you're a terrible liar."

Orson didn't need his troopers to report an extra bed or a toy left out in the fields. There would be no more delays for Galen, no hope of hiding his family's presence on Lah'mu.

He prayed that Lyra would fare better. She had never failed him before.

Galen put aside even that thought to picture his daughter in her arms.

Lyra ran, her fingers wrapped around the fragile wrist of her daughter. She pulled without tenderness. She heard Jyn whimper in pain, felt the girl stumble beside her, and longed to hoist her in both arms, carry her across the rocks and clutch her to her breast.

She longed to, but she couldn't carry her daughter and crouch low enough to take advantage of the concealing hills. She couldn't add another twenty-five kilograms onto the supplies she carted on her back and still maintain her speed. Lyra loved her daughter, but love wouldn't save them today.

Lyra had always been the practical one in the family.

Damn you, Galen, she thought, *for sending us away.*

She caught a flash of motion out of the corner of her eye, turned to confirm that it wasn't the wind, and tugged Jyn down as she dived onto moist soil. Her stomach already hurt from the run. The cool dirt felt good on her body, but her forehead prickled with sweat and fear. She peeked around the rocks to watch a half dozen figures—black-clad Imperial troopers led by a uniformed officer in white—stride rapidly toward the farmhouse.

No, not just an officer in white. *Orson Krennic* was leading a death squad to the farmhouse. Toward Galen.

"Mama—" Jyn was whispering, tugging at her hand. "I know that man."

That caught Lyra by surprise. But Jyn had her father's mind, if not his obsessions. Her memory was better than Lyra's had ever been.

That's your father's special friend Orson, she wanted to say. *He's a lying bastard who thinks he's a visionary.* Instead she whispered, "Shh," and pressed two fingers to Jyn's lips before kissing her on the forehead. "We need to keep going. Don't let them see you, okay?"

Jyn nodded. But she looked terrified.

They moved together, as swiftly as Lyra could manage while squatting out of sight. Her hips were cramping as she led Jyn around the base of a comm spire and stopped again to peer toward the farmhouse. She couldn't make out Krennic past the troopers, couldn't see if Galen had emerged, but the group had halted near the front door. Lyra suddenly pictured the armored figures raising flamers, reducing the house to ash and charred metal while her husband screamed inside . . .

She knew better. So long as Krennic was in control, Galen would stay alive long after the rest of them were dead. He would have no choice but to work for that man until he was old and feeble, until his intellect began to fail him and the Empire determined he was no longer useful.

Lyra realized she'd made a decision.

She unslung her bag, rooted through the contents until she found what she needed. She set a bundle of clothes in the grass and placed her hands on Jyn's shoulders. The girl was trembling. She met her mother's gaze.

"You know where to go, don't you?" Lyra asked. "Wait for me there. Don't come out for *anyone* but me."

Jyn didn't answer. Lyra saw the moisture in her eyes. A voice told

Lyra, *If you leave her now, she's done. You've taken all her strength away.*

But Lyra had committed herself to a path. Her husband needed her more than her daughter.

She hurriedly reached to her own throat, pushing away coarse cloth until her fingers caught a fraying string. She pulled off her necklace, watched the pendant swing in the breeze. The jagged, cloudy crystal was etched with writing on one side. Gently, she put the necklace over Jyn's head. The girl didn't move.

"Trust the Force," Lyra said, and made herself smile.

"Mama—"

"I'll be there," Lyra whispered. "Now go."

She wrapped Jyn in her arms—*Don't hold her too long, don't give her time to think*—and turned the girl around, pushed her away. Lyra watched her daughter stumble amid the rocks, disappearing out of sight.

It was time to refocus. Jyn would be safe. Safer if Lyra did this, safer still if she succeeded, but safe either way. She looked back to the farmhouse and the group gathered around the doorstep, lifted the bundle of clothes, and walked back the way she came. She kept her body low, picked up her pace as she saw four troopers enter the house and reveal Galen and Krennic standing together. She heard their voices, faintly. Krennic unctuously declaring *We have to start somewhere.*

She hadn't expected to see an opening so quickly. She'd wanted more time to plan. But there was no guarantee she'd catch Krennic with fewer bodyguards anytime soon. She straightened and hurried, kept the bundle clutched close.

Krennic saw her first, though he spoke only to Galen. "Oh, look! Here's Lyra. Back from the dead. It's a miracle."

Galen turned in her direction. She'd rarely seen such pain on his face. "Lyra . . ." But he was looking past her, searching the fields for Jyn.

Lyra almost wanted to smile.

The black-clad troopers raised their weapons. "Stop!" Krennic snapped.

Lyra let the clothes fall from her arms and raised the blaster she'd concealed beneath the pile. She aimed the barrel at Krennic, felt the chill metal of the trigger under her finger. She didn't look at the troopers. If they killed her, all she needed to do was twitch.

The troopers kept their weapons low. Krennic smirked at Lyra. "Troublesome as ever."

"You're not taking him," Lyra said.

"No, of course I'm not. I'm taking you all. You, your child. You'll all live in comfort."

"As hostages."

She'd lived that life before, or close enough. She had no desire to do it again.

Krennic seemed unperturbed. "As 'heroes of the Empire.'"

Lyra heard Galen's voice to one side. "Lyra. Put it down." The concern in his tone felt like a weight on her arm, a hand on her wrist. She kept the blaster up anyway, ignoring her husband.

Krennic wasn't smiling anymore. Lyra let the words, the threats, roll out. She'd imagined this before, made speeches in her mind to the man who'd ruined her life again and again, and the actuality felt, in turn, dreamlike. "You're going to let us go," she said. "You're going to do it because you're an egomaniacal coward. And I'm sure if your superiors let you live you'll come after us again, and that's fine. But *right now* we go free. Do you understand?"

Krennic merely nodded and said, "Think very carefully."

She sensed the troopers tensing. She knew, somehow, that Galen was staring at her in horror. And she suddenly realized that she'd misjudged Orson Krennic's cowardice—that he'd changed in the years since she'd known him, or she'd never understood him even in the old days.

Jyn would still be safe.

Maybe she could still save her husband.

"You'll never win," she said.

Krennic cocked his head. A patronizing gesture to an outmatched opponent.

"Do it," he said.

Lyra pulled the trigger, felt the blaster jump even as light flashed nearby and hot pulses ravaged her chest. She heard the troopers' shots only after she felt the pain—dull, almost numb pinpricks up and down her body, each surrounded by a halo of excruciation. Her muscles seemed to vibrate like plucked strings. Galen was shouting her name, rushing toward her as she fell, but she couldn't see him. All she saw was Krennic, clutching a black and smoking shoulder as he snarled through pain.

If Lyra could have screamed, she would have screamed not in agony, but in rage. She could not scream, however, and she went into darkness bitterly.

Her last thought was: *I wish Galen weren't here to see.*

The last things she heard were Galen shouting her name and a furious voice calling, "They have a child. Find it!" But she was too far gone to understand the words.

Jyn wasn't a bad girl. Jyn didn't like to misbehave. When her parents told her to do something, she *almost always* did it. Not fast, but eventually (*almost always* eventually). She didn't deserve to be punished.

She knew she shouldn't have stayed to watch her mother talk to Papa and the man in white. But she couldn't have known what would happen. She couldn't have known what the troopers would do . . .

Had they been talking about her? Was it her fault?

Mama wasn't moving. Papa held her in his arms. Jyn couldn't stop herself from crying, but she held back a scream because she had to be brave. She *had* to be.

She'd seen how scared Mama had been. Whoever the strangers were, Jyn knew they would hurt her, too.

And she knew what she was supposed to do. She needed to behave now. She needed to make things better.

She had trouble breathing as she ran. Her nose and eyes streamed, and her throat felt swollen and clogged. She heard voices in the distance, electronic voices like droids or garbled comms. The troopers were coming after her.

She was wheezing with a high-pitched sound that would give her away. Her face felt like it burned hot enough to see for kilometers. She knew where she was going, though. Papa had tried to pretend it was a game, all those times he asked her to race and find the hiding spot, but she'd known better. She'd asked Mama about it once; she'd held Jyn's hand and smiled and said, "Just pretend it's a game anyway. It'll make your father feel better."

She wanted to pretend now, but it was hard.

She found the spot Papa had showed her among the piled rocks. She dragged open the hatch cover embedded in the hillside, almost shaking too hard to tug it free. Inside, a ladder led to the lower compartment, but Jyn stayed by the cover and pulled it shut. A sliver of light escaped through the hatch, illuminating the dusty gloom.

She pulled her knees to her chest and sang one of her mother's songs, rocking back and forth, ignoring her tear-streaked face and filthy hands. This was part of pretending, too. All she had to do was wait. That was all she'd ever been told to do in the hiding spot.

Mama or Papa would come for her.

She smelled smoke, and the smoke stung her eyes worse than her tears. She could see the shapes of troopers moving among the rocks, but even though they went back and forth and back and forth they never noticed the hatch. Never saw her shelter. When the daylight began to fade, they left and Jyn climbed down the ladder.

The lower compartment was too small for comfort, made cramped by stockpiles of food and machines and containers, but she could sit. She found a lantern and watched its feeble light wax and wane through the night as she listened to the rumble of a storm outside and the splashing of rainwater down the hill above her. She tried to sleep, but she never slept for long—raindrops crept into the cave and tapped at her forehead and sleeves no matter how she arranged herself.

Even her dreams were about that insistent tapping. Those wet, random strikes. In her dreams, sometimes Mama fell down when the raindrops hit Jyn.

When morning came, she woke to the sound of metal scraping above her. For an instant she confused dreams with reality and thought Mama or Papa had arrived at last—she believed what she'd seen the day before was a nightmare, and that this was another of Papa's games.

But only for an instant.

She looked up. The hatch opened, and silhouetted above her was an armored figure with a dark face graven with scars. The man looked down at Jyn with eyes that gleamed in the lantern's light and spoke in a voice of command:

"Come, my child. We have a long ride ahead of us."

Orson Krennic observed Galen aboard the shuttlecraft and wondered when the man would finally pry himself from the gurney where his wife's corpse sprawled. "We'll bring her home," Krennic said. "I promise."

Galen said nothing and stroked his wife's hand.

What more did I expect? Krennic wondered.

Lyra would have survived if not for her own foolishness. Krennic had risked his life for Galen and his family, given Lyra every opportunity to stand down rather than immediately signaling his troops to fire. *That* would have been the safest bet—his death trooper elites were *unkind* men who, given their druthers, would have ended the standoff far less mercifully.

She'd *shot* him!

He'd tried to spare Lyra for Galen's own comfort, out of an understanding that genius worked best without distractions—and yes, out of a desire to honor the cordiality, if not friendship, he and Galen had once shared. Yet self-imposed exile had changed Galen: He was no longer a man of dispassionate contemplation, able to interpret facts without prejudice. Whatever Krennic said, every action he took, was to be interpreted by Galen as the ruthless ploy of a scheming power-monger.

This irked Krennic—of course it irked him, to have the rapport of years so neatly dismissed—but he could *use* it. If Galen refused to readjust (perhaps a man who changed so swiftly once could swiftly change again?), then Krennic could play the monster to ensure his cooperation.

The bandage around his shoulder rendered his arm immobile. He'd need weeks, if not months to fully recover, with who-knew-how-many hours spent immersed in medicinal bacta tanks. The pain would be considerable once the analgesics wore off, yet he could forgive that; not so the loss of time.

Any debt he owed Galen was now repaid.

"We will find the child," he said, more insistent.

Galen did not look away from Lyra's body (another gift from Krennic—who else would have brought her home for a proper funeral?). "I think if you haven't found her already," Galen murmured, "you are very unlikely to succeed."

Krennic bristled, but there was truth to the words. Jyn had clearly received outside aid—the signal sent from the farmhouse suggested as much—and Krennic was not prepared to underestimate her rescuer's competence. He hoped investigation of the comm stations, no matter how badly Galen had damaged them, would reveal the particulars; the results would determine how he turned the situation to his advantage.

If Galen was unsure of his daughter's fate—if he'd sent out a general distress call or offered a reward for retrieval to every smuggler or bounty hunter in receiving range—then Krennic's dogged pursuit of the girl would incentivize Galen to cooperate. Galen would never admit to it, of course, but he would be soothed by the certainty of knowing his daughter was in Imperial hands.

Conversely, if Galen knew *exactly* who had rescued Jyn, then perhaps it was best to leave well enough alone and use the threat of Imperial interference as impetus for cooperation.

All of which, Krennic realized with a start, was a worry for another day. He'd been so consumed by his mission that he had failed to appreciate his own victory.

After a long search, Galen was back in his hands. The scientific setbacks, the engineering problems plaguing Krennic's teams would soon vanish. The constant needling from men like Wilhuff Tarkin—

bureaucrats without any true sense for the *scope* of Krennic's accomplishments—would soon be over. These were truths worth celebrating.

Krennic smiled at Galen and shook his head fondly. "Your wife will be honored. We'll have the service as soon as we reach Coruscant. But meanwhile . . . shall we discuss the work?"

Galen finally turned and looked at Krennic with loathing.

Then, almost imperceptibly, he nodded.

SUPPLEMENTAL DATA:
REBEL ALLIANCE INTELLIGENCE UPDATE

[Document #NI3814 ("Situational Analysis Regarding Jedha, et al."), timestamped approximately thirteen years after the conscription of Galen Erso by Orson Krennic; from the personal files of Mon Mothma.]

There is no hard evidence of an interplanetary engineering project consuming Imperial resources (living, financial, and material) on a massive scale. That remains the bottom line, as it has since our investigation began.

Yet as before, we consider this statement insufficient and our situation grave.

Major tactical deployments of Imperial forces to strategically insignificant worlds continue on Jedha, Patriim, Eadu, Horuz, and twelve others of note. Frequent communications blackouts make analysis of these deployments exceedingly difficult, and we strongly suspect our list is neither accurate nor complete. Nonetheless, we know that a majority of the worlds in question contain facilities for resource harvesting, manufacturing, or scientific research and development. More recently, we have learned that several of these worlds share a set of nonstandard security protocols far exceeding the Imperial norm.

We have intercepted multiple communiqués sent to Orson Krennic, the Empire's advanced weapons research director, from these worlds. We are not yet able to decrypt them.

We have intercepted multiple communiqués sent to one "Galen Erso" from these worlds. We are not yet able to decrypt them or confirm that the "Galen Erso" referenced is the former head of multiple high-energy research projects (including "Celestial Power"—see notes) once housed on Coruscant.

We have intercepted multiple communiqués referencing a future weapons test of indeterminate scale.

Our attempts to surveil Imperial activities related to this matter have resulted in the loss of several operatives. We request additional personnel. Attempts to obtain the cooperation of Saw Gerrera on Jedha have been ended at the recommendation of General Jan Dodonna.

We understand that our concerns are considered controversial inside Alliance council leadership. We do not dispute that intelligence resources should be focused on the Senate if there is to be any hope of a peaceful political resolution to the larger struggle. Several analysts have declined to attach their names to this document for fear of giving it "undue credibility."

But this is not a conspiracy theory, and ignorance will not protect us from whatever the Galactic Empire is building.

Full report is attached.

CHAPTER 1

THE RING OF KAFRENE WAS a monumental span of durasteel and plastoid anchored by a pair of malformed planetoids within the Kafrene asteroid belt. It had been founded as a mining colony by Old Republic nobility, built for the purpose of stripping every rock within ten million kilometers of whatever mineral resources the galaxy might covet; its founders' disappointment, upon realizing that such valuable minerals were scarce at best in the Kafrene belt, had earned it the unofficial slogan that arced over its aft docking bay in lurid, phosphorescent graffiti: WHERE GOOD DREAMS GO BAD.

Now the Ring of Kafrene was a deep-space trading post and stopover for the sector's most desperate travelers. Cassian Andor counted himself among that number.

He was already behind schedule, and he knew that if he hadn't drawn attention during disembarkation he was certainly doing so now. He moved too quickly down the throughway, shouldering aside men and women and nonhumans of indeterminate gender who had the proper, plodding gait of people sentenced to live in a place like Kafrene. Between the road and the distant rock warrens stood a thousand sheet-metal shacks and shoddy prefabricated housing units recycled from foreign colonies; outside the main throughways there was no plan, no layout that didn't change almost daily, and even the workers proceeding home in the artificial twilight stuck to the major arteries. Cassian tried to moderate his pace, to ride the crowd's momentum rather than apply force. He failed and imagined his mentor's disappointment: *The Rebel Alliance taught you better than that.*

But he had been traveling too long, from Coruscant to Corulag and onward, tugging at the loose threads of an elaborate tapestry that was outside the scope of his vision. He had paid dearly in time and credits and blood for precious little intelligence, for the reiteration of facts he'd already confirmed. He'd spent too much to return to Base One empty-handed. His frustration was starting to show.

He cut across the street and smelled ammonia wafting from a ventilation shaft—exhaust from an alien housing complex. He suppressed a cough and stepped into the gap between one tenement and another, working his way through a maze of corridors until he reached a dead-end alleyway barely wider than his arm span.

"I was about to leave," a voice said, full of nervous irritation. The speaker emerged from the shadows: a human with a soft round face and hard eyes, dressed in stained and fading garb. His right arm hung limply in a sling. Cassian's gaze locked on the man even as he sorted through the distant sounds of the street: voices, clattering merchandise, something sizzling, someone screaming. But no commotion, no squawking comlinks.

That was good enough. If there were stormtroopers hunting him, they weren't ready to shoot.

"I came as fast as I could," Cassian said. He stashed his paranoia in the back of his brain—out of the way but within easy reach.

Tivik started toward Cassian and the alley mouth, wiping one palm on his hip. "I have to get back on board. Walk with me."

"Where's your ship heading?" Cassian asked. "Back to Jedha?"

Tivik didn't stop moving. In another moment, he'd have to squeeze past Cassian to continue. "They won't wait for me," he said. "We're here stealing ammo—"

Cassian shifted his weight and broadened his stance, blocking Tivik's path; he wasn't a large man, but he knew how to feign *presence*. Tivik flinched and took an abrupt step backward.

As informants went, Tivik was one of the more maddening Cassian had worked with: He was, for all his faults, a true believer; he was also an abject coward, forever looking to escape the moral responsibilities he assigned himself. He responded well to pressure. And after the past few days, after rushing to extricate himself from Corulag based on Tivik's oblique message, Cassian was in the mood to press.

"You have news from Jedha?" he growled. "Come on . . . I came across the galaxy for this."

Tivik met Cassian's gaze, then relented. "An Imperial pilot—one of the cargo drivers on the Jedha run? He defected yesterday."

"So?" Low-level defectors from the Empire weren't uncommon. They made up half the Rebellion's foot soldiers, give or take. Tivik knew that as well as Cassian.

"This pilot? He says he knows what the Jedha mining operation is all about. He's telling people they're making a weapon." Tivik spat the words out like bitter rind. "The kyber crystals, that's what they're for. He's brought a message, says he's got proof—"

Cassian sorted through the barrage of information, cross-referenced against what he already knew, and reprioritized his concerns. This was why he'd come, but it wasn't what he'd expected. There had been leads about a *weapon* before, and every one—on Adalog, in Zemiah's Den—had turned to dross.

His pulse was quickening. Maybe he wouldn't return to Base One empty-handed after all.

"What kind of weapon?" he asked.

Voices rose in the street, distorted by echoes down the alleyways. Tivik somehow shrank into himself, the small man making himself smaller. "Look, I have to go."

"You called *me*. You knew this was important—"

"You shouldn't have come late!" Tivik snapped. His eyes were glassy with distress.

Cassian hoisted Tivik under both arms, dug his fingers into the sling and coarse cloth and soft flesh. The man's breath had the scent of cinnamon. "What kind of weapon?" Cassian repeated, louder than he'd intended.

"A planet killer," Tivik whispered. "That's what he called it."

Cold crept down Cassian's spine.

He tried to bring to mind old reports, speculative intelligence documents, tech readouts, anything to put the lie to Tivik's words. A planet killer was a myth, a *fantasy,* an obscenity dreamed up by zealots who viewed the Emperor as a wrathful deity instead of a corrupt tyrant.

Along with the cold came a shameful mix of excitement and revulsion. Maybe for this, *any* price would be justified.

He set Tivik down as gently as he could. "A planet killer?"

"Someone named Erso sent him, sent the pilot. Some old friend of Saw's."

That much fit the puzzle. "Galen Erso?" Cassian asked, trying to tamp down his own intensity. "Was it?"

"I don't know! I shouldn't even have said this much." Tivik shook his head. "The pilot, the guys who found him, they were looking for Saw when we left."

Saw Gerrera. A defector pilot. Jedha. Kyber crystals. A weapon. A planet killer. Galen Erso. Cassian sorted through them and found it was too much to deal with, a hand built of too many playing cards. Tivik was on the verge of bolting, and Cassian didn't have time to figure out the right questions. "Who else knows this?" he asked.

"I have no idea!" Tivik leaned in, his cinnamon breath coming in quick little bursts. "It's all falling apart. Saw's right—you guys keep talking and stalling and dealing and we're on fumes out there, there're spies everywhere—"

Tivik didn't finish the sentiment. As he stared past Cassian's shoulder, Cassian heard movement behind him and turned to face the alley mouth. Positioned to block the entrance, as Cassian had blocked

Tivik, were two figures in white armor with helmets like stylized skulls: Imperial stormtroopers, rifles hoisted casually and aimed in Cassian's direction.

Cassian cursed silently and made himself smile.

"What's all this?" The stormtrooper's voice buzzed with distortion. He was curt, authoritative, but not scared. Cassian could use that.

"Hey," Cassian said, and gave an exaggerated shrug. "Just me and my friend. If we're bothering someone, we'll get out of the way—"

"You're not leaving." The second stormtrooper spoke now, impatient. "Come on, let's see some scandocs."

Cassian kept his eyes off Tivik. There was nothing he could do to coax the man into playing along, to urge him to *make no move*. He kept smiling his small, reassuring smile at the stormtroopers, even as his blood pumped fiercely with the promise of a *weapon*, a *planet killer*. "Yeah, of course," he said. "My gloves?"

He indicated a pocket with a gesture. The stormtroopers didn't object. Thieves were common on Kafrene, and they'd doubtless seen stranger hiding spots.

Neither stormtrooper reacted in time as Cassian reached down and touched the cool metal of his pistol's grip. He barely moved his wrist and squeezed the trigger twice, averting his gaze just enough to avoid the glare of the energy discharge. The electric noise was low and sickly, muffled by an illegal silencing device that was *almost* effective.

A moment later the stormtroopers lay dead in the alleyway. It was a miracle, Cassian thought, that the silenced blaster bolts had penetrated their armor. In a fairer world, he would be the one lying in filth with a burning hole instead of a heart.

"No . . ." Tivik was shaking his head. "What've you done?"

Cassian caught another glimpse of white, heard a garbled voice beyond the alley mouth. There would be more troopers coming, *many* more, and next time they wouldn't hesitate to fire. He seized Tivik by the elbow, hurried deeper into the alley, and scanned the walls. There were no exits, no air shafts or back doors, but the rooftops weren't more than a meter or two out of reach. Unaided climbing wasn't his specialty; still, he could be up and over in seconds, and he'd disappear in the labyrinthine depths of the Ring of Kafrene.

Tivik recognized his intent. "Are you crazy? I'll never climb out of here." He tugged himself away from Cassian's grip—Cassian released him after a moment—and adjusted his sling. "My arm . . ." He rotated his body awkwardly to watch the alley mouth.

Cassian heard footsteps and a distant, distorted yell. He looked Tivik up and down and realized that, in all likelihood, the man was right: He really couldn't make it up the wall, not without help and not swiftly. In the best-case scenario, by the time both he and Cassian were up on the roofs, the stormtroopers would already have identified them and initiated a cordon.

"Hey," Cassian said, and touched Tivik's shoulder—gently now, his voice stripped of all force. "Calm down. Calm down. You did good—everything you told me, it's real?"

"It's real," Tivik said. His voice was the voice of a confused child.

One more payment.

"We'll be all right," Cassian said. And for the third time that day, he squeezed the trigger on his blaster. He heard the sickly electric squawk, smelled burning fibers and worse as Tivik fell to the ground. The informant let out one last little groan, like he'd been troubled in his sleep, and lay still.

They would've caught you, Tivik. You would've broken. You would've died. And neither of us would deliver your message.

Cassian's hands were shaking as he pulled himself up and over the wall, grabbing at handholds along pipes and stained sills, kicking at the surface for support. He heard the stormtroopers behind him counting bodies and hurried on, chest flat against the rooftop.

Less than an hour later, he was on a shuttle departing the Ring of Kafrene. His face and beard were dripping where he'd wiped them with a cold sponge in the sanitation station—not just to hide the sweat on his brow, but to shock himself back into focus. He had a lot to occupy his mind, and farther to go before he could transmit it to Draven and Alliance Intelligence.

He closed his eyes and sorted the cards in his hand:

Jedha. The pilgrim moon. A wasteland world intimately linked to a vast Imperial project only visible through its ripple effects.

The kyber crystals. Jedha's only natural resource of any value. The Empire had been shipping crystals offworld, their ultimate destination unknown.

A defecting pilot carrying a message to Saw Gerrera. Possibly trustworthy, possibly not.

Saw Gerrera. Nominally part of the Rebellion. In practice, not so easily categorized.

Galen Erso. The legendary scientist, connected—again—to the Imperial mega-project whose existence the Alliance could only speculate about. The man whose message the pilot supposedly carried.

And the weapon. The *planet killer*. The galaxy's nightmare, designed and built and polished to shine by Erso and his cronies.

It was more than Cassian had hoped to bring back from this mission; a treasure hoard of facts and speculation and possible connections, enough to keep the analysts busy for weeks or months or years.

If he was lucky, it would even be enough to keep him from replaying—over and over in his head, on the long shuttle ride to safety—the last dying groan of the man he'd murdered.

Bodhi Rook had only ever doubted himself, and today was no exception.

His captors hadn't hurt him. Threatened him, yes; refused him food and water and left him with a headache that seemed to squeeze his skull tight around his swollen brain, yes; but they treated him more like an object than a man. They rarely spoke as they dragged him across the frigid Jedha desert, grasping him by the arms and marching at a pace that he—insulated by the Imperial flight suit he wore under a loose kaftan—couldn't quite match. His soles touched sand twice for every three steps his captors took; and so every three steps he flew, and their grip became painfully tight.

He could survive this, he told himself. He'd chosen *right*, found the right people. And when he delivered his message, they would all understand. They would accept him as a good man, a brave man.

He could only hope that was all true.

"How much farther?" he asked.

His captors stayed close around him, so close he couldn't see much of the wasteland: just pale and freezing sun, low mountains that formed the borders of the valley, and the occasional crumbling monolith of one of Jedha's great statues—a stern humanoid head with lips worn smooth over millennia, or a pair of broken legs embedded in the cracked and rusty valley floor. When the wind rose, loose wisps of long, dark hair drifted before his eyes.

"I know you're being careful," he said, struggling to sound reasonable. "I know that's smart—you think I could be a spy, and spies have to be a worry for people like you."

Don't make them think about spies! He told himself that, even as another part of his brain assured him: *Hide nothing. Only honesty will save you.*

He fought to regain his train of thought. "But—but!" He spat air through dry lips. "You also have to give me a chance. Not for my sake, but for yours. I want to help you . . ."

His captors—five revolutionaries in ragged local attire, each armed with an illegal blaster rifle—yanked him hard, and he scrabbled over the dust. No one met his gaze. Instead scarred, unwashed faces watched Bodhi's bound hands or the endless desert.

An interminable time passed before he spoke again.

"Do you have a family?" he asked a towering man with a blade half concealed in his boot.

For his troubles, he got the briefest of glances.

"*I* have a family," Bodhi said, though it was only somewhat true.

The revolutionaries began to spread apart, wordlessly changing formation to put Bodhi at the center of a broad semicircle. With his newly expanded field of vision, Bodhi now saw a second group standing ahead of them in the wastes—small, dark figures on a bright horizon.

"Is that him?" Bodhi asked, and received no reply.

The semicircle closed the distance to the second band. The new-comers resembled Bodhi's captors but carried their ordnance more conspicuously: A white-furred Gigoran hoisted a rotary cannon, while the humans wore bandoliers and detonator belts. At the fore of the newcomers was a Tognath: a lanky figure dressed in dark leath-ers, whose pale, skull-like head was set in the vise grip of a mechani-cal respirator. The Tognath turned his sockets onto Bodhi and said in a thickly accented dialect, "It's the pilot. Look alive!"

The Tognath gestured once, and the two bands merged with swift and soldierly precision. Bodhi flinched under the Gigoran's glower and felt a flush of shame; nonhumans hadn't made him nervous be-fore he'd signed on with the Empire.

He made himself focus. "Okay, so you're—you're Saw Gerrera?" he asked, more in hope than genuine belief.

Someone snickered. The Tognath examined Bodhi with an expres-sion that might have been disdain.

"No?" Bodhi shook his head. "Okay, we're just wasting time that we don't have. I need to speak to Saw Gerrera! I keep telling them—" He lifted a shoulder at one of his original captors. "—before, before it's too late."

He thought he heard another snicker. It might have been the wind playing on sand, but it was enough to raise his ire.

They need you. You need to make them understand.

"We need to get to Jedha City. We're out here in the middle of nowhere—" His voice rose to a shout, thick with frustration. "What part of *urgent message* do you guys not understand?"

He saw the shadow above him, then felt coarse cloth drag over his hair, catch on the goggles perched on his forehead, and slide tight against his nose, mustache, and beard. He saw the glow of the sun through the stitching of the sack over his head. "Hey!" he said, trying not to bite the fabric. "Hey—we're all on the same side, if you just see past the uniform for a minute . . ."

You always talk, his mother had said, *but you say so little! Learn to listen, Bodhi Rook.*

Talking was all he could do now.

"I've got to speak to Saw Gerrera," he cried. He was pleading as one set of hands released his arms and new hands, the terribly strong hands of the Gigoran, took their place. "You know what? Just tell him—tell him what I told you, and then he'll *want* to speak to me."

I gave up everything to come here. I'm here to help!

Someone pulled the sack tight around his neck. It scraped at his throat when he breathed.

Bodhi Rook thought about the reason he'd come back to Jedha and found himself hating Galen Erso.

Jyn had been at the Empire's mercy before. Sometimes she'd even deserved her troubles—she couldn't blame some petty dictator for ordering her dragged off the street and slammed into holding when she really, truly was planning to blow up his ship and steal his guns. She'd had rifles pointed at her, felt stun prods deliver jolts to her spine, and generally suffered the worst a stormtrooper was authorized to deal out.

What made her circumstances different *now* was that, for the first time, Jyn had no escape route. No partners outside the prison walls waiting to bust down the doors; no *in* with a greedy security officer she could promise (lying or not) to pay off; not even a knife she could hide where the guards wouldn't find it.

She'd run out of *friends*. She'd come to Wobani Labor Camp alone. She expected to die there that way and, very likely, it wouldn't take long at all.

She opened her eyes, flinched away her thoughts as a drop of filthy water smacked into her forehead and took a circuitous route down the side of her nose. She smeared it away with her palm and glanced about her cell as if it might have changed since lights-out. But there was no gap in the wall, no blaster tucked discreetly beside her slab. The blanket-draped lump of her cellmate moaned and wheezed, loud enough to wake Jyn even if she did manage to sleep.

She waited for the stormtrooper on patrol to pass her door, counted to five, then slid to her feet and crept to the bars. Outside was an endless march of more cell doors, more prisoners sleeping or, in a few cases, feeding their own private demons—clawing their arms or sketching invisible mandalas on the floor. Wobani didn't care about treatment or rehabilitation any more than it did about punishment. Order and obedience were the priority; everything else was left to rot.

"Bad dreams?" The moaning and wheezing had stopped. The voice sounded like claws on slate.

"Not really," Jyn said.

"Then you should not be up," her cellmate huffed. The tentacles protruding from her pinched, wormlike face writhed in irritation.

The woman called herself Nail. The other prisoners at Wobani called her Kennel, for the parasites she hosted in the filthy cloth jacket that half covered her leathery chest. Only the guards called her by her real name, which—along with her species and actual gender— Jyn hadn't bothered to learn.

They both fell silent as the patrol came around again. Jyn returned to the slab that served as her bed, considered rising a second time solely to irritate Kennel, then decided against it. If she was going to pick a fight, better to be awake enough to enjoy it.

"Do you want a warning?" Kennel asked. "Before I do it?"

"Not really," Jyn repeated.

Kennel grunted and rolled from one side to the other. "I will give you one anyway. Next work crew we are on together. I will kill you then."

Jyn laughed breathily and without humor. "Who's going to keep you company?"

"I like a quiet cell," Kennel said.

"What if I kill you first?" Jyn asked.

"Then I hope *you* like a quiet cell, Liana Hallik."

Liana Hallik. Not Jyn's favorite name, but probably her last. She twisted her lips into a smile that her cellmate wouldn't see.

"Were you always like this?" she asked after the stormtrooper had passed by. "Before Wobani? Back to when you were a kid?"

"Yes," Kennel replied.

"Me, too," Jyn said.

Neither of them spoke again. Jyn lay on her slab and didn't sleep and toyed with the necklace tucked under her shirt—the crystal she'd managed to keep, smuggled into the prison when she should have been worried about weapons or a comlink. She didn't think much about her would-be murderer, knowing that if Kennel didn't kill her something else would.

No one survived Wobani for long. Jyn was supposed to serve twenty years, but anything more than five was a death sentence. All she could do was try to pick the most interesting end possible.

The next morning, the stormtroopers gathered up the work crews, selecting prisoners at random (supposedly at random, though everyone knew the guards had *favorites*) for their day on the farms. Jyn preferred work to sitting in her cell—she handled strained and quivering muscles better than agonizing boredom—and she'd almost given up hope when a guard waved a rifle at her cell door. A short while later she and Kennel were chained by the arms to a bench in the back of a rusting turbo-tank, bouncing and rocking with three other convicts as a trio of stormtroopers looked on from the front.

None of the prisoners looked at one another. Jyn took that as a good sign: If Kennel was planning to kill her, at least she didn't have allies.

The transport stopped so suddenly that Jyn whipped forward, the metal of her shackles raking the flesh of her wrists. There was shouting outside. Curiosity wormed its way into Jyn's brain; they'd been in transit too little time to be at the farms. The other prisoners shifted restively, glancing at the stormtroopers and the forward door.

"Nobody moves!" a trooper snapped. His two partners had their weapons up. All three turned to face front.

Jyn heard the dull *thunk* of something metallic and a faint, high-pitched whine. One of the other prisoners was looking up now, grinning with excitement like he'd figured it all out.

Then the front of the transport exploded.

The roar of the detonating grenade—it *had* to be a grenade, Jyn knew the noise too well—made her ears throb and turned the screams and shouts and blaster shots that followed into a tinny, incomprehensible buzz. Smoke carrying the odor of ash and burning circuits flooded the rear compartment, stinging Jyn's eyes and nostrils. She tried to follow what was happening, watch the movements of the stormtroopers, but it hurt to look and she had to blink away grit. She kept her gaze on the floor. In her peripheral vision she saw the stormtroopers die one by one, felled by a barrage of particle bolts that burned through their armor and sparked against the transport walls.

"Hallik!" a muffled voice called, barely audible above the ringing in her ears.

Jyn lifted her chin with a jolt and turned toward the front of the turbo-tank. Three armed figures in battle-stained attire picked their way among the bodies. They wore no insignia, but she knew them by their movements, by their uniformity of manner and their scowls.

They were professionals. Soldiers.

They weren't with the Empire; that made them rebels.

They'd *found* her.

She couldn't stop the thought. It leapt into her head, demanded that she fight, that she *run*. But it made no sense. Why would they even be *looking* for her? Maybe it was a coincidence, maybe they were after a different prisoner and she'd misheard . . .

"Liana Hallik!" the leader—a man so thoroughly covered in gear that his exposed face seemed out of place among the cloth and leather—called again.

Jyn slowly lowered her gaze to the chains around her wrists. Her hands were shaking. She gripped her seat to make them stop.

"Her," another rebel said, and gestured in Jyn's direction.

Her deafness was abating. She waited, half expecting a blaster bolt to the head. She wondered how it would feel. People died fast from blaster bolts; she'd seen it enough. She didn't think it would hurt much.

"You want to get out of here?" the rebel leader asked. His tone was neutral, guarded—as if he was as cautious of Jyn as Jyn was of him.

Jyn tried to imagine what had brought the rebels to her. Had Saw decided to bring her back? Had one of his people decided she knew too much?

She nodded at the man, lacking any better option.

One of the rebel grunts fumbled with her shackles, finally unlocking them with a key from a stormtrooper's corpse. Jyn snapped upright, dizzy from the smoke and the blood rushing to her head but determined not to show it. Her rescuer started to say something when, from the other side of the transport, a prisoner called, "Hey! What about me?"

The rebel standing over her turned away. Jyn recognized it as an opening.

She was halfway across the transport floor in a second, her foot driving firmly into the leader's soft gut to slam him against the wall. Momentum kept Jyn upright as she spun toward a second body closing in. She swung a fist, landed a solid blow to the newcomer's face, felt his teeth through his cheek. She stumbled forward, still light-headed, and grabbed the first weapon she could find among the farming tools stored nearby: a shovel, solid and long enough to give her reach. She'd seen the damage a shovel could do in a prisoner's hands.

She let the shovel's weight carry her through her first swing, gave a solid, fleshy *smack* to the leader as the man bounced back from where she'd kicked him into the wall. She swung again to strike the rebel who'd unshackled her as he came up from behind. Jyn saw a clear path to the front of the transport and dashed for the twisted and broken doors.

The world was a blur, but she was *out,* feet striking the gravel trail.

She could find a way off Wobani. Forge new scandocs. Retire *Liana Hallik* and start over yet again, pick whatever name she wanted, one the Empire wouldn't care about and the Rebel Alliance would never *find*—

"You are being rescued," a voice said. It was electronically distorted, but too high-pitched to be a stormtrooper. A cold metal hand snagged her collar, hoisting Jyn until she was wriggling half a meter in the air. Before her towered the spindly chassis of a sunlit security droid, black as night save for the Imperial insignia on its shoulder plates and the dead white bulbs of its eyes. "Congratulations."

The droid flicked its arm and tossed her to the ground. Pain flashed up Jyn's spine, crashed through her skull. Tilting her head back, she saw an angry, bloody-mouthed rebel pointing a rifle at her chest.

Damn Saw Gerrera anyway. Damn the whole Rebel Alliance.

CHAPTER 2

SOMEWHERE INSIDE JYN'S BRAIN THERE was a cave sealed shut by a heavy metal hatch. The cave wasn't for her protection. Instead it was where she locked away the things she was *done with* but couldn't altogether forget: The Rebellion. Saw Gerrera. People and places buried in the dark for so long that she barely recognized their names as more than cruel, hurtful impulses.

She loathed the cave and everything inside it. Everyone who *knew* about it. It wasn't real, of course, though she'd described it to someone once—someone she trusted—and admitted what the image meant to her. She'd immediately regretted it and sworn to keep it hidden forever after. Now the grenade that had ruined the prisoner transport had exposed the hatch—blasted away the concealing soil, put it in open view of Jyn and the world.

On the long, harrowing flight from Wobani, the U-wing's navigation computer malfunctioned, forcing her rescuers to hail a fleet of Rebellion fighters for help. Although the X-wings were meant to de-

fend them, Jyn felt herself trapped between the armed rebels surrounding her and the hatch inside her mind.

Once again, she had no escape.

A moist film swaddled Jyn as she disembarked onto the jungle moon
of a red gas giant. Warm breezes carried the aroma of rotting vegetation from the forest floor, masking the subtler stench of mildew. The
shadow and shelter of a great stone ziggurat provided only a sem-
blance of relief—just enough to remind a person how pervasive the
heat and humidity and stink really were.

It wasn't the most uncomfortable rebel outpost Jyn had ever visited. But it was the first she'd seen while under armed guard or without knowing where she was. Maybe the star system was too obscure
to even have a name.

"Keep walking." The man who'd led the raid on Wobani marched
Jyn down the outdoor tarmac and onto the slick stone floor of the
ziggurat's makeshift hangar. The man's name was Ruescott Melshi.
He hadn't bothered to introduce himself, but she'd overheard him
talking to the pilot.

"You're still mad, aren't you?" she said.

"About what?"

"Being hit with a shovel."

Melshi grunted. "They're waiting," he said, and she didn't ask *Who?*
because she knew it was what he expected.

If it was Saw who was waiting, she knew how to deal with him.

They walked together, past pilots in jumpsuits chattering at technicians; past starfighters and freighters and transports sitting in orderly rows. It was more than a mere rebel *outpost* should have had.
Wherever Jyn was, it was important. Even without knowing what
system they'd arrived in, she suspected she'd seen too much to be allowed to ever regain her freedom.

She fantasized about tripping Melshi on the wet stone, smashing
his face into the rock, grabbing his weapon, dragging him bodily
back to the hangar entrance, and using him as a human shield. The

rebels wouldn't let her offworld, but she could escape to the jungle where she would—what?

Poison herself trying to live off the local flora?

She let Melshi guide her deeper into the ziggurat.

A troubling thought came to her: *Saw would never let a prisoner see all this.*

The rebels hadn't built the ziggurat. That much was obvious. But they'd made it their own, strung cables across ancient etchings and set flashing consoles like offerings on the slabs of altars. Melshi seemed unmoved; Jyn recalled her mother's love of history with the faintest of pangs and banished the memory. When they arrived at a chamber deep below the surface—a bunker, maybe, fortified to withstand an attack while the ziggurat crumbled above it—Melshi gestured her inside.

"Try what you tried on Wobani—" he began.

She finished for him. "—and I'd better succeed."

The bunker was dimly lit and subdivided by a conference table. Melshi steered Jyn to a chair, and she surveyed the faces arrayed against her: Two men wearing the insignia of rebel generals—one elderly, pale and soft-eyed; the second a decade or more the first man's junior, wearing a perpetual scowl under hair like rust. A third man—dark-haired, mustached, closer to Jyn's age—stood to one side as if unconcerned with the role he'd been assigned in the rebels' drama. He looked at Jyn with an expression of dispassionate curiosity.

Saw Gerrera was not present.

"You're currently calling yourself—" The rust-haired general stepped forward, glancing deliberately between Jyn and the datapad in his hand. "—Liana Hallik. Is that correct?"

He stood above her as if he could intimidate her.

Jyn waited. *Let him try.*

"Possession of unsanctioned weapons, forgery of Imperial documents, aggravated assault, escape from custody, resisting arrest . . ." He lowered the datapad and cocked his head smugly. "Imagine if the Imperial authorities had found out who you really were.

"Jyn Erso? That's your given name, is it not?"

She flinched.

She felt as much as saw the general's smile at his petty victory. Nothing about his words surprised her—the rebels wouldn't kidnap *Liana*—but hearing *Jyn Erso* aloud for the first time in years felt like a violation. The general had taken a cutting torch to the hatch in her brain, crudely attempting to burn through the barrier.

He kept talking. "Jyn Erso? Daughter of Galen Erso. A known Imperial collaborator in weapons development."

She could have struck him once, maybe twice, to stop him from saying *Erso, Erso*. The mention of Galen sent a black, charred crack through the hatch, and she felt her pulse quicken in response.

Before Jyn could act, however, she saw movement from the bunker's far entrance. A woman in white robes emerged from the shadows, at once tired and steely. Her face was lined and her copper hair impeccably styled—not like a soldier's or a general's at all. The men, nearly in unison, took half a step away as she claimed the head of the table.

"What is this?" Jyn hissed at the newcomer.

"It's a chance for you to make a fresh start," the woman said. "We think you might be able to help us." The words were gentle, but her voice was unforgiving.

"Who are you?"

"You *know* who she is." The rust-haired general again. A fleck of spittle touched Jyn's forehead, but she kept her attention where it was. The woman gestured at the general, and he fell silent.

"My name is Mon Mothma," the woman said. "I sit on the council of Alliance High Command, and I approved your extraction from Wobani."

Mothma. The Alliance chief of state. That made the ziggurat rebel headquarters. The place where decisions were made, where orders were given while people far away died—

Why was she *here*? Where was Saw?

"There's a bounty on your head," Jyn said, because it was better than not speaking; because she'd spotted a vulnerability she could jab like an unprotected eye.

Mon Mothma didn't laugh, but Jyn caught her smiling before she gestured to the third man. "This is Captain Cassian Andor," Mothma said. "Rebel Alliance Intelligence."

Cassian moved toward Jyn but feigned a respectful distance—one that would also give him space to maneuver if she lunged. The rust-haired general retreated to the edge of the room with a shake of his head.

"When was the last time you were in contact with your father?" Cassian asked.

Jyn didn't flinch this time. A second crack spread through the hatch. Sparks poured from the cutting torch.

"Fifteen years ago," she said. It was a guess, but close enough.

"Any idea where he's been all that time?" While the general had tried to intimidate, Cassian's tone was casual and his eyes were keen. As if these were questions he'd ask over dinner to show he was *interested in you as a person.*

"I like to think he's dead," Jyn said. "Makes things easier."

"Makes things easier," Cassian echoed. "Easier than what? Than him being a tool of the Imperial war machine?" Despite the baiting, he kept the same casual tone.

"I've never had the luxury of political opinions."

Jyn spotted another trace of a smile from Mothma. But Cassian became sterner. "Really? When was your last contact with Saw Gerrera?"

Shouldn't you know?

If Saw wasn't here—if Saw hadn't helped the rebels find her—then what was any of this about?

"It's been a long time," she said.

Cassian's warmth was all spent. His keenness was the keenness of an interrogator. "He'd remember you, though, wouldn't he? He might agree to meet you, if you came as a friend."

Jyn opened her mouth to argue, to swear, but she said nothing. She needed time to figure out an approach, time to decide who she was ready to betray to save herself.

"We're up against the clock here, girl," the rust-haired general snarled. "So if there's nothing to talk about, we'll just put you back where we found you."

Fine. The simple answer, the honest one. The one you already know.
"I was a child," she said. "Saw Gerrera saved my life. He raised me. But I've no idea where he is. I haven't seen him in years."

The elderly general nodded as if this confirmed something he had suspected. He exchanged a glance with Mothma, yet Cassian was the one who spoke next. "We know how to find him," Cassian said. "That's not our problem. What we need is someone who gets us through the door without being killed."

Jyn fought down a smirk. "You're all rebels, aren't you?"

"Yes, but Saw Gerrera's an extremist. He's been fighting his own war for quite some time," Mothma said. "We have no choice but to try to mend that broken trust."

So that was it? Even when Jyn had first met Saw, he'd been on the fringes of the Rebellion. If he'd parted ways with the Alliance altogether, it meant his course had held steady. And now the rebels had kidnapped her from the labor camp to use her as a peace offering.

Only that didn't explain everything.

She dug her nails into her palms and asked the question she didn't want answered. "What does this have to do with my father?"

Mon Mothma gave Cassian a prompting look.

"There's an Imperial defector in the Holy City of Jedha. A pilot. He's being held by Saw Gerrera." Cassian paused, sought Jyn's eyes as if to emphasize the gravity of what he said next. "He's claiming the Emperor is creating a weapon with the power to destroy entire planets."

This time, Jyn couldn't help but laugh.

"That's a *terrible* lie," she said.

She expected Mon Mothma to offer another wan smile. Instead, the woman looked at Jyn for a long while before saying, "I believe it's the truth. I may be wrong, and I pray that I am—but I believe a weapon that murders worlds is the natural culmination of everything the Emperor has done."

You're all crazy, Jyn wanted to say. Yet she held back.

"You're right, though," Mothma continued. "If this were just about Saw Gerrera, we would have other approaches."

Cassian resumed, apparently untroubled by the interruption and Jyn's mockery. "The pilot," he said, "the one Gerrera has in custody?"

"What about him?" Jyn asked.

"He says he was sent by your father."

The hatch inside Jyn's mind shattered like baked clay.

The *things* inside the cave, damp and soiled by darkness, seeped unwelcome into her brain. Foreign thoughts spread like stains, obscuring everything else: *My father is alive. My father is a traitor. My father is building a weapon to destroy worlds.*

My father is a hero. My father is a coward. My father is a bastard.

Galen Erso is not my father. Galen Erso didn't raise me . . .

Her palms were bleeding where she'd dug in her fingernails. She wiped her hands on her hips, looked around the suddenly vertiginous room, barely heard Mothma say, "We need to stop this weapon before it is finished," or the condescending tone of the rust-haired general:

"Captain Andor's mission is to authenticate the pilot's story and then, if possible, find your father."

It was too much. Too much to think about now, maybe too much to think about ever. But the others were watching her. Jyn focused on the sensation of her breath, her clammy skin against the metal chair, the awful stinking humid air. She forced her mind's eye away from the broken hatch above the cave, forced revulsion and loathing and doubt down like bile.

Mon Mothma was speaking again. "It would appear Galen Erso is critical to the development of this superweapon. Given the gravity of the situation and your history with Saw, we're hoping that Saw will help us locate your father and return him to the Senate for testimony."

"And if I do it?" Jyn asked. She spat the words out bitterly, though she didn't hear them.

"We'll make sure you go free," Mon Mothma said.

It was the best answer Jyn could hope for.

She wasn't calm by the time she walked out of the hangar and onto the tarmac, but she was calmer. Her body felt bruised and sore, like the morning after a fight, but she breathed without struggle. If she didn't think about *it*—the mission, the meaning *behind* the mission— she'd be okay.

And when it was over, she could go back to her old life. Make a new life. Find somewhere away from the Rebel Alliance, away from Saw Gerrera and *Galen Erso* and—

Just don't think about it.

"Captain Andor!" a voice called.

Cassian halted mid-stride beside Jyn, glanced toward the hangar, and spotted the source of the yell—the rust-haired general from the bunker, who'd been all snide remarks and grunts instead of mute senility like his partner. "General Draven," Cassian murmured. "Give me a moment."

"No rush," Jyn said.

Cassian dashed ahead to the boarding ramp of a battered U-wing transport, unslung the duffel he carried over his shoulder, then hurried back in Draven's direction. Jyn followed his path to the ship, giving the vessel a cursory once-over. While the base as a whole was larger, busier, and better equipped than anything she'd seen from the Rebel Alliance before, the U-wing was in line with her expectations. Like the one that had retrieved her from Wobani, it looked like a set of engines with a cargo bay strapped to it, maintained and repaired over the years by a droid with pistons for hands.

She'd been aboard worse.

"Jyn Erso! Alias Liana Hallik, prisoner six-two-nine-five-alpha!"

She flinched—again—at the sound of her name. She would have to get used to it.

She looked up the boarding ramp to the main cabin. Towering above the communications console stood the security droid emblazoned with Imperial symbols that had captured her on Wobani. "I'm Kay-Tuesso," he went on, with a cheerfulness Jyn could only interpret as threatening. "I'm a reprogrammed Imperial droid."

"I remember you," she said.

She'd heard stories about reprogrammed droids going *wrong*—about safeguards reasserting themselves, about old code suddenly resurfacing for reasons no one could explain. She wasn't overly concerned; if K-2SO reverted to type, the ranking members of the Rebel Alliance would be his top priority. Jyn, an escaped convict drafted into the mission, wouldn't be strangled until second or third, at least.

"I assume your presence indicates that you will be joining us on our trip to Jedha," the droid went on. A statement, not a question.

"Apparently so."

"That is a bad idea. I think so, and so does Cassian. What do I know? My specialty is *just* strategic analysis."

Jyn was barely listening. She'd turned away from the droid, looking across the hangar to where Draven and Cassian huddled together. They stood too near each other, leaning in to avoid being overheard by passing pilots and technicians.

To her surprise, Jyn realized she trusted Draven: He was an ass, but that made him predictable. Cassian—the *intelligence operative,* the spy, the casual liar—could be trouble.

"Can you tell what they're saying?" she asked K-2SO, with a glance over her shoulder.

"Yes," the droid said, and retreated to the cockpit.

Fair enough, she thought. Left alone in the cabin, she took the opportunity to examine Cassian's duffel and its contents: nothing but gear. Weapons and portable medpacs and signal boosters. No holo-image of a dutiful wife or tattered childhood security blanket. He packed impersonal and he packed light.

Jyn pulled out a blaster pistol, tested its heft and grip, and strapped it on her hip. A BlasTech A-180 wasn't her weapon of choice, but it was sturdy and low-profile. By the time Cassian had turned back to the U-wing, Jyn was moving to peer into the cockpit herself. The droid, adjusting one setting or another on the flight console, ignored her.

She heard the exterior door shut and seal. "You met Kay-Tu?" Cassian asked.

"Charming," Jyn said.

Cassian lifted his shoulders in a boyish, what-can-you-do? shrug. "He tends to say whatever comes into his circuits. It's a by-product of the reprogram."

The droid's vocabulator increased in volume, loud enough to hear in the cabin. "Why does she get a blaster," he asked, "and I don't?"

Jyn kept her hand off her weapon but shifted her weight into a defensive stance as Cassian shot her a look. "I know how to use it," she said.

"That's what I'm afraid of," Cassian answered. Jyn watched the humor, the warmth, evaporate in a flash. The expression of the calculating spy emerged. She felt a certain sour satisfaction. "Give it to me," he said.

"We're going to Jedha. That's a war zone. You want me to risk my life to help find Saw?" She shrugged. "Trust goes both ways."

Cassian stared a moment longer. The look of calculation, too, vanished, and Jyn could no longer read him at all. He returned her shrug and hauled himself into the cockpit.

Off to a grand start, Jyn thought, and went to find a bunk or, at worst, a half-comfortable surface. She hadn't slept since Wobani, on the night her cellmate had promised to kill her.

"You're letting her keep it? The blaster?"

Cassian Andor pulled himself into the pilot's seat of the U-wing—worn, thinly padded, stained by the sweat of a dozen species—and swept a hand over the controls, refamiliarizing himself as best he could. It had been a while since he'd flown a transport.

K-2 waited for a reply that didn't come, then asked: "Are you interested in the probability of her using it against you?"

Humidity had fogged the cockpit viewport, rendering the jungle a green smear. Cassian sketched out a course in his head. Flight control recommended skirting the canopy briefly before attempting full ascent from the moon of Yavin 4—a halfhearted attempt at disguising Base One's exact location from any Imperial probes.

"It's high," the droid said.

Cassian shook his head. "Let's get going."

"It's very high."

You don't know the half of it, Cassian nearly said.

He thought back to his conversation with General Draven in the hangar. The assurances of trust, of confidence in Cassian's judgment, were swiftly being pulled into the amorphous eddies of his memory, but Draven's orders were etched in steel:

Galen Erso is vital to the Empire's weapons program. There will be no "extraction."

You find him, you kill him. Then and there.

Draven wasn't wrong to want Galen Erso dead. It would be a righteous killing as well as a practical one, the execution of a man surely responsible for the deaths of countless civilians. Erso's years inside the Imperial war machine could have no innocent outcome. If killing Erso saved a single life, then that was cause to celebrate—but if not, his assassination was no less justified.

Nor did the contradiction between Mon Mothma's orders and those of General Draven trouble Cassian. The notion of bringing Galen Erso to a Senate hearing—of exposing the Empire's planet killer, of creating such an uproar inside the civilian government that the Senate would move openly against the Galactic Emperor—was absurd on the face of it.

Mothma desired a leveraged détente—a political solution made possible through rebel military action—that was, to Draven and Cassian, self-evidently impossible. The Imperial military was loyal to its commanders, and its commanders believed that they, rather than the Senate, already effected complete control over the Empire. They were right. No peaceful transfer of power could occur.

Yet Mothma was an idealist. Cassian suspected she wanted a Senate hearing not because she thought it would *work,* but because she felt obligated to *try.*

Cassian admired Mothma. Galen Erso's assassination would free her from the obligation of a doomed peace effort.

And yet Cassian was troubled nonetheless.

He was escorting a girl not much older than a teenager to see the father she had believed she'd lost. A girl who—genetics notwithstanding—had clearly inherited Saw Gerrera's burning rage and icy competence. The *need* in her eyes frightened Cassian.

Had the others seen it? Had he imagined it?

He wasn't sure what troubled him more: what he was doing to Jyn Erso, or what she would do to him if she ever learned the truth.

CHAPTER 3

BODHI BELIEVED HIS SUFFERING WOULD end soon. That Saw Gerrera would hear him out and set him free. That the weeping sores on his feet would be treated and his wrists would be unbound and the coarse cloth hood torn from his face so that he could see and hear and *breathe* again.

If he didn't believe these things, he knew he would go mad.

He had marched with the rebels for most of the day, only sure of the passage of time by virtue of the sunlight that passed through the fabric of his hood. From the desert they'd entered a shelter of some kind—a building or a cave where the feeble warmth of the sun vanished. Now he knelt on a rough stone floor and waited. He heard bodies shuffle nearby, distant footsteps, voices in adjacent rooms. He didn't try to speak. His mouth was parched.

These were not the rebels Galen Erso had described: gallant men and women whose righteous hearts led them to oppose the horrors Bodhi had seen, the deeds in which he'd been complicit. Instead, these were the rebels the Empire had always warned of: the murderers, the criminals and terrorists who concealed their viciousness in a patriotic wrapping. The ones who saw the deaths involved in spaceport bombings as a small cost for smaller victories.

Saw Gerrera would be different, though. He *had* to be different.

"Lies!"

The hoarse, ghostly bellow echoed in the chamber. Along with the voice came a rhythmic metallic clanking, like the firing of a piston.

"Deceptions!"

There was nothing but fury in the voice.

"Let's see it."

A demand, hissed from terrible depths.

Bodhi listened to more shuffling and scraping, craned his neck and strained to see something other than silhouettes and stitching.

"Bodhi Rook. Cargo pilot." Hands suddenly grasped Bodhi and yanked him to his feet. He would have fallen if the hands hadn't clamped his shoulders. "Local boy," the ghost scoffed. "Anything else?"

"There was this." A second voice in another language. Bodhi recognized the speaker as the Tognath with the respirator. "A holochip. Unencrypted. It was found in his boot when he was captured."

Bodhi jerked forward in the hands that held him—not to escape, but to demand attention. "I can hear you! You made your point! I'm scared, you made me scared, but he didn't capture me—I came here *myself*." He couldn't tell if they understood him through the cloth. "I defected," he called around a mouthful of fabric. "I *defected*!"

"Lies," the ghost repeated. "Every day, more lies."

"Lies?" Bodhi was almost screaming now, violently sucking in breath through the sack to give his fury strength. "Would I risk everything for a lie? We don't have *time* for this!

"I have to speak to Saw Gerrera before it's too—"

Someone grabbed the sack and *tugged,* yanking the hood free and scraping the work goggles back on Bodhi's scalp.

Bodhi could see again. He almost wished he was still blind.

He was in a room—not a cave, but a chamber hewn from ancient stone and sparsely appointed as a living space. Three of his captors stood nearby, while a fourth man, a stranger, stood before him. This man—the ghost, Bodhi assumed, the hoarse and chilling voice—had wild, graying hair and a face knotted with scars. He leaned on a thick, metal-shod cane to support the weight his artificial leg could not.

"Saw Gerrera?" Bodhi asked.

This time no one snickered.

Saw pinched a holochip between two fingers. Bodhi nodded toward it. "That's for you," he said. He heard himself babbling, protesting, couldn't stop the flood of words: "And I *gave* it to them, they did not *find* it. I gave it to them.

"Galen Erso. He told me to find you."

Saw Gerrera laid his cane aside and grasped an oxygen mask attached to his armored chest plate. Without looking from Bodhi, he brought the mask to his face, inhaled, and returned the mask to its place.

Please believe me, Bodhi thought. Or maybe he said it aloud; he wasn't entirely sure.

I did this for you. I did this to do something right.

Saw turned his head to signal the Tognath. "Bor Gullet," Saw said.

"Bor Gullet?" Bodhi asked.

Then the cloth scraped over his forehead and nose and lips again, and arms dragged him backward, spun him away from Saw—away from the man he'd been sent to find, away from salvation and vindication and redemption. "Galen Erso sent me!" he cried through the sack. "He told me to find you!" He said it, and things like it, over and over, and it did him no good at all.

Orson Krennic, advanced weapons research director of the first Galactic Empire, had never received the respect he was due.

This was not an accident of fate, nor a symptom of some personal weakness. While Krennic could acknowledge that he lacked the scientific prowess of a man like Galen Erso, even the most arrogant researchers under his command largely accepted that genius, when bound to Krennic's vision, accomplished more than genius could alone. It was Krennic who, across two decades, had directed a thousand brilliant minds like a maestro with his symphony; Krennic who had focused the energies of a million scientists and engineers and strategists and laborers into a singular creation; and this, all while playing the games of the Emperor's Ruling Council, all while assuaging the petty jealousies of admirals and Joint Chiefs.

Orson Krennic had built the *Death Star*—the greatest technological achievement in galactic history, a feat of engineering that rivaled the transformation of the city-world of Coruscant or the invention of the hyperdrive; *his* achievement as much as anyone's. If that extraordinary and all-consuming venture had left him vulnerable, it was no failing on his part.

Instead, responsibility for his circumstances rested squarely on one man—the very man who had summoned him to meet aboard the Star Destroyer *Executrix*.

Grand Moff Wilhuff Tarkin was Krennic's true bane. While Krennic *created*, Tarkin fought to keep Krennic from rising above his station. From earning the attention of the Emperor himself.

The old governor's back was to Krennic as Krennic strode onto the *Executrix*'s bridge. Behind Krennic came an escort of his personal troops; an intimidation tactic lost on Tarkin as he stared out a viewport toward the massive Death Star battle station.

Today the firing array of the station's primary weapon was scheduled to dock. Six thousand detachable thrusters were maneuvering the colossal dish above the spherical superstructure of the station, where droids, technicians, and mechanical arrays awaited; once the dish descended, they would lock it permanently into place. The operation had taken months of planning, and required the shutdown of many of the Death Star's power systems to eliminate any risk of an energy surge. Krennic should have *been there*, sealed in a full environment suit in the temporarily airless corridors of the battle station, to supervise and observe the final stages.

"Most unfortunate about the security breach on Jedha, Director Krennic," Tarkin said, and turned his frail body around at last. He gave Krennic's death trooper escort not a glance, and reserved his most withering look for the hem of Krennic's white cloak.

"I'm afraid I'm not sure what you're referring to," Krennic lied, with a quizzical expression.

You think I'm a fool, Tarkin? he wanted to say. *You believe I don't have my own people within your ranks, telling me everything they tell you?*

But if Tarkin thought him a fool, best to play the part.

The governor kept speaking. "After so many setbacks and delays— and now this. We've heard word of rumors circulating through the city. Apparently you've lost a rather talkative cargo pilot."

"And what does a cargo pilot know that's of consequence to us?" Krennic asked, as lightly as he could. "You acknowledged yourself that secrecy was becoming an impediment to progress some time ago. Rumors were bound to spread—"

"The rumors are not the concern. The concern is *proof.* If the Senate gets wind of our project"—Tarkin spoke with distilled contempt— "countless systems will flock to the Rebellion."

Krennic countered instinctively. "When the battle station is finished, Governor Tarkin, the Senate will be of little concern."

Tarkin's lips looked as chiseled as a crevice in a cliff, and just as good-humored. "*When* has become now, Director Krennic. The Emperor will tolerate no further delay—you have made time an ally of the Rebellion."

As if you speak with the Emperor's voice.

"I suggest," Tarkin said, "we solve both problems simultaneously with an immediate test of the weapon. Failure will find you explaining *why* to a far less patient audience."

Krennic was taken aback. It was not the way the conversation should have gone.

An immediate test?

Look for the trap. Tarkin demands nothing that doesn't serve him.

But the old governor was waiting for an answer. If Krennic appeared less than confident in the Death Star's capabilities then that, too, would be turned against him.

"I will not fail," he said. "A test of the weapon to wipe Jedha clean."

In a better world, he would have been able to say such a thing with triumph and anticipation. To see the battle station fully functional would be a glorious thing; and Tarkin had found a way to poison it.

Tarkin turned away in dismissal and disinterest.

Later, back aboard the Death Star, Krennic stalked through the voluminous corridors that honeycombed the massive station, inspecting the results of the day's work. The black floors were polished to a mirror sheen, and the reflection of Krennic's white uniform shone like a guiding beacon. Though he made a show of interrogating engineers and droids, of personally scanning conduits for microfractures, he knew there was nothing meaningful he might discover that wouldn't appear in the daily activity reports. He walked because it helped him *focus;* because vigorous exercise gave him an outlet for his frustrations. His meeting aboard the *Executrix* raised too many questions, and he analyzed and clarified circumstances and stakes with every harried step.

Lay it out as you would for a new development team. Solve the problem.

Did Tarkin believe the Death Star was not ready to be tested? That the primary weapon would fail?

Revealing the Death Star as impotent above Jedha carried substantial risk—it would be humiliating, as much for Tarkin as for Krennic. Yet Krennic had heard rumors that the Emperor's right hand—Darth Vader himself—kept Tarkin as a close ally.

Was it conceivable Tarkin sought to use Vader as a shield?

A bold man, Tarkin. Bold and arrogant enough to orchestrate a public failure and deflect responsibility.

Which raised another question: Why did Tarkin believe the test would fail at all? He had long belittled Krennic's own ability, mocked Krennic's every recitation of the engineering challenges before them, so perhaps his disdain had blinded him to success, but to build a risky plan on an ungrounded assumption seemed unwise even for Tarkin.

Was it mere coincidence that Tarkin had summoned Krennic while the firing array was being placed?

Would Tarkin go so far as to sabotage the installation?

Krennic halted in his walk, spun about, and made for the outer decks where the firing array had been locked into place. His pulse quickened and his blood burned with ire. He commandeered a maintenance turbolift and dismissed its occupants with a gesture; only when he had arrived at the force field blocking a still-airless corridor did he begin to calm. Behind the shimmering field stood two stormtroopers equipped with oxygen tanks, as vigilant as ever.

There were a hundred other entry points to the construction areas that a saboteur might take, of course. Even the stormtroopers might have been in Tarkin's employ. But the scene was tranquil enough to drain Krennic's rage.

Sabotage. The possibility galled him, yet he could adjust. He would reach out to his contacts within Tarkin's inner circle, learn what—if anything—they knew.

Meanwhile, he had a day, perhaps two, until the evacuation of Imperial assets from Jedha was complete. In that time, he could order every diagnostic imaginable for every focusing lens and kyber crystal and conduit in the firing array. If there *was* sabotage, his people would find it.

Nothing aboard the Death Star could be hidden from Krennic. He alone—or at most he and one other—could comprehend its magnificence as a work of mortal invention.

With those thoughts to comfort him, Orson Krennic finished his walk-through and returned to his sparely elegant quarters—his home, more than any planet or moon. He sat at his desk and drank wine and distributed orders and read his reports. His confidence was renewed. The Death Star would soon be complete—every last toggle operational and every hull plate ground smooth. The test on Jedha would be a triumph rather than a failure, and he would see the galaxy respond in awe and terror.

No one—certainly not *Wilhuff Tarkin*—would deny Krennic that pleasure.

.   .   .

In her dream, Jyn was five years old—or maybe four, or maybe six; it was long ago—and she lay in the most comfortable bed she would ever know in her life. She clutched Beeny (her favorite toy, her best friend) against her face, so close that Beeny's fur was damp with Jyn's breath. She held Beeny tight and she *listened*.

"Whatever atrocities they seek to commit, they have no movement, no organization. That's the upside of having anarchists as an enemy."

Jyn didn't understand the words. She didn't like that. Sometimes it was nice, lying in the dark (she wasn't afraid of the dark at all) listening to the grown-ups talk, but tonight wasn't nice. They were talking about fighting.

"Even the Separatists wanted more than just destruction." Mama's voice. "And if they're so far gone, how is building a shining new Empire going to win them over? We're talking about—"

"We're talking about a very delicate time in our history." The first voice again. Jyn rolled over, peering through the door at the gathering in the living room: Mama in her pretty cloak, Papa in his gray uniform, and Papa's friend in white. They were gathered around the dessert table, and the man in white was pouring a drink, offering to refill glasses as he spoke. "If people believe in the Empire, military victory over Separatist holdouts and malcontents is inevitable. If people lose faith—" Mama was trying to interrupt him; the man waved her off. "—well, you know about Malpaz. Coruscant will be fine, of course, but we'll all feel guilty enjoying these meals while terrorism flourishes in the Outer Rim . . ."

Mama laughed. Not a real laugh, but the quiet sort of laugh she used when she was *supposed* to laugh but didn't really want to.

Papa looked over at Jyn's bedroom, at *Jyn,* and she saw that he knew she was watching.

Mama was talking again as Papa stood and walked toward Jyn. Jyn drew her knees up, shrank back into her bed, as if she could hide. She didn't want Papa to shut the door. Not because she was afraid of the dark (she wasn't afraid of the dark!), but because she wanted to keep listening, she *deserved* to keep listening . . .

Papa didn't close the door. Instead, he stepped inside and sat beside Jyn on her bed. She felt the mattress sink under her. "What's the matter, Jyn? You look frightened," he said, and pushed back a strand of her hair. He smelled like his uniform, sour and scrubbed clean.

"I'll always protect you," he murmured.

Then the dream changed.

Papa's body looming over Jyn was no more than a shadow. Jyn was alone in a cave, slamming a hatch shut, trapping herself in the dark. Mama was a corpse in the dirt by the farmhouse, and Jyn had nothing. Even her song wouldn't emerge from her lips—she couldn't speak, and her lungs were full of smoke and ash and soil.

"Why do people fight?" she asked, and she was back in her bedroom again, the horrors of her future forgotten.

Papa took a long time to answer. When he finally spoke, he spoke as if he were thinking about it for the first time. "That's a good question," he said. "My friend Orson says some people just fight because they're angry. But I think—" He stopped talking and half closed his eyes. The voices in the other room continued. "I think, usually, people are unhappy, and they don't agree how to make things better."

Jyn watched her father, tried to tell what he thought of that idea. "Maybe they'd agree if they stopped fighting first?"

Papa looked at her kindly. Jyn thought she'd surprised him, in a good way. "Stardust. Don't ever change."

He leaned in to kiss her on the forehead. She wrapped her arms around him, felt his smooth and sour-smelling uniform press against her. "I won't," she promised. Then, softer: "I love you, Papa. You're a good man."

Papa returned the hug, in her bedroom in the city and in her bedroom on Lah'mu, both at once. With her chin on his shoulder, Jyn looked past her father to her bedroom door. Mama stood in the living room, watching them. She smiled very gently. Behind her stood the man in white.

The arms around Jyn's shoulders became thin and rough like string. Now Mama was right in front of her, putting her crystal necklace around Jyn's neck.

The hatch opened, and Saw Gerrera looked down.

·   ·   ·

When Jyn woke up, she was no longer a child and she was no longer in a comfortable bed in an apartment on Coruscant. Her mother and father and Beeny were long gone. (Beeny had been the first casualty of her private war, never even making it as far as Lah'mu.)

The hatch, she knew, was irreparably broken.

The U-wing trembled as Jyn, in the dark of the ship's cabin, fumbled to find her mother's crystal necklace against her breast.

SUPPLEMENTAL DATA: BATTLE STATION DS-1

[Document #YT5368 ("Official Statement on Battle Station DS-1 General Directive"), timestamped approximately two years prior to Operation Fracture, sent from the office of Grand Moff Wilhuff Tarkin.]

To Director Krennic:

I find these communiqués distasteful, but since you evidently require written reminders of your duty I will oblige. It is incumbent upon everyone involved in the construction of the battle station (of clearance level DS/30 and above) to share a unified vision for the technologies involved and, in turn, our doctrine of use.

The time for painstaking compartmentalization of development cells is past. Lying to your engineering teams about our ultimate goal let you recruit energy researchers and materials experts more interested in revitalizing Coruscanti infrastructure than in building a weapon; for this, I give you credit. But we *are* building a weapon, one with a *specific* purpose that must not be compromised.

Quite simply, it's time to stop playing games.

A project of this scope has never before been attempted. I do not care what motivates your engineers, but it is imperative that they comprehend our priorities. In a battle station with eight billion component parts, even a handful of poor decisions could compromise our ultimate effectiveness.

Shall I elaborate? I shouldn't have to, but to wit:

The battle station is not a military force unto itself. It is part of a system, and individual elements must be manufactured to Imperial standard. If there are *incompatibilities* with the Star Destroyer fleet, these must be remedied.

The battle station is not a testbed for new technologies. Promising your people opportunities for innovation was a mistake. Update only where necessary, and if we must add a hundred reliable, proven reactors instead of developing a single new one, so be it.

The battle station is certainly not *symbolic*, meant only to demonstrate the Empire's might in ceremonial planetary executions. The main weapon must be built to fire repeatedly within a short span, as it might during the course of a single fleet battle. Both the mechanisms and the control scheme *must support this practice*.

We are building a weapon not to prevent a war, but to end one. Time and again we have seen the galaxy dissolve into instability and chaos, and the rise of the rebel terrorist movement is only the latest iteration of a cycle. The rebels have no chance of overthrowing us, but they threaten our order nonetheless.

The Death Star will not put an end to treason. Yet never again will a conflict consume our galaxy as did the Clone Wars. When an enemy rises, we will strike with decapitating vehemence. If one strike does not suffice, we will repeat the process and burn planets until either our enemy is annihilated or the galaxy is so terrified that further resistance is unthinkable.

The new peace will last until the cycle begins again. At which point the battle station will be redeployed. The interruption of stability will be brief and *illuminating*.

Are we of like minds now, Director? The Death Star is the ultimate weapon of war. It serves no other purpose. It is not a monument to your workers' scientific prowess or the cornerstone of a new navy designed to your personal ideal. *Crude but functional* is an acceptable watchword.

See to your staff immediately.

[Document #YT5368A ("Reply to Official Statement on Battle Station DS-1 General Directive"), sent from the office of Orson Krennic, advanced weapons research director.]

Respectfully, Governor, I request clarity.

My understanding is that the battle station project was initiated at a level above either of us. I know you have the ear of the Emperor; can you confirm that the vision you've elaborated comes directly from him?

I would hate to see anything spawned from his mind described as *crude but functional.* Indeed, I endeavor to exceed his expectations.

[No follow-up documents found.]

CHAPTER 4

IF JEDHA HAD EVER BEEN more than a barren rock of a moon, some years or centuries past, Jyn couldn't see it now. There was nothing *to* see from space—no great oceans, no churning clouds. No glittering cities of metal and glass that spread across continents like mold. Only amber dust and cold desert.

"That's Jedha," Cassian announced. "What's left of it, anyway."

Winds tore at the U-wing as it breached the atmosphere, rocking the vessel and causing Jyn to sway in the cockpit doorway. It was enough to leave her nauseated—Cassian and the droid seemed unperturbed—and she retreated to the cabin for the landing. Unwanted images of Saw Gerrera, of Galen Erso (*My father is alive. My father is a bastard . . .*) crept into her mind, spilling out of the hatch and crawling behind her eyes like parasites.

She couldn't afford to sit and think. She'd go mad. *Ignore the nausea and do something useful,* she told herself.

By the time the transport alit on a cracked desert mesa, Jyn had already sorted through everything she might need on the moon's surface: thermal layering—gloves and jacket and hood—to ward off the chill; a pair of combat truncheons for close-quarters fights; a satchel full of codebreakers and ration packs and maps, because she'd found them on the U-wing and she had an empty satchel to fill. While Cassian and K-2SO were still in the cockpit, she left the ship and found a seat on a boulder like an icy knife.

From there, she looked onto the valley and toward the distant walls of the city—the Holy City, Jedha City, NiJedha, depending on whose data bank you checked. Dust and smoke obscured dully painted spires and palisades, ancient stone plazas and gold-topped manors. From so far away, the settlement looked like a smudged painting of a history Jyn didn't recognize. All she could make out with certainty were the shuttlecraft drifting like flies near the belly of an Imperial Star Destroyer hovering overhead. Where the city was rough and decayed, the Destroyer was sleek and impermeable.

Cassian and the droid emerged from the U-wing behind her, sending small pebbles tumbling down the side of the mesa.

"What's with the Destroyer?" she asked.

"The Empire's been sending those since Saw Gerrera started attacking their cargo shipments," Cassian said.

That didn't surprise Jyn. *You don't stop Saw Gerrera with a few extra TIE fighters.* She wondered if she was proud or simply resigned to Saw's doggedness.

"What are they bringing in?" she asked.

"It's 'what are they taking out?'" Cassian passed a set of quadnocs to Jyn. She raised them to her eyes, scanned the horizon, let the automatic tracking systems fix and zoom in on one of the shuttlecraft. She saw a half dozen cargo crates colored hazard-orange strapped to the undercarriage, but she didn't spot any markings.

"Kyber crystal," Cassian went on. "All they can get. We believe the Empire is using it as fuel for the weapon."

"The planet killer?" She sounded more sardonic than she felt.

"You don't think it's real?"

Jyn shrugged and passed back the quadnocs. "Could be. Your boss was right when she said it seems like the sort of thing the Empire would do—"

"The *natural culmination of everything the Emperor has done*," Cassian corrected. His lips curled in a wry smile.

"Either way. It's not surprising the Empire *wants* a planet killer. It'd just be surprising if it *works*."

The droid spoke cheerfully. "It might not. Not much crystal left at this point."

Jyn glanced at K-2 and found herself eyeing his Imperial markings. "Maybe we should leave *target practice* here behind."

"Are you talking about me?" the droid asked.

Cassian straightened and tugged his jacket tighter as the wind picked up. "She's right," he said. "We need to blend in. Stay with the ship."

"I can blend in," K-2SO returned. It wasn't so much a protest as a declaration.

Jyn snorted. "With Saw's forces? Or the Imperials? Half the people here want to reprogram you. The other half want to put a hole in your head."

"I'm surprised you're so concerned with my safety."

Jyn turned back to the city and the valley, trying to guess at the distance they'd need to cover. *You overpacked*, she decided, and tossed her satchel to K-2SO. "I'm not concerned," she said. "I'm just worried our enemies might miss you and hit me."

Cassian had already started walking. Jyn followed. When the droid called, "Doesn't sound so bad to me," she pretended not to hear.

Bodhi Rook couldn't see the creature in the cave. When he craned his neck, tried to squirm out of his bonds or pull himself away from the chair, the shadows of the cave seemed to crawl—*wriggling*, like the ocean creatures he'd seen in an aquarium as a child. The shadows writhed and played in long wisps and blunt stubs—but when he tried to focus on them, to bring a single tendril into view out of the dark, he saw nothing. No motion but the flicker of lanterns in his peripheral vision.

"Bor Gullet can *feel* your thoughts," said the ghost.

Saw Gerrera was watching. He was outside the cave, the cell that contained Bodhi and the creature. Safe. But watching.

"Don't do this," Bodhi said, barely loud enough to hear. "Don't do this, please." He mumbled things, incoherent things, pleading things, because it was all he knew how to do.

The sores on his feet, the chill in his fingers, the dehydration and bruises—these were discomforts he could survive. They were discomforts he understood. He'd suffered before, gone through sleep deprivation during pilot training. He was afraid of pain, yes; but the thing in the shadows repelled him, offended him on a level too intimate for words.

"No lie is safe," Saw Gerrera said.

The shadows were crawling toward Bodhi now, swirling around the base of his chair. They smelled cloying as blooming flowers. He held his breath, tried to shrink back into his seat.

"What have you *really* brought me, cargo pilot? Bor Gullet will know the truth."

Bodhi felt a touch on his shoulders, on his neck, feather-light and almost gentle. When he trembled, however, the touch became painful, like his flesh was being pinched in a vise. He thought he was saying, *I never lied to you. I never lied!* But he couldn't hear his voice.

The tendrils found his forehead. He felt his hair press tight against his skull as something wrapped about him. He closed his eyes. His body felt cold and clammy with sweat he was too dehydrated to exude, and pinpricks of fire burned at his temples.

These are a few of the things that Bodhi saw:

His mother, her hands over his own, showing him how to cut a vegetable stalk with a knife in the family kitchen. His mother never let Bodhi handle knives, but this time was different because she felt sorry for him and he couldn't recall *why*. He was certain the reason would break his heart. There was something he had lost. He would have wept if he had not begun to see—

Misurno, his teacher, his copilot on the Fentersohn run, who would while away the journey talking about his years shooting pirates and rebels and Separatist holdouts in a starfighter; whose breath stank and who joked loudly about how badly he'd treated cadets, but who'd drunkenly called Bodhi his *best* friend, his *only* friend.

Galen Erso, who looked not entirely unlike Misurno, telling Bodhi, "There is nothing brave about blind obedience. The simplest droid does what it's told—never questioning or deciding. If you want to know what we're building, Bodhi Rook, you could simply ask." *And he hadn't asked, not then, not yet.*

His cargo shuttle in flames, his hands burning as he worked the controls, trying to gain altitude, to keep out of the streams of particle bolts from the ground as the rebels shot at him. Someone was scream- ing in the aft compartment but he couldn't *do* anything, just fly, just hope the stormtroopers or the TIE fighters would intervene . . .

Bodhi wasn't sure if these things had happened at all.

He could no longer remember how to breathe, and felt the strain in his lungs.

"The unfortunate side effect," the ghost voice of Saw Gerrera said, "is that one tends to lose one's mind."

From a distance, the city had seemed as silent as the desert—its desolation broken only by the rumble of starships like wind. But up close, the streets were awash with the sounds of daily life in Jedha: the shuffle of foot traffic and the shouts and clatter of merchants, the monotone chanting of pilgrims and the hum of machinery. Threaded among these noises were the sounds of occupation: distorted voices of stormtroopers demanding scandocs at checkpoints, the roar of uncontrolled fires in contested sectors, and the echo of distant, spo- radic blaster volleys.

Jyn knew the sounds of occupation well. They were the sounds of *home.*

"We've got a good few hours of daylight left," Cassian said. Jyn fol- lowed him through a curtain and into a pockmarked alley-turned- living room for a colony of Kubaz; the two ignored the long-snouted aliens and picked their way around blankets and sizzling cookpots as they walked. "We'll probably need them. There's a curfew at sunset, and I don't fancy a walk back through the desert after dark."

"No sightseeing, then?"

"No sightseeing."

As they turned a corner and exited a second curtain, they passed into a tightly packed crowd constrained by a narrow street. Jyn brushed against a passerby, then felt a jolt as someone shoved her to one side. Her hand went under her jacket, sought her truncheon, as her assailant snarled, "You better watch yourself!"

Spoiling for a fight. Her gaze caught the man's face—a barely human mien distorted from burns or scarring—and moved to a second individual—Aqualish, all tusks and bulbous black eyes—behind him.

She could take them both. Her heart was suddenly racing. She smiled coldly.

"No, no—" Cassian grasped her arm, tugged her back into the flow of the crowd. "We don't want any trouble. Sorry."

The surge of adrenaline left her. Without a distraction at hand her mind returned, unprompted, to an image of her father's face—a face nearly fifteen years out of date, but still the face of the man who'd abandoned her to serve the Empire. She kicked at the dust, shook her head when Cassian started to speak. "So what now?" she asked.

If he noticed her discomfort, he didn't show it. *Good for him,* she thought.

"I had a contact," he said. "One of Saw's rebels, but he's just gone missing. His sister will be looking for him."

"Sweet family."

"The temple's been destroyed but she'll be there waiting. There're enough pilgrims around to make it a decent place to hide in plain sight, use as a dead drop. We'll give her your name and hope that gets us a meeting with Saw."

"Hope?" She eyed Cassian dubiously. "Is that the best Rebel Intelligence can do?"

Cassian might as well have shrugged. "Rebellions are built on hope," he said.

The crowd thinned out one street over. Jyn drew up her hood as they passed a squad of stormtroopers knocking on doors and manhandling residents. She didn't reach for a weapon this time; she'd be too tempted to use it. She tuned out the pleas of the Jedha citizens

instead and zeroed in on the words of an Imperial propaganda hologram shimmering nearby. Something about an armed fugitive in a
stolen Imperial flight suit.

She waited until they were out of earshot of the troopers and then
asked, "Is this all because of your pilot?"

Cassian didn't bother answering the question. "Wait for me," he
said, and disappeared into the crush of bodies.

Jyn grunted an assent and began a slow orbit of a tight cluster of
merchant stalls. She made a show of turning her head to study the
contents of the shops—hand-knit fabrics, fruit so brown and spotted
that it had to have been grown locally, shards of stone ostensibly from
ruined shrines within the wastelands—and avoided eye contact with
the hawkers. She could still hear the propaganda hologram in the
distance ("goes by the name *Bodhi Rook*"), but a pilgrim's chanting
rose in volume until it drowned out almost everything else. Over and
over, a simple refrain: "May the Force of others be with you."

She picked up a palm-sized heater that a merchant promptly
slapped from her hand. Her mind began to drift and she feared she'd
start thinking of Saw again, of Galen Erso, yet the chant resounded
inside her skull. It followed her as she walked, until she was sure that
the pilgrim responsible had fallen in behind her.

She snapped a glance over her shoulder. The chant ended. At Jyn's
back was an ancient woman with withered hands, currently haggling
over the heater Jyn had set down. Not her chanter.

"Would you trade that necklace for a glimpse into your future?"

The voice of the pilgrim. Jyn frowned and took another step forward, trying to locate the source.

"Yes, I'm speaking to you." Without the monotone sobriety of the
chant, the voice seemed touched with gentle humor.

She found the speaker at last, seated on the ground a few steps
down the line of stalls. He was dressed simply, in a dark shirt and
charcoal robe in the local style, and his smooth skin fought gamely
against the years that infected his words. His eyes were milky and
unfocused, and at his side lay a sturdy wooden staff in the dust. *Are
there trees left on Jedha?* Jyn wondered.

"Your necklace?" the man repeated.

Jyn felt the crystal against her skin. Her necklace was still hidden, buried under layers of cloth.

And the man was blind.

"I am Chirrut Îmwe," the man said.

"How did you know I was wearing a necklace?" Jyn asked, and felt like a fool, like a *mark,* even as she spoke.

Chirrut's next words only confirmed her instinct. "For that answer you must pay."

It was the reply of a con artist. Jyn shook her attention from Chirrut to search for his partner (he *must* have had a partner, one who had spotted her necklace somehow) and immediately found her quarry: a hulk of a man with hair as wild as Chirrut's was neat, in a filthy civilian flight suit and battered red plastoid armor half concealed under a wearable tarp. On his back was a generator unit connected to the blaster cannon he held casually in one hand. He stood with the stoic confidence of a bodyguard, unafraid of thieves or stormtroopers.

"How did *you* know I was wearing a necklace?" Jyn asked the second man, who shook his head slowly and snorted. Under other circumstances, she might have admired his weapon. Now she didn't want to give him the satisfaction.

"What do you know of kyber crystals?" Chirrut asked. His tone was patient, prompting.

She should have turned away. Refused to be lured in. Yet Chirrut's voice seemed to resonate like his chant and demand an answer.

"My father," she eventually said, and it tasted less bitter than she expected. "He said they powered the Jedi lightsabers."

Chirrut nodded approvingly. Jyn half parted her lips, tried to speak before the blind man's voice could enter her skull again, but another sound broke the spell instead. *"Jyn."* Cassian, sharp and low. "Come on."

She wrenched away from Chirrut, took three strides at Cassian's side before the pilgrim's next words found her: "The strongest stars have hearts of kyber."

Her necklace seemed to burn in the cold.

"Let's *go*," Cassian urged.

She couldn't help glancing back once at the pilgrim (or the con man) and his partner. But she shrugged off Cassian's guiding hand and trailed him willingly down the street. "We're not here to make friends," he muttered. "Not with those guys."

"Who are they?"

"The Guardians of the Whills. Protectors of the Temple of the Kyber. But there's nothing left to protect, so now they're just causing trouble for everybody."

She frowned. "What kind of trouble?"

Cassian turned his head in a slow arc as if checking for pursuit. "For the Guardians, anyone who's not a pilgrim is intruding on holy ground. The Empire calls them strays . . . used to be domesticated, still beg for scraps, but they've really gone feral. Look at them wrong and they'll bite your hand in a second."

"You'll make me like them," Jyn said. She tried to push their faces, Chirrut's voice, out of her brain. They probably *were* con men, even if they'd been zealots once. Beyond that, she didn't know enough about the local religions to speculate; pilgrims from a hundred faiths came to the moon from across the galaxy, and all of them blurred together into the same pathetic cult, chanting and moaning and squirming under the Empire's boot.

Cassian didn't reply. His pace picked up.

"You seem awfully tense all of a sudden," she said. "What were you doing back there?"

"Spotted an old associate. He didn't have any better line on Saw Gerrera, but he's been hearing rumors."

"What *kind* of rumors?"

They were drawing closer to the Holy Quarter, and the character of the streets was changing. The roads grew wider—just as ancient, but no longer touched by the centuries of expansion, of the layering of building onto building by residents and merchants. The vendors and their customers were fewer, replaced by pilgrims in bright-red kaftans and hoods and shawls.

"This search for the pilot," Cassian said. "The door-to-door inspections . . . there were shootings last night, an elderly couple dead in their home, others civilians rounded up. No one's sure if they were innocent or if they knew something about the defector, but word is out that Saw Gerrera is planning reprisals."

"That doesn't sound like Saw," Jyn said. Cassian threw her a skeptical look, and she hastily explained, "Not that he wouldn't arrange revenge attacks, but if he were *that* easily baited they'd have caught him long ago."

Cassian frowned in thought and seemed to process the words.

"Could be my associate was wrong," he said. "Could be it's one of Saw's people arranging the attack without oversight from Saw himself. Or it could be Saw thinks the Empire is vulnerable right now—distracted by the search or something else we don't know about.

"Regardless, we have to hurry. This town—it's ready to blow."

They passed a mural, colors long since faded to muddy indecipherability. Jyn saw chips in the stone and a grenade fragment lodged into the wall. She laughed gutturally. "We're a little late for that," she said, though she didn't slow her stride.

They arrived on an upper-level street overlooking a large plaza. The shadow of a descending Imperial cargo shuttle spread over the ground while a squad of stormtroopers rousted sleeping forms out of doorways and shoved them headlong into neighboring streets, waved blaster rifles at pilgrims, and barked orders. Jyn was surprised by the aggression—at close quarters, one squad couldn't suppress a riot—until she saw the assault tank rumbling around a corner to join the Imperial forces. Its blaster cannons could have leveled a city block. Jyn didn't doubt its pilots were eager for a challenge.

Secured to the back of the tank were the same orange cargo crates she'd seen while spying on the city from afar. The kyber crystals, mined from the ground or stolen from holy sites.

The strongest stars have hearts of kyber.

She indicated the crates to Cassian with a nod. His attention was elsewhere. He was scanning the rooftops, his gaze flickering back periodically to the civilians lined up along the edge of the plaza. To a person, the onlookers were garbed in thick, bulky cloaks and over-coats.

When Jyn recognized what was happening, she was surprised the stormtroopers hadn't already opened fire. But the Imperials appeared entirely—almost pitiably—oblivious.

"How far is your contact? The sister of Saw's man?" she asked, barely louder than a breath.

"Half a dozen blocks over," Cassian murmured. "But I don't think she's going to stick around."

A wrinkled Duros scampered up the stairs from the lower level and past Jyn and Cassian, red beetle eyes avoiding the now grounded shuttle, the tank, and every living creature nearby.

"Tell me you have a backup plan," Jyn said. "You want to tap one of these guys on the shoulder, ask if they can spare some advice before the shooting starts?"

"We've got to get out of here." Cassian spoke the words like a curse.

Jyn didn't see who threw the first grenade. She heard it strike pavement despite the noise of the vehicles, recognized the sound despite the murmuring from the rooftops and the sharp commands of the stormtroopers. A glint of sunlight drew her eye to the metal sphere and she saw it bounce once, roll half a meter in the direction of the tank, then disappear in an eruption of street fragments and smoke and shrapnel. She felt the resonant *boom* in her teeth. She heard a dozen cloaks and overcoats being shucked in unison, then the dull *clack* of pistols and rifles being brought to bear.

The air turned bright with the arterial glow of a hundred particle bolts.

Sparks burst off ancient stone walls. The noxious smell of burning plastoid armor and the ozone of vaporized Jedha atmosphere stung Jyn's nostrils. A volley of blasterfire coursed across the plaza's upper level—originating from stormtrooper or insurgent, Jyn wasn't sure—and Jyn reacted instinctively, dashing with Cassian into the flimsy shelter of a doorframe and squeezing tight against him.

"Looks like we found Saw's rebels," she said. Her blaster was in her hand. Her finger was on the trigger.

If Cassian replied, Jyn lost the words in the bedlam. She tried to read the battlefield, pinpoint every combatant, and found the chaos overwhelming. This wasn't her kind of fight anymore; there were too many people on each side deploying tactics she hadn't thought about in too long. All of Saw's training, the long months staring at holographic carnage and the years of staging ambushes with his soldiers, churned wildly in her brain. She spied only *moments:* a stormtrooper shot in the visor while swapping blaster packs; a rebel bleeding on the stairs and desperately searching for cover; the guns of the tank elevating, aiming toward a shop whose rooftop supported a trio of rebel attackers.

Beneath the awning of the shop stood a girl, ten years old at the most. *Probably a pilgrim,* Jyn thought. The girl was trembling, staring at the battle. Utterly paralyzed.

Jyn left the cover of the doorway and ran for the shop. Cassian called her name, but it meant nothing.

Jyn didn't see the tank open fire. She grabbed the girl, scooped up her too-light body, and didn't stop running as stone burst and sparks spattered her back like rain. Fury drove her forward, a sudden revulsion that had lain buried and forgotten under the hatch in her brain: a violent horror at Saw Gerrera and his people, and the cost of his tactics.

Jyn might have kicked the woman who stepped forward to intercept her if the girl she carried hadn't writhed and twisted, almost leapt into the woman's outstretched arms. Jyn let the girl go, ignored the woman's babbling and waved her off.

You cluster together, you die, she thought. The old training was resurfacing after all.

She was too exposed. She knew that. She searched the plaza for cover and for Cassian. She spotted him out of the shelter of the doorframe, stupidly, *dangerously* near the tank, and realized he'd already seen her. He had his own blaster out and fired a cluster of tight shots above her head. She craned her neck around in time to see Cassian's target: a rebel stationed on another rooftop behind her.

An instant later Cassian's target and his rebel comrades disappeared in the fiery bloom of a grenade. Jyn could only guess one of the rebels had been aiming the explosive her way.

Cassian had shot one of Saw's rebels to save her life. Jyn supposed she should have been anguished, torn at the thought.

She wasn't.

She sprinted toward Cassian. Clustering *would* get them killed, but she didn't plan on staying in the plaza and she didn't relish the thought of escaping Jedha on her own. She bowled into Cassian as another grenade impacted the tank. She slammed him to the ground and shielded him as metal shredded the air.

Cassian dragged her to her feet and uttered a breathless "Come on!" He didn't thank her, and Jyn was grateful for it.

They made it fifty meters from the plaza before hitting another stormtrooper squad. Half a dozen soldiers obstructed the alley Jyn and Cassian had turned down, advancing gingerly through the Holy Quarter like they expected the streets to be mined.

Jyn swore to herself. Cassian pivoted around, but the stormtroopers reacted faster, turning their rifles on the man. One might miss; together they'd cut him down in seconds. Jyn called Cassian's name and barreled forward, pulling her truncheons from her coat.

The fight in the plaza had numbed her senses. Her body had acclimated to the roar of explosions, the glare of particle bolts, the heat of flames, and the blasts of demolished stone across her face. The brief respite from combat had let her *feel* again, and now her cheeks prickled and her legs throbbed with fatigue. She gripped her truncheons too tight, afraid she'd lose one as she slammed the metal rods into the joints of stormtrooper armor. She targeted throats and behind knees, felt the cushion of bodysuits underneath the troopers' plating and struck again, *again*, crushing her own fingernails bloody in the pressure of her grasp. She knocked aside rifles with her shoulders, wedged herself into the fray to deny her opponents the opportunity to aim. She let her strikes determine her balance, moved from blow to blow, and ignored the flat *smack* of a rifle butt against her rib cage. When her truncheon found air, when no foe stood within reach, she stumbled back against the alley wall and exchanged a truncheon for a blaster.

She fired two shots, dispatched two more troopers bringing their weapons to bear on her. She kicked one of the men she'd left on the ground and turned in time to see Cassian execute their last upright opponent.

She was ready to drop from exhaustion. The blow to her ribs made her want to vomit. But she saw a long, spindly shadow extend down the length of the alley and forced herself to turn. In the stormtroopers' wake came the black metal body of an Imperial security droid, marching on thin, titanium-strong legs.

She dropped her second truncheon, gripped her blaster in both hands, and felt her aim waver as she fired. Despite her unsteady hands, the shot hit its mark. The droid's chest sparked and something internal popped. It tumbled to the ground, only to reveal a second, identical droid marching behind it.

The second droid shuffled to a halt. The heat of the blaster barrel warmed Jyn's cold fingers. She took aim.

The second droid bent his head to study his fallen comrade. "Did you know that wasn't me?" he asked.

Jyn furiously searched her memory and recognized the voice of K-2SO.

"Of course!" she snapped.

Cassian joined them as she tucked away her blaster and recovered her truncheon. "I thought I told you to stay with the ship," he growled.

"You did," K-2SO replied. "But I thought it was boring, and you were in trouble. There are a lot of explosions for two people blending in."

A series of short, resonant blasts echoed from the direction of the plaza. A new column of smoke, threads of blue mixed in with the black, wafted above the rooftops. *Another assault tank?* Jyn wondered. *Maybe a walker?*

"We could find one of Saw's people," Cassian said. Jyn noticed he was sweating despite the cold; despite his matter-of-fact tone. "Preferably someone down but still breathing. Maybe he could help us."

"If you want to drag someone out of that death trap"—Jyn jutted a thumb toward the plaza—"you're welcome to try. But I'm guessing the rebels here aren't feeling *trusting* right now."

"Just keep an eye out," Cassian said.

K-2SO turned his head. Jyn couldn't tell if he was listening to something—concentrating on whatever sorts of frequencies an Imperial security droid might pick up—or looking at Cassian askance.

"The Imperial forces are converging on our present location," K-2SO said.

The droid's head jerked again, and Jyn followed the machine's gaze to the stormtroopers left sprawled on the ground. One trooper had risen to a knee, a small metallic cylinder in his left hand. He threw the grenade limply; before Jyn could move, as she tensed to leap away, K-2 extended an inhumanly long arm and caught the cylinder in one hand. A moment later the grenade retraced its arc perfectly.

Jyn winced and turned away from the explosion. A cold voice inside her said, *No more witnesses.*

"I suggest we leave immediately," K-2 declared, and they left.

For the first time since crossing the desert to the Holy City, Cassian noticed the cold. The insulating press of bodies in the street had kept him warm much of the day; then, during the fighting, the chill hadn't registered at all. Now that sunset was approaching and his undershirt was soaked with sweat, he found himself shivering and watching his breath steam from his lips.

If it was this bad for him, he couldn't imagine how Jyn was still standing.

The *need* in her eyes had been subsumed by an almost feral anger, a survival instinct that guided her with frightening surety through the chaos. But while he didn't doubt her alertness, she was slowing physically. The bruises she'd sustained brawling with the stormtroopers left her wincing with every other step. Cassian wondered, too, if she'd been concussed when she'd saved his life in the plaza—the grenade had gone off with stunning force, and she'd shielded him from the brunt of the blow.

She needed a medical droid. A chance to recuperate. Instead she traveled with Cassian and K-2 through the maze of the Holy Quarter, her head low and her breathing strained.

"We'll find shelter soon," he said. He kept his eyes averted and his tone matter-of-fact. He doubted she would respond well to pity.

Even so, she didn't argue. That struck Cassian as a bad sign.

He tried to focus on practicalities. They had to escape the Holy Quarter before it was cordoned off. They would need to reach Saw Gerrera—and the pilot—without the help of Cassian's contact. And while Jyn was right that Saw's people wouldn't be *trusting* right now, Cassian couldn't see any other leads.

Could Saw Gerrera put aside bad blood in the face of a planet killer? It seemed madness to have to ask. But by all accounts, the rift between Saw and the Alliance was profound, nurtured by years of bitterness that had curdled into violence; and Saw Gerrera was not a man who knew how to forgive.

He'd passed that on to his adopted daughter. Or maybe she'd taught it to him.

Jyn blocked Cassian's path with an outstretched arm. From a passageway too narrow to be called an alley, they watched a dozen stormtroopers pass through an intersection.

Cassian recognized a side street across the way. "That should bring us out of the quarter," he said.

Jyn waited for the patrol to move on, then promptly sprinted through the crossroads. Cassian and K-2 followed, only to stumble to a halt as Jyn abruptly stopped. Blocking the side street, nested in a pile of rubble, was the dusty wreck of an X-wing starfighter.

Cassian swore. It wouldn't be difficult to climb across, but it would leave them exposed for precious seconds—

"Halt! Stop right there!"

The trio turned together toward the voice. The stormtroopers who'd passed by were now spread out to block their retreat.

Too many to fight, Cassian thought, and his hand drifted to his blaster anyway. His power pack was almost empty, but there was no point in saving his bolts. Jyn's shoulders sagged, yet she stared at the stormtroopers like she was eager to enter the fray, glad to have nowhere to run.

The squad leader nodded to K-2SO. "Where are you taking these prisoners?"

Cassian felt something very similar to hope.

The droid stared back at the squad leader as if struggling to process a response. "These are prisoners," he said.

Cassian winced. The feeling like hope evaporated.

He flicked through a deck of possibilities. Maybe K-2 was trying to access Imperial behavioral programming and coming up short. Maybe overwritten Imperial loyalty protocols were coming back to life, thanks to hardware damage or some personal memory of the squad leader.

Most likely, and worst of all: K-2 was *that bad* at lying. He always had been, since the reprogram. Relentless honesty was his natural state.

"Yes," the squad leader said. "Where are you *taking* the prisoners?"

"I am taking them"—K-2 spoke with stilted care—"to imprison them. In prison."

Cassian channeled his irritation into a growl of anger—a sound he prayed resembled something a defiant captive might make. "He's taking us to—"

The droid swung a metal arm into Cassian's face. "Quiet!" The blow nearly took Cassian off his feet and left his nose and chin throbbing painfully, his lip stinging. K-2 loomed over him. "And there's a fresh one if you mouth off again!"

"We'll take them from here." The squad leader again. Cassian tried to refocus as the stormtroopers approached the trio. They kept their weapons out, maintained a tight formation, demonstrated all the discipline Imperial soldiers were supposed to. As one retrieved two sets of stun cuffs, the others watched Jyn, Cassian, and the droid.

K-2 was babbling now. "That's okay. If you could just point me in the right direction, I can take them, I'm sure. I've taken them this far—"

Jyn looked to Cassian and reached for her truncheons as the trooper with the cuffs approached. Cassian shook his head. *Wait for a chance,* he mouthed, and Jyn looked ready to bite as the trooper snapped the restraints onto her wrists. A few seconds later Cassian, too, was cuffed.

"Hey," he murmured. "Hey, droid. Wait a second."

Whatever the troopers' suspicions, they clearly didn't believe K-2 had been subverted. If Cassian could make his intentions known, the droid could locate them in holding, access the Imperial database to free them.

It wasn't a *good* plan, but it was *a* plan.

"Take them away," the squad leader called. The stormtroopers circled and moved in unison. Cassian felt a rifle muzzle nudge at his back.

"You can't take them away!" K-2 protested.

"You stay here," the squad leader said. "We need to check your diagnostics."

"Diagnostics? I'm capable of running my own diagnostics, thank you very much."

Don't argue, Cassian wanted to snap. He gave the droid as intent a look as he dared, but K-2 was too invested in his debate with the squad leader. A stormtrooper shoved Cassian from behind and he stumbled forward.

If they were taken captive and K-2's reprogramming was discovered, then they truly had no way out. They could claim they were residents of Jedha City, but that would fall apart on a cursory investigation. They could say they were deserters from Saw's band, but they'd gain no leniency.

You messed up bad, Cassian told himself. *This time, you get to pay the price yourself.*

Then a voice cried out, steady and commanding, and everyone—stormtroopers, captives, and droid—stopped to look.

"Let them pass in peace!"

Chirrut Îmwe stood in an archway staring at the stormtroopers with blind eyes. Jyn wanted to laugh.

Cassian had called him a Guardian of the Whills, whatever that really meant. He'd played games with Jyn to try to buy her necklace. And now he was, what? Martyring himself?

Maybe he was more zealot than con man after all.

"Let them pass in peace," he said again, leaning lightly on his staff. The stormtroopers were repositioning themselves, fanning out to defend against Chirrut or another rebel ambush.

Chirrut began chanting, and the words throbbed in Jyn's aching skull: "The Force is with me, and I am with the Force." He emerged from the archway, stepped toward the stormtroopers. He was in the middle of the street now, separating most of the squad from Jyn, Cassian, and K-2SO. "And I fear nothing, for all is as the Force wills it."

"Hey! Stop right there!" The squad leader's voice was angry. *Not used to being ignored by civilians,* Jyn thought, and smiled grimly.

"He's blind," a second trooper called.

"Is he deaf?" the squad leader asked. "I said: Stop right there!"

Chirrut raised one foot from the pavement, and the squad leader fired a single shot. It was too late to shout a warning, too late for anyone to intervene, and Jyn felt an unexpected ache, a pang of guilt over the death of a man who had tried to save them.

But Chirrut was not dead. The bolt had been aimed with precision, yet Chirrut was *not dead*. The merest twitch of his head, a glance to one side, had saved him and sent the energy flashing by, toward the captives and over Cassian's shoulder.

Stormtroopers who had previously hesitated to shoot a blind man adjusted their weapons with nervous hands and a renewed sense of duty. Jyn shifted her wrists in her cuffs, glancing at the two stormtroopers who remained within her reach.

Chirrut was inside the bulk of the squad in two strides. His staff was suddenly in motion, sweeping behind legs and twisting arms back unnaturally. Jyn felt clumsy and graceless—where she had thrown her whole body into every strike with her truncheons, Chirrut dropped stormtroopers with a delicate whirl, a flick of his wrist.

He was *mocking* them now, in a voice full of gentle mirth. "Is your foot all right?" Like a dancer, he leapt a step to the side as another stormtrooper fired his rifle. The bolt found one of the trooper's squad mates, and Chirrut only shook his head sadly.

The two stormtroopers by Jyn were staring at the melee, as if debating whether to join their squad. Jyn chose her moment and swung her cuffed hands into the helmet of the trooper nearest. The metal bit fiercely into her wrists as she impacted. Graceless or not, exhausted and cold and hurting or not, she'd do what she could.

She'd caught the stormtrooper by surprise. She took advantage of the man's shock by throwing her shoulder into his chest, forcing him to his knees. She heard Cassian and K-2SO fighting, too, heard continued shouting from Chirrut's direction, but she focused on her own opponent. She brought her shackles down on the back of the trooper's head, pounded at his helmet, drove him low—drove the plastoid against his skull again and again, until he finally slumped to the ground. If she'd been sure of his unconsciousness, Jyn might have stopped there; instead she kicked him fiercely, viciously, three times, until she was certain he couldn't rise.

Cassian and K-2SO's opponent was down as well. Chirrut stood calmly over a pile of bodies. Jyn rolled aching shoulders and felt blood on her raw wrists.

But the fight wasn't over. A second squad of stormtroopers—reinforcements, maybe, or just drawn by the noise—rushed in from the intersection. Chirrut was too far away to intercept them before they could take aim. Jyn scanned for cover, saw none within reach, and prepared to drop flat onto the dust.

She heard the crackling snap of a particle bolt, but none of the stormtroopers had discharged his or her weapon. One collapsed, then another, as sniper fire struck them faster than Jyn would have thought possible. When the last was dead, the shooter emerged from across the way.

Jyn recognized him: Chirrut's silent partner from the alley, the one with wild hair and red armor. In one hand, he bore his repeating cannon. In the other was an ornate, gold-trimmed bowcaster at odds with his battered and practical gear; this, the man passed to Chirrut.

"You almost shot me," Chirrut said.

"You're welcome," his partner replied. Without looking, he fired a bolt into the back of a stormtrooper crawling nearby.

Then Chirrut's partner turned toward Jyn and Cassian. He raised his cannon, expression wary but not outright hostile. Chirrut watched with blind eyes. *You both saved us,* Jyn thought. *You won't kill us now.*

"Clear of hostiles!" K-2SO announced, striding forward to survey the remnants of the battle.

Immediately, Chirrut's partner aimed at the droid. K-2SO halted and amended, "One hostile!"

"He's with *us!*" Jyn cried.

"No." Chirrut spoke to his partner gently. "They're okay."

The red-armored man lowered his weapon again. Jyn thought he looked disappointed.

Jyn nursed her scraped wrists and flexed her fingers, glad to be free of the cuffs. She'd spent too much time in restraints, gone to too much trouble to ensure her freedom. Even a few minutes was more than she wanted to endure.

K-2SO was freeing Cassian as Chirrut and his partner looked on. "Go back to the ship," Cassian told the droid. "Wait for my call."

"You're wasting your most valuable resource," the droid returned, but he strode away obediently. Jyn looked to Cassian for an explanation. They were still in danger, and while the droid brought unwanted attention he'd also proven useful. She didn't much like K-2; he was still more reliable than their new allies.

Cassian, evidently, had other things on his mind. He watched Chirrut's partner. "Is he Jedi?" he asked, with the hushed doubt of a man on the verge of a great discovery.

Jyn thought of the spinning staff, of Chirrut's graceful dance of battle. Was that what Jedi were like? Her mother had told her stories: the mystic warriors and guardians of the Republic in the centuries before the Empire, believers in a Force that guided living creatures.

She'd never really believed in the stories. The *Jedi,* yes, but not the *legend.*

"No Jedi anymore," Chirrut's partner said. "Only dreamers like this fool."

Chirrut shrugged mildly. "The Force *did* protect me."

"*I* protected you," his partner replied.

If Cassian was disappointed by his answer, Jyn couldn't tell. She was willing to take Chirrut's partner at his word; easier to believe in what existed now rather than what *might have been* long ago.

She bit back her next words, savored the sour taste before asking, "Can you get us to Saw Gerrera?"

She'd already committed to the mission. *Might as well see it through.*

Neither Chirrut nor his partner had the opportunity to reply before someone called: "Hands in the air!"

Rebel fighters emerged from alleys and rooftops. Jyn recognized several from the plaza. She wanted to shout in rage—for hours, it seemed, she'd done nothing but fight, and her body had been sapped of every erg of strength; had turned to nothing but a collection of bruises and aching muscles.

Cassian was the first to drop his weapon. Jyn followed suit. Cassian mouthed something to her: *Not the enemy.*

"Can't you see we are no friends of the Empire?" Chirrut asked. He'd set his bowcaster in the dust. Even his partner had relinquished his cannon.

One rebel stepped forward: a thin, skull-faced Tognath in leathers who breathed through a mechanical respirator and spoke in his native dialect. "Tell that to the one who killed our men."

Jyn looked to Cassian. In her mind's eye, she saw him fire his blaster in the plaza, felt the grenade explode over her head. She remembered the cold, guiltless sensation that had passed over her then; shame found her now, gripped her heart, and she tore through it with anger.

These were Saw's people. If Saw was alive, she knew how to deal with them.

"Anyone who kills me or my friends will answer to Saw Gerrera," she called.

The rebels shuffled, murmured to one another. One of them

chuckled hoarsely. The Tognath cocked his head, as if trying to recognize Jyn's face.

"And why is that?" he asked.

"Because Saw *knows* me," she said. "Because I know *him*. Because I was battling at his side when most of you were still crying in your beds instead of fighting back." She'd begun by choosing her words carefully, but now they spilled from her lips unwanted. "I've seen that man at his worst. I know exactly what he does when he feels betrayed, and I'm still *alive*."

The broken hatch made it easy to stumble upon unwanted memories. The battle in the plaza had already dredged up a hundred bloody conflicts she'd barely survived, thirteen or fourteen or fifteen years old and already trusted with a blaster. Now she remembered the *looks* from her fellow rebels, the whispers behind her back. The things they wondered about her. The things they believed.

"Because," she finished, "I am the daughter of Galen Erso."

The Tognath watched her for a long moment. Everyone, friend and foe, was still.

"Take them," the Tognath said.

Two rebels grappled Jyn. She didn't fight. Coarse cloth scraped over her nose, and she fought to breathe through the sack that clung to her face. She heard Cassian groan nearby, a growl from Chirrut's partner, and then Chirrut's own voice:

"Are you kidding me? I'm blind!"

SUPPLEMENTAL DATA: PILGRIMS OF JEDHA

[Document #DN4624 ("Faith and the Force of Others"), fragment excerpted from the archives of the Order of the Esoteric Pulsar; author unknown.]

What is the Force of Others? To ask this, you must ask one question and a thousand.

To a cultist of the Huiyui-Tni, you must ask, "What is the exhalation of the true, amphibious god?" To a Jedi, you must ask, "What is it that binds and defines all life?" To a child of the Esoteric Pulsar, you must ask, "Show me the secret pages of the Book of Stars." To a faithless man, you must ask, "What power enables prophecy and sorcery in a world controlled by logic and law?"

These thousand questions will garner a thousand answers, all pointing toward the same truth.

Now ask, "*Where* is the Force of Others?" and one answer becomes inevitable: the kind and cold moon of Jedha. For a thousand faiths see truth in Jedha's mysteries, no matter that their stories differ; no matter that not one history of the Temple of the Kyber can explain each brick in its foundation, or that our legends entwine and part in paradox.

I ask you to believe that Jedha is a nexus for faith, life, and the Force of Others in all their forms. If the Force can be embodied in a vision or a living creature, why not a place? Or why not an *idea*? Why can *pilgrimage* not be Jedha, and Jedha not *be* the Force?

I ask you to believe this not because it is *true,* but because it is a beginning.

Imagine these things and you must conclude that every visit to Jedha is a pilgrimage—that every visit to Jedha is an expression of faith and a search for truth, intended or not. When a thief comes to Jedha to prey upon the vendors in the markets, she does so in accordance with her nature; she will trick and lie and steal, and if she does *not* trick or lie or steal then her faith and nature are altogether different.

You say, "Why a thief? Why such a cynical conjecture?" To which I say, "Do you not wonder why the Guardians of the Whills protect their temple so? Why the Jedi carry their cruel swords of light, even here?" It is because our pilgrimages *are* in accordance with our faiths, and faith can bring terrible conflict. A thief is but the kindest example I can offer.

Jedha does not give answers to those who do not know what answers they seek. Jedha does not bring into harmony those things that cannot harmonize. Jedha does not express faith and the Force through its pilgrims; pilgrims express faith and the Force through Jedha.

Pilgrims express faith and the Force through life.

For what is life but pilgrimage? And what is life but conflict?

There have been worlds and tyrants who have tried to prevent their people from journeying to Jedha. But such a thing cannot be stopped. Living beings will always find their way to the kind and cold moon, as they always have. Through the Force and Jedha, they will act as they must, for good and ill.

And we will know them by their actions there.

CHAPTER 5

CASSIAN WAS BLIND BENEATH HIS hood, but although he lacked Chirrut's preternatural senses, he knew how to *listen*.

During the long march from the Holy City, he listened to his captors. He listened to the code words they murmured to unseen allies who granted them passage out of the settlement and into the desert. He listened to their confusion, the short-lived cheering and then the grim silence, as the Star Destroyer above Jedha shrank into the twilight sky. He listened to the Tognath state coolly, "Saw will know what it means."

He listened to Chirrut's endless chanting (*May the Force of others be with you. May the Force of others be with you.*), muffled by the cloth sack. The combined effect seemed simultaneously profound and absurd.

Most of all, he listened for Jyn. He listened for her struggles. He listened for her voice. He tried to determine which steady tread on the sand was hers.

For all Cassian heard, she might have vanished from the face of Jedha.

Was it concern that made him fixate on her? His mission was to find Saw and, through Saw, find the pilot; find proof of an Imperial weapon that could mutilate the galaxy. If possible, he was also to find and eliminate Galen Erso—a man very likely culpable in that weapon's creation. Jyn was first and foremost a means of finding Saw. She'd already served that purpose, which meant she was now expendable.

She dominated his thinking nonetheless. Cassian believed neither pity nor pragmatism explained it.

He had sacrificed Tivik without hesitation.

Maybe it was the *need* he'd seen in Jyn, the fire that had carried her through the fighting in the Holy Quarter. It seemed obscene to leave that need unanswered, abandoned to the dust.

It was late into the night when the band left the desert for the rocky slopes of a mountainside, then on from the mountain to the echoing corridors of a stone shelter. Cassian recognized the heavier tread of Chirrut's partner at his side and risked a low murmur. "We're half a day out. A shrine?"

"A monastery," the man said. "The Catacombs of Cadera, down among the dead."

The name meant nothing to Cassian.

He tried to count rebel voices in the distance, but he rapidly lost track. They'd reached a base of some kind: Weapons clattered and heaters hummed, and heavy doors opened and slammed shut. Shouts of triumph and the click of wooden game pieces suggested the presence of bored guards or off-duty soldiers. Without prelude, Cassian's hood was torn off and a solid kick delivered to his lower back. He pivoted in time to see the blurred shadow of a cell door slam shut. He blinked furiously to adjust to the dim light.

The cell was little more than a cramped alcove in the rock. Chirrut and his partner shared the space with Cassian. The former man chanted softly (*May the Force of others be with you . . .*) in one corner, while the latter stood with arms folded across his chest, staring into the darkness of the cavern beyond the door.

Jyn was missing.

"Hey!" Cassian called. He rushed to the bars, cried out, "Jyn Erso! Where is she?"

No one answered.

You're a fool, Cassian told himself. *They won't talk to you. But they'll try to spot your weakness.*

He mollified himself with the dubious pleasure of inhaling musty air unencumbered by a hood. The walls of the catacombs were inlaid with humanoid skulls—thousands of them, from what had to have been generations of monks—and draped with power cables leading from generators to heaters to comm stations. A handful of rebel guards sat on squat stools nearby, not far from where the group's gear had been splayed on a table. Other cells neighbored Cassian's own, silent and dark.

He turned his attention to the door itself and pushed himself against the bars to peer at its outer control panel. The lock was mechanical, but wired into the systems of the rebel hideout. He could definitely reach it, suspected he could pick it, but not without triggering an alarm.

"You pray?" Chirrut's partner asked.

Cassian turned to find the man speaking to the still-chanting Chirrut.

"You pray," the man said, and barked a laugh. He glanced at Cassian. "He's praying for the door to open."

"Pray I get a chance to work," Cassian murmured, but both men seemed to ignore him.

Chirrut stopped his chant abruptly. "It bothers him," he said, "because he knows it is possible."

Chirrut's partner laughed again. The sound was brief and ugly, but Chirrut only shrugged and told Cassian, "Baze Malbus was once the most devoted Guardian of us all."

Baze Malbus. Cassian ran the name through his mental database and came up empty. "Now he's just *your* guardian?" he asked.

Neither man took the bait. Cassian ran his hands over his face, scratched at his beard. Both of the Guardians were formidable fighters, to be sure; and Chirrut, Jedi or not, half mad or overzealous or sincere, was an echo of an era the Empire had nearly erased.

Even the leaders of the Rebellion rarely spoke about the Jedi. Had men like Chirrut been common? Men so certain in their faith that they wielded it like a shield? Men so disciplined that, even blind, they could down a dozen stormtroopers with nothing more than a stick?

How many people were alive to remember?

Before the rise of the Empire, Cassian would have considered the Jedi his enemies. But he'd been *so* young, too young to understand who he'd been fighting or who he'd been fighting *for*. Now the Separatists were as forgotten as their Jedi foes.

"Why did you save us?" he asked.

"Maybe I only saved her," Chirrut said.

Cassian grunted. "I'm beginning to think the Force and I have different priorities."

"Relax, Captain," Chirrut answered. "We've been in worse cages than this one."

"Yeah? Well, this is a first for me."

"There is more than one sort of prison, Captain," Chirrut said. "I sense that you carry yours wherever you go."

Baze laughed again, but there was no boisterousness this time— just a coarse, hollow sound.

Cassian frowned and turned back to the lock and the cavern. It was some minutes later that he realized no one had told Chirrut he was a *captain*.

Jyn recognized the soldiers in the monastery, though she'd never met most of them. She knew their scars: the burn marks on their palms from overheated blasters, the short, jagged lines on cheeks and neck drawn by slivers of shrapnel. She knew their carriage: the proud, compact manner they maintained that readied them to take or return a blow. She recognized these things, recognized the soldiers not only as rebels but as *Saw's* rebels, trained in his image, and she instinctively mirrored their posture, reflected their mistrustful glares.

All these years later, she was still one of them—and they hated her for it.

She couldn't really blame them. They were mourning casualties in the Holy City because of her. They were mourning their brothers and sisters, dead at her hand (or close enough).

She waited in the central chamber of the monastery, a place stacked with cots and cook stations attended by Saw's people. The Tognath had left her there after guiding her away from Cassian, her hood off and her hands bound. The question of where Cassian might be now was no more than a distant distraction to Jyn—like the sound of a rat scuttling along rafters.

She had other concerns on her mind. Saw Gerrera was somewhere close. She could almost smell the oil on his favorite rifle. For years, she had anticipated, *fantasized* about confronting him; picked hurtful words and braced herself for the wrath of the *first, last, and only true warrior to stand against the Empire.*

That confrontation had never come, and she'd let the fantasy die. Now she wasn't sure she was ready for the fight.

"I remember you."

Jyn turned to see a woman approaching. She was pale, almost chalk-skinned, but human, dressed in an armored jacket two sizes too large. Her speech was slurred. One of her arms hung limp.

"Were you on Fashinder Prime?" the woman asked, as if trying to place an acquaintance.

"No," Jyn said, and furrowed her brow. "Must've been after my time."

Jyn tried to recall the woman's face and caught other memories instead. She saw comrades she hadn't thought about in a lifetime.

"Is Staven still alive?" Jyn asked.

Staven, who'd lectured her for hours one night for miswiring a detonator. Staven, who'd given Jyn her first sip of fermented bantha milk and let her sit with the adults telling dirty jokes before anyone else.

"No," the woman said.

"What about Codo?"

Codo, who'd taught Jyn how to swim in the mudhole they'd called a grotto. Codo, who'd tried to kiss her, and who wouldn't talk to her after she refused.

In response, the woman lifted her good hand, put an imaginary blaster to her head, and pulled the trigger.

"Maia?" Jyn asked. But that was stupid; she remembered now, she had *been there* when Maia died. Jyn had been the one to inherit—and promptly lose—Maia's synthskin gloves, the gloves that had been so soft and smelled like carbon scoring.

People didn't talk about the dead much among Saw's rebels. It made it easy to forget when someone was gone.

The woman grunted and drifted away. The Tognath emerged from a doorway and returned to Jyn's side. With a swift, unkind motion, he cut the bonds around her wrists.

"He'll see you now," the Tognath said.

No more distractions, Jyn thought.

Saw Gerrera had recruited hard soldiers and made them heartless. Staven and Codo and Maia, everything Jyn had loved and hated about them—all of it was shadow in Saw's fiery light.

She shut down a tremor and steeled herself to meet the man who'd saved her from the cave.

"In there," the Tognath said, and gestured at a curtained doorway. Jyn stepped through the ragged fabric, which parted like a cobweb. The Tognath did not follow.

The small chamber beyond was a spartan living area built for a lonely abbot. It peered onto the valley of the Holy City through a window in the rock. A pale-gray dawn had crept up behind the horizon, and Jyn realized that she was no longer tired; sometime during the night, during the march across the desert, she had lost the capacity for ordinary exhaustion and taken on a deeper weariness.

She heard a harsh metallic *clank*. She shifted her weight instinctively, ready to take a fighting stance.

"Is it really you?" a hoarse voice asked.

She was ready, she told herself.

Jyn turned her head and looked at Saw Gerrera.

The wreck that had *been* Saw Gerrera.

Where she had once known a soldier, scarred but strong, now she saw an old man held together by the scaffolding of armor and braces. His dark hair was frosted with white, grown wild and unkempt about his face. His eyes were keen as ever, but they were trapped inside a rusting cage.

Saw Gerrera had been the strongest person Jyn had ever known. Even sealed within the hatch in her mind, buried in the darkness, he had shouted to be heard.

She loathed him for so many reasons. She had been prepared to fight. Witnessing him like this, she wanted to cry.

"I can't believe it," he whispered. "Jyn . . ."

He strode toward her, the metallic rhythm of his leg echoing in the chamber.

"Must be quite a surprise," she said. She spoke in the voice of the Jyn who wanted a battle. It was the voice of a soldier, the voice that terrified prisoners and demanded cold, merciless retribution.

It was supposed to be Saw's voice.

But there was no harshness in his rasp. "Are we not still friends?" he asked.

"The last time I saw you," Jyn uttered, as casual as if she were butchering a rat on a spit, "you gave me a knife and loaded blaster and told me to wait in a shell turret until daylight."

"I knew you were safe," Saw said. He sounded *wounded.*

"You left me behind."

"You were already the best soldier in my cadre." Saw shook his head. "You were ready, and I saw that, even if you did not."

Her words came too fast, too hot. "I was *sixteen.*"

"I was protecting you." Her error seemed to give strength to Saw. His rasp became sharper, a swift slap of correction.

"You dumped me," Jyn sneered, but it wasn't much more than a murmur. She had come full of savagery, ready to pit her fire against his; instead he'd stolen her heat, and all either of them had now was embers.

"You were the daughter of an Imperial science officer," Saw said. He spoke more gently than Jyn could bear. "People were starting to figure that out. People who wanted to—to use you as a hostage.

"Not a day goes by I don't think of you . . ."

"Stop," she said. She didn't want this. The *kind* Saw Gerrera, the *gentle* Saw Gerrera, who could afford to look at the girl he raised and pity her. *Fight me,* she wanted to beg.

Then Saw's eyes narrowed, and Jyn caught a glimpse of the warrior she knew.

"But *today,* of all days?" he asked.

He took another step forward, stared at her, unblinking.

"It's a trap," he said. "Isn't it?"

"What?"

The soldier *was* somewhere in the wreck of the man, inside the armor and the braces, gasping defiance against his dying body. "The pilot," Saw said, with impotent urgency. "The message. All of it." He grasped at the oxygen mask built into his armor, pulled it to his face and sucked in a mouthful of air before resuming. "Did they send you? Have you come here to kill me?" There was no humor in his voice as he added: "There's not much left."

Jyn shook her head slowly. The words drifted like motes of dust, like ash, and she began to comprehend. This *was* still the Saw Gerrera she knew, albeit enfeebled and drained of life. This was the man who knew compassion, who cared for Jyn as his own daughter, only so long as there was no battle to fight; no paranoid fantasy of traitors or Imperial plots to lure him astray.

"I don't care enough to kill you, Saw," she said.

"So what is it, Jyn? Why come to Jedha in the name of the Rebel Alliance?"

He'd done his research, apparently. He wanted to talk about her mission? About the pilot? *Fine.*

"The Alliance wants my father," she said. "They think he's sent you a message about a weapon. I guess they think by sending me you might actually help them out."

"*Who* sent you?" he asked, as if he'd caught her at a lie. "Was it Draven?"

"General Draven, Mon Mothma, the whole damn council," Jyn snapped. "I don't know them, Saw. I'm doing this job because I have to."

Saw turned away, snatched up a cane, and leaned heavily against it. His hand was trembling. "So what is it that *you* want, Jyn? Did you expect I could welcome you back? Ignore the deaths in the city?"

She almost laughed. She held it in, smiled bitterly instead. "I want to be left alone. They wanted an introduction, they've got it—you should be talking to your prisoners, not me." Again, that distant, distracted thought of Cassian. "I'm out now. The rest of you can do what you want."

The cane wobbled in Saw's hand. She saw him lurch, catch himself. "You care not about the cause?"

Jyn tried to find words to respond. *Do you think you're testing me? Do you think I've been hiding anything from you?* "The cause?" she finally managed. "Seriously?"

"You were the best soldier in my cadre," Saw hissed. "Not because of your skill, but because you *believed.*" The cane rose and snapped back to the floor, the sound bellowing through the room. "Because you knew our enemy like I did. Because you were willing to die for our cause and our army."

She had believed. Saw was right about that. But that belief hadn't been preserved in the dark cave in her mind. It had withered there, dried and cracked and turned to dust.

"The Alliance?" she said. "The rebels? Whatever it is you're calling yourself these days? All it's ever brought me is pain."

Saw's throat worked with effort. His nostrils flared. He didn't reach for the oxygen mask. "You can stand to see the Imperial flag reign across the galaxy?" he asked.

Jyn shrugged.

She could have walked away then; turned her back on the shadow of the man she'd known, walked into the desert and called an end to her obligations.

But Saw had hurt her.

"It's not a problem if you don't look up," she said.

She had seen Saw Gerrera face disloyalty before. She had seen him spill blood over worse offenses than her own, seen him bind and blindfold a would-be deserter and toss him from an airspeeder in front of an Imperial barracks. She knew, too, that he had hidden the worst from her—secret methods of torment and interrogation that he hadn't wished to show a fifteen-year-old girl.

She wanted to hurt him.

She wanted his old fire back, in the hope that it might rekindle her own. She had come into his chamber prepared to fight and found herself suffocating, her rage perishing without fuel. The exhaustion of the night's trek, of the battle in the Holy Quarter, rose to reclaim her after all.

You taught me to survive.

But Saw only took a drag from his oxygen mask and closed his eyes. The trembling of the cane ceased. When he looked at her again, he seemed to have found a new clarity.

"I have something to show you," he said.

So much could go wrong, Orson Krennic thought, but in the moment before action—in the instant when both triumph and defeat remained possible—the galaxy seemed wondrous.

He observed the evacuation of Jedha on a dozen viewscreens across the Death Star's overbridge. The smaller craft, the personal shuttles of high-ranking officers and the transports of specialized stormtrooper units, were the last to lift off. The Star Destroyer *Dauntless,* once stationed above Jedha City, had already repositioned itself some distance from the moon. Despite the protests of local garrison commanders, the forces assigned to Jedha would be safe from whatever followed.

One of the bridge officers called out a number: 97 percent. Krennic amended the thought: *97 percent* of Jedha's assigned military forces would be safe.

That would suffice. Jedha was a meat grinder. A 3 percent loss in return for total victory would win any general a commendation.

"It's past time, Director." The unctuous voice came from the direction of the turbolift.

Krennic pivoted on his heel and smiled a broad, *respectful* smile at Wilhuff Tarkin as the old man eyed the bustle of officers and technicians. "I couldn't agree more," Krennic said, and inclined his head. "But under the circumstances, it seems only respectful to await the Emperor's command."

"The Emperor is awaiting *my* report," Tarkin retorted.

Krennic's smile faded only a touch. "One had hoped that he and Lord Vader might have been here for such an occasion."

Tarkin's voice was laced with irritation and feigned exasperation. "And I thought it prudent to save you from any potential embarrassment."

My embarrassment, or your own?

Tarkin's objective was transparent: The man believed (with typical grandiose certainty) that a demonstration on Jedha would diminish, rather than enhance, Krennic's stature. Yet *why* remained an open question. Krennic had turned up no evidence of sabotage; nor had his contacts close to Tarkin revealed anything of use regarding the governor's plot. And while Tarkin's disdain for Krennic was supreme, he would surely have arranged for the Emperor to bear witness if he assumed Krennic's "incompetence" would result in the station's failure.

No. The most likely possibility was that Krennic's precautions against sabotage or failure had shaken Tarkin's confidence. The man was now hedging his bets. If Krennic succeeded in annihilating Jedha, Tarkin would attempt to take credit in the eyes of the Emperor. If Krennic failed, all the better.

But Krennic would not fail. The Death Star was ready. Once Jedha was destroyed, he would receive his private audience with Emperor Palpatine—and he was confident he could persuade the Emperor that it was he, not Tarkin, who deserved the accolades.

It even happened to be true.

"Your concern is hardly warranted," Krennic said. "The finest scientists and engineers in the Empire have dedicated their lives to this project. You will not find *our* faith in them misplaced."

"If saying it would only make it so," Tarkin murmured, just loud enough for the officers to hear him above the din.

Krennic barely withheld a snarl. "All Imperial forces," he announced, striding along the command stations, "have been evacuated, and I stand ready to destroy the entire moon." The officers faced him, uniformly at attention; the technicians slowed but did not cease working, as Krennic had earlier instructed.

"What we do today was once inconceivable—a scientific heresy. Yet our Empire and our Emperor have ensured our success and granted us the moral authority required to take this step toward peace. The death of a world—"

He stopped at the sound of brisk applause from Tarkin. "Inspiring," he said, "but that won't be necessary. We need a statement, not a manifesto."

Krennic's smile twisted into a grimace. "What is it," he asked, "that you suggest?"

Tarkin shrugged. "The Holy City will be enough for the day."

Krennic tugged at his gloves, felt sweat on his palms as his ire grew. His assessment of Tarkin had been incomplete: The old man was hedging against both success *and* failure, ensuring that even a perfect performance would be unspectacular at best.

Could he subvert Tarkin's orders? Arrange the destruction of the moon regardless and claim that the station's sheer power had been unanticipated? He glanced from a control console to Tarkin and back.

Not with him *watching*. Not on short notice.

He would find another way.

"Target Jedha City," he snapped. "Prepare single reactor ignition."

Krennic concealed his resentment, calmed himself with the sounds of his breath and the tidal rush of the station reactor. This wasn't how he'd imagined the culmination of twenty years' work—a diminished attack, a grand moff's power play—but it was the reality he contended with.

"Fire when ready." His voice was steady. He had earned his pride, no matter the outcome.

CHAPTER 6

CASSIAN HAD A PLAN. HE'D tested the cell door's locking mechanism while the guards were fixated on a game of dejarik, pressing against the metal with his thumb and probing the limits of its tamper alarm. He'd feigned fatigue, leaning against the door's bars so he could inspect the lock visually and find its make and model. He'd mentally cataloged the picks hidden in his boot and selected the tools he intended to use. He guessed he could escape the cell in under three minutes.

As soon as the guards were gone, anyway. But the guards weren't moving, and now he was stuck with two thoughts he had no desire to dwell upon:

Had killing Saw Gerrera's people ruined any chance of reconciliation with the Rebel Alliance? Even against the threat of a planet killer?

And where was Jyn?

"Who's the one in the next cell?"

Cassian tore his eyes from the guards and glanced over to Chirrut. It was the first time the blind man had spoken for nearly an hour.

Baze grunted and shuffled to his feet. "What? Where?" He crossed the alcove, lightly shouldering Cassian aside to make room at the door. He peered into the darkness of the cell across the way; all Cassian could see was shadows, but Baze pulled back abruptly, snarling. "An Imperial pilot."

Cassian scowled and leaned in, trying to see what Baze saw. "What pilot?"

"Imperial." Baze shrugged, squinted, seemed to assess the distance between himself and the ragged pile Cassian was starting to discern. "I'll kill him."

Cassian tried to interpose his body between Baze and the cell door as the Guardian straightened with purpose. "No—wait!" *Damn religious crazies.* He wasn't sure what Baze could do from behind bars, and he wasn't keen on learning. "Back off!" He tapped the larger man's chest with his hands, tried to seem insistent without starting a brawl. Baze shoved Cassian once but then returned to his corner, slumping to the floor.

Cassian crouched at the bars. The ragged pile shifted awkwardly. Shadows crystallized into limbs, hair, a dirt-encrusted face, and a battered uniform with Imperial markings on the arms. The man didn't seem to see Cassian, staring between his knees, huddled as if in fear of the dark and the cold.

Even from a few meters distant, he stank of sweat and filth.

Is this what Saw does to prisoners?

Is this what he's doing to Jyn?

"Are you the pilot?" Cassian called. The man didn't look up. "Hey, hey—are you the pilot? The shuttle pilot?"

The man blinked. Cassian watched dim lights from the guards' chamber gleam in wet eyes. Then the man made a noise, a groan, that Cassian had trouble interpreting as a word: "Pilot?"

Chirrut spoke softly. "What's wrong with him?"

Cassian shook his head and tried to recall the words of the Imperial holograms in the city. "Bodhi Rook?" he asked.

The man squeezed his eyes shut and shrank back. Cassian swore to himself.

If he's broken, he's no good to us anyway.

"Galen Erso," Cassian tried. He meant to sound gentle, but he heard urgency slip into his voice. "You know that name?"

The man hissed, turned his cheek as if he'd been slapped. His breath picked up, swift and loud like a hound's panting.

Cassian held still.

Come on . . .

The man opened his eyes again. His breathing slowed.

"I brought the message," he said. "I'm the pilot."

Then, in surprise and horror and hope:

"I'm the pilot. *I'm the pilot.*"

Saw Gerrera clenched one trembling hand around the edge of his console. The other hand moved assuredly, inserting a holochip into the comm unit and tapping in a command. "This is the message from the pilot," he said. "For what it's worth, he believed it was real."

Jyn's throat seemed to tighten. She rocked half a step backward, as if to withdraw from the chamber. She hadn't wanted to see Saw. She didn't want to see this.

For reasons she couldn't justify, she stood still and watched.

The holoprojector flared and a man she didn't recognize appeared etched in sapphire light. He was gaunt, but not haggard, like someone dying under the gentlest of care, and his eyes looked beyond the recorder instead of at it. His face stirred something in Jyn she couldn't verbalize—some primordial recollection warped by the weight of years.

When he spoke, she knew his voice.

"Saw, if you're watching this," Galen Erso said, "then perhaps there is a chance to save the Alliance." The words had the air of a deathbed confession.

My father is alive. My father is a coward. My father is a bastard.
Galen Erso is not my father. Galen Erso didn't raise me . . .

Jyn wanted (madly, childishly) to rush to Saw's side, to cling to him for protection. She wanted to drive her fist into the holoprojector, to bleed from shards embedded in her knuckles and then tear the holochip out, crush it under her heel.

She stood and listened.

"Perhaps there's a chance to explain myself and, though I don't dare hope for too much, a chance for Jyn, if she's alive, if you can *possibly* find her . . ." He trailed off, shook his head briskly. "A chance to let her know that my love for her has never faded and how desperately I've missed her."

From the ruin of the hatch, from the cave in her mind came images, sounds, scents: Jyn's father holding her, declaring *I love you*, smelling as sour as his Imperial uniform.

She wanted to shout at the hologram, *Your love? Who gives a damn about your love? You sent me to Saw.*

You let my mother die.

You did this to me.

She didn't say anything, and the recording kept speaking.

"Jyn, my Stardust, I can't imagine what you think of me.

"When I was taken, I faced some bitter truths. I was told that, soon enough, Krennic would have you. He toyed with me that way; for months, he would pretend to forget you, and then act in conversation as if he'd slipped up—make mention of a new lead on you or Saw. Part of me longed for those mentions. I realize now it was a kind of torture.

"As time went by, I knew that you were either dead or so well hidden that he would never find you. But I knew if I refused to work, if I took my own life, it would only be a matter of time before Krennic realized he no longer needed me to complete the project." He spoke these words swiftly, almost slurring them in his haste. In the silence that followed, his mouth worked noiselessly. Then he began again. "You may think that's an excuse. That I was fearful, and should have died. In the interests of objectivity—" Here, for the first time, he smiled. It was an ugly, effortful thing. "—I should admit the possibility. History will forgive me or excoriate me, as is appropriate. I only wish it would forget me."

Jyn listened to her father's explanations—his *justifications*—as they piled on, one after another. Too many to consider, too many to argue against, years of Galen's personal analyses and self-recriminations spat out in the space of seconds. He was trying to answer her every question, anticipate every response, and the torrent denied her any opportunity for logic or fury.

How could she not loathe him?

How could her heart not break?

She needed to sit. Her legs were swaying beneath her, as unstable as Saw's cane.

She stood and watched.

"So I did the one thing that nobody expected: I lied." His voice grew steadier, as if *here* he stood on sure ground. "Or I *learned* to lie. I played the part of a beaten man resigned to the sanctuary of his work. I made myself indispensable, and all the while I laid the groundwork of my revenge.

"You may have heard rumors by now, leaks regarding a battle station integrating an advanced laser prototype. The battle station is real. Its primary weapon has been built to penetrate the crust of a planetary object, to pour energy into a world until the bonds of matter fray and break. The ultimate result, we believe, would be the planet's violent obliteration. Nothing would survive. Nothing could ever be rebuilt.

"This battle station . . . we call it the Death Star. There is no better name."

Jyn heard the horrors her father described, but it was only his spellbound tone that allowed her to notice at all; her thoughts were fixed on his simple *presence*, his story of years of desperation and labor and doubt.

My father is alive. My father is a traitor. My father is building a weapon to destroy worlds.

Galen Erso is not my father. Galen Erso didn't raise me . . .

She looked in vain to Saw, looked for the compassion she had derided and defied minutes before. Yet he, too, was watching the message, his expression cold and somber—as if for the first time, he was hearing Galen's words and dwelling on their implications instead of searching for a trap.

"My colleagues," Galen said, "many of them, have fooled themselves into thinking they are creating something so terrible and powerful it will never be used. But they're wrong. No weapon has ever been left on the shelf. And the day is coming soon when it will be unleashed."

His head turned from the recorder as if what he said next, more than anything, he feared to say aloud.

"I've placed a flaw deep within the system.

"A scar so small and powerful, they'll never find it."

Jyn knew the words mattered. Her father spoke with the breathless agony of a man baring his soul.

It wasn't what she needed to hear. Not now.

She no longer felt the swaying of her legs. Darkness crept around the edges of her vision, as if the hatch in her mind and the cave where the hatch had been were rising up to engulf her. As if she were descending, falling, to be locked away in her own skull with everything she'd denied.

Galen shivered like a man dying in icy rain. The confession appeared to have been too much. "Jyn, if you're listening . . ." He was slurring again, stumbling and urgent. "My beloved, so much of my life has been wasted. I try to think of you only in the moments when I'm strong, because the pain of not having you with me . . . Your mother. Our *family*." He paused, seemed to try to refocus with limited effect. "The pain of that loss is so overwhelming I risk failing even now. It's just so hard not to think of you. Think of where you are.

"I assume logically, rationally, that you fight with the Rebellion. It's difficult to imagine Saw steering you any other way, and you always had the same anger—" He smiled for a second time. Here it was unforced, without self-mockery or bitterness. "—the same insistent sense of *righteousness* as your mother. It frightens me to imagine you grown, somehow working to oppose injustice in the galaxy, whether from a laboratory or a starfighter; it frightens me, and I think the Rebellion could ask for no better friend.

"Yet if it isn't so? If I'm wrong, and you left the Rebellion and Saw behind but this message still finds you? You make me no less proud, Jyn. If you found a place in the galaxy untouched by war—a quiet life, maybe with a family—if you're *happy*, Jyn, then that's more than enough."

Jyn's jaw ached, clamped shut to hold in her screams. She couldn't swallow, could barely breathe. The cave walls rose around her until the only light in the blackness was the sapphire glow of the hologram.

If you're happy, *Jyn . . .*

Galen snapped back into focus, no longer hesitant or soft. "Saw, the reactor system, that's the key. That's the place I've laid my trap. It's unstable, so one blast to any part of it will destroy the entire station."

She was losing her balance. Her legs shook and her head swam. Galen's words were fading behind a roar, like the rush of blood in her ears. She tried to concentrate on his voice as if it were a lifeline to haul her out of oblivion.

"You'll need the plans, the structural plans, to find your way, but they exist. Sabotage from the inside is impossible: Krennic is too paranoid. But I've thought about this, Saw, prepared everything for you I could."

The roar was growing louder. The stone seemed to tremble and Jyn fell to her knees, a shock of pain driving back the darkness of the cave long enough for her to realize that Saw, too, was shaking. His cane tapped rapidly on the floor.

"I know there's at least one complete engineering archive in the data vault at the Citadel Tower on Scarif. Use what I've told you, run the analysis, and you'll be able to plan your attack. Any pressurized explosion to the reactor module will set off a chain reaction that will—"

Without prelude, the hologram vanished. Not even the control lights on the console still gleamed. The voice was gone. Saw Gerrera cried out something as the monastery lurched and a choking wave of dust billowed through the window.

Something terrible was happening on Jedha. Jyn knew that.

But she'd lost her father. The cave beneath the ruined hatch swallowed her, enveloped her in night.

CHAPTER 7

KRENNIC PACED THE OVERBRIDGE UNDER Tarkin's watch, observing the technicians and referencing every step against the control protocols he'd memorized long ago. Levers were flipped, rotating focusing lenses deep within the station's core. Engineers adjusted radiation baffles and ventilation pumps as the main reactor shook with effort and its comforting roar turned to an eerie scream. Krennic saw more than one hand shaking, more than one face flushed or daubed with sweat. But his officers knew their duty. They would do everything necessary to destroy Jedha City at the bidding of their commander.

Obedience and skill, of course, might not be enough.

Eight separate beam generators came online in the Death Star's heart. Here the process became too much for Krennic to observe in its entirety—a dozen officers on the overbridge alone chattered into their comms, relaying information through a dozen more teams responsible for monitoring and controlling the primary weapon's final ignition. Krennic turned from the technicians to the monitor screens, saw readings gently crest as the eight beams reached minimum coherency.

From the focusing dish on the station's outer shell, the beams of light and charged particles poured into a single vertex controlled and suspended by the kyber fields. The overbridge's main display blazed with green fire set against the void of space, and Krennic stepped forward, staring in awe at the conflagration. The radiance of the display splashed over his white uniform, over the black helmets of the technicians, over Tarkin's grave face, and rendered the room in carved emerald.

For a moment, the blazing nexus of energy hung in the void. Krennic tensed involuntarily. This was the moment where so many tests and computer simulations had failed him. He had seen the nexus sputter and die, or expand to consume the station itself. He had seen calculations collapse under their own weight as predictions gave way to haphazard guesswork. He had seen successes, too, but they gave him no confidence now.

Then the last stage was triggered: From the center of the focusing dish came another particle beam, invisible to the human eye. It carved through the nexus and tunneled a path for the energy's release, funneled the conflagration away from the battle station and toward the rust-brown sphere of the Jedha moon.

The atmosphere seemed to flare where the beam struck. Krennic tried to imagine the incineration of the Holy City and the ensuing shock wave. He found his mind failed him.

Surely no one could imagine such a thing.

He had killed a city.

He could kill a world.

Every morning, Meggone ate her breakfast before the smoke ceremony. According to certain ancient customs, this was an act of heresy; but she'd done it every day for sixty-odd years and no cosmic power had ever smacked the eggs from her withered hands or turned the water in her canteen to blood.

Besides—it seemed to Meggone that a dollop of heresy kept a person from getting too wrapped up in the particulars of tradition. "Smoke ceremonies and pilgrimages don't put one in touch with the Force," she'd once told a disappointed visitor to her shrine. "Best they can do is focus head and heart."

It was while making breakfast over her portable stove, just outside her tiny shrine in the mountains beyond the city, that Meggone noticed the dark silhouette in the sky. It was no more than a smear to her rheumy eyes, and she tried to rub it from her vision with her knuckles. It remained despite her efforts, a blemish on the dim gray heavens.

She trembled as she adjusted the stove's heat. Her body had been failing her more and more lately. The dull pain in her ankles had worsened the past few weeks, and the mole she could feel on the nape of her neck had gotten larger. "Admit it, Meggone," she mumbled. "You're finally getting old."

She looked back to the smudge in the sky. It wore a fiery halo now, and the world seemed darker, as if the smudge had eclipsed the sun itself. Mixed with her confusion was the elated thought: *Maybe it's not my sight after all.* Then the smudge flashed a brilliant emerald, and her vision spotted as if she'd been staring into a fire.

Meggone felt the heat wash over her body but she felt no pain. She ignited in an incandescent burst of burning air, turned to ash and less than ash in an instant.

At the age of ninety-three, she was not ready to die.

Pendra was pouting. Larn was praying the pout didn't sour and become a full-blown tantrum. He loved his daughter, but he'd seen her shriek for an hour straight and he was late for work already. "You're going to stay with Aunt Jola today," he said. "She has those toys you like, remember? The ones that belonged to Cousin Ked?"

Larn knew very well that his daughter had ignored the toy starship models the last time they'd gathered at Jola's. Still, if he lied in a soothing enough voice there was always the chance Pendra would believe him.

Instead, his daughter ignored his words as he adjusted her boots. "I want to go with Mom," she whimpered.

So do I, Larn thought, then cursed aloud as he tried to stand and banged his shoulders against the kitchen table. Pendra was continuing her protests, but he wasn't listening anymore. He scooped her up in both arms, glancing about the cramped apartment to make sure he hadn't forgotten anything.

So far as he could tell, Pendra didn't remember the fight in the Holy Quarter. She didn't remember nearly dying and being saved by the whim of—who had it been? Not a rebel and not an Imperial, but, according to Huika, some woman caught in the crossfire.

When had Jedha become such a death trap? It hadn't always been this way. And now they were going to work, doing their shopping, like nothing had happened. Maybe, Larn thought, he could talk to Huika. Maybe she was right about finding a way offworld . . .

But not tonight. Tonight he just wanted her home safe.

Larn and Pendra Sillu didn't see the emerald light or hear the thunder before they died. Pendra never left her father's arms.

The order to evacuate had come while JN-093 was in the outlands doing recon on suspected rebel hiding spots. All she and her squad had turned up was a shallow cave packed with empty supply crates. Now she was waiting for pickup; so far from the city, they'd never make it back on foot in time for liftoff.

"You know *why* we're being moved offworld?" JN-092 asked. He was pacing awkwardly by the edge of a long-dry lakebed, occasionally digging the toe of his boot into the dust.

"I don't," JN-093 said, though she doubted she would have told Two if she *did* know. He was a stormtrooper; he should've known better than to ask.

JK-027 laughed into the comm in his resonant bass. He was nearly out of sight, scanning the horizon from atop a boulder. "You getting cozy here? Afraid to leave?"

Two grumbled something insulting that didn't quite cut through the static. JN-093 shook her head in irritation. There was something going on between Kay and Two—she wasn't sure what, but it had started after they'd come back from a night at the cantina. She made a note to question them if they didn't reconcile soon; she didn't need her squad members at one another's throats.

Where was the blasted pickup, anyway?

Kay was looking at the sky now. JN-093 felt a shadow fall across the valley, allowed her helmet visor to automatically compensate. She scowled as she tried to contact transport control. The comms seemed to be working, but no one was answering.

Two prized off his helmet and tossed it to the ground. He, too, craned his neck to look skyward. JN-093 prepared to scold him when a surprised voice finally came through: "Jayen-Oh-Nine-Three, please confirm. Your squad's still on the ground?"

You forgot *us?* she wanted to ask. "Affirmative," she said. "Still waiting for pickup."

"Sorry, Oh-Nine-Three. You may be stuck out there awhile. Just got—" A pause. "I'm really sorry."

The voice cut out. The comm hissed. JN-093 kicked at the dirt. Kay and Two were standing by the lakebed together now, both with their helmets off, still staring at the sky. She started to stroll toward them. *Maybe they're making up,* she thought, and Two started laughing when the sky turned emerald.

JN-093 was thrown into the dirt as the ground bucked and a gale whipped across the valley. In the direction of Jedha City, the horizon glowed as if a new sun were rising—a sun of white and green fire that swelled and burst, spilling forth destruction. JN-093 instinctively screamed orders into her comm, though no one was listening. She pushed herself to crawl toward her team as the gale grew stronger and black clouds rose and shrouded the distant fire.

She fought against the battering wind and dust for what felt like minutes. The next time she could think and see, she was behind a ridge of boulders dragging Two by one arm. He was coughing and brushing sand from his face. A wall of churning ruin filled the horizon, rapidly marching closer. Kay was nowhere in sight.

JN-093 finally thought to look at the shadow in the sky. She stared at the structure, indefinably large and eclipsing the sun.

She knew a weapon when she saw one, no matter how incomprehensible. "They did it," she murmured. "The rebels finally did it."

Two sputtered weak laughter.

"I don't think that's the rebels," he said.

When the storm front hit them, JN-093's armor protected her just long enough to make her death painful. In her last flicker of brain activity, she felt she'd failed her squad.

Saw Gerrera looked from the window of the Cadera Monastery and saw his death on the horizon.

The Holy City was gone. In its place was a roiling storm of sand and fire, like the work of some primal deity. The bed of the valley flowed like an ocean, save where fissures opened and drew the land into itself. The wind battered him, burning with heat and stinking of ozone; he inhaled one scorching lungful of dust then clamped his oxygen mask to his face.

He found himself transfixed by the monstrosity before him. Saw had seen many terrible weapons over the years: disruptor beams that tore soldiers apart; screamers that left the residents of whole city blocks hallucinating and bleeding from their ears; viruses that spread on the wind and adapted to every species imaginable. He had *used* those same weapons and numbed himself to the outrage of the Rebel Alliance. Yet now he saw something beyond all his dark dreams, and he remembered fear.

No. Don't lie to yourself. You've feared your death for a long time, and more with every day.

He turned away from the window, stumbled, and saw his console spark with one last surge of power. He thought of his soldiers in the catacombs, considered what order to give. But they were surely evacuating already. His lieutenants knew the next rendezvous, and they knew their duty.

Well enough to also know he would only slow them down?

He envisioned dragging his failing body, trapped in its unwieldy armor, down the collapsing corridors of the monastery with the support of a warrior under each arm. It was a humiliation. It was a fantasy.

It's time, Saw. Past time.

There was only Jyn, then.

The girl was on her hands and knees, still staring at the dead holoprojector. Saw felt a jolt of ire and shame (had she become *soft,* after all these years?), which he routed from his mind. Whatever had become of Jyn, she was still *his.* Still his best soldier.

Still his only family.

The floor jumped and the tip of his cane skidded out from beneath him. Saw crashed to the ground as chips of stone pelted him from the ceiling. His armor cushioned him from the worst of the blow; the pain was, as always, in the act of *motion,* in lifting himself back to his feet and clambering to Jyn's side.

He tried to speak, cursed his enervated lungs and the coughing fit that followed. He sucked at his oxygen mask and watched Jyn reflexively rise off her hands without turning from the projector.

She was better than this. Better than behaving like an Imperial pilot ravaged by Bor Gullet.

He found his comlink, rasped a demand for aid, and heard no response but static. He could count on no one else to rescue Jyn.

Saw had to make her remember. Remember that she was his best soldier. Remember that she had a mission to complete, a war to fight, a Death Star to destroy, an Emperor to execute for all the crimes of a nation.

He grasped her shoulder as tight as he could and spat her name.

"Jyn!" he cried.

"My daughter!"

But Jyn didn't seem to hear.

CHAPTER 8

"What was the message?" Cassian asked. "You can tell me the message."

Baze grunted behind him. The pilot refused to look directly at Cassian. They'd gone around twice already, Cassian asking questions and the broken man answering in jumbled words and mumbles. There were hints of insight to be found—Cassian had heard the words *planet killer* more than once—but little else. He wanted to tear the answers bodily from the man he'd come so far to find.

This had to be worth it. The message, the mission, it had to be worth the cost.

"Brought the message," the pilot finally said. "Brought it from Galen. Brought it from Eadu."

Eadu.

He dimly recalled the name from some Alliance Intelligence file—a planet somewhere in the Outer Rim. It was a thread Cassian could follow.

Then the catacombs began to rumble.

Outside the cell, skulls skittered out of their niches on the walls and shattered on the stone floor. The lights flickered, and guards rushed to exit the outer chamber. An absurd, obsessive instinct in Cassian urged him to ignore the quake, to keep the pilot talking, but he tamped down the compulsion enough to recognize the opportunity he'd been provided.

"Proton bombs," Baze said, turning his eyes to the ceiling.

Chirrut shook his head. "No." But he ventured no alternatives.

Cassian freed his security kit from his boot and began work on the cell's lock, clipping wires and shifting tumblers. The quake's force steadily increased, causing his hands to jerk and slip. Finally the lock made a satisfying click and the door slid open; he had barely enough time to pull his arms out from the bars. He dashed for the table where the group's gear had been stashed as Baze tugged Chirrut along after.

"Let's go!" Baze snapped.

Cassian snatched up his blaster in one hand, fumbled for his comlink with the other, and signaled. "Kay-Tu? Kay-Tu, where are you?"

Please be at the ship. Please don't say you followed me. We're so close here . . .

The comlink crackled with static and an almost incomprehensible voice replied, "There you are! I'm standing by as you ordered. Though there is a problem on the horizon."

"What problem?" Cassian spat.

"There is no horizon. On a positive note, I may have found our planet killer."

The catacombs shuddered and bucked, nearly tossing Cassian to his knees. It wasn't until he regained his balance that he understood what the droid was talking about.

What was happening on the surface?

And did it matter? The planet killer was *real*.

It's here.

He felt a thrill, realizing what they'd found; realizing he would return to the Rebellion not just successful, but wildly so, with an eyewitness account of the monster they faced. Realizing that he was imperiled by a menace unheard of in galactic history, and that he would survive or not according to his own skill. The thrill was arrested by the chill that worked its way down his back and the sweat on his brow.

"Locate our position," he said. "Bring that ship in here now!"

"Five minutes to extraction," the droid replied. "If I make it at all."

Cassian glanced sidelong at Baze, who was either inspecting or caressing his blaster cannon. *Five minutes.* It wasn't nearly fast enough, and far *too* fast for what he wanted.

Jyn was still missing, in the hands of Saw or whatever torturers Saw had sicced on Bodhi Rook. She was extraneous now: Cassian no longer needed Saw, and Bodhi could lead the rebels to Galen Erso on his own.

Worse than extraneous, he told himself. *She'll try to stop what comes next.*

All Cassian had to do was forget the *need* in her eyes. Leave her behind, as he'd *left behind* Tivik on the Ring of Kafrene. As he'd left behind men on Eiloroseint and Chemvau . . .

"Where are you going?" Chirrut shouted.

Cassian was already halfway to the cavern exit.

"I've got to find Jyn," he called. "You get the pilot. We need him. Then if you want a ride out of here, meet me up top."

It was as much a threat as an offer.

There was barely enough light to navigate the catacombs. Cassian followed the flashes of swinging overheads and, as he caught up, the handhelds carried by Saw's fleeing soldiers. The rebels all traveled the same path, and Cassian raced up stairs and around corners in their wake. No one seemed to notice a lone prisoner in pursuit.

He scaled the steps to the main floor of the monastery and heard new noises over the rumbling of the mountain and the shouts of evacuating rebels: the engines of starships and, beyond, a terrible howling wind like the hurricanes of Squarr. The soldiers scattered from a central chamber, gear slung over their shoulders or abandoned on the ground. Cassian wondered if any of them would survive to see the stars.

As a Twi'lek rebel bolted past, Cassian caught the man by his cyan head-tails and tossed him against a wall. "Where's Jyn Erso?" he asked. "Where was she taken?"

The Twi'lek pushed back instinctively. He was young and slim—slim enough that Cassian had underestimated him—but he was still a fighter, still one of Saw's. He slammed a fist into Cassian's ribs. Cassian caught the next blow and forced his opponent to the wall again. "I'm not here to fight. What's your name?" he growled. The boy stared, uncomprehending. "What's your *name*?"

"Rai'sodan," the boy said.

"Rai'sodan." *Making him angry won't help you. Keep him calm.* "We can beat each other up while this place falls apart, or you can tell me where you took Jyn Erso. The prisoner from before. The one separate from the rest."

The boy took barely a moment to decide. "Saw's chambers. The upper level. But I haven't seen him since—"

Cassian turned and sprinted away. Saw had left the pilot behind. Maybe—if Cassian was lucky—he was cruel enough to leave Jyn, too.

He ascended another stairway two steps at a time. The monastery made a noise like thunder as some part of the structure collapsed altogether. Cassian was forced to put his sleeve over his mouth and nostrils to keep himself from choking on the dust. Power cables led him to a doorway filled by a tattered curtain, where he tripped on something soft: the heap of a rebel body, a youth with a rifle longer than her arm.

No blaster marks, Cassian thought. *Poor kid must have come for Saw and cracked her head during one of the tremors.*

She might have been alive, but she wasn't his concern.

He called Jyn's name, pushed forward through the curtains, and found what he was looking for.

Jyn was squatting on the floor of the chamber within, her shoulders slumped and her arms limp. With each shudder of the monastery she shifted her weight, straightened to avoid toppling over, but those were the only motions she made. She was staring sightlessly across the room. She didn't seem to notice the armored figure crouched before her.

Saw Gerrera. Older, much older than the images Cassian had seen in the dossier at Base One, but unmistakably Saw.

What had he done?

Saw lifted his head. Bloodshot eyes met Cassian's own. The man squinted in thought, then rasped, as if reading the rage and the question on Cassian's face, "This was not my doing. She wasn't ready for what she saw."

Cassian wanted to yell, *What does that mean?* But Saw spoke again in a voice that defied interruption. "If you can save her," he said bitterly, "take her."

The monastery was falling apart. If K-2 was coming, he'd arrive momentarily. There was no time; Saw's answer would have to be good enough.

Cassian knelt by Jyn. Her eyes were glassy, unfocused. "We've got to go," he said, soft and stern.

She flinched at the sound. Nothing more. Cassian swore to himself.

Leave her behind.

It would be easier than he'd expected. The *need* had burned out of her eyes. The feral instinct to survive had been buried kilometers deep. He'd be leaving behind an empty shell . . .

"I know where your father is," he said.

Jyn blinked. Her eyes flickered toward Cassian.

"Go, Jyn!" Saw's voice, commanding even in its frailty. "You must go."

Jyn rose to her feet on trembling legs. Her breath hissed between barely parted lips. She turned a blank face to look over the room, over Cassian and Saw, and reached out to grasp her mentor's arm.

Something passed between Jyn and Saw that Cassian couldn't begin to read. Saw spoke simply, softly: "Save yourself. Please."

Jyn's face seemed to flash with anger. But her fingers unclenched from Saw, and Cassian grabbed her other arm, tugging her toward the doorway. "Come on," he said, and she stumbled one step, then two.

"Go!" Saw urged, somehow stronger now, his voice competing

against the tumbling rocks that clattered beyond the chamber window. Jyn took another step, but her gaze remained on the old rebel.

"There's no time," Cassian snapped. He pulled at her again and now she was moving, unsteady yet swift, making for the corridor at Cassian's side.

Saw's bellow seemed to shatter stone behind them and dwarf even the roar of the cataclysm: "Save the Rebellion!" he cried. "Save the dream!"

Bodhi Rook understood the distinction between past and present, between recollection and reality; he just wasn't sure which was which anymore.

Bor Gullet had taken everything Bodhi was—every intimate thought and dream, every cherished or forsaken memory—and torn through it with tendrils like scalpels. A scrap of *first kiss* drifted, ripped and sodden, into a pile on the right; a ribbon of *kyber crystals* floated to the pile on the left, pressed and preserved for further examination.

When Bor Gullet and Saw had completed their investigation, Bodhi had tried to stuff every memory back into his mind. He was certain they hadn't all fit quite right.

"*I'm the pilot!*"

Who had he said that to? Someone had *listened* to him at last. Or was that a memory from long ago?

Was he still in the cage with Bor Gullet?

No. But he was in another cage. It smelled of his own putrid scent. His flight suit chafed his icy flesh, irritated his sores, and ground dirt into his wounds.

The whole world was rumbling like a ship taking flight. Surely *that*, Bodhi thought, was a memory?

"The *pilot*," a voice said, low and full of scorn.

He focused on the source and saw through the bars of his cage a hulk of a man with dark, wild hair. Behind him stood a slimmer man who carried a staff.

The first man—the name *Baze* surfaced in Bodhi's brain, though Bodhi couldn't have guessed where he'd heard it—raised a blaster cannon and pointed it at Bodhi's chest.

Panic helped Bodhi find words. "Wait!" he cried. "No . . ."

He stumbled to his feet, readied himself for the pain of death. He heard the blaster shot and felt nothing.

The door to his cell slid open. Baze was scowling at him, pointing his weapon at the burnt and sparking control panel.

"Come on!" the second man called. *His name is Chirrut.* "Let's go!"

Was this reality?

Was this a *rescue*?

Bodhi nearly twisted an ankle on his first step. The ground bucked on his second. Then he was running, chasing after Baze and Chirrut and praying that he had found his salvation at last—found the welcome Galen Erso had promised him when he had said to seek out the Rebellion, to *make amends*.

Maybe, Bodhi thought, just *maybe* his torment was over.

He recognized some of the faces running with him. There were whole crowds beyond Baze and Chirrut, clattering through the stone hallways with rifles and duffels slung over their shoulders. Among them were Bodhi's captors, the men and women who'd bound him, blinded him, marched him at gunpoint across the desert when he'd begged simply to help them. They didn't look at him now, didn't seem to see him. He pushed his aching legs and cold lungs harder to keep pace.

"They'll kill us," he whispered to Baze. "You don't know these people."

Baze laughed so loud that Bodhi was terrified the rebels would look back. They kept running.

"Forgive my friend," Chirrut said. "You would think it's funny, too, if you knew *he* wanted you dead most of all."

Bodhi didn't find that funny in the slightest. But a rescue was a rescue.

They ran out of the catacombs, up ancient steps worn smooth over centuries, and burst into the frigid dawn. Sunlight slashed Bodhi's eyes with cuts of blue and green and silver. He couldn't recall when he'd last *seen* sunlight, though Bor Gullet would have known.

He staggered to a stop behind Baze and Chirrut, standing on a broad mountain ledge overlooking a valley. The rebels were gone, scattered—somewhere. In the valley there was nothing but dust: a billowing, blooming storm of sand, expanding outward in all directions and rolling across the valley floor.

Baze's lips parted without words. He watched like a man in shock.

"What do you see?" Chirrut asked Baze.

Bodhi blinked away the scars of light. When his eyes had adjusted, he realized that the valley was now *too* dim. He raised his stiff neck, looked to the sky, and saw a shadow like a moon eclipsing the sun.

"What do you *see*?" Chirrut asked again.

Realizations crashed together. Bodhi was on Jedha, had never *left* Jedha, and he was looking onto the valley where the Holy City had been. And above him, in the sky . . .

"No," he whispered. "No."

This was not a rescue. This was a trick of Bor Gullet. This was the reason he had left the Empire, abandoned his friends, trusted the words of Galen Erso, suffered torment and humiliation—to stop the battle station, stop the planet killer from coming to life. What he saw was not real. It could not *be*.

"It wasn't supposed to happen yet," he whispered, though no one listened.

He was too late. This was his fault.

Scalding wind cut through the cold, nearly blasted him from his feet. The dust storm was getting closer.

Then he heard another noise, a screaming *boom* separate from the thunderous rumble of the storm. Descending toward the mountain was a ship: a UT-60D U-wing transport. It dipped awkwardly in the buffeting wind, trying to match the level of the ledge.

Baze wrapped an arm around Chirrut, started toward the ship. "Okay, let's go!"

What was the point? Bodhi wondered. They'd already lost.

An open palm smacked Bodhi between the shoulders. "Move!" a

man called. He rushed past, pulling a woman by the hand. Bodhi had seen the man before, he thought; he remembered a gentle, almost pitying voice.

What was the *point*?

He didn't want to die.

He followed the man, followed Baze and Chirrut, through the air that was growing ever-thicker with dust. Sand beat his flesh and raked his hair. He couldn't hear the U-wing's boarding ramp descend, but he saw the aperture, a window in the storm. The others were ahead of him, sprinting inside, making the final jump with apparent ease. Bodhi leapt, but his quaking legs failed him. He was falling onto the ramp when a hand caught him, yanked him violently forward an instant before the cabin door shut.

He didn't see who it was who'd saved his life.

"Get us out of here!" a voice yelled. "Punch it!"

The cabin lurched and swayed. Baze, Chirrut, and the woman clutched at the seats, at support struts, to keep from being dashed against the walls. But even with the floor unsteady beneath him, even with the metallic wail of the wind against the bulkhead, Bodhi felt comforted. He was on a ship now. He *knew* ships.

The hull shrieked as something heavy bounced off the top of the U-wing. The deck dropped, sent Bodhi onto his hands and knees and drove spikes of pain into his wrists. He went sliding as the ship banked. He recognized the sound of the engine (an Incom Corporation rebuild of their 9XR standby . . .) as it strained against the storm.

Bodhi dragged himself forward and clambered into the cockpit. He'd never seen a U-wing cockpit before.

Seated at the controls were a droid and the man who'd passed by him before. (*Cassian?* Was that his name?) They were adjusting thrust madly, trying to ride the waves of the dust storm, trying to turn the ship away from the epicenter and maneuver through the mountains as they cracked and shattered.

Bodhi didn't interrupt. He watched their hands play over the controls. He read the instruments and the scanners (nearly useless, never meant for these conditions). He felt the U-wing rise on a crest of the storm, shuddering all the way as it tried to match speed, and saw a shadow creep over the cockpit as a heavier, hotter cloud raced overhead and began to fall.

He was going to die after all. His rescue was over. And it was his own fault. If he'd been faster, the rebels might have stopped the planet killer.

"I'm sorry," he whispered.

Cassian and the droid didn't hear him.

He understood that Bor Gullet was gone from his mind. Yet the memory that seized him was every bit as vivid as those the creature had evinced. Bodhi looked out the viewport and saw, instead of the dust storm, the emerald and turquoise hues of titanic gas clouds. Lightning volleys like alien dancers leapt from one cloud to the next, causing each to ignite and burst. Bodhi was laughing as his shuttle, a *Nu*-class transport barely viable for training runs, bounced and twirled, and his classmates cheered him on . . .

It was a memory of utter serenity. Then his flight through the gas giant of Bamayar IX was over and he was gazing into the dust storm again as darkness closed around the U-wing.

"Look!" he cried, and reached toward the viewport—toward a speck of light, a gateway through the dust, collapsing as the wave above them crashed down.

Cassian didn't turn toward Bodhi. Maybe he hadn't heard. But the rebel snarled "Come on!" as he diverted power again, urged the ship through that speck of light as oblivion raged around them. And the sky turned blue, then black, and the viewport filled with stars.

The U-wing leapt into hyperspace, and Bodhi laughed on the floor of the cockpit in giddy joy.

CHAPTER 9

THE DEATH STAR'S OVERBRIDGE WAS dark except for the lit rows of instrumentation and the glow of the main display. Dominating that vast screen was what remained of the valley of the Holy City of Jedha: a churning, whirling, burning storm of sand and rock shards. The air, ionized by the energy of the Death Star's weapon, flashed with lightning. At the storm's epicenter, the crater of the incinerated city smoldered where the beam had sublimed the outermost layer of the moon's crust.

This was not the fate Krennic had envisioned for Jedha. The Death Star was designed to obliterate worlds, not maim them. Yet he wondered if the moon would ever recover from such an attack, or whether the cascading effects of a burning atmosphere and broken crust would result in a tortuous death played out across millennia. He felt in his bones that his weapon had exposed something profound— about the nature of worlds, about their lifeblood and their death throes—though he could not have put it into words. *Maybe,* he thought, *that's what poets are for.*

"It's beautiful," he murmured, breaking minutes of near-silence on the bridge. Even Tarkin had respected the crewmembers' shared awe as they spoke in whispers and muffled their keystrokes.

"I believe I owe you an apology, Director Krennic," Tarkin replied. "Your work exceeds all expectations."

Krennic did his best to conceal his surprise. "And you'll tell the Emperor as much?" *Too eager.* He moderated his tone; he could afford humility if it would comfort Tarkin. "After all, this is *his* triumph—the triumph of his insight and will—more than any other single man's." *There. Enough for you to save face, but not enough to deny me credit.*

Tarkin cut the air with a dismissive gesture. "The Emperor desires facts, not flattery. Your tenure on this project has been rife with setbacks—setbacks you have, it seems, overcome. I will tell him his patience with your misadventures has been rewarded with a weapon that will bring a swift end to the Rebellion."

"You're too kind, Governor." *Condescending bastard.* "But you express my hopes as well. We've seen that the Death Star might destroy a city or a rebel base unimpeded by planetary shields or defense grids. And what you witnessed today? That is only an inkling of the destructive potential—"

The same gesture as before: a demand for silence. Smiling acidly, contritely, Krennic obliged.

"I will tell him," Tarkin said, "that I will be taking control over the weapon *I* first spoke of years ago . . . effective immediately."

Taking control?

Krennic curled gloved fingers into fists and looked about the over-bridge as he quelled his first and most vicious response. The duty officers were not watching the confrontation; they remained busy at their stations, checking and rechecking the Death Star's primary weapon status and scanning the system for survivors.

That was a very small comfort.

Krennic stepped as close as he dared to Wilhuff Tarkin and snapped, "We are standing here amid my achievement—not yours!" He forced his voice into a hiss. "My people are loyal. And *my people* are the only ones capable of operating this station."

He knew it was unwise to threaten Tarkin openly. He could berate a subordinate without repercussions, but not the grand moff. And there was no imminent scenario in which Krennic could remove or replace Tarkin; he would need to suffer the man's existence for some time to come.

But Krennic was not a man to smile meekly forever.

Tarkin shrugged as if he hadn't heard the threat; as if he were certain that the officers' *loyalty* was far too malleable to be a problem. He might have been right. "I'm afraid these recent security breaches have laid bare your inadequacies as a military director. Your place, I think, is among the engineers; there are many initiatives that could benefit from your organizational skills—"

"The security breaches have been filled," Krennic retorted. "Jedha has been silenced."

There was a flaw in that argument, too, Krennic knew. The ignition of the weapon and the ensuing storm had left the Death Star's sensors momentarily blind. It was conceivable that survivors had escaped the moon; conceivable, but unlikely.

Tarkin had a different countermove in mind. "You think this pilot acted alone?" He let out a wheezing half laugh. "He was dispatched from the installation on Eadu. Galen Erso's facility."

Galen Erso.

Galen Erso.

Fury made a fool of Krennic. This time, he could not hide his surprise.

"We'll see about this," he snarled, and turned to leave the overbridge.

General Davits Draven was the bane of his peers and a hero to his subordinates. It wasn't the role he wanted to play, but he believed it was a necessary one.

As an organization, the Rebel Alliance was held together more by external pressure than by internal bonds. Mon Mothma's almost pathological need to make political overtures toward peace— regardless of their success—was a poor match for General Jan

Dodonna's policy of covert strikes that minimized attention from the Empire and its Senate. Dodonna's approach, in turn, was incompatible with Bail Organa's desire to rapidly intervene wherever Imperial atrocities occurred. Saw Gerrera had effectively withdrawn from the Alliance over strategic disagreements; but there were other council members who shared his more aggressive agenda. If not for the Empire's overwhelming strength—if not for the need for the rebels to work together to even *survive*—the Alliance would have fractured in a matter of months.

If not for the Empire's strength . . . and if not for General Draven.

While his peers argued and mapped out roads to an imaginary ultimate victory, Draven maintained a singular focus on protecting the Alliance itself—on ruthlessly defending the organization and its people while correcting their mistakes. If that earned him a reputation for arrogance or intrusiveness, it was a small price to pay.

In the matter of the supposed planet killer, Draven feared there was nothing *but* mistakes to correct. A few of those mistakes were even his own. Yet he had no intention of shirking his duties.

He marched into the comm center on Yavin 4 with his head held high and his shoulders stiff, the way soldiers imagined a general. He hoped the rebels on duty would forgive the sweat on his brow from the jungle heat. "What do you have?" he demanded.

Private Weems leapt to his feet. "A coded message from Captain Andor, sir," he said.

That was fast. Andor was smart, thorough, and not particularly inclined to make contact during the course of a mission. This time around, he also had the Erso girl to contend with. Draven hadn't expected to hear from him for a week, at best.

"What's he got for us?" Draven asked.

Weems read in the deliberate tone of a man pretending not to see what he was seeing. " 'Weapon confirmed. Jedha City destroyed. Mission target located on Eadu. Please advise.' "

"*Destroyed?*" Draven echoed. Weems only nodded.

The planet killer is real.

Doubt followed instantly in the wake of that thought. Andor was a fine agent but not flawless. His message was vague. The transmission could have been intercepted and altered en route. There were a thousand reasons why *weapon confirmed* might not be confirmation at all.

But Draven had seen too many commanders use *doubt* as an excuse to deny the obvious.

He hadn't really believed in the planet killer before—not rationally, not in the cold, strategic part of his mind that was (he could admit, if to no one but himself) his only true value to the Rebel Alliance. If the weapon was active, then the strategic framework of the entire galaxy was in flux. Everything the Rebellion had built, every scheme from every council member, would have to adapt.

But urgent decisions had to be made first.

Andor's message contained nothing new on Galen Erso. *Those* assumptions remained intact, and if Erso was instrumental in the planet killer project then maybe Draven could give the Alliance breathing room. A chance to evolve before worlds instead of cities started dying.

"Proceed," he told Weems. "Tell him my orders still stand. Tell him to proceed with haste and keep to the plan. We have to kill Galen Erso while we have the chance."

The first time Jyn had been orphaned was on a farm on a shoreline of the planet Lah'mu. She had seen her mother shot by a death squad and watched her father surrender to the man responsible, abandon her to a soldier she barely knew.

The second time had been in the deserts of Jedha, when she had seen the man who raised her—the man who had taught her everything, whom she hated more than *almost* anyone—buried beneath a mountain after being nothing but kind. Or as kind as he knew how to be.

Perhaps she'd never been orphaned at all, however. Galen Erso was alive. Not the gentle farmer she remembered; nor the coward and monster who'd left her behind to become an Imperial weaponeer, earning years of spite. Both of *those* men had died on Jedha as well.

There was another Galen Erso. All she knew of him was a sapphire light in the cave in her mind—the cave where she lived now—

repeating the same words over and over. Words about love and happiness and loneliness. Excuses for deeds done long ago. Plans and lies about a Death Star, a planet killer . . .

My love for her has never faded.

She couldn't stop the words. Each one tore at her, and she clung to them for solace.

She sat in the cabin of the U-wing and stared out at her companions from the cave's depths. She watched their faces through the distant pinpoint of the broken hatch. A very small part of her was aware of how she must have looked—a disheveled and battered and dirt-encrusted creature, all but catatonic as she observed the room blankly—and hated herself for her weakness.

"Baze, tell me." Chirrut's voice. The blind Guardian of the Whills who had saved her life. "All of it? The whole city?"

Baze. Chirrut's partner had a name. He sat beside the blind man with his eyes on the bulkhead. The strobing blue-white light of hyperspace splashed on his cheeks from out of the cockpit.

"*Tell* me," Chirrut said again.

"All of it," Baze answered, short and bitter.

Jedha City is gone. Jyn examined the thought numbly. The death of Jedha City meant the death of Saw; the deaths of many or all of his soldiers; the deaths of red-robed pilgrims and blustering water vendors. It meant the death of the girl she'd swept into her arms during the fighting in the plaza—the brutal, *pointless* death of the only person she'd helped in any way since this mission began . . .

We call it the Death Star. There is no better name.

The planet killer was real. She had mocked it, mocked the Alliance for believing in it, and it was *real.*

If she had believed sooner, kept faith in her father, would anything have been different? Would they have found Saw faster, acted in time to do—what?

Was Jedha City her fault? Even a little?

"Understood." It was Cassian speaking now, a murmur into the comm unit. Then, calling to the droid in the cockpit: "Set course for Eadu."

Jyn repeated Cassian's phrase in her head, tried to hear it over her father's words in the dark of the cave.

"Eadu?" she asked. Her voice sounded thick and hoarse.

"Sodden lump of a world, according to the files," Cassian said. He looked at her with a hint of surprise, swiftly hidden. "Small native population, mostly rural nerf herders. Officially, the Empire designates the planet for research and chemical processing."

"Is that where my father is?" Jyn raised her chin, tried to force out the hoarseness.

She tried to picture the reunion. Tried to picture meeting the man in the hologram for the first time and telling him who she was. Telling him *I saw your message.* She should have felt joy at the idea. Her father was a hero.

But *who she was* was Liana Hallik and Tanith Ponta and Kestrel Dawn, a bloodstained fighter and a thief and a prisoner who had spent nearly fifteen years *loathing* Galen. Locking him in a prison of contempt until, when he needed her, she hadn't believed his warnings about the Death Star at all. She'd have to tell him that, too. The thought brought bile up from her stomach.

Could she have been someone else, if she'd only known?

I try to think of you only in the moments when I'm strong.

"I didn't have a lot of time to question our friend Bodhi," Cassian said. He gestured at the fifth occupant of the cabin—a long-haired man dressed in a stained Imperial flight suit and wearing battered goggles, weaving and unweaving his fingers together. Occasionally, the pilot whispered something without looking up. "But Eadu's where he said his message came from. So is your father there? I think so, yes."

Jyn nodded distantly. Bodhi's whispers became louder—a stuttered, indecipherable series of sounds. Then he leaned forward in his seat, fully intent on Jyn. "You're Galen's daughter?" he asked.

He looked like he hadn't slept in days. Like he expected everything nearby—Baze, the seats, the bulkhead—to clamp jaws around his neck if he dared to blink. He looked almost as pathetic as she did.

"You know him?" she asked.

What did he think of the stranger in her hologram?

"Yes."

She had a hundred questions, none of which she wanted the answers to. "Did he tell you anything?"

"He said—" Bodhi ducked his head. "He said I could get right by myself. He said I could *make* it right, if I was brave enough and listened to what was in my heart. Do something about it." His lips worked, over and over again, forming and swallowing whole sentences before he stilled.

"Guess it was too late," he said at last.

Jedha City was gone. Saw was gone. His people were gone. The little girl was gone.

"It wasn't too late," she said. At least the pilot had *tried*.

"Seems pretty late to me," Baze growled.

In the silence of the cabin, in the darkness of the cave, Jyn listened to her father's recording. *That's the place I've laid my trap* . . .

Saw's dying howl echoed, *Save the dream!*

Galen and Saw tore at her together now, asking for what she'd refused them already, demanding recompense for every way she'd failed them and every day Liana and Tanith and Kestrel had lived their own glorious, petty existences. But she had nothing to give them—she was hollow, and even what she'd kept in the cave was lost to darkness. All she had left was the voice of a hologram.

Yet she broke anyway. She gave in to the demands, because her shame was too great to do otherwise.

"No," she whispered. The single word demanded the attention of the ship. "We can beat the people who did this. We can stop them."

She would make a deal with the hologram of Galen Erso. She would obey his demand, and he would—if not forgive her—cease to remind her of her failures and her guilt and her loathing.

And by the time she met the true Galen Erso on Eadu, she would have something to show for it.

She spoke evenly, slowly, enunciating each word like she was whetting a blade. "My father's message," she said. "I've seen it. They call it the Death Star. But they have no idea there's a way to defeat it."

The tension in Cassian's expression dissipated as he donned his spy's face, his innocently cerebral face. Jyn caught it and knew exactly what it meant. "You're wrong about my father," she said. "You think he's still working for the Empire."

"He did build it," Cassian said. As if that fact changed everything, and only he was clear-eyed enough to see it.

"Because he knew they'd do it without him." She dragged a breath between her teeth and waited for Cassian to object again. She might not know the true Galen Erso, but she spoke with the hologram's voice now; echoed his claims in submission to his cause. To Saw's cause.

"My father made a choice," she said, steadying her intonation. "He sacrificed himself for the Rebellion. He's rigged a trap inside it, inside the Death Star." She spoke only to Bodhi now. "That's why he sent you. To bring that message."

"Where is it?" Cassian asked.

Everyone turned to face him.

"Where's the *message*?" he asked.

"It was a hologram," Jyn said, sharp and fragile as glass.

Cassian didn't back down. "You have that message, right?"

"What do you think?" she snapped. He knew what had happened to her; he'd witnessed her state in Saw's chambers. She wanted to lunge across the cabin, slam him against the bulkhead, force the calm from his demeanor. She wanted to crack open her skull, let the light and sound of the hologram pour from the cave. "Everything happened so fast. But I've just *seen* it!" She heard her own ragged insistence as petulant. Childish. *You were better off catatonic.*

Cassian looked to Bodhi now. "Did you see it?"

The pilot shook his head and avoided Cassian's gaze.

"You don't believe me," Jyn said.

Cassian almost laughed. "I'm not the one you've got to convince. I'm not the one who can authorize a strike against a Death Star because it *might* have a weakness. Maybe Mon Mothma—"

"I believe her," Chirrut interjected.

Cassian shook his head in a show of exasperation. "That's good to know. You're also not part of the Alliance."

Throughout the exchange, Baze had been slumped forward, as if drowsing. Now he righted himself, spoke past Cassian and Chirrut. "What kind of trap?" he asked. "You said your father made a trap."

"The reactor." On this point Jyn was utterly certain. "He's placed a weakness there. He's been hiding it for years. He said if you can blow the reactor—the module—the whole system goes down."

She fixed her gaze on Cassian. "You need to send word to the Alliance," she said.

"I've *done* that."

She said the words the hologram needed her to say, bolstered its voice with her own zeal. "Then they have to know there's a way to destroy this thing. My father said we could find the weakness in the structural plans—"

"We don't have those." Firm but gentle. *Patronizing.*

"He said we can *find* the plans," she insisted, "that they're in a data vault on the planet Scarif. Tell the Alliance: They have to go to Scarif and get the plans."

Cassian was silent long enough that Jyn thought she had a chance.

"I can't risk sending that," he answered at last. "Even if everything you say is true, we're in the heart of Imperial territory. If the message were intercepted, the whole Alliance fleet could be lured into a trap."

He might have been lying, so far as Jyn knew. Avoiding further argument by positing a threat she couldn't disprove and couldn't counter.

In the darkness of the cave, Jyn heard her father's recording repeat. *If she's alive, if you can possibly find her . . .*

"You still want to go to Eadu?" she asked.

"Yes," Cassian said.

There would be no redemption, then. No ameliorating her choices or hiding her sins. She would, after all, tell the Galen Erso she'd never met *exactly* who she was and *exactly* what the Death Star had done. The only balm would be whatever he did after; whatever they *both* managed, with whatever deal they struck.

That would have to be enough to keep her sane in the dark.

She had nothing to guide her but the sapphire hologram. Everything else was gone.

"Then we'll find him," she said. "My father. And we'll bring him back, and he can tell the whole Alliance himself."

She spoke with conviction she did not feel. Cassian nodded—but he wore his spy's face, and Jyn couldn't read him at all.

Orson Krennic toured the corridors of the Death Star as he had so often before. He listened to the main reactor's muffled roar, like the ebb and flow of a distant ocean's tide; he felt the gentle tremors in the deck plating as the station reconfigured for hyperspace transport; he could even trace the power couplings through the walls, imagine their end points in vast artificial caverns.

He walked and he could not focus. Tarkin was *taking control* of his masterwork.

Perhaps it was for the best. Perhaps Krennic had spent too long fettered to a single place, a single project. Let Tarkin have the Death Star—he'd soon find the responsibility overwhelming and fail to grasp the battle station's subtle potential. Meanwhile, freed from the behemoth, Krennic would have a flexibility he'd formerly lacked. A hundred small victories across the course of a year might be preferable to one great work over decades. He would have his audience with the Emperor soon enough.

But this rosiest of scenarios was only possible because Tarkin had outmaneuvered him over Jedha.

And Tarkin had outmaneuvered him thanks to the betrayal of Galen Erso.

That the grand moff had become aware of Erso's treason before Krennic had was unforgivable. Krennic had already determined how his people inside Tarkin's organization had been kept in the dark; leaks and obfuscation were the nature of the game. But how had he not *personally* seen the betrayal in Galen? For all Galen's faults, he had never been an equivocator. Nor had he ever failed to take pride in his own genius.

For him to disrupt the work—to disrupt *their* work, all they had built these past decades? To have somehow hidden his motives from Krennic, who knew him so well? How was it possible?

Had he miscalculated? Could another scientist at the Eadu laboratory be responsible instead?

Have I become blind?

But no. While Galen was a fluke, Krennic had not failed to spot Tarkin's greed; only failed to anticipate its precise manifestation, thanks to Galen's interference. Therefore, Galen was the priority and needed to be dealt with swiftly. Much as Krennic loathed to leave the Death Star now, he could not afford to let his problems accrue. He would eliminate them in sequence, leaving Tarkin for last.

He had found weapons he might use against Tarkin already. He only needed an opportunity.

He boarded his shuttle, accompanied by his death troopers, just after midnight station time. He'd settled himself in his seat with a glass of wine and a datapad by the time they'd left the docking bay.

"Course set for Eadu, sir," his pilot announced.

Krennic barely heard.

Galen Erso.

Galen Erso, whom he'd given every chance. Galen Erso, whom he'd nearly died for once on that sad scrap of farmland.

"I thought we were past this," Krennic murmured to himself, with a bitter smile. And his thumb dug into the screen of his datapad until the surface cracked and he began to bleed.

SUPPLEMENTAL DATA: "NO CONFIRMATION"

[Document #RJ9002C ("Jedha Query"), forged timestamp unreadable; actual timestamp presumed concurrent with the Jedha crisis. Sent from Mon Mothma to General Draven and six other recipients ("Operation Fracture Oversight").]

I just received a troubling message from a contact in the Senate. She claims that a total evacuation of Imperial forces has taken place on Jedha and that there are rumors of a massive energy burst in orbit. Her source conducts illegal asteroid mining at the far edge of the Jedha heliosphere, and she stresses that "instrument error" is a possibility.

Nonetheless, she's seeking additional information from me. Whether she knows more than she's sharing and what exactly she suspects, I'm not sure.

Can we confirm this data? Do we have an update on Operation Fracture?

[Document #RJ9002D ("Reply to Jedha Query"), sent from General Ria to Operation Fracture Oversight.]

I don't have any new information, but can you clarify: Did you tell this contact about the rumors of a planet killer?

If not, this could be a fishing expedition by the Empire. She may want to see how you react to a false story.

[Document #RJ9002E ("Reply to Jedha Query"), sent from Mon Mothma to Operation Fracture Oversight.]

Some brief background: My contact refuses to aid the Alliance directly but she's kept in touch with me since my departure from the Senate. If she can be won over, she could be important to our political strategy. I don't think she's serving Imperial military interests.

I have not shared anything about the planet killer with her. If we can't confirm her data, however, I'd like to judiciously broach the subject. It may serve us in both the short and long terms.

[Document #RJ9002F ("Reply to Jedha Query"), sent from Admiral Raddus to Operation Fracture Oversight.]

We have a cargo freighter outfitted for long-range scans four stops down the nearest hyperlane from Jedha. She's tasked on another operation, but I can divert her if Captain Andor doesn't report in soon.

I find the possibility that the planet killer is at Jedha extremely troubling.

[Document #RJ9002G ("Reply to Jedha Query"), sent from General Draven to Operation Fracture Oversight.]

I'm working as we speak to obtain solid intel on Jedha. For now, there is no confirmation of any unusual Imperial activity. Strongly recommend that we do *not* share our intelligence and do *not* initiate new investigations.

I will update the group on Operation Fracture and Captain Andor's status when I have reliable information that can be securely shared. Until then, suggest we shut down this conversation as a precaution.

CHAPTER 10

CASSIAN ANDOR HAD MADE AN error. Like a hairline fracture in a blaster barrel, it was nearly invisible on cursory inspection. When its repercussions manifested, however, they would do so with devastating effect—Cassian would very likely die, though that wasn't what bothered him most.

He knew now that he should have left Jyn Erso on Jedha. Better yet, he should never have taken her off Yavin 4.

"You're showing indications of stress," K-2 declared. He sat beside Cassian in the cockpit, monitoring the instruments. "You should be careful—you're a much worse pilot when you're stressed."

Cassian offered a wan smile. "How can you tell?"

"You overcorrect with the throttle control."

Not what I meant, he thought, but he didn't clarify his question. For all K-2's social dysfunction (or perhaps his disinterest in organic socialization—who could fathom the mind of a droid?), he knew Cassian better than anyone. He'd seen Cassian commit acts even Draven wasn't aware of.

On Jenoport, he'd found Cassian staring at his blaster with tears on his face. K-2 had volunteered for a memory wipe in case Cassian's "continued dignity and service demanded it."

K-2, Cassian knew, would gladly subdue Jyn Erso and lock her somewhere safe. If the Guardians of the Whills hadn't been aboard, Cassian might have been tempted to try.

"We're approaching Eadu," the droid said. "Exiting hyperspace in four minutes."

"Set our approach vector and get Bodhi in here. I want his eyes on the landing zone."

As K-2 obeyed, Cassian returned to his thoughts. Jyn's fervor in the cabin had been almost inspiring. Maybe it *had* inspired Chirrut and Baze and Bodhi—none of whom he really knew, none of whom he could trust—just as her fire had spread to him, made him view her with a sort of awe in the Jedha Holy Quarter. But the stakes were different now: The planet killer, the Death Star, was real. General Draven had determined that eliminating its creator was the best way of ensuring the survival of the Rebel Alliance. If Cassian could stop one more incident like Jedha City, his duty was obvious.

Jyn would have argued that her father had already provided another way; that his sabotage gave the Rebellion a chance to stop the Death Star *now*, albeit at a terrible risk. Jyn's judgment, however, was compromised.

Her fire would burn them all.

When Cassian had found her in Saw Gerrera's chambers, she'd been lost in oblivion, awaiting her own death. He couldn't imagine the forces that had shaped her in life. He didn't doubt she was a woman of extraordinary strength, yet whatever message Saw had shown her had broken her completely.

She was feigning strength now. She clung to her father's instructions for reasons entirely unrelated to the galaxy or the Alliance. If those instructions led her and everyone around her to their doom, would she even notice? Would she care?

Her terrible *need* had returned. It couldn't end in anything but disaster, no matter how prettily she dressed it in the clothes of the Rebellion.

And if Cassian denied her what she wanted? If he assassinated Galen Erso?

She would surely be twice as dangerous.

Eadu was a night world even during the day, shrouded in storm clouds so thick that Cassian was forced to rely on scanners as they descended through the troposphere. From above, there was nothing to see but slate-gray thunderheads and flashes of light; the panorama was nearly peaceful. But the moment the U-wing broke through the cloud cover, gales battered the ship as water drummed on the hull and streamed down the viewport.

"Low," Bodhi hissed, gripping the back of Cassian's seat. He was freshly scrubbed and bandaged, and smelled distractingly of cheap cleaning products and disinfectant. His formerly distant, terrified voice sounded almost human again. "Lower!"

Cassian angled downward as much as he dared. He imagined the rainwater wriggling into a hundred metal seams wedged open during the Jedha sandstorm; droplets creeping among exposed electronics and shorting critical systems.

"This ship was not meant to be flown this way," K-2 observed.

The U-wing emerged from a fogbank to reveal the landscape below: a hundred jagged rock formations, broad mesas, and narrow spires, rising from an uneven ground. A narrow canyon wove between the deadly ridges, its boundaries barely discernible in the storm.

"They have landing trackers," Bodhi said. "They have patrol squadrons. You've got to stay in the canyon, keep it low."

Cassian nodded, adjusted his altitude, and checked his scanners for TIE fighters. He found nothing, though he wondered whether ships so small would even show up in the maelstrom. K-2 increased thrust as the wind momentarily dropped off; the U-wing lurched and Cassian's teeth smacked together.

"If we proceed," K-2 said, "there's a twenty-six percent chance of failure."

"How much farther?" Cassian shot at Bodhi.

"I don't know," Bodhi said. "I'm not sure, I never really come this way—"

I figured that, Cassian thought. They were skimming over a spire, no more than ten meters above the summit.

"—but we're close. I know *that.*"

"Now there's a thirty-five percent chance of failure," K-2 interjected.

Cassian toggled the landing lights. They'd be easily spotted by any patrol squadron overhead, but his visibility was nil. "I don't want to know," he said, not glancing at the droid. "Thank you."

"I understand," K-2 said. "I'd prefer ignorance myself."

The spire fell away beneath them and Cassian descended farther into the canyon. The broken walls curved one way and then another, following the course of a dozen writhing streambeds. The rocks were too close, came up too fast, but if Cassian reduced speed any more they'd be at the total mercy of the storm.

"Now!" Bodhi shouted, and slammed a hand on Cassian's seatback. "Put it down now!"

"The wind—" K-2 started, but Bodhi was squeezing between the seats, gesturing at something through the rain.

"If you keep going, you'll be right over the shuttle depot. Put it down now!"

Cassian swore. Bodhi was right—what he'd mistaken for refracting raindrops on the viewport was a series of distant floodlights. A landing pad for Imperial spacecraft.

He cut the ship's speed. Almost immediately the wind caught beneath the starboard wing, sent the U-wing veering toward the side of the canyon. K-2 tried to bank, but a ridge of black stone came up too fast for even a machine's reflexes; a ledge clipped the U-wing and Cassian slammed forward in his restraints, crying out as the ship trailed sparks and went into a steep decline. The dashboard was red with warning lights.

"Hold on tight," Cassian shouted. "We're coming in hard!"

Whether anyone in the cabin heard him in the tumult, he couldn't guess.

K-2 extended the landing gear and activated the retro-rockets in a futile attempt to break their speed. When they struck the planet surface, the U-wing's underbelly screamed violently against mud and stone while momentum carried them forward. For almost half a minute, they plowed on as the ship's hull threatened to shred.

When the U-wing finally stopped, cockpit cracked and half buried in gravel and mire, Cassian was certain the ship wouldn't fly again.

The rain had tapered to a cold, cruel drizzle by the time Cassian finished a cursory inspection of the damage. His initial assessment had been correct: The U-wing was largely intact, but the port engine had been dashed into the rocks and was beyond repair. Most of the other components—long- and short-range comms included—were salvageable but nonfunctional.

He could still complete his mission. He could still kill Galen Erso. But he hadn't planned to end the day stranded on Eadu. He pictured himself picking his way through the canyons, hunted by both stormtroopers and Jyn.

He was in a sour mood when he marched back into the cabin. He looked at the faces before him—the zealots, the defector, the madwoman, and K-2—and felt a new rush of ire. They'd had opinions on the mission until it had gone south; now they expected a solution from him.

The only one he even trusted was the Imperial droid.

"Bodhi," he snapped. Rainwater streamed down his forehead onto the cabin floor. "Where's the lab?"

Bodhi straightened and took an awkward step forward, like a soldier being called to attention. "The research facility?"

"The place you made deliveries and met Galen Erso. *Where is it?*"

Bodhi trembled for a moment. Cassian debated whether to push harder or coddle the man; but then the pilot stilled and said crisply, "It's just over the ridge."

"And that's a shuttle depot straight ahead of us? You are sure of that?"

"Yes," Bodhi said.

A satellite image would have been preferable, but Cassian had worked with worse than the word of a scared traitor. "We'll have to hope there's still an Imperial ship left to steal. The U-wing is scrap."

No one looked surprised. Baze smiled sardonically.

"Grab anything that might be useful," he went on. "K-2 will burn anything sensitive." Alliance ships were programmed not to keep navi records, and all identification had been scrubbed long ago. Cleanup wouldn't be hard. "After that, here's what we're doing."

He waited for an argument that didn't come. Bodhi still stood at attention. Baze regarded Cassian like he was judging him at trial. Chirrut looked distracted, cocking his head as if listening to the rain.

And Jyn? Jyn seemed pale and gaunt compared to the woman he'd met on Yavin. Even her momentary zeal after leaving Jedha was gone, revealed as a pretense to drag them into her madness. She watched him somberly, sadly, like she was sure he would disappoint her.

She was probably right about that.

"Hopefully," he said, "the storm keeps up and keeps us hidden down here. Bodhi, you're coming with me. We'll go up the ridge and check out the *research facility.*"

"I'm coming with you," Jyn said.

That didn't take long. But he'd planned for it.

"No," he said. "Your father's message—we can't risk it. You're the messenger."

Jyn scowled. "That's ridiculous. We *all* got the message. Everyone here knows it."

K-2 spoke for the first time. *"One blast to the reactor module and the whole system goes down. That's how you said it. The whole system goes down."*

"You"—Cassian shot toward K-2—"get to work fixing our comms." He forced himself to moderate his voice, to sound *reasonable,* before returning to Jyn. "All I want to do right now is get a handle on what we're up against. And even if I were ready to extract your father, I wouldn't be stupid enough to try on my own. I need you for fire-power; and at *this* moment, I need you protecting the ship."

She returned to that intense, somber stare. *Good enough.*

"So," he said, and nodded at Bodhi, "we're going to go very small and very carefully up the rise and see what's what. Let's get out of here."

There were no questions, and Cassian kept his eyes on his gear as he checked his equipment and reconfigured his blaster, slapping scope and extended barrel into place with rapid, familiar motions. *At least,* he thought, *the weaponry survived the crash.* He heard Bodhi's footsteps behind him as he trudged back out into the rain and the mud, his soles sucking noisily at the drenched soil.

"Do I need one, too?" Bodhi called. Cassian cast a look backward at the man as he crept down the slick boarding ramp. "A weapon?"

"You sound like my droid," Cassian said. Then he grunted, and shook his head. "We won't be long. You'll be fine."

It was probably true. And there was a fringe benefit: If Bodhi sided with Jyn over Cassian, it meant one fewer person who might shoot him in the back.

Jyn hadn't spoken to the others during the journey from Jedha. When Bodhi had approached her, tried to ask about Galen, she'd managed a gentle smile before waving him off. Chirrut and Baze had known better than to try talking; or perhaps they, like Jyn, wrestled with truths too difficult to express in words.

So she had listened to the hologram of her father in her mind and watched the dark of the cave become the darkness of Eadu.

The fact that she had no way to leave the planet lay discarded in her consciousness, untouched and irrelevent.

"Does he look like a killer?"

She was watching Cassian and Bodhi descend into the mud when she heard Chirrut's voice. She turned to look and saw he was speaking to Baze.

"No," Baze said, after a moment of thought. "He has the face of a friend."

"Who are you talking about?" she asked.

Baze eyed her appraisingly. "Captain Andor," he said, flat.

She should have been irritated by the curt explanation. Instead she could muster only vague confusion. "Why do you ask that?" she said, looking to Chirrut now. "What do you mean, *Does he look like a killer?*"

"The Force moves darkly near a creature that's about to kill," Chirrut answered. He might have added, *As simple as that.*

"Fascinating," K-2SO called, heading for the cockpit. "His weapon *was* in the sniper configuration."

Jyn pictured Cassian assembling his weapon and exiting the ship. She remembered the first time she'd held a sniper rifle, staring down the scope under Saw Gerrera's direction, measuring her breath so she could confidently, quietly, kill a man from a kilometer away.

It might have meant nothing.

Her heartbeat quickened. She spun toward the boarding ramp and started down into the mud. The chill crept through her boots, up her legs and her spine. She couldn't see the path Cassian and Bodhi had taken, couldn't hear them over the steady rain, but she could see the dim, distant light of the Imperial compound.

There, she would find her father.

Baze Malbus watched a gust of wind spatter raindrops across the cabin floor, discoloring the metal in a thousand pinpoints like bleak stars in a gray sky. The rain smelled like fecund soil with an undertone of acrid stink.

Baze was not a young man. He had seen rain before. But Jedha's rains—rare, powerful torrents that were cause for celebration, that he had taken such joy in as a child—had never smelled like this.

Soon, Baze thought, he would forget the smell of Jedha's rain altogether.

Chirrut rose abruptly, swept his staff before him, and marched toward the boarding ramp.

"Where are you going?" Baze growled.

Chirrut paused but kept his back to Baze. "I'm going to follow Jyn. Her path is clear."

"Alone?" Baze asked. The word was volatile with meaning. "Good luck."

He was certain Chirrut understood his warning. But the blind man, once brother to Baze among the Guardians of the Whills and now the fool Baze was cursed to entertain, started forward again. "I don't need luck," Chirrut said. "I have you."

Baze watched Chirrut descend the ramp. He listened to the foot of the staff rap on metal. When the rapping ended and Chirrut stepped onto soft ground, Baze heaved himself to his feet. Without a glance at the cabin, he followed his brother into the storm of an alien world.

The tragedy of K-2SO's existence was this: The skills he most cherished were skills his rebel masters disdained; and the skills he considered crude and trivial were skills his masters were helpless to learn.

Thus, his present circumstances: Instead of traveling to the research lab to manhandle, capture, restrain, and extract the scientist Galen Erso—a mission virtually *requiring* the talents of an Imperial security droid, and which might (if handled delicately) permit the exercise of multiple underutilized procedures hardcoded into K-2SO—he was rewiring a communications array and locating faults in each of eighty-four connectors by touch.

Such a task required a bare minimum of computational power. K-2SO had more than enough to spare to listen to the goings-on in the cabin and observe the landscape from the half-buried cockpit viewport.

He watched Jyn depart with disinterest. The woman had always verged on disrespectful toward him.

He watched Baze and Chirrut depart with more robust disapproval. He posited an array of scenarios involving their separation from the U-wing, few of which ended in their continued well-being.

"What are they doing?" he asked sharply.

K-2SO was not a protocol droid, but he was designed for biological interaction. He found that verbal discussion, even with himself, spurred his creativity.

He soon came to a solution he was satisfied with.

"If Cassian comes back," he said, "we're leaving without them."

CHAPTER 11

CAPTAIN CASSIAN ANDOR HAD FAILED. That was the assumption Draven had to make.

He had activated the homing beacon aboard Andor's U-wing immediately after receiving his agent's supposed confirmation of the planet killer. The beacon was a risk, but a minor one—its signal was disguised as pulsar radiation and relayed through a dozen unstaffed rebel outposts before reaching Base One—and under the circumstances, Draven thought it wise to keep tabs on Andor.

He had the utmost respect for his agent—for *Cassian*—but only a fool would stake the fate of the Alliance on a single man. Much as Draven detested the fact, this mission had taken on such unlikely proportions.

"Try them again," he said.

He stood behind Private Weems in the communications room, looking over the man's shoulder as he tapped at his console. Two of Draven's captains stood with him—officers he trusted as well as Andor, albeit for different reasons.

"I am trying, sir," Weems said. "The signal's gone dead."

"Guess wildly for me. *Why?*" He turned toward his captains. Better to get the speculation over with.

"We know Andor made it to the Eadu star system." It was Captain Nioma who spoke first: analyst and technical adviser for Alliance Intelligence, a mumbling genius who hadn't slept since she'd first heard rumors about the planet killer. "Could've been shot down. Could've been shot *at*, though the beacon's rugged enough to survive a lot of damage. We don't have much intel on Eadu, though, so for all we know the signal's blocked by a high-energy thermosphere—"

"How likely is that?" Draven asked.

"Not likely."

He grunted, leaned his weight against the back of Weems's chair. "Say we wanted to send in Blue Squadron. How long to Eadu?"

Captain Vienaris had been, of all things, a spaceport control officer before joining the Rebellion. He had the numbers for half a dozen hyperspace routes at hand; he factored in variable atmospheric conditions and rapidly ran through the lot with Draven. "Short version: We're in striking range, but if the Empire's begun to evacuate we won't catch them. Best case, Blue Squadron arrives just in time to see the Imperials jump out."

But would the Empire bother to evacuate at all? Draven tried to put himself in the mind of the commander in charge of Eadu's garrison. *I just caught a transport—a Rebel Alliance Intelligence U-wing— making a recon run over my base. I shot the ship down and even took prisoners . . .*

It was only *one* ship. It was a threat to operational security, but it wasn't cause for panic. If the Alliance knew for certain what was on Eadu, they'd come en masse. And the work being done on Eadu was vital; if the decision was made to uproot, the base's chief scientist would need to be the *last* to go to ensure everything was safely relocated. You couldn't trust stormtroopers with the delicate equipment.

So Galen Erso was still onsite. The planet killer might not die with him, but—if Erso really was responsible for its main weapon—it would be a hell of a lot harder to keep operational after he was gone.

"Squadron up," Draven said. "Target Eadu. We must take out Galen Erso if we have the chance."

Captain Vienaris was running from the room, speaking into his comlink almost before Draven had finished. Nioma was looking at him with bloodshot eyes. "Do you have authorization?" she asked. "A full-scale attack on a major Imperial installation . . ."

Anyone else, Draven would have taken aside and rebuked for questioning him in public. But Nioma had never possessed a military mindset, and she looked like she'd turn to dust at a stern word. "The mission's under my department," he said. "I don't need the council's sign-off."

That was true. What he didn't tell Nioma was that, authorized or not, the mission had crept well outside the council's intended parameters.

He'd been hoping to withhold Andor's report of the planet killer over Jedha until after debriefing the captain himself; revealing the truth (if it *was* true) to the council members without context would only encourage them to pursue their own leads, activate their own contingencies, all without coordination or strategy. Half the Alliance would run and hide while the other half would take the offensive. Word would spread outside the council in a matter of hours, inciting panic. Any hope of using knowledge of the planet killer as a form of *leverage*—to manipulate a vote in the Senate, to bring Saw Gerrera's zealots back on-side—would be lost.

Draven worked for Alliance Intelligence. His job wasn't to share every secret he came across. It was to explain what secrets *meant,* if and when they were safe to share. He couldn't do that yet.

But the council was going to hear about his activation of Blue Squadron. Mon Mothma was going to want to know when the mission had become about assassination rather than extraction.

Blue Squadron would be en route to Eadu in a matter of minutes. Draven had until it arrived to prepare for the conversation.

"No, no," Bodhi called, rivers of rainwater dribbling off his hair and beard. "We've got to go up."

Cassian frowned at Bodhi, then glanced down the slope of the muddy canyon at the distant shine of the laboratory lights. He could have questioned the pilot, but his mood was still sour and he didn't see the use. Either Bodhi knew the topography or he didn't; either he was lying or he wasn't.

He shrugged and followed Bodhi up the rocky, rain-slick slope. At least it took them out of the worst of the mud.

As they trudged up the ridge, Bodhi nattered on about his time on Eadu. Cassian half listened to the pilot's stories of running cargo flights, delivering kyber crystal from Jedha to the local scientists. Bodhi had barely been authorized (he claimed) to access the mess hall while onsite, to refresh himself and refuel before heading back to Jedha. "If I hadn't started a conversation with Galen in the meal line, asked him which droid to grab a bite from, maybe I never would've wondered what was going on here. What they were *working* on . . ."

It sounded too much like a lie for Cassian to really believe it. But it also sounded like a lie for Bodhi's benefit, not Cassian's. If that was the story he wanted to tell about meeting Galen, so be it. If Bodhi was *scared* of Cassian, desperate to convince him his defection was genuine, that was fine with Cassian, too.

Eventually Bodhi stopped talking as the path grew narrower. Cassian saw the pilot stumble and noticed the stiffness in the man's legs—the way he bent his knees as little as possible, more so the longer the hike went on. He noticed, too, the dark bruises and the raw, scraped flesh at the base of Bodhi's neck. These were largely concealed by the collar of his flight suit, but the rain had tamped the suit down and left them more evident than before.

"How long did Saw Gerrera's people hold you?" Cassian called.

Bodhi flinched but kept walking. "What?"

Cassian repeated his question.

"A few days, maybe," Bodhi said, not looking back.

Cassian thought back to the rumpled pile of a man he had found in the catacombs, malnourished and battered and deranged with trauma. Less than a day later, the man leading him through the canyons of Eadu was transparently terrified and far too eager to chat; but he was also doing his damnedest to feign *normalcy* on what looked likely to be a suicide mission. He was even doing a decent job of it.

Cassian laughed. It was a brief, guttural sound that seemed drowned in the rain. Bodhi did look back now, surprised and a touch alarmed. "What?" he asked.

"Nothing," Cassian said. Then he added, blunt and almost humbled: "Must've been a hell of a few days."

Bodhi smiled—just a twitch of his lips—for the first time since Cassian had known him.

They climbed higher. Cassian could make out a platform across a narrow valley now—a raised landing pad separate from the shuttle depot. But the path up the ridge was turning increasingly treacherous. Soon it almost disappeared altogether, and Bodhi drew up against the rock face as scree poured from beneath his feet.

"I'll be right behind you," Cassian said, with as much reassurance as he could muster.

Bodhi looked sickly, but he nodded. "Come on."

They crossed the next switchback with agonizing care. Beyond, the path widened again, and after a final ascent they crested the ridge and looked down onto the Imperial installation from above. The flat metal sweep of the landing pad abutted a series of military-spec housing and laboratory stations. Cassian recognized the prefab designs, but the labs, at least, looked heavily customized—he spotted whole swaths of unfamiliar antenna equipment and generators.

He shuffled forward and knelt behind a boulder, felt the cool jab of damp pebbles against his knees. Next, he pulled Bodhi down beside him and fished out his quadnocs, magnifying and surveying the installation. There was activity on the landing pad—stormtroopers emerging in formation from one of the buildings, followed by figures in blue-and-white engineering jumpsuits.

Cassian held the quadnocs out to Bodhi without taking his own eyes off the platform. "Take a look," he said. "You see Erso out there?"

Bodhi raised the quadnocs, shook his head incrementally, and then stilled. "That's him," he said after a moment. "That's him, Galen, in the dark suit—"

His voice hitched in excitement. Cassian snatched the quadnocs and scanned the platform again. Among the engineers was a man in gray and blue, with a sharp, angular face and a scalp covered in wisps of frosted hair. Cassian sought a resemblance to Jyn and found it in the man's eyes, deep-set and staring.

Galen was speaking to the other engineers. The rain made them all look sodden and haggard, displeased at being brought outside so late.

Cassian frowned. Why *were* they there? Had he and Bodhi tripped some alarm? Were they waiting for evacuation?

He almost didn't notice the rumbling in the distance, wrote it off as part of the storm. But the sound was too even in pitch and grew louder too fast. He wrapped an arm around Bodhi and pulled the pilot flat onto the ground as a broad-winged Imperial shuttle swooped overhead and made for the platform.

"Do they ever bring the engineers out for deliveries?" Cassian hissed.

Bodhi coughed as rainwater caught in his nostrils, then shook his head vigorously. "Not like this. Not this time of night."

Then something's off. Maybe it wasn't related to the arrival of the U-wing. Maybe it was connected to Jedha—the Empire cleaning up its production facilities now that the Death Star was operational. The shuttle was a *Delta*-class long-range model, used for passengers more than cargo. Whatever was happening, *now* might be the only opportunity to act.

Cassian put the quadnocs to one side and unslung his rifle. He checked its settings, balanced it on the rocks, and shifted his position as he spoke to Bodhi. "You need to get back down there," he said, "and find us a ride out of here. You understand?"

"What are *you* doing?"

Cassian put an eye to the rifle's scope, saw nothing but a blur atop the platform. He adjusted his magnification and filters, let the internal computer compensate for the sheets of rain.

"You heard me," he said. He made his voice hard, tried to erase any warmth that had sparked between him and the pilot. He couldn't afford an argument now.

"You said we came up here just to have a look," Bodhi snapped back.

Lie to him. Tell him you need to keep Galen alive and on Eadu, and you don't know what that shuttle could mean.

"I'm here," Cassian said. "I'm *looking.* Go."

The platform crystallized. More Imperials were emerging from the buildings. He adjusted his aim and began seeking the face of Galen Erso. He heard Bodhi's soft, rapid breathing at his side. "Hurry!" Cassian snarled.

Bodhi's boots tossed flecks of stone onto Cassian's jacket as he ran.

During the flight to Eadu, Krennic had stoked the fury in his heart. Fueled by outrage and humiliation, its fire burned bright enough to warm him in the chill that swept through the shuttle; to ward off the ice of the raindrops that assailed him as he descended the boarding ramp onto the landing platform.

The boots of his death squad squealed against wet metal as he drew to a stop and surveyed the assortment of stormtroopers, officers, and engineers before him. The troopers had corralled the engineers—miserable as wet hounds, standing in a loose, indecorous cluster—at one end, while the facility's senior officers were aligned about the shuttle, doing their best to ignore their indignity in the presence of their director. The garrison commander stepped forward to offer a welcome, but Krennic waved her off. He had no interest in delaying what he had come to do.

The engineers looked nervously at one another. Krennic noted each in turn, recalled his name, studied his posture. Most he did not know overly well. He had hand-selected Uyohn out of the Brentaal Futures Program—the same program Krennic and Galen had completed together—and been mildly disappointed in the results ever since. Uyohn stood straight-backed, expression vacillating between fear and deluded, desperate hope. Onopin, conversely, looked ready to curse loudly about *bureaucratic interference* and bury his obvious worry beneath a thin layer of professional pride. Krennic liked Onopin, but he hoped he would remain silent this once.

None of them showed any hint of *defiance*.

Krennic looked to Galen Erso. The man stepped forward, blinking the raindrops out of his eyes. He held himself as if Krennic's presence neither surprised nor concerned him.

"Well, Galen," Krennic said. "At last it's complete. You must be very proud."

"Proud as I can be, Krennic."

It was false humility, of course. Krennic was certain of that. "Gather your engineers," he said. "I have an announcement to make."

Galen barely gestured. The engineers drifted, herdlike, from one side of the platform to the other until they stood before Krennic and Galen together. They huddled as if to share heat in the spitting storm and ward off their collective dread. "Is that all of them?" Krennic asked, though he already knew the answer.

"Yes," Galen said.

Krennic smiled acidly and said the words he had selected with care aboard the shuttle: "Gentlemen. One of you has betrayed the Empire. One of you conspired with a pilot to send messages to the Rebellion. I urge that traitor to step forward."

On cue, Krennic's death squad took position and leveled its weapons at the engineers.

There were too many people on the landing pad. Cassian kept his rifle propped against the stone, ignored the trickle of rain like sweat down his spine, and tried to draw a bead on Galen. But there were stormtroopers in the way now, and his shot became no clearer once the shuttle landed and the crowd reconfigured itself. He swore to himself and waited.

He dredged his memory to try and identify the officer in the white cape and found the name Orson Krennic—some sort of project director apparently attached to the planet killer. If by some miracle Cassian got off a second shot, he decided Krennic would make an excellent target. The Empire could only be improved by the loss of another high-ranking blowhard.

But that would be a bonus. He had his mission. He just needed a few inconvenient stormtroopers and engineers to get *out of the way.*

At least Bodhi was gone. No one to witness what happened next.

Krennic and Galen were speaking. Still too many people in the line of fire.

Cassian would need a story for Jyn. He knew that. She wouldn't believe him no matter *what* he told her, but if he offered her something plausible and Bodhi backed the portions of his tale that were true, she might not act rashly. She'd suspect Cassian in the back of her mind, and he'd need to watch himself so long as they were together; but the uncertainty might suffice to drag her down. Without her father and without a target, her obsession and *need* would drain out of her like pus.

If they made it off Eadu, if she survived to return to Yavin, he would be done with her then. Even with her fire gone cold, she'd be better off than she was in prison.

Galen was gesturing. The crowd was reconfiguring again, the other engineers stepping forward. Still no shot.

Destroying Jyn—*that's what it would be, you can admit that much*—was his best option. If she *did* realize what he'd done, she'd turn that feral need against him. She'd want him dead, probably sway the Guardians of the Whills and Bodhi against him as well.

The engineers were arrayed in front of Krennic and Galen. Krennic's retinue of black-clad troopers fanned out. A few more steps . . .

Maybe that wouldn't be such a terrible way to go. He'd assassinated better men than Galen—an Imperial collaborator, the man who'd built a *planet killer,* remorse be damned. And if Jyn came after Cassian, he'd die for his crimes. There were worse deaths.

Was that what it had come to?

Galen stepped forward. Cassian had the shot.

But he was breathing too hard now. The rifle rose and fell. He clamped a hand on the barrel, lodged it firmly against the rocks.

He was tired of crimes he never answered for.

The Death Star is your answer. Finish this mission, and all is forgiven.

He looked at Galen Erso through his scope and saw his daughter's eyes.

With a hoarse and ragged cry, he swept the rifle away from the rocks and set it in the mud at his side.

None of the engineers answered Krennic's accusation. He hadn't really expected them to.

"No one?" he asked. "The traitor will still be executed, but at least he can die making a stand. Maybe he'll convert someone here"—he swept a gloved hand around the platform—"with his dying words."

Onopin was opening and closing his mouth, as if caught between begging for the traitor to step forth and attempting a show of silent indignation. Two of the other engineers were looking at their fellows intently, as if frantically conducting their own investigations.

Galen, standing beside Krennic, took a single step forward and did nothing else.

"Very well," Krennic said. "I'll consider it a group effort, then."

The words were cruel and sweet. Krennic felt no shame in deriving satisfaction from justice ruthlessly applied. "Ready," he said, and his troops checked the settings on their rifles with a metallic *click*.

"Aim," he said, and the death squad took aim.

"And—"

Galen took action at last.

He dashed between Krennic and the engineers, spun about and nearly slipped on the wet platform. "Stop," he cried, again and again, spreading his arms as if he could block the troopers' shots. "Krennic, stop. It was *me*. It was me. They have nothing to do with it."

Krennic looked into the face of the man he'd befriended long ago. He waited.

"Spare them," Galen said. Drenched and tired and wild-eyed, he looked like a man whose genius had deserted him.

Krennic crooked a finger at Galen. As if reluctant, the begging man stepped back toward Krennic.

"Fire," Krennic spat.

He didn't watch the crimson bolts flare from his troopers' rifles, didn't bother glancing at the bodies of engineers tumbling to the ground and sizzling in the rain. His eyes were on Galen, and he saw the explosion of shock and fury in the scientist's face—saw him try to hide it the next instant behind a mask of iron.

But they were long past hiding things, and Galen should have known better. Krennic swung his fist in a tight arc and felt the back of his hand strike Galen's cheek and chin. Galen staggered and dropped to his knees.

"I fired your weapon," Krennic said. "Jedha. Saw Gerrera. His band of fanatics. The Holy City. The last reminder of the Jedi." He paused. "An entire planet will be next."

Galen stared up and neither trembled nor shouted.

"You'll never win," he said softly.

Such a perfect delusion. It was almost beautiful.

"Now where," Krennic asked, "have I heard that before?"

Somewhere in the mud and the rain and the dark, Jyn had lost track of Cassian and Bodhi. That wasn't important; she'd found her way down the canyon by the lights of the research facility and on to the base of a landing pad. It was where she needed to be, where her mission to find her father had guided her. It was the answer to the recording that played in the blackness of her mind, and the words of Galen Erso became clearer and louder with every step.

She'd needed time to find a way up—there was no unguarded path to reach the platform or the abutting structures from the bottom of the canyon—but she'd located a service ladder built against the canyon wall and begun to climb. The rungs were half slick with water sprayed against them by the breeze, and where she couldn't get a strong grip, she hooked her arm over the metal and pulled, straining her shoulders and kicking until she found purchase. She did this again and again, driving thought and hope and despair blessedly from her mind, until she was only the *body* of Jyn, who would climb to the top or who would fall. She did not return to herself until the platform was within reach and she heard soft voices muffled by the patter of rain.

She didn't hesitate to pull herself up and over. It wasn't a safe choice, but her gloved hands had gone numb and she'd begun slipping a bit more with each rung. She preferred to die moving than to die out of caution.

The platform's cold metal felt comforting against her prone body. She had no time to rest, however. A pair of white boots stepped in front of her and the barrel of a rifle lowered at her head. She reached up to twist the blaster away, lunged to wrest it from the stormtrooper's grasp. In a single motion she was up and spinning, sweeping the trooper off the platform's edge and sending him into the abyss. His head struck the rock wall instantly. He never screamed.

Jyn nestled the rifle under her arm and looked around. She could still hear voices, but she'd been lucky; she'd ascended behind a row of cargo crates, and her skirmishing had gone unnoticed. She crept forward, head low, and peered around a crate at the gathering on the platform.

What she saw was this:

Stormtroopers in white, spread across the platform and observing the proceedings with their weapons at their sides.

Imperial officers of various ranks, standing unhappily in the rain.

Half a dozen corpses, freshly killed with wounds still smoking.

Stormtroopers in black, like the ones who had executed her mother on Lah'mu.

The man in white who had ordered her mother's execution.

And her father, on his knees before the man in white and looking up with pity in his eyes.

It was a scene out of her memory playacted on a new stage—an impossible, nightmare re-creation for the benefit of the little girl who had run to the cave.

But that girl was buried in the wet dirt below the hatch in Jyn's mind. Her wails of anguish and terror were muted.

With shaking hands, Jyn raised her rifle and aimed for the man in white.

.   .   .

Cassian sat among the rocks on the ridge and watched.

He had *chosen* to watch. By setting aside his rifle, he had forfeited his mission, betrayed his oaths—spoken and implicit—to Draven and Alliance Intelligence. Under other circumstances, such a betrayal might have felt freeing. As it was, he could do nothing while the man he'd spared was readied for execution.

He'd been powerless to stop the slaughter of the engineers. If he'd fired into the crowd, he might have picked off a stormtrooper but done no lasting good. Not that intervention was necessarily in his interests—the lives of Imperial researchers weren't lives that roused emotion in his chest.

But it seemed obscene for fate or the Force or ancient Eadu gods to slay Galen Erso so soon after Cassian had made his choice. He watched the scene on the platform through his quadnocs, scanned the vicinity for anything that might disrupt what seemed likely to happen next.

What he found, to his shock, was Jyn—hoisting herself over the edge of the platform and throwing a stormtrooper to his doom.

What was she *doing* there?

He guessed the answer the moment he posed the question.

He didn't have time to consider how he could act on the information before his comlink hissed with static and K-2's urgent voice came through. "Cassian, can you hear me?"

He snatched up the comlink in one hand, brought it to his mouth. "I'm here." He tried to keep watch on Jyn as she crept along the cargo crates stacked at the side of the platform. "You got the comms working."

"Affirmative, but we have a problem! There's an Alliance squadron approaching." Cassian struggled to hear the words through the distortion and the rain. "Clear the area!"

His brain filtered the meaning from the noise a second later. "No," he spat. "No, no, no—tell them to hold up! Jyn's on that platform!"

If Draven had sent a fighter squadron, he'd done so in order to complete the mission—to eliminate Galen Erso by leveling the research facility and picking off any soft targets on the ground.

The pilots wouldn't know about Cassian and the others. Draven likely wouldn't have bothered informing them; wouldn't have sent them out if he'd thought Cassian was still alive.

Cassian looked at the platform, at the shadowy figure of Jyn, and thought to himself: *I've killed us all.*

Draven's countdown was nearing zero. There were rumors spreading around Base One that *something* had happened on Jedha, and if rumors were spreading on Yavin, they'd certainly crept to more civilized regions of the galaxy. He had to brief the Alliance High Command council on the planet killer and the mission to Eadu.

More precisely, he had to brief Mon Mothma. He didn't have *time* for the council as a whole, and Mothma—much as Draven vigorously disagreed with her strategies—could be brutally straightforward when backed into a corner. The ex-senator and current Alliance chief of state wasn't above playing dirty politics, and Draven had occasionally caught her playing dirtier than she liked to admit; but in the matter of the planet killer, he trusted her to put pragmatism above brinksmanship.

He was halfway to Mothma's office on the upper levels of the ziggurat when he was summoned back to the comm center. He hustled down two flights of stairs; his uniform was clinging to the sweat on his back when he arrived.

"General!" Private Weems saluted and gestured him to a terminal. "Faint signal from Eadu. It's Captain Andor's U-wing—full voice, no encryption."

"What?" *They must have lost the whole comm array, jury-rigged something in its place.* He took a seat and hunched over the console. "Put it through."

A faint, tinny voice spoke. The tone was almost relaxed. "Captain Andor requesting a delay on squadron support." *Andor's pet droid.* Draven leaned closer to the console speaker, clenched his jaw as he heard the remainder of the message: "Alliance forces onsite. Please confirm."

Draven swore inwardly and gestured rapidly at Weems. "Get the squadron leader on," he said. "Get him on *now!*"

Weems looked as aghast as if he'd been accused of desertion. "They sent word three minutes ago. They're already engaged, sir."

Damn it all.

Draven nodded slowly. Possibilities sprouted in his mind. Desperate options bloomed. One by one, he cut down each.

If the squadron was engaged, asking the pilots to abort now would only give the Imperials time to entrench. The dead wouldn't come back to life. Any survivors of Cassian's team would be left without support and made vulnerable to capture. The mission would certainly fail.

"If you can get a message through," he said, "let Blue Squadron know what we know." Not that there was anything the squadron could do about it. "And as for Andor's team . . ."

He sighed. *Sometimes good people meet bad ends.*

"Tell them," he finished, "may the Force be with them."

CHAPTER 12

BAZE HAD ALLOWED CHIRRUT TO lead them up the ridge. He'd taken point often enough—pushed Chirrut to the side to stomp at a crumbling stretch of narrow rock, or gone hunting switchbacks where the ridge became less sheer—but it had been Chirrut to insist "Higher," until they stood together on the apex, looking far below onto the twisted paths and the research facility.

"You said we were following *Jyn*," Baze growled.

"Why are you so literal?" Chirrut asked. His smile was playful, almost smug.

Baze grunted in reply. It was an old habit, a way to assure Chirrut of his presence without words. He doubted his companion appreciated it in the slightest.

A short while later, he had his cannon adjusted and the scope to his eye. There was a gathering on the facility's landing pad. He spied stormtroopers and officers, a shuttle descending. He looked at the pale, clean-shaven face of a young Imperial captain, haughty and smirking at something his neighbor had said.

It was the face of a man who had the luxury of thinking of something other than death. Something other than the ruin of everything he had loved.

"Baze," Chirrut said.

Baze readied himself to pull the trigger on his cannon. To burn the platform with more blaster bolts than there were drops of rain on Eadu.

"I sense anger in you," Chirrut said.

Let the Imperials sense it, too, Baze thought.

"This is not what we came for," Chirrut said. There was no playfulness in him now. "This solves nothing."

Baze jerked his weapon down and turned to his companion. "They destroyed our *home*. I will kill them."

Chirrut said nothing. But the blind man's unflappable calm, the wind tugging at his clothes and the rain beating against his scalp, seemed to leach some of Baze's ire. In time, Baze spun back and lodged himself among the rocks, observing the goings-on on the platform with his naked eye. The Imperials were only smudges that way. *Harder to hate a smudge.*

"So what did we come for," Baze asked, "if not vengeance? Are we lackeys of the Rebellion now?"

Chirrut tapped at the ground with his staff, searching out the edge of the cliff before crouching at Baze's side. "Captain Andor is the only lackey of the Rebellion here. And even he may not last much longer."

"Then why follow *Jyn*?" Baze asked.

He had allowed Chirrut to lead the way up the ridge. He had allowed Chirrut to lead him in many things, and learned long ago not to demand answers. But grief had turned all his lessons to tatters. Today was not a day for the evasions of a Guardian of the Whills.

Chirrut knew, of course.

So many years together, how could he not?

"Because she *shines*," Chirrut said, and placed a hand on Baze's shoulder.

For a few short minutes, there was serenity in the rain on the mountaintop.

Then the sky roared and starfighters blazed trails of fire above them, silencing the storm.

The alarm began to wail seconds before the first blast hit. Jyn's aim slipped from her target. Then she saw the X-wing diving, saw its laser cannons flare. The volley cut across the platform, setting fire to metal and sending waves of sparks skidding in all directions. The storm-troopers and officers struck squarely by the blasts died instantly, burned to char. Those on the edges of the volley screamed and clutched their wounds and ran.

Jyn retreated behind the cargo crates, dragged in a ragged breath of the suddenly smoky air. The X-wing leveled out of its dive. She heard its cannons continue pulsing, the sound rapidly falling off as the vessel flew past the platform.

She didn't bother to ask herself where the attacker had come from. She knew, however, it wouldn't have come alone. The alarm's wail seemed faint in the aftermath of the assault. Someone was screaming orders to scramble fighters, to return fire. Jyn took the opportunity to creep out from behind her cover and scan the platform for her father.

He was where she had left him, still near the furiously yelling man in white—the ghost standing in the midst of mayhem, threatening to kill Jyn's mother again with the mere fact of his existence.

But her father was pushing himself upright, standing unsteadily. He was *alive*.

She wanted to run to him. She forgot every fear she'd had of their reunion. But now two more X-wings had begun a strafing run and the blinding crimson of laserfire, the heat of boiling rainwater against her cheeks, overwhelmed Jyn for one second, two, three. She blinked spots from her eyes and cinders from her lashes and sprinted, head low and rifle cradled in both arms. She shouldered a panting officer to one side, leapt over the burning body of a stormtrooper.

"Papa," she screamed.

Galen turned. He *saw* her. For the first time in nearly fifteen years, Jyn's father was *looking* at her.

She kept running, struggling to find traction on the wet metal. She saw the man in white stop shouting orders and whirl toward her, drawing his sidearm. She didn't break stride; she brought up her rifle, ready to kill the ghost to reach her father.

Whether the man in white ever fired, Jyn didn't know. Her body went numb as a shock wave slammed into her, as thunder and shattering metal assailed her ears. She felt her feet leave the ground and her skull strike steel. All she saw of the proton torpedo that hit the platform was a blinding incandescence.

She wondered whether her father had even recognized her.

The platform was burning. There was nothing Cassian could see besides oily smoke, low-burning flames, and silhouettes crawling through the pandemonium. He had no target, no means to intervene.

"Jyn," he whispered. "No."

He didn't even know if she was alive.

With his rifle slung over one shoulder, he ran. He half slid down the muddy ridge, digging his front heel into the scree to avoid doubling over into a roll. When he had enough purchase to maneuver, he set out toward the research facility and the platform, hoping his path would be clear through the darkness.

He knew he was running toward catastrophe. The odds of him reaching Jyn—*if* she'd survived—were slim. The Imperials would shoot at him on sight, and there was no time for stealth. The rebel squadron would continue attacking until it was driven off or until the facility was buried in rubble. But he was free of his mission now, and if he failed to save Jyn . . .

He had to save her.

The sky was ablaze with green and red energy. TIE fighters had joined the battle, swooping to intercept rebel X-wings and slower Y-wing bombers. Volleys of turret fire from points around the research facility and along the canyon rim glimmered and hummed. Cassian spotted an X-wing caught in crossfire; it spun and plunged toward the rocks. He couldn't see where it struck, but the roar of its death echoed across the valley.

He fell as much as he ran, dropping through open air and landing on his heels or tumbling before he rose and resumed his stride. A thought sparked in his brain: If he found Jyn, where would they go? They were still trapped on Eadu. But it didn't matter; didn't change the immediacy of his needs.

A great bright bolt streaked overhead like a meteor. The bolt lanced one of the TIE fighters, sending it spiraling through the rain until it collided with a turret. The white bloom that followed illuminated Eadu as far as Cassian could see. When he glanced behind him, traced the afterimage of the bolt's path toward its source, he saw two humanoid silhouettes standing far above him on the ridge.

One of the silhouettes was carrying a staff.

The U-wing was on fire, struck—intentionally or not, Bodhi wasn't sure—during a TIE fighter's berserker maneuvering over the canyon. The Rebel Alliance X-wing squadron, much like Saw's rebels on Jedha, seemed to have no particular interest in whether Bodhi lived or died. And of the companions he'd taken up with—the companions who'd almost started to tolerate him—the only one left was the droid who, Bodhi suspected, wanted him locked away.

"Would you like to be carried?" K-2SO asked as they hurried away from the burning hulk of the U-wing. The droid's strides were markedly slower than Bodhi's, but his spindly limbs crossed twice the distance with every step.

"No!" Bodhi said. It was more breath than he had to spare.

"I could carry you anyway," the droid said. "That way you wouldn't have to choose."

Bodhi staggered to a halt and clapped his knees, hung his head panting for what he knew was too long. "No," he managed at last. "No, listen. I need you to trust me, all right? You need to follow my lead and not say *anything* unless someone asks you to."

Rain bounced off the droid's chest plate. K-2SO looked at Bodhi appraisingly. "*Trust* is a matter of degree," he said. "I really don't know you, Bodhi Rook."

Bodhi cringed and shook his head. *There's no time!* The others were waiting. Galen Erso was waiting. He wanted to shout. Instead he talked.

"You *do* know me," he said. "Look—you, me." He jabbed his finger at the Imperial emblem on the droid's arm, then at the identical symbol on his flight suit. "We've both got them, and we're both here *anyway*. We both want to stop the Death Star, right? Both want to help the Rebellion?"

The droid didn't answer. Bodhi was talking too fast now, but if anyone could understand him it would be a machine. "Cassian reprogrammed you, right? Maybe? You're loyal to him, I get that. Galen Erso reprogrammed *me*. We can still get this mission right, and we want the same thing, but you have to let me lead the way . . ."

Something exploded on the canyon ridge. The light made K-2SO look wraithlike—a gaunt shadow with deathly bright eyes.

"All right, then," K-2SO said.

Bodhi nodded briskly, raggedly, and turned to face the shuttle port.

He had never intended to come back to Eadu. He'd never meant to set foot in an Imperial garrison again after defecting. Galen had made it sound *simple,* like he could turn the message over to Saw Gerrera and sneak away somewhere outside the Empire, somewhere the Rebellion would hide him and pay decent money for all the good he'd done.

He suspected that plan had never really been in the cards. But he'd never been a good gambler, and he couldn't blame the dealer for that.

"If a fight starts," Bodhi said, "try not to hurt anyone we don't have to."

"I always try," the droid replied.

Bodhi started toward the shuttle port's bright lights and prayed he could find a way offworld.

.   .   .

Jyn woke to something burning in her lungs and the smell of death in her nostrils. When she coughed, the jolt sent needles of pain from her neck to the small of her back. She rolled onto her chest and climbed to her knees and reached with her right hand to steady herself on the platform, only to find her fingers tracing the hot, charred edges of a hole that spanned much of the landing pad. To her left was a corpse too black and bloody to identify.

She concluded she was alive.

Where was her father?

"Director!" someone called. "We have to evacuate!"

She looked toward the noise. Through thick smoke she spotted two officers supporting the man in white, leading him past sputtering fires up the boarding ramp of the shuttle. As the ramp began to close, the man in white cast a final glance toward a body across the hole from Jyn.

Galen's body.

Jyn forced herself to stand and felt agony wrench her spine. She tried to run and took awkward, plodding strides instead. If anyone had tried to shoot her she would've died instantly, but no one bothered. She heard footsteps and shouting. She saw no one else through the smoke.

Raindrops sprayed against her and a harsh gust of warm air dropped her to her knees again. As the shuttle lifted off the platform, its engine backwash built until Jyn was sliding back toward the platform's edge. She prostrated herself, clawed at the slick metal with her fingertips, and only the shuttle's final ascension saved her from the fate of the stormtrooper she'd killed earlier. As she dragged herself from the precipice and stumbled upright, she saw her fingernails were cracked and caked with soot.

Trembling, she retraced her path. Soon she was steadier. Then she was running to her father's side. She knelt in ashes, wrapping her arms around Galen and drawing him against her chest.

He was so *light*. A crumpled leaf of a man.

But he was warm. He was breathing.

"Papa," she whispered. "It's Jyn."

His head lolled and he stared at the clouds before finally turning her way. There was pain in his face, bewilderment, and a joy he seemed not to entirely trust.

"Jyn?" he said, and she nodded. Her eyes stung with smoke and tears.

My father is alive.

My father is dying.

"Stardust," he said, lips moving with overwrought care—as if he wanted her to recognize the word even if his breath failed him.

She stroked his wet and grimy hair. Like Saw, he was a shadow of the man she remembered. Where she had grown, he had withered. Even the man in the hologram had been more *solid* than the man she held now.

She was surprised to realize she felt no hate at all. There was nothing *to* hate. Just a dying man who loved her and who had exhausted everything else he was.

Her confessions, too, fled her. This was not a man who needed to hear what the Death Star had done, or the faith she'd lost in him, or the deeds Liana and Tanith and Kestrel had committed when he'd been telling himself, *If you're* happy, *Jyn, then that's more than enough.*

He was speaking again, watching with sad intensity.

"It must be destroyed," he said.

"I know," she said, soothing, reassuring, shivering as she leaned as close as she could. "I've seen your message."

She wasn't sure he heard her.

He wet his lips. "Someone has to destroy it."

Painfully slowly, he lifted one arm. His wrist was twitching almost imperceptibly as his muscles strained. Three soft fingertips dragged across Jyn's cheek and then fell.

"Papa . . ." Her throat felt thick. "No. No . . ."

She smoothed hair away from his forehead. He was warm, but his chest no longer rose and fell—not even with the tiny, wounded-animal breaths he'd struggled to take before.

"Papa . . . Papa! Come on."

She looked inward, to the cave in her mind, but the hologram was gone and its words no longer echoed. Now there was only darkness and emptiness. Nothing to shelter her or guard her or guide her remained.

She didn't let go of Galen, of her father, as a white-armored body stepped out of the smoke and took aim. She felt for her rifle and found nothing; she couldn't remember when she'd dropped it. She clutched the body tighter and braced for one last shock of pain.

She heard the shot. She watched the stormtrooper fall. Cassian emerged from the smoke behind him and was by her side in an instant, hands on her arms and trying to coax her upright, tug her away from Galen. "Jyn, we've got to go. Come on."

She didn't understand where he'd come from, in the same way she didn't understand the attack by the X-wings. Understanding wouldn't make any difference.

"I can't leave him," she said.

"Listen to me." Firm, but not harsh, he uncurled her fingers from her father's body. Galen's warmth slipped away, replaced by the chill of the rain. "He's gone," Cassian said. "He's gone. There's nothing you can do. Come on."

Her father dropped to the metal. "Help me," Jyn said, and she was surprised to hear the force in her voice.

"Come on," Cassian pressed. He hoisted Jyn to her feet. The pain raced through her body and seemed to activate her nerves. The smoke hurt to breathe. Footsteps were racing toward them. The platform itself was groaning.

She had to leave or die with her father.

"Move!" Cassian urged.

She took his hand and let him show her the way out.

Cassian had seen Jyn broken and trapped inside herself in the monastery on Jedha. What he saw now was different—she was alert, keenly aware of her surroundings and her decisions. He only needed to make sure she decided to stay alive.

He'd failed her father already.

He kept one hand on Jyn's arm and the other on his rifle as he picked his way around the fires and gaping holes of the platform. He knew their time was short. He'd seen the rebel squadron pull out of the sky shortly before he'd found Jyn; now the Imperials were scrambling as the inferno unleashed by the bombs spread through the facility. Half the garrison was hunting for intruders while the remainder raced to evacuate.

Cassian had found a cargo turbolift, unguarded in the chaos, to bring him to the platform. He'd led Jyn half a dozen meters to the door when a stormtrooper squad emerged from one of the neighboring structures. Cassian raised his rifle—too many to take out, but he could give Jyn cover—and watched a rapid volley of particle bolts topple the soldiers like toy dolls.

The bolts had come from the direction of the ridge. He'd only ever seen a sniper eliminate a squad so quickly once before.

Thank you, Baze, he thought, and sprinted for the turbolift. "Come on," he called at Jyn. "Come on!"

He snapped off three shots as more stormtroopers poured onto the landing pad. He didn't see whether he hit his targets; instead he glanced over to Jyn. She was looking toward her father.

When she turned back to Cassian, there was ice in her eyes. But she ran with him.

Soon they were on the canyon floor, splashing through puddles and kicking stones behind their heels. Endless barrages of crimson bolts strobed down from the landing pad. As Cassian and Jyn rounded the base of a rocky pillar, more particle blasts sounded behind them. Cassian tried to raise K-2 on his comlink and failed. He spoke Baze and Chirrut's names into the comlink before remembering they had no comms at all.

He caught sight of the stormtroopers in the canyon fanning out, taking a hunting formation. On familiar ground, Cassian might have eluded them. But he could barely see a stone's throw ahead and he would glow like a beacon to any heat sensors. Without a reprieve, he and Jyn would both be dead soon enough.

"The starfighters," Jyn said, with gravel in her voice. "Can you call them back?"

Her hair was plastered to her face. Streaks of ash covered her cheeks and chin. She looked like she'd stepped out of her own cremation to take vengeance on the world that had done her wrong.

"I can't," Cassian said. "They're gone."

"But they're Alliance?" It sounded like an accusation more than a question. "They're *yours*."

"They don't take my orders," Cassian said, "and I don't have a way to contact them. *They can't save us.*" He couldn't tell what she was thinking, couldn't guess what she might fixate on next in her distress. "We're on our own, Jyn."

A volley of blaster bolts sparked against the rock nearby. Jyn looked impassively past Cassian at the ghostly troops in white armor.

A sudden roar and a blast of wind nearly smashed Cassian against the stone. Rising above the crest of a ridge, diving toward Cassian and Jyn came an Imperial shuttle—not the one Cassian had seen on the platform, but a worn and battered *Zeta*-class vessel built for cargo hauling. It rode the storm winds like a boat bobbing in a whirlpool, yet it steadied as it came closer to ground. Laser cannons twitched on its undercarriage, acquiring targets, and spat toward the soldiers in the mist. Stormtroopers cried out and fell in burning heaps.

Cassian wanted to laugh. To *shout*.

The shuttle's boarding ramp screeched as it descended from the hovering ship, metal sheeting singing in the wind. A voice came from inside: "Let's go, let's go, let's go!" Silhouetted against the interior light was Bodhi, waving frantically.

Cassian and Jyn ran together and clambered up the ramp. Bodhi was grinning broadly, but when he saw Jyn—somber, implacable—his face fell. Cassian felt the ship lift beneath him and turned around, nearly stumbling out the door and peering through the shroud of rain.

He saw what he was looking for and cried toward the cockpit, "Wait, *wait*, Kay!"

Chirrut was scrambling down a rock slope, tapping at the ground with his staff in one hand and carrying his ornate lightbow in the other. Baze followed, twisting his torso and never lowering his cannon as he watched for pursuit. Both men burst up the ramp and into the bay of the cargo shuttle.

Cassian eyed Chirrut's lightbow with newfound appreciation. "You take out a TIE fighter with that thing?"

"Don't praise him," Baze growled, chest heaving with breath. "You're lucky he didn't hit you."

Bodhi threw a switch and the ramp began to close. As he raced for the cockpit ladder he called, "Kay-Tu, all aboard! Let's go!"

"Copy you," the droid's voice returned faintly. "Launching and away."

The cabin shook as the shuttle lifted out of the canyon, banked around an outcropping, and began a rapid ascent skyward. A series of distant, thunderous blasts—some clipped and clustered together, others protracted—followed. *The laboratory,* Cassian thought. The fires had found the kyber crystals, or some other volatile material onsite.

That limited the likelihood of pursuit, at least.

As the sounds of the storm and the destruction faded away, the shuttle steadied. They were leaving the atmosphere. Cassian slumped against the cargo webbing to catch his own breath and felt the exuberance of escape replaced by fatigue. He looked to Baze and Chirrut and saw that both wore bleak expressions.

They were expecting Galen Erso.

Bodhi almost certainly had been, too.

Cassian didn't look at Jyn at all.

Krennic woke to the taste of dust and smoke, immediately coughing and expelling a black wad of phlegm.

He was aboard his shuttle, strapped into a seat. Pterro, his aide, knelt beside him. Krennic waved away a question about his health and tried to piece together how he'd arrived. He remembered the torpedo blast. He'd made it to the shuttle before blacking out.

"The rebels," he growled. "An assassination attempt?"

"Yes, sir," Pterro replied. "Spotters on the ground and an X-wing squadron, so far as we can tell."

Something troubled Krennic about that summary—he felt the absence of some element like a missing tooth, caught a flash of dark hair and felt a long-forgotten hitch in his shoulder—but it was a problem for later. He continued reviewing the jumble of images in his mind. "Galen Erso?" he asked.

"He didn't survive the attack, sir."

Krennic's jaw tightened. For an instant the smell of ashes was overpowering, flooding his brain until nausea and vertigo assailed him.

You'll never win.

But he had won, or close enough. Galen had admitted to treason—though of course he'd needed Krennic to play the role of oppressor. As he had on Lah'mu, Galen had arranged a scenario in which they would walk away hero and villain; in which Galen could wrap himself in righteous outrage when he began the work anew.

Only Galen really hadn't walked away this time.

The X-wing pilots had given Krennic revenge without reconciliation. He might have still used Galen somehow, albeit under close watch. Now he would remember the man not as a brilliant scientist but as wasted potential; as little more than Wilhuff Tarkin's cat's-paw.

Krennic coughed as dust and bile rose again in his throat. He waved off Pterro's aid, dragged his gloved fingers over his face, and stilled himself. Maybe Galen's death was for the best, he thought. There were degrees of treason, and some could never be forgiven.

"Sir?"

Pterro was standing over him, the corner of his mouth quivering.

"Spit it out, man," Krennic growled. He'd lost enough time to unconsciousness on a very busy day.

"We received new orders while you were occupied," Pterro said. Again, he hesitated. "You've been ordered to Mustafar. Lord Vader wants to speak with you."

Darth Vader?

The Emperor's right hand and executioner. Ally of Wilhuff Tarkin.

A summons from Vader boded poorly, but the meeting might also be the opportunity Krennic needed.

"Set a course." Krennic shrugged. "We don't want to keep his lordship waiting."

He looked down at himself and straightened his uniform with a tug. He noted black smudges from smoke and charred metal, a patch of red where someone—probably him—had bled. He wondered if he would have time to clean up before arriving.

Or maybe Lord Vader would respect a man who'd seen combat.

SUPPLEMENTAL DATA:
BATTLE STATION ENGINEERING NOTES

[Document #YM3884L ("Waste Radiation Distribution Solutions"), timestamped approximately eighteen months prior to Operation Fracture, sent from Engineering Operations Manager Shaith Vodran to Galen Erso.]

Erso:

I had the droids generate a new Systems Safety and Compatibility Report incorporating your team's proposed adjustments to the reactor core. The new plans triggered a dozen subsystem warnings and spat out one blazing red stain on the line labeled "Hypermatter Annihilator Unit." I didn't bother asking my astromech *how bad* that could be—a redline on a critical system speaks for itself.

Why are we even making reactor modifications this late in the game?

Have your engineers check their work better next time. Suffice to say, *no changes* are approved.

[Document #YM3884M ("Reply to Waste Radiation Distribution Solutions"), sent from Galen Erso to Engineering Operations Manager Shaith Vodran.]

Vodran:

Sincere apologies. I fully agree that this is unacceptable. The modifications are intended to reduce primary weapon recharge times to satisfactory levels (I'm sure you saw Tarkin's directive) but sloppy work is sloppy work.

I assume you alerted Director Krennic to the report as well? More as soon as I've spoken with my team.

[Document #YM3884N ("Reply to Waste Radiation Distribution Solutions"), sent from Engineering Operations Manager Shaith Vodran to Galen Erso.]

Director Krennic is copied on all SSCRs, but if he wants oversight on these particular modifications, it's your responsibility to brief him on your problems.

[Document #YM3884O ("Reply to Waste Radiation Distribution Solutions"), sent from Galen Erso to Engineering Operations Manager Shaith Vodran.]

Vodran:

I alerted the director personally, at your suggestion.

I also spoke to my team and we identified the problem. The reactor core modifications are resulting in radiation buildup, which in turn has the potential of interfering with the hypermatter annihilator.

The buildup is caused by the inner shield actively reflecting excess particles and metaphorically "cooking" the reactor core. Had the shielding team's research not been so heavily compartmentalized this might have been avoided.

Nonetheless:

The reactor core modifications must remain as-is. Therefore, we are left with three possible ways of avoiding radiation buildup.

Option one: construction of a particle funnel and recycler. This is known and tested technology. I am confident it will function. Physical requirements mean the recycler would need to replace existing noncritical mechanisms under the northern command sector, but I estimate the needed disassembly would take under two weeks.

Option two: further refinement of our reactor technology to reduce waste particles. I have several team members keen on this possibility. They are excited about the potential for a technological breakthrough.

Option three: construction of manual venting shafts and thermal exhaust ports. This should reduce particle buildup to within tolerances but not to a degree I find personally acceptable. In addition, adding venting shafts risks additional incompatibilities with noncritical systems.

Please alert me if you have concerns.

[Document #YM3884P ("Reply to Waste Radiation Distribution Solutions"), sent from Engineering Operations Manager Shaith Vodran to Galen Erso.]

I oversaw construction of the northern command sector myself. Tarkin has already toured the facilities. If the particle funnel and recycler can't go anywhere else, stick with options two and three.

You might want to give Krennic the final decision. He's concerned about the timetable.

[Document #YM3884Q ("Particle Buildup"), sent from Galen Erso to Advanced Weapons Research Director Orson Krennic.]

Director:

As we discussed, attached are preliminary reports on two methods for reducing particle buildup. I made my preferences clear in person, but I defer to your judgment.

[Document #YM3884R ("Reply to Particle Buildup"), sent from Advanced Weapons Research Director Orson Krennic to Galen Erso.]

Galen:

New research and technological development is out of the question at this juncture. Work up a full proposal for the exhaust port solution and send the plans to Vodran for SSCR.

[Document #YM3884S ("Venting Shafts"), sent from Engineering Operations Manager Shaith Vodran to Galen Erso.]

Erso:

What is this trash? The Systems Safety and Compatibility Report quit running after two hundred redlines. I only reviewed the first dozen, but it looks like you're flooding half the station with radiation?

I thought these venting shafts were supposed to solve the problem.

No changes are approved.

[Document #YM3884T ("Reply to Venting Shafts"), sent from Galen Erso to Engineering Operations Manager Shaith Vodran.]

I repeat myself, but: I apologize.

As you know, an engineer may be single-minded in his or her focus on a particular task. I, along with my team, have fallen victim to the sin of hubris.

Of course I should have warned you that your droids might register dangers. The venting shafts are designed to expel the *majority* of the heat and particle buildup, but some radiation leakage is inevitable. We estimate that human crewmembers stationed in any of fifteen sections would—in the event that the battle station fires the primary weapon three times within one hour—be placed at increased risk for a wide variety of long-term health problems. The SSCR, of course, detected this in those "two hundred redlines."

I am instructing my team to look into all options. To expedite matters, I must request the use of your droids in running several alternative scenarios.

This will be an inconvenience, I realize, but the safety of the battle station's crew is paramount.

[Document #YM3884U ("Reply to Venting Shafts"), sent from Engineering Operations Manager Shaith Vodran to Galen Erso.]

Are the command sectors or officer quarters in the affected radiation zones?

[Document #YM3884V ("Reply to Venting Shafts"), sent from Galen Erso to Engineering Operations Manager Shaith Vodran.]

No.

[Document #YM3884W ("Reply to Venting Shafts"), sent from Engineering Operations Manager Shaith Vodran to Galen Erso.]

Send me your final plans. I'll declare the droids in error and override the next SSCR.

I'm not burying Krennic in redline reports while you figure out how to keep a handful of stormtroopers from developing a cough.

[Document #YM3884X ("Reply to Venting Shafts"), sent from Galen Erso to Engineering Operations Manager Shaith Vodran.]

That's not necessary. I'm certain we can resolve this. Even if a technical solution fails, we may be able to alter crew rotation schedules to mitigate any health risks.

> [Document #YM3884Y ("Reply to Venting Shafts"), sent from Engineering Operations Manager Shaith Vodran to Galen Erso.]

You may be too obtuse to realize it, Erso, but I'm doing you a favor. This project needed to be done *weeks* ago.

Send me the final venting shaft and exhaust port plans. I'll bypass SSCR and submit them for production, manufacturing, and installation.

Changes have been approved.

CHAPTER 13

JYN FELT THE CHILL OF her drenched clothes acutely. She felt *everything* acutely, as if the dark of the cave that had swallowed her also intensified her senses. Bodhi was giving instructions to K-2SO while climbing down from the cockpit. Baze and Chirrut sat motionless, dripping and somber, their attention on her. Cassian was stripping off his wet gear, dropping jacket and quadnocs and rifle in a pile.

Cassian, who had betrayed her.

When had she figured it out? During the race from the landing platform? When the first X-wings had streaked across the sky?

It didn't matter. Over the years she'd developed a sense for betrayal. She'd mostly grown numb to it, accepted it as the price of living free among killers and thieves.

Why had she expected more from the Rebellion?

"You lied to me," she said to Cassian.

He flinched like a man struck by a blow he'd known was coming.

"You're in shock," he said. He met her stare, held it as he turned to face her fully. Trying to bring her to heel.

"You went up there to kill my father."

His answer came instantly. "You don't know what you're talking about."

"*Deny* it," she snapped. And then again, more slowly, "You went up there to kill my father."

Her father, who hadn't been a hero or a traitor in the end. Just a frail man she hadn't had the chance to know. She recognized the pain welling up at the thought and made it hard and sharp as a weapon; it was an old and practiced reconfiguration.

Bodhi was gazing at Cassian as if wounded—but like Cassian, he seemed unsurprised by the accusation. Jyn was confirming something he'd chosen to disbelieve. Baze looked at Cassian with all the disgust he'd shown dead stormtroopers on Jedha.

Chirrut's head was down. Jyn thought he might have been praying.

"You're in shock," Cassian repeated, "and looking for someplace to put it. I've seen it before—"

Jyn grinned nastily, rose from her seat as she spat the words: "I bet you have." She jutted a thumb to one side, toward the others. "*They* know. You lied about why we came here and you lied about why you went up alone. Alliance starfighters didn't come to Eadu by *coincidence*." She didn't care if Cassian confessed—not really. Not if she could drive accusations through him like spikes, watch him twist and writhe rather than face the truth. "Maybe you've been lying since the rebel base. My father was always just a target for you."

She could hear water dribbling off clothes and onto the deck in the silence that followed. When Cassian spoke again, he did so slowly, enunciating his words and trembling all the way. "I had your father in my sights. I had every chance to pull the trigger.

"But did I?"

He spun toward Chirrut and Baze, flashed a look of fury at Bodhi. "*Did I?*"

No one spoke. Jyn hadn't expected them to.

She stabbed at Cassian again, letting resentment bolster her while her teeth chattered. "You might as well have. My father was living proof and you put him at risk. Those were Alliance bombs that killed him!"

She was *right*. She tried to find the pleasure in being right. There was none; not in the cave in the dark.

"I had orders! Orders that I disobeyed!" There was nothing calm about the man who stood before Jyn. The spy's face had been torn away, leaving something vicious and raw. "But you wouldn't understand that."

"Orders? When you know they're *wrong*?" The memory of a fourteen-year-old Jyn and her solo mission from Saw flashed through her mind; she banished the painful shade, searched for a spike to drive straight through Cassian's heart. "You might as well be a stormtrooper."

Yet Cassian didn't back down, didn't flinch anymore. He marched toward her, stopping a handspan distant and nearly yelling, "What do *you* know? We don't all have the luxury of deciding when and where we want to care about something." He matched her earlier sneer. "Suddenly the Rebellion is real for you? Now that you've got a *stake* in it, and—*and*—now that you don't have another life to go back to?" He raised a clenched hand. Jyn readied herself for a fight, but he put his arm down again just as quickly.

"Some of us *live* this Rebellion," he said. "I've been in this fight since I was six years old. You're not the only one who lost everything." His breathing was swift, but his words were deliberate. "Some of us just decided to do something about it."

Jyn stared into the face of her betrayer.

You lied to me, she wanted to say again. *You went up there to kill my father.* But the cold was deep in her bones now, biting at the marrow.

"You can't talk your way around this," she said.

"I don't have to," Cassian snarled.

She didn't look away. Nor did Cassian. They stood locked together until at last the cold and the dark became too much for Jyn to bear; until she had no words to hurl, no weapon left to stab with, and all that remained was for her to drive a fist against his ribs, dig her knee into his chest, and watch him fall.

But that wouldn't make him beg forgiveness for killing her father. It wouldn't make her feel any less *petty.*

She turned around.

"Yavin Four!" Cassian yelled toward the cockpit. "Make sure they know we're coming in with a stolen ship." Out of the corner of her eye, she saw him whirl, fix Bodhi, Chirrut, and Baze with a stare. "Anybody else?"

Nobody spoke. What more was there to say?

"You should have told me," Mon Mothma said. But there was no venom in it.

She stood at her office window: a broad aperture in the ziggurat overlooking the endless jungle, its antiquity refuted by the hung plastic tarp Mothma used as a shade during rainstorms. General Draven watched her from his seat at her desk, periodically glancing at the clock on her console.

"None of it would have made a difference," he said. His voice was bitter, but the bitterness wasn't directed at Mothma. "We didn't hear about Jedha until too late. As for Galen Erso, once we lost Captain Andor—once we *thought* we'd lost Captain Andor—I had to make the call on the spot. Assassination instead of extraction."

That was a lie, but Mothma didn't need to know assassination had been the plan all along. Draven wasn't afraid of defending his choices, yet there were larger issues at play, and it was best not to muddy the waters.

"You don't *know* what would have made a difference." Mothma spun, brow crinkled in dismay. "You have no idea what I've been doing these past days, General. Since we first heard rumors of the planet killer, I've been straining to organize our allies in the Senate so they might push through a vote: a declaration of intent for the Empire's demilitarization and a reconciliation with the Rebel Alliance."

Draven hadn't known that, though such a vote had always been part of Mothma's long-term plan. He *should* have known, certainly. It was a humbling, unwanted reminder of Alliance Intelligence's blind spots.

Mothma wasn't finished. "I could make do with uncertainty. The possibility, the *rumors* of a planet killer months or years from completion could have driven votes our way. Galen's testimony regarding its power and purpose might have been even better. But this . . ." She sighed and sat on the windowsill, smoothing the folds in her white robe. "A fully operating planet killer, ready to deploy, and the Alliance has next to nothing? If I revealed *that,* half the senators wouldn't believe us, and the others would panic. I can't control panic."

Draven digested the statements, filed parts away for later investigation, and did his best to separate what was aimed at *him* from what was simply a cry of frustration.

"Does that mean," he asked, careful to show no judgment, "that you're giving up on a political solution?"

"Never," Mothma said quietly. "But peace may be deferred a little longer."

Draven barked a laugh and immediately regretted it. After a moment, Mothma gave one of her rare, self-deprecating smiles.

"We'll need to gather the Alliance council, of course," she said. "As soon as possible. Brief everyone together and determine our strategy in the face of a crisis."

Draven had anticipated that. A gathering of Alliance leaders was a bad idea on the face of it—one traitor with a thermal detonator or one careless transmission would put an end to the Rebellion—but he didn't have a better option. The military commanders were used to traveling covertly, despite the danger; the civilian council members, the scattered Alliance agents in the Imperial Senate and elsewhere, would be more difficult to summon discreetly to Base One.

"I'll handle it," he said. It would be like moving a mountain on short notice, but he *would* handle it. "There's a good chance we'll have Captain Andor and Erso's daughter back in time for the meet."

"Good. Captain Andor's testimony might help calm and persuade the more skeptical councilors." She didn't sound like she believed it.

"Andor may not have a lot to say. Turns out the message that kicked this whole thing off? The one from Galen Erso?" Mothma nodded and cocked her head. Draven sighed. "Erso's daughter is the only one alive who saw it. She saw Erso, too, before he died. We'll debrief her, but I don't know how *calming* she's going to be in front of a crowd."

Mothma smoothed her robes again, examined them for half a minute or more. Then she stood. "I want Jyn Erso in that conference," she said. "Make sure of it."

More than anything else she'd said, *that* surprised Draven. *Jyn Erso?*

"The girl's a thief and a liar," Draven said. "She was in prison for a reason. Practically bit the heads off my extraction team." Mothma had pushed to get Jyn off Wobani from the start; anyone else, Draven would have assumed she didn't want to admit to a bad call. "You really see something in her?"

"Fire," Mothma said, as if that explained anything.

"Sure." Draven hesitated, thought of ending the conversation while he was on comparatively firm ground and decided to take another chance instead. "Whatever the council decides," he said, "we'll need to move fast. I'll see if I can recall some specialists, air and ground troops; they'll be in reserve if we need them."

"Thank you, General," Mothma said.

"When I say *whatever* the council decides . . ." He stood from her desk, released a slow breath. "I can't promise to be on your side once that meeting starts."

"I know," Mothma said. "I imagine we'll both be trying to make up for our mistakes."

Draven had no retort for that, so he nodded brusquely and left the room. He had enough to keep him busy without resorting to self-reflection.

Mustafar burned like an ember in the dark, seething with oceans of lava and spotted with continents of black rock. Krennic looked upon it and thought of the Death Star, wondered if the power of his weapon tempered *just so* could reduce a world to such a state; crack its skin and bleed it until it died in its own heart's fire.

The power of planets failed to rival Krennic's creation. But the Death Star was not with him today.

His shuttle pitched and rolled as it entered the atmosphere, riding rivers of black clouds tossed by howling winds. The shuttle's stabilizers and gravity units maintained an interior equilibrium, but Krennic found the experience no less unsettling for the relative lack of discomfort. He grasped his chair tight, kept his chin raised, and reviewed for the sixth time everything he knew about Darth Vader, recounted every one of a dozen tactics he might use in conference with the man who had made Mustafar his base of operations.

The shuttle dipped beneath the clouds. The life support units clicked softly as they switched from warming to cooling the air. Through the viewport, Krennic glimpsed a geyser of molten rock dancing a dozen meters from the ship.

Was Vader mad? Was this his *homeworld*? Perhaps he wasn't human beneath his armor; perhaps that forbidding black suit did more than replace lungs and limbs damaged in battle, and instead allowed a creature born in magma to survive the chill of space.

Or maybe he lived on Mustafar because he enjoyed burning his victims alive.

What did it say about Emperor Palpatine that he chose such a man as his enforcer?

No. Krennic shook his head, refusing to nurture *that* thought. The Emperor was vindictive, but not mad. He was a gamesman, a being of vast vision and vaster ambitions who'd begun his life as an ordinary politician and seized extraordinary opportunities as they arose; used each to its utmost advantage. Palpatine had *tamed* Vader, but he had not *created* the self-styled mystic and lord of the dead Sith cult.

That gave Krennic hope. If a senator from Naboo could leash Vader, then surely Krennic could as well. Whether he was here for accolades or castigation, he could creep into Vader's inner circle and break the alliance between Vader and Tarkin. He had the means: The seed planted in his mind at Jedha had reached maturity on Eadu, and he had found Tarkin's weakness. He only needed a chance to exploit it.

The shuttle swept toward a stark black mountain against the blazing sea: an obsidian monolith bound in metal, towering over fiery oblivion. When the shuttle landed, Krennic disembarked into the heat and was greeted with a gesture by a black-cloaked aide. As the aide led him through the monolith, Krennic wondered how many visitors the man had led to execution. *No wonder he's not talkative.*

But such thoughts were self-indulgent. Krennic reproached himself for his morbidity and suspected Galen was to blame—the demise of a man Krennic had known for decades made him aware of his own mortality at the worst possible time. He smoothed down his uniform, tugged at the hem of his shirt, assured himself he was presentable. In a rotunda deep within the monolith, he was bade to wait while the aide proceeded through the iris of a door.

The scent came to Krennic first—chemical, medicinal, like ointment on a scrubbed droid. Then came the sound of fluid draining from a vast enclosure and the mechanical whining of a hundred gleaming manipulators. Steam spilled from the iris, and as Krennic's eyes adjusted he heard a new sound: a hollow, metallic rasp that resonated in the chamber; the desperate, hungry breathing of a creature that should not have been alive.

Krennic's guide reemerged and disappeared into the corridor. Krennic barely noted his departure, trying to assemble the glimpses of shadow before him into an image he could recognize.

"Director Krennic." The words of the *thing* that breathed in the dark, deep and puissant as the voice of an abyss. Krennic felt his teeth vibrate, forced himself to bow.

"Lord Vader." His voice did not tremble, and he was grateful.

The steam was dissipating. Shadows coalesced into a silhouette and stepped forward. Before Krennic loomed a black-cloaked figure in ebon armor, lights glimmering on a chest plate engraved with controls and readouts. The helmet was a skeletal horror, polished to a gleam and colorless save for crimson lenses in the place of eyes.

"You seem unsettled." Vader had no face to read. Krennic tried to assess him by his posture, by the cadence of that agonized breath, and failed on both counts.

But he speaks like any other man, Krennic told himself. *This will be a game of words.* And the Sith Lord did not strike Krennic as a man apt to waste time prior to an execution; he had already revealed more than he intended.

"No," Krennic said. "Not unsettled. Just pressed for time. There're a great many things to attend to."

"My apologies." Vader stepped forward. The red eyes stared out of steam and darkness. "You do have a great many things to explain."

Such as? he could have asked, but better to present his victories upfront. "I've delivered the weapon the Emperor requested," Krennic said. "The test on Jedha has proven its power. Yet I fear Governor Tarkin may have—as a relative stranger to the project—failed to articulate to the Emperor the essence of our success."

Vader is a warrior at heart. He'll respect boldness.

Krennic finished: "I deserve an audience to make certain he understands its remarkable potential."

The terrible mask looked down upon Krennic. The voice spoke. "Its power to create problems has certainly been confirmed. A city destroyed. An Imperial facility openly attacked." A swift step forward and to Krennic's side, like a hunter circling his prey.

An Imperial facility openly attacked. Vader blamed Krennic for the strike on Eadu. Was this, then, the opportunity Krennic had sought? The chance to reveal Tarkin's error so soon?

"It was Governor Tarkin that suggested the test," he began.

But the voice spoke again, resonating in Krennic's skull: "You were not summoned here to grovel, Director Krennic."

Krennic swore inwardly. He'd been too transparent. "No, I—"

"There is no Death Star," the voice said. "We are informing the Senate that Jedha was destroyed in a mining disaster."

"Surely the Senate—"

"—is not without uses, so long as it remains pacified. It will be dealt with by the Emperor according to *his* timetable."

"Yes, my lord," Krennic said. He straightened his back, took the rebuke with dignity.

Vader had completed his circuit. He didn't deign to glance at Krennic as he strode toward the door. "I expect you to not rest until you can assure the Emperor that Erso has not compromised this weapon."

Was that all? A swift interrogation and a warning?

"So I'm—" Krennic began. The words sounded faint and he found himself suddenly parched, his throat raw. "I'm still in command of the station? You'll speak to the Emperor about—"

Vader gestured, his back still to Krennic. Krennic tried to swallow and discovered the act was difficult—as if an unseen hand had grasped his neck and, in utter control of the pressure it exerted, begun to squeeze.

As he coughed and then stopped coughing, fighting desperately for air, Krennic thought of the stories he'd heard of Vader, the time at a military conference when he'd seen Vader strangle an officer. He'd told himself in the days after that Vader had wrapped his hands around the man's neck until it cracked, but Krennic had lied to himself.

The Jedi were dead, but their power persisted. Mad cultist or not, the Sith Lord's sorcery was real.

The unseen hand clenched Krennic's throat for a final moment—long enough for him to believe that somehow, death had found him after all—then released. Krennic fell to his knees, caught himself on his hands, felt the cold floor through his gloves.

"Be careful not to choke on your aspirations, Director," the voice from the abyss said.

Then Vader was gone and Krennic was panting as he scrambled backward, not even fully upright by the time he left the rotunda. The cloaked aide was waiting. With a tip of his head the man indicated for Krennic to follow, retracing the paths they'd walked earlier.

Krennic smiled a giddy, unpleasant smile as he limped away.

Vader had let him live. Vader had judged him too valuable to kill—and by extension, the Emperor recognized his value as well. Tarkin's mutiny, his seizure of the Death Star, had been forestalled. And Krennic had yet to reveal Tarkin's greatest error—how in destroying Jedha City, Tarkin had failed to blockade the moon, failed to ensure against survivors. For how else could the rebels have infiltrated Eadu? The traitorous pilot had *come from* Eadu and fled to Jedha; his message had escaped.

Only Tarkin could be held responsible for that.

Krennic could wait to deploy that weapon against Tarkin, though. Vader was correct that the extent of Galen's treachery remained unclear.

Could Galen—not Krennic or the facility—have been the rebels' true target on Eadu? Had the rebels feared Galen would submit to Imperial interrogation and reveal even greater betrayals and sabotage?

Krennic needed to know. He needed to be certain.

The cloaked aide spoke for the first time, jolting Krennic from his thoughts. "Few people have the honor of seeing Lord Vader in his sanctum." They had reached the door to the landing pad. "I suggest you keep all you witnessed to yourself."

Krennic drew himself up, studied the aide, and found him as unreadable as Vader's mask. He said nothing as he stepped back into the heat.

He was ready to leave the madhouse that was Mustafar, but he was suddenly uncertain he could ever escape Vader's shadow.

Aboard his shuttle, he ordered a course set for Scarif.

Jyn huddled in the cramped engine compartment of the Imperial cargo shuttle and waited for the mechanisms' heat to warm her. She was beginning to believe it never would.

She had gone there after the shouting match with Cassian. She'd needed a place to be alone, away from *him* and away from the pity of the others. As the shuttle thrummed, the engine pulsing steadily as it propelled the vessel through hyperspace, she let her mind wander in her personal endless dark.

For a while, she fantasized about revenge.

She could wait until Yavin. Find a way to collapse the whole ziggurat on Cassian and General Draven and Mon Mothma and everyone who had been complicit in the murder of her father. She'd told

Saw that all the Rebellion had ever brought her was pain; since it had come crashing back into her life, stolen her from Wobani prison, that was more true than ever. It seemed only right to return the favor.

She luxuriated in thoughts of retribution awhile. Then she stopped. Whatever else she was, whatever she'd done in her short, brutal life, she wasn't a murderer. She'd killed, yes; to save her life, to save others, and in war. But she wasn't *Cassian,* and she didn't want to be. Even the fantasy of hurting the people behind her father's death couldn't sustain her; after the initial rush, the notion left her exhausted and empty.

She thought of her father's recording: *If you found a place in the galaxy untouched by war—a quiet life, maybe with a family—if you're happy, Jyn, then that's more than enough.*

Was that correct? She didn't know if she remembered it anymore. The words had stopped replaying when she'd seen her father die, and she hadn't been able to bring them back.

So if her choice was not revenge, was it better to walk away? Steal a few credits and hunker down out of the line of fire? She could scrape by as she'd done before, while the Empire went around blowing up planet after planet, burning the Rebellion to the ground.

It can be destroyed. Someone has to destroy it.

Her father's final words. Not a declaration of love, not *I missed you.* When he was dying and seeing his daughter for the first time in years, all he could think about was the machine that had taken over his life. The machine he'd spent decades building and then sabotaging; the machine that had led the Rebel Alliance to kill him.

Jyn should have been angry at him for that. Angry that she had gone to Eadu for nothing, for *less* than what his message had given her. Instead of remembering the man overcome with emotion, the man who struggled to say *my love for her has never faded,* the image in Jyn's mind of her father was the heap of a body in her arms; a confused old man who was as mortal as anyone.

She *wasn't* angry at him. She was angry at the Rebellion and Cassian. And even that anger, it seemed, was pointless; it only brought her back to the beginning, to the revenge she didn't want.

She had no answers. Eventually the thrum of the engine lulled her to sleep.

In her sleep, Jyn dreamed.

She dreamed of Saw Gerrera, the man who'd raised her for just as long as her father and barely smiled for the length of it. She dreamed of being a scared eight-year-old girl in the care of a soldier who wouldn't take fear as an excuse for anything; a soldier whose roar left Gamorreans twice his size quaking and who'd never encountered a fight he hadn't known how to win. She dreamed of the time she'd come home to Saw with a bloody face and a broken leg; of the dozen scars she'd earned during her time with his cadre. She still wore those scars today.

Saw had given her fire. Saw had given her *teeth*. And she'd never thanked him before his death.

Jyn dreamed of Galen, too. She dreamed of their apartment on Coruscant and the farm and her father presenting her with *toys,* so many toys, all of which she would name and whose names he would somehow remember: Beeny and Stormy and Lucky Hazz Obluebitt and more, others who were only shadows in her mind. So many nights he'd come into her room—wherever her room was, it didn't matter the planet—and place a toy in her arms. His love had never been extravagant. Always simple. Always unmistakable. She'd hated him for so many years.

She dreamed of Galen dying, executed on Lah'mu by black-clad stormtroopers and burning in a hail of TIE fighter bombs. She dreamed of the light of the Death Star, *his* Death Star, incinerating buildings and canopies and people in the Holy City of Jedha. She raced forward in a plaza, reaching to scoop up a tiny girl, and she didn't make it in time. By the time her arms were around the child, all she held were bones. Then the bones turned to dust. She dreamed of more stormtroopers—stormtroopers dragging people out of doorways, stormtroopers patrolling cell blocks, stormtroopers shooting at blind men, rows and rows of stormtroopers marching endlessly, firing at *her* now and burning a thousand holes through her chest.

She dreamed of the man in white surveying the work of the stormtroopers, their execution of Jyn, and speaking words Jyn could not hear. He looked pleased. He never spared her a glance. He had more important things to do. The stormtroopers, now clad in black again, continued to shoot her.

And when Jyn felt she could endure the nightmare no longer, felt she had to wake up, she dreamed of her mother.

Jyn lay on her back, dead, in their Coruscant apartment while Lyra diligently packed gear for some one-woman planetary survey mission. Lyra nearly stepped on Jyn as she grabbed a portable scanner off the dessert table.

"Oh, for—" Lyra shook her head, reached down, and pulled Jyn upright.

Was this a memory? Jyn didn't know anymore. Her hand was shaking in her mother's grip.

"Mama?" she said.

Lyra laughed and poked Jyn on the forehead with one finger. "You need to *not* lie down in the middle of the floor. I'm going to trip and fall and land on you, and your father's going to blame *me* when you bruise."

She went back to packing. Jyn watched her. "Mama," Jyn whispered again. "I don't know what to do."

Lyra held up a hand for silence. She reviewed the contents of her duffel, nodded with satisfaction, then walked slowly to Jyn's side. She smiled gently, sadly. "I know, sweetheart," she said. "But you're a big girl. You have to decide for yourself."

They were no longer in the apartment. They were in the endless dark that had once been the cave.

"I don't know how," Jyn whispered, though she was ashamed to say it aloud.

Lyra glanced over her shoulder conspiratorially, then looked back to Jyn. "I'll give you one hint, okay?"

Jyn nodded awkwardly.

Lyra leaned in until her nose brushed Jyn's. "You're your father's daughter," she said. "But you're not *just* that.

"It's okay. We all trust you."

Jyn felt small. She was four years old again, and her mother was so much bigger than her.

Lyra whispered in her ear, so soft Jyn had to strain to hear it: "*The strongest stars have hearts of kyber.*"

Lyra's necklace seemed to burn around Jyn's neck.

Then the dream was over, and Jyn was awake in the engine compartment of an Imperial cargo shuttle, weeping harder than she had since she'd been a child—weeping until her face was red and her nose was stuffed; weeping until the dark that had been the cave seemed to be growing brighter; weeping until the tears wiped away the rain of Eadu and she felt clean at last.

CHAPTER 14

JYN FELT READY IN A way she hadn't for as long as she could remember. She sped toward Yavin 4 with a purpose; and not simply a purpose, but a *plan,* flimsy and delicate as a petal. She had emerged from the shuttle's engine compartment with only a single answer, and she had found it was enough.

Her anger and resentment toward the Rebellion remained. But left unstoked, they diminished. They were both as real and as irrelevant as her old anger toward Saw Gerrera and his people.

Besides, she needed the Rebellion for what came next.

She would tell them all the truth. *It can be destroyed. Someone has to destroy it.*

As she stepped off the shuttle, Jyn was struck again by Yavin 4's oppressive perfume of mildew and rotting vegetation. She was near the back of the group of her shipmates, close beside Bodhi and behind the Guardians of the Whills; Cassian had taken the lead, hurrying ahead to consult with a cluster of Intelligence officers waiting inside the hangar. K-2SO observed them all from the rear, as if he expected everyone but his master to attempt an escape.

During their landing, they'd seen other starships thundering through the atmosphere toward the ziggurat. "They're bringing in everyone for an Alliance council meeting," Cassian had warned them—brusquely, eyes averted. Bodhi, Chirrut, and Baze were to be interviewed by Alliance Intelligence while Cassian and Jyn spoke to the council directly. Baze had shown his teeth, but Chirrut had said something about showing courtesy as *guests* in the rebels' home.

Now armed rebel soldiers hustled ornately dressed aristocrats off the tarmac and toward the temple interior. Bodhi looked over-whelmed, craning his neck to watch each ship come in to land. "That's a Firefeather starcutter," he murmured, pointing to a black dot in the blue-gray sky. "You can tell by the whistling sound. They're really rare—someone important must be aboard."

"You don't get on the council without money, guns, or influence," Jyn answered.

Bodhi laughed nervously. After a moment, he scraped the sole of his boot against the stone and turned halfway to Jyn. "I'm sorry about Galen," he said.

It took Jyn by surprise, though she couldn't say why. "Thanks," she returned.

Bodhi shrugged. "I liked him a lot. Not that I knew him very well, but I did like him—"

"You probably knew him better than me."

Bodhi's smile was smaller now, but there was no nervousness to it. "I don't think so."

Jyn was starting to sweat in the heat. She shifted uncomfortably and watched an astromech droid drift from one starship to the next without apparent purpose. Bodhi seemed to be trying to keep silent—for her benefit, probably, given his usual habit of running on.

Jyn took pity on him and gestured at his Imperial flight suit. "Bet you'll be glad to get out of that. Got to be a change of clothes some-where here."

"What?" Bodhi glanced down at his arms, eyed the Imperial emblems on his shoulders. "No. No, I—I'm thinking I'll keep it. As a reminder."

"A reminder of what?" she asked.

Bodhi leaned in, as if embarrassed to be heard. "That I *volunteered* for all this. You know?"

Jyn was saved from answering by a yell from the cluster of Intelligence officers. The rebels rapidly arranged themselves around Baze, Chirrut, and Bodhi. "I'll see you around," Jyn called as a lieutenant gently led Bodhi away.

Cassian signaled Jyn to follow him, and they joined the stream of life flowing deep inside the ziggurat. "Come on," Cassian said. "They're about to start."

The briefing room was as crude as the rest of the rebel base. Stone walls wept moisture onto bolted pipes and cabling that led between consoles and a central holoprojector. The chairs arrayed inside were far too few for the crowd: Admirals and generals in boldly stenciled uniforms stood shoulder-to-shoulder with guerrillas in piecemeal armor; nobles and civilian bureaucrats (dressed in *simple* clothes made of more expensive fabric than Jyn had ever owned) huddled in compact cliques. Jyn overheard murmurs suggesting some of the councilors present were Imperial senators; if she'd bothered to follow politics, she might have recognized them.

She let the bulk of an Ithorian militia commander wedge her into a corner and lost sight of Cassian. A short while later, Mon Mothma—the grave, robed woman Jyn had met days and a lifetime ago—stepped up to the holoprojector and drew the mob's attention.

"I want to thank you all," Mothma said, "for coming on short notice. Many of you undertook journeys whose dangers I cannot begin to appreciate. You risked exposure, crossing Imperial lines because you believe in our Alliance. Because you believed what you were told when we informed you of an *unprecedented crisis.*

"I wish I could say the crisis isn't real. I wish I could say you came

all this way for nothing." Mothma offered a ghost of a smile. Someone in the audience laughed gruffly and tried to hide it in a cough.

"But the evidence we will present is not speculative. It is *secretive,*
yes—and by showing it here, we must reveal certain sources and
methods used by Alliance Intelligence; sources and methods we cannot take to the public or the Senate. You will hear testimony from
both trusted rebel operatives and newfound allies. If you doubt their
word, remember that all of them are marked for death by the Empire." There were murmurs in the crowd, shuffling feet and skeptical
faces. "I would ask all of you to refrain from speculation until the end
of the briefing. At that time, we may discuss what we have all seen
and determine the future of our organization and our galaxy together."

Mothma hesitated. Jyn spotted General Draven shouldering his
way toward the center, but he stilled when Mothma spoke again.
"What we face," she said, "is the natural culmination of all the Emperor's evils."

Jyn recognized the words, amended from her first encounter with
Mothma. *You've been working on this speech awhile,* she thought.

"It is a weapon designed to murder planets," Mothma went on. "To
turn thriving worlds and billions-strong populations to dust. You
will see today that it is *not* intended for use solely against military
outposts, but as a weapon of absolute destruction and absolute fear.

"We believe the Empire has code-named it Death Star."

Now Mothma did step aside. Draven took her place and began the
briefing proper. Jyn tuned out his voice, the series of reports about
kyber crystal mining and Imperial research credit trails, and observed the councilors instead. With few exceptions, the military officers were rapt—they had *faith* in Draven, for whatever reason, and
they took his words as truth. The politicians maintained, as a whole,
an air of neutrality, as if they'd spent their lives learning how to look
open-minded.

Mon Mothma was speaking in a hushed voice with the councilors
in her immediate vicinity. The woman kept busy.

Soon Draven turned the briefing over to a series of Alliance Intel-

ligence officers. Bodhi was brought in for terse questioning about
Galen Erso and the construction he'd personally witnessed. Cassian
came next, every bit the professional, reporting the story of "Operation Fracture." It was a story whose broad strokes—an attempt to
contact Saw Gerrera regarding an Imperial defector, an attack on the
Holy City by the Death Star itself—resembled the truth Jyn knew.
The holoprojector showed the crater and the dust storm left behind
on Jedha.

"The Empire is saying it was a mining accident," a man muttered,
two rows ahead of Jyn. "They're not ready to go public, either."

Then Cassian was lying about Eadu, calling it an aborted attempt
to extract Galen. The councilors started interrupting, asking for spe-
cifics about the Empire's plans that Cassian couldn't provide. Jyn
looked away in disgust and almost jumped when she saw that Mon
Mothma had crept to her side. In the packed crowd, she felt intimately close.

"Am I up next?" Jyn asked. She laughed caustically as she guessed
why Mothma had approached. "You here to prompt me?"

There had to be versions of Jyn's story that Mon Mothma, chief of
state of the Rebel Alliance, wanted told—and others she wanted silenced.

But Mothma shook her head. "No. I wanted to say . . ." Her gaze
held on Jyn's face as she searched for words. Jyn thought through all
the trite, meaningless statements the woman might make: *I'm sorry
for your loss. The Rebellion is proud of you. Good luck with the crowd.*

"I won't forget what we did to you," Mothma said.

Jyn stared and tried to comprehend the sadness in her voice.

She might have asked a question, but then Jyn heard her name
being called and a gloved hand was escorting her to the front. She
squared her shoulders and readied herself. She knew what she'd come
to say.

Jyn told her story as concisely, as bluntly, as honestly as she was able.
She recited all she could recall of Galen's message, though the words

had continued disappearing from her mind one by one. She suffered the questioning of a red-shirted senator (someone called him Rebel Finance Minister Jebel, which struck her as a title rich in potential for mockery) who seized on her extraction from Wobani; he asked whether she'd been bribed with freedom to serve as a witness, and she snapped "Yes" before spotting a grimacing Bodhi in the crowd and amending her answer. Admiral Raddus—a Mon Calamari with skin mottled like storm clouds and unblinking amber eyes—sternly asked her about her initial parting from Saw Gerrera; she made up a lie about her discomfort with Saw's methods that seemed to satisfy him.

She spoke too softly one moment and too loud the next, unsure how well her voice carried in the briefing room. Her eyes skimmed the crowd, never landing anywhere for long. Over the course of an hour, then two, then three, she saw the councilors grow restless. Cassian and Bodhi slipped out into the depths of the ziggurat. Jyn finished by telling what had transpired on Eadu and repeating her father's dying words.

"*It can be destroyed*," she said. "It was the last thing he thought. It was the most important thing in his life."

She felt a huskiness in her throat and stepped away from the projector before anyone could shout another question. Vague disappointment settled onto her; a sense that her words should have carried more weight, or that she should have felt the same rush from testimony as she did firing a blaster.

No one stepped up to take her place. The briefing was over.

"Senator Tynnra Pamlo of Taris." A woman in an ivory hood and a ceremonial medallion announced herself and seized the floor, despite soft murmuring within a dozen subgroups intent on their own discussions. "It seems clear that Senator Mothma's description of this situation as *a crisis* was an underexaggeration by half. General Draven and his people make a convincing case: This Death Star is an existential threat not only to our Alliance but to all life as we know it."

New voices rose in affirmation and dispute. Pamlo was undaunted. "I say this with sincere regret and moral certainty: We *cannot* in good conscience risk entire worlds for our cause. The Death Star's existence is an ultimatum we cannot refuse. Until we know that the Empire will not use it on a populated planet, we must scatter the fleet and disband our military units. We have no recourse but to surrender—"

The gathering's pretense of civility evaporated like water droplets on an engine block. Arguments and murmuring erupted into bedlam. At once, twenty grand speeches began and rabid voices competed to be heard. Generals loosed rhetorical volleys they'd been preparing since the briefing had begun.

Jyn stood openmouthed, uncomprehending. She found herself awaiting the end of Pamlo's speech, as if it might pivot and become a rallying cry.

She caught fragments of fervent inquiries and proclamations:

"Are we really talking about disbanding something that we've worked so hard to create?"

"We can't just give in—"

One of the civilians and Admiral Raddus, their fury immediately matched and countered by a haughty man in a heavy blue cape:

"We joined an Alliance, not a suicide pact!"

Jyn swore—aloud or silent, she wasn't sure—and spun hard enough to jostle her closest neighbor as she sought to see and absorb the will of the mob. Of all the outcomes she'd anticipated, all the ways she'd expected the Rebellion to be useless, *surrender* hadn't been one of them.

"We've only now managed to gather our forces," Raddus's civilian ally—a middle-aged man entirely in brown, who seemed to command attention disproportionate to his simple garb—was saying. "If we coordinate at last—"

Finance Minister Jebel interrupted and made no attempt to hide his mockery. "*Gather our forces?* General Draven's already blown up an Imperial base! I thought the Alliance was disavowing Gerrera's tactics—"

"A decision needed to be made," Draven snarled from across the room. "You know how this works. By the time we finish talking today there'll be nothing left to defend!"

Jyn's breaths became rapid hisses through clenched teeth. The briefing room was too small. The sweaty mob was crushing her. The darkness that had been the cave was creeping in at the edges of her vision, compressing her, compressing everything.

Pamlo reentered the fray. "The blood of all Taris will not be on my hands. If it's war you want, you'll fight alone!"

"If that's the way it's going, why have an Alliance at all?" asked the haughty man in blue.

"If she's telling the truth, we need to act now!"

If.

And that from Admiral Raddus, one of the councilors Jyn had thought was *listening*.

What had she done wrong? What had she *said* wrong?

"Councilors, please!" Mon Mothma was trying to regain control. "We are *all* troubled by our situation, but I beg you to open yourselves to solutions from your colleagues instead of—"

Mothma's effort did nothing. More shouting, more arguments:

"It is simple," a general in a flight suit declared. "The Empire has the means of mass destruction. The Rebellion does not."

"The Death Star," Jebel sneered. "This is *nonsense*."

If she's telling the truth.

Jyn was shouting before she realized it, shoving her way back toward the projector. "What reason would my father have to lie? What benefit would it bring him?" She was mimicking the cadence, the language of the senators. She sounded awkward to herself, but she saw Mon Mothma—the woman who'd been practicing her speech for a week—nod surreptitiously in her direction.

"Your father," Draven said, steady and hard, "may have been an Imperial or a fool until the end. Everything he said could have been bait, knowingly or not, to lure our forces into a final battle. To destroy us once and for all."

Jyn fumbled for a reply. "That's insane," she snapped. She'd lost her senatorial poise already. "You know the Death Star exists—"

But Draven was ready. "We know a dangerous *battle station* exists, able to destroy a city. We have no confirmation of its full capabilities or weaknesses. This is how the Emperor has *always* operated, back to the time of the Republic—the gun is less threatening than the lie."

The man in blue ignored Jyn altogether, stalking toward Admiral Raddus. "You want us to risk everything—based on what? The testimony of a criminal? The dying words of her father—an Imperial scientist?"

Jebel laughed in anger and frustration. "Don't forget the Imperial pilot."

Jyn sought Bodhi and found him, back in the room again and forlorn against the wall. He didn't speak up, didn't defend himself. Jyn might have screamed at him if he'd been closer. If the darkness hadn't been closing in so fast.

She squeezed her eyes shut and thought of the girl in her arms from the Holy Quarter. She thought of the broken temple and the Guardians of the Whills and her mother's whispers.

She had delivered her father's message, and it wasn't enough.

"My father," Jyn said, "gave his life so that we might have a chance to defeat this."

"So you've told us," a deep, steady voice replied. She saw the white-haired general she'd met her first time on Yavin; the man who hadn't said a thing.

He seemed to be prompting her.

She wasn't *just* Galen's daughter. This wasn't just *his* mission.

"If the Empire has this kind of power," Senator Pamlo called, "what chance do we have?"

"What *chance* do we have?" Jyn echoed. She wanted to scream, *Who the hell cares?* But she needed a better answer. "The question is *What choice?* You want to run? Hide? Plead for mercy? Scatter your forces?" Her breathing was too fast and loud. Her skin felt hot. The councilors were falling silent one by one. Mon Mothma watched her, lips parted as if she could feed Jyn the right words.

She heard Saw Gerrera instead. *You can stand to see the Imperial flag reign across the galaxy?*

She didn't stop speaking, wrapped herself in her own momentum and found the senators' language again, backed it with ferocity. "You give way to an enemy this evil with *this much* power and you condemn the galaxy to an eternity of submission. The Empire doesn't care if you surrender. The Empire doesn't care if you're hopeless. I've given up before, and it doesn't help. It doesn't *stop*. I've seen people lose everything because they happened to be in the way.

"The time to fight is *now*, while we're still alive to try. Every moment you waste is another step closer to the ashes of Jedha."

There were new voices rising in the room. She saw none of the speakers, recognized no one:

"What is she proposing?"

"Just let the girl speak!"

So Jyn spoke. "Send your best troops to Scarif." The crowd was an undifferentiated blur behind a veil of sweat or tears. "Send the whole rebel fleet if you have to. We need to capture the Death Star plans if there is any hope of destroying it."

She strained to breathe again. As she did, a smeared ivory figure parted the crowd and approached. Through the blur, Jyn recognized her voice as belonging to Senator Pamlo.

Pamlo was very nearly pleading. "You're asking us to invade an Imperial installation based on nothing but hope?"

Jyn shrugged, unable to feign a senator's diction any longer. "Rebellions are built on hope."

"There is no hope," the man in blue said, like a preacher pronouncing an omen.

With that, the arguing began anew. Calls to fight and calls to surrender filled the chamber. The movement of dozens of bodies struggling for a place near the projector pushed Jyn back and she limply permitted it. The momentum was gone and her strength with it. She waited for the darkness to return.

She'd tried.

"I'm sorry, Jyn." Mon Mothma touched her upper arm, turned her gently. "Without the full support of the council, the odds are too great."

I won't forget what we did to you.

Jyn said nothing and walked out of the briefing room.

Jyn spotted Bodhi hurrying after her in the dank maze of hallways beyond the briefing room. She was trying to retrace her path out of the ziggurat—not really sure of her ultimate destination, but set on putting distance between herself and the council. Maybe she'd keep walking into the jungle; if Bodhi wanted to follow, she wouldn't argue. She'd kept worse company.

She thought about apologizing to him. She'd blamed him for not speaking up during the chaos, which on reflection hardly seemed fair. He wouldn't have changed anything.

They stepped into the hangar bay before she could decide whether to say anything. Jyn shielded her face from a shower of sparks as a technician and her astromech welded armor plating onto a nearby X-wing. When she lowered her arm she saw Chirrut and Baze standing before her.

"They didn't lock you up?" she asked. "The debrief really was just a debrief?" She tried to force levity into her voice. It came out bitter.

"You don't look happy," Baze said.

Jyn shrugged. "They prefer to surrender." It wasn't true—not for every councilor—but it was close enough.

"And you?" Baze was as somber as ever.

Chirrut gestured toward Jyn with his staff. "She wants to fight."

It's all I've ever done, she thought. *It's the only answer I have.*

Only this time, she believed it was the right one.

"So do I," Bodhi said, stepping around to her side. "We all do."

"The Force is strong," Chirrut said, and it sounded like a promise.

She looked at the blind man, the killer, and the coward in front of her in wonder and confusion.

She didn't *know* them—not really, not when they'd barely spoken outside of shouting matches aboard the U-wing. She'd half expected to never see them again after the briefing.

But in front of the councilors, she had wrestled with the words to convey the horrors of the past days. Tried to express all that had happened, all the Empire had taken, without exposing her wounds to the rebels' eyes—without revealing the shame of her most pitiable, contemptible moments, when she'd been shaken by loss and trapped in her own fears.

Bodhi and the Guardians already knew the horrors and her shame. They'd fought and nearly died together. They'd seen Jyn fall and claw her way back. And they were still *with her*.

They looked willing to take on the galaxy, no matter that they didn't have a chance. She couldn't help but smile, small and sad and sincere.

"I'm not sure four of us is quite enough," she said.

Baze grunted dismissively and looked to Bodhi. "How many do we need?"

"What are you talking about?" Jyn asked.

Baze jutted a finger, pointing behind Jyn. When she turned around, she saw more than a dozen rebel soldiers marching down the corridor, pouring out into the hangar and blocking the entrance to the ziggurat. She recognized Melshi, the rebel she'd hit with a shovel on Wobani; the others were strangers, young and old men dressed in sandy combat fatigues too patchwork to be called uniforms. Their weapons gleamed with well-oiled care. An amphibious Drabatan with skin worn and gray as baked leather showed a mouthful of crooked yellow teeth; a bald-headed man with bright, dangerous eyes offered a nod. Towering in the back was K-2SO; emerging at the fore came Cassian, chin high and back straight.

He looked like he was ready to arrest her.

"They were never going to believe you," Cassian said. "Not the council. Not today."

"I appreciate the support," she said. Her voice was frigid. Her hands balled into fists. She was surprised how little she wanted this fight.

She positioned herself between Bodhi and Cassian. After what the pilot and the Guardians had said, she was ready to do what was necessary to save them from the Alliance's goons.

"But I do," Cassian said. "I believe you."

Her eyes flickered from Cassian to the soldiers. They were armed, but their postures were relaxed. Their weapons were down. A few even looked *amused*.

"We'd like to volunteer," Cassian said.

She didn't trust him. She didn't trust anything the galaxy could throw at her. "Why?"

He smiled, and it died on his face. "Some of us—" He hesitated, waited until Jyn's gaze had met his. "—most of us, we've done terrible things on behalf of the Rebellion." He spoke matter-of-factly, as if it were the most obvious truth in the world. "We're spies. Saboteurs. Assassins."

Jyn spared another glance at the soldiers. They were looking at her, one and all, as if awaiting judgment.

Was this a confession?

"Everything I did," Cassian said, "I did for the Rebellion. And every time I walked away from something I wanted to forget I told myself it was for a cause that I believed in. A cause that was worth it." He was almost stumbling over his sentences, forcing each out before he lost his nerve. Like a man wrenching a dislocated limb into place, one agonizing pull at a time.

He went on: "Without that—without a cause—we're lost. Everything we've done would have been for nothing. I couldn't face myself if I gave up now. None of us could."

Don't do this, she wanted to say. *I can't give you absolution.*

Instead she looked at the band he'd assembled and whispered with a sort of awe, "How did you find them?"

"It's been a busy day," he said, too dry to be devoid of humor. "I didn't need to see the whole briefing to know where it was going."

"I can't—" she started. *I can't give you a cause.* But she stepped back unsteadily and saw the ferocity, the *need* in Cassian's eyes mirrored in each of the soldiers. Whatever they'd seized on, it was no longer hers to give. She could no more refuse them than Cassian could have refused her after Jedha.

She gave a curt nod. Someone in the group laughed.

"It won't be comfortable." Bodhi was speaking behind her, looking between the soldiers and the tarmac where the cargo shuttle sat. "It'll be a bit cramped, but we'll all fit. We could go."

"Okay," Cassian said. The emotion was gone from his voice, the confession done. He turned to the soldiers. "Gear up. Grab anything that's not nailed down—we don't know what we'll find on Scarif and we don't have long to prep. Go!"

The soldiers scattered, moving with purpose and surety. Bodhi and the Guardians joined them. Only Cassian and K-2 remained. The droid looked down at her. "Jyn," he said. "I'll be there for you. Cassian said I had to."

She held back a laugh and looked to Cassian. The man who'd betrayed her. The man who'd admitted his guilt and decided to fight for her. He saw her staring and looked back at her quizzically.

It wasn't how betrayals were supposed to go.

And she remembered that while Cassian—and Bodhi and the Guardians—had seen her at her worst, she had seen them broken, too. Bodhi, who had been tortured; the Guardians, who had lost their home; and Cassian, who had betrayed himself as easily as he had Jyn. They all had their shame.

With one another, at least, they had no vulnerabilities left.

She thought of Wobani again, when she'd been alone among a thousand other prisoners.

"I'm not used to people sticking around when things go bad," she said, by way of explanation.

She didn't know if Cassian really understood, but he said, "Welcome home," and she knew she was.

Twenty minutes later, weighed down with weapons and duffels full of stolen gear, Jyn and Cassian stepped out of the bright Yavin sunlight and into the cabin of the cargo shuttle. There were, Jyn thought, even more faces than before, more scarred and sweaty and determined soldiers than she'd seen in the hangar. She realized with a pang that she likely wouldn't have time to learn their names before they arrived on Scarif—that soon they'd all be fighting for their lives together on a mission that was very likely to fail.

Jyn spotted Baze and Chirrut among the rebels. Chirrut's head was turned toward her, and he raised his staff like a salute or a toast. She remembered a saying from her days with Saw Gerrera and spoke loud enough to be heard through the shuffling of the unit.

"May the Force be with us."

"Cargo shuttle, we have a pushback request here. Read back, please: Request denied. You are not cleared for takeoff."

Bodhi winced at the comm and peered out the viewport at the tarmac. The flight droids had already tugged the shuttle away from the ziggurat hangar; that gave him room to initiate a vertical lift-off without worrying about igniting an inconveniently placed fuel tank.

"Yes, yes we *are* cleared," he said. "Affirmative. Requesting a re-check."

It was a bad plan. It had *all* been a bad plan, of course, starting with Galen's message and ending with this unauthorized raid on Scarif. Now he was, what—defecting from his defection? If he survived, he'd be an Imperial traitor and a rebel mutineer. He'd be lucky to see the inside of a Yavin prison cell.

He wondered if there was a Bor Gullet on Yavin, too. He doubted it. He could take comfort in that.

"I'm not seeing this request here," the comm said.

He thought about his passengers. Like him, they were going rogue, courting treason by defying the Alliance council. They'd already pilfered enough Alliance weapons and gear to supply an army; and Bodhi had seen enough of the operation on Yavin to know equipment was in short supply.

He wasn't sure if that made the personnel on-base more or less likely to shoot the shuttle down. They'd want to recover the stolen gear, at least . . .

"Are you sure everything's been processed?" Bodhi tried. "Someone should've authorized it by now."

He flipped a series of toggles and checked for warning lights. The mass–volume ratio was confusing the computer—a packed cargo pod normally meant forty tons of ore, not a ship full of soldiers—but it wouldn't do any harm.

He thought about all the bad bets he'd made in his life—the times he'd sunk everything on a long shot in order to win back what he'd lost, only to end up with nothing. Was that all he was doing now with Jyn and the others? Doubling a bad bet?

It didn't *feel* like that. There was none of the heady uncertainty, the mix of hope and despair. When he thought about what he was doing, he was almost calm.

"What's your call sign?" the voice on the comm asked.

"Yes, we have it . . ." *Just take off!* "It's, ah—"

Think, Bodhi. Give them something. Give them anything.

If you give them something, they might not shoot.

"—call sign Rogue. Rogue One."

He transferred power to the thrusters, felt the familiar wobble of a cargo shuttle taking off under his control. The officer on the other end of the comm was squawking at him. Bodhi ignored it.

"Rogue One," he declared, "pulling away!"

At the age of fifteen, during the winter when she'd discovered smash-ball, romance, and her parents' profound imperfections, Mon Mothma had decided to devote her life to studying history; decided to turn her back on her family's political dynasty and to spend her days in a cramped study reading thousand-year-old diaries and letters and cargo manifests until her eyes burned. She would be detective, coroner, and philosopher all at once, examining means and motive and cause of death for entire civilizations.

She hadn't become a historian, of course. By the next summer, Mon's moment of rebellion had been forgotten. Inertia and family pressures and a genuine love of governance had returned her to the road to politics. She'd gone on to become a senator (far too young, she thought now) and scrabbled for votes and smiled and kept her head above water until she'd learned how to play the game for real.

She'd campaigned for an end to one war and now—with even-handed hypocrisy—had built an army while trying to prevent another. She'd fled her home and a life to become the Empire's most wanted woman and leader of a revolution. And she couldn't help but wonder what her fifteen-year-old self would have said about the Rebel Alliance, looking back on it from some distant future:

For all their self-importance, the rebel leaders lacked the courage to transform their network of paramilitary cells and sympathetic politicians into more than a curiosity. Their inability to commit to a course of action ensured the Empire's growth and the delegitimization of any future protest movements . . .

Mon was accustomed to failure and self-judgment. But the thought still stung.

The briefing room was nearly empty now. Voices worn from screaming had gone silent, and men and women who'd traveled across the galaxy to reach Yavin had retired to their ships or to more private consultations. There had been no consensus or formal vote, and Mon was grateful for that much. Given the tenor of the discussions, a swift decision could only have ended badly.

Mon would not sleep tonight. She planned to spend the hours until the council reconvened in discussion with her peers and reaching out to allies who might salvage *something* from the situation. And while she wasn't yet sure *what* there was to salvage, she knew who to start with.

Bail Organa, the former senator from Alderaan, seemed to be waiting for her near the briefing room door. "You spoke well," he said as she approached, with funereal gravity.

She smiled wanly and wondered if she looked as exhausted as he did. She had considered Bail a partner since the day they'd first discussed opposing Palpatine's rise to power. In all the years since— throughout all the arguments over Bail's *charitable interventions* and her covert dealings—she couldn't remember the lines in his face ever seeming so deep.

"Despite what the others say, war is inevitable," she mused with a sigh. "Senator Pamlo has noble instincts, but she's wrong: If the Empire used the weapon at Jedha, it will use it again. We can't prevent these genocides, but only resist them."

Bail nodded, the motion so small it seemed like all he could muster. "I agree. I must return to Alderaan to inform my people that there will be no peace." Mon heard his pain at that admission and wondered what it would cost him. "We will need every advantage," he added grimly.

It took Mon a moment to comprehend. Then she glanced to the closest other councilors and lowered her voice. "Your friend," she said. "The Jedi."

Bail nodded again. "He served me well during the Clone Wars and has lived in hiding since the Emperor's purge." He appeared to wait for Mon's verdict, but she had nothing to offer. At last he finished, "Yes, I will send for him."

A Jedi, returning to fight against the Empire. It seemed an impossible thought, so Mon focused on what was not. "Captain Antilles's ship is docked with the *Profundity* for repairs, but it's nearly ready to go. The extraction should be simple; if it's not, his skills will be an asset."

"My assessment as well," Bail said.

"Whoever makes contact with the Jedi will have a terrible responsibility." Mon knew who Bail had in mind—it was clear in the tired lines of his face; in the fear of a man who had never previously feared the Emperor's blackest vengeance. She was reluctant to doubt his decisions, but she needed to be certain. "You'll need someone you can trust."

"I would trust her with my life," he said.

You'll need to trust her with more, Mon thought, but he was already on his way out the door. And for all her reservations about Bail's agent (the girl was so *young,* no matter anything else), she could think of no one better.

The matter was resolved, then.

Mon Mothma squeezed the exhaustion out of her eyes and considered who to speak with next.

CHAPTER 15

J YN STILL LIVED IN THE cave in her mind. But it was larger now, so large it felt like it could contain worlds and armies, and so filled with light from above that she didn't feel trapped at all.

She could only hope it wouldn't close on her again. Not before the mission was over. Not before she was through with Scarif.

Jyn was climbing into the cockpit as the shuttle lurched out of lightspeed. The azure mists of the hyperspace tunnel collapsed beyond the viewport and stars streaked into visibility, fixed into place by real matter and real gravity. In the center of the stellar vista was a planet wrapped in deep-blue oceans and speckled with clouds and rocky archipelagoes. If not for the massive ring-shaped orbital station above the northern hemisphere, Scarif would have looked almost pristine.

"Okay," Bodhi said. "We're coming in." He sat beside K-2SO at the console, waving Jyn between them with barely a backward glance. It was strange, Jyn thought, to see him so confident, so *comfortable.*

"What am I looking at?" she asked, squinting at the ring. She made out the specks of starships descending through its center, but then a shimmer outside the ring's edge caught her eye—the subtly distorting gleam of an energy field.

"There's a planetwide defensive shield with a single main entry gate," Bodhi said. "This shuttle should be equipped with an access code that allows us through."

"Assuming," K-2 added, "the Empire hasn't logged it as overdue."

"Or stolen," Bodhi said.

"And if they have?" Jyn asked.

"Then," Bodhi answered, "they shut the gate and we're all annihilated in the cold, dark vacuum of space."

Jyn let out a huff of a half laugh. She was starting to like the confident, comfortable—and *cynical*—Bodhi.

"Not me," K-2 said. "I can survive in space."

Jyn dug her fingers into the back of the cockpit seats and tried not to lean in. The shuttle veered gently in the direction of the gate, and the specks swiftly grew larger. The great wedge-shaped masses of twin Star Destroyers loomed like monstrous statues over the orbital station's portal, dwarfing the swarms of cargo shuttles and transports and TIE fighters. Jyn tried to remember the last time she had seen so much Imperial activity in one place and failed.

"Okay, this is good," Bodhi said. He glanced up at the Star Destroyers and then back to his scanners. "It's not normally this busy. I think this is good. We're just one more ship, nothing worth noticing." Jyn heard his confidence crack, then reassert itself. "Okay. Here it goes . . ."

The shuttle's thrusters rumbled and the deck plating trembled as, course locked, the vessel accelerated through the vast distance separating itself from the gate. Bodhi worked the comm with one hand and said without a hitch, "Cargo shuttle SW-0608 requesting a landing pad."

Jyn straightened off the cockpit chairs and backed away carefully. *Confident, comfortable, and Imperial.* She might have wondered what Bodhi had been like—what *any* of her companions had been like before the Death Star—if she hadn't been intent on not making a sound.

"Cargo shuttle SW-0608, you're not listed on the arrival schedule," the voice on the comm said. The operator sounded vaguely puzzled. Bodhi had a ready reply.

"Acknowledged, Gate Control. We were rerouted from Eadu Flight Station. Transmitting clearance code now."

Jyn flinched as she heard a sound from the ladder into the cockpit. She glanced over to see Cassian, who seemed to sense the mood and paused in his climb.

She knew enough about what the spy had been like before the Death Star. She wasn't sure if she'd forgiven him for it, or simply decided to abandon it like a used-up blaster pack.

"Transmitting," K-2 said. The console hummed softly and went silent as the dispatch finished. Cassian completed his climb, swift and hushed. Jyn found her hand tangling in the string of her necklace, drawing the kyber crystal into starlight.

Cassian had said *we've done terrible things*. If this went wrong now—if they failed before they'd even landed—Jyn was sure the only unforgivable choice would be her own.

She wrapped her fingers around the crystal. She imagined praying like she'd seen Chirrut pray. She nearly laughed, dangerously loud, and squelched the sound.

"Cargo shuttle SW-0608?" The voice on the comm had returned. "You are cleared for entry."

Jyn dropped the crystal and squeezed her hand in a fist, almost shouting in triumph. She spun and was startled to see Cassian standing close to her. On instinct, riding the joy of the moment, she grabbed his arm and squeezed.

He looked at her with a wry, curious smile. She dropped her hand and brushed past him. "I'll tell the others," she said.

The cave was getting brighter all the time.

Jyn was changing. It was evident in her fluid movements and her lucid stare. She no longer hunched her shoulders, no longer maintained the compact posture of a woman ready to absorb a hit before she hit back. She'd shed none of her intensity, but it came with what Cassian could only interpret as a confidence bordering on invincibility.

She'd always struck him as a person unafraid to die. Now she seemed like someone who couldn't.

He should have been terrified of following her into battle. He no longer understood her, could no longer locate her old need for answers, her desperate grasps at meaning. Yet he'd faced down her loathing during the return from Eadu, walked a razor-fine edge before the briefing on Yavin, uncertain what would happen after.

He'd told the story of his mission before the council. Jyn had told the story of hers. And Cassian had realized that setting his sniper rifle aside had roused a hunger in him. He'd tried to imagine executing another coldly elegant mission for Draven and finding nourishment in the stale, momentary thrills of danger and triumph.

He couldn't survive that way anymore.

After realizing that, recruiting the rest of the team had been easy.

Jyn was changing. And through her, Cassian would do what was required of him. They all would.

Careful. You're starting to sound as zealous as Chirrut.

The descent through Scarif's atmosphere was so smooth as to be almost unnoticeable, save for the slow fading of the stars and the paling of the sky from black to blue. The ocean below, once Cassian could see it, seemed utterly still; only the telltale ripples of light suggested waves.

The shuttle hurtled over the specks of jungle-riddled volcanic islands and finally slowed as it approached a wheel of landmasses connected by sandy tombolos and transit tubes. Other shuttles and starfighters circled the islets, spiraling down or rising from the two dozen landing pads supporting the wheel's sprawling Imperial installations. The layout was, so far as Cassian could tell, roughly as Bodhi had sketched out during the hyperspace journey.

A voice came through the comm, bored and professional. "SW-0608 clear for landing pad nine. Acknowledge, please."

"SW-0608 proceeding to LP9 as instructed," Bodhi said.

The shuttle banked, dipping below the top of a monolithic Imperial fortress rising from the centermost islet. "The main building down there," Cassian said. "What is it?"

"That's our goal," Bodhi said. "The Citadel Tower. Command and control for this whole facility."

Cassian was tempted to ask Bodhi to do a second flyby, but it wasn't worth the risk of drawing suspicion. "Can you access the shield gate from inside?"

"Don't think so. But if the Death Star plans are anywhere, they'll be there."

They'd better be. They'd built their whole scheme around finding the Citadel's data vault. If by some chance Galen Erso had been wrong, if Bodhi was wrong now, if the Empire had moved the one data tape they needed to another location . . .

Movement caught his eye atop the tower: the subtle readjustment of a massive signal array. "And the dish at the top? What's it for?"

Bodhi shrugged. "That's the communications tower. Every communication in and out of this base goes through that dish. Normal transmissions can't penetrate the shield, and a normal rig wouldn't have the bandwidth to handle everything on-base at once."

Cassian pictured the soldiers in the cabin below, scanned their faces and dossiers. He stopped at Corporal Pao—he had a vague recollection that the SpecForce commando had taken out a similar comm unit in a demolitions job on Foerost. He made a note to ask him about it before leaving the shuttle.

"Landing track engaged," K-2 said.

Cassian stepped away from the viewport. He didn't expect anyone to spot him from the ground, but why take the chance? "Security?" he asked. "How's it look right now?"

"I don't know," Bodhi said. "I've made twenty cargo runs in and out of the place. They've never let me off a landing pad, so I don't have much to compare it to. Security's tight."

Cassian watched green treetops and white beaches flash by. For an instant he caught a glimpse of the boxy metallic body of an All Terrain Armored Cargo Transport—a four-legged walker whose militarized cousins he'd seen devastate bunkers. He'd almost never seen full-sized walkers outside a war zone.

"Well," he murmured. "We've faced longer odds."

"No," K-2 said. "We haven't."

There were almost two dozen soldiers in the main cabin. Two dozen people waiting to fight and die. And all of them looked at Jyn like Saw's troops had looked at him.

She'd listened to their chatter during the flight, caught a handful of names. Many of the troops had fought together before as Special Forces Pathfinders. Some had worked directly with Cassian, while he'd sought others based on their reputations; a few had caught wind of the Scarif operation and volunteered to come along instead of turning them all in. The rebels who didn't know one another rapidly swapped war stories or jokes or barbs, bonding the way soldiers did. Or they sat alone, staring contemplatively at their hands.

Private Calfor was a half-deaf grenadier who'd once owned a bloodhound kennel on Mykapo. Eskro Casich was a braggart and a glory hound, and Jyn pegged him instantly as a man terrified of being the mission's sole survivor. An unassuming middle-aged man with a thick accent had tasked himself with inspecting every blaster aboard, polishing away carbon buildup and swapping out energy packs. A pale woman had started shouting at one of her teammates about how the Alliance was dead, how they were all traitors now, and then sat back down mumbling apology after apology. Corporal Tonc had spent half the flight at Bodhi's side, skeptically questioning the pilot about his suitability for the operation—whether Bodhi was competent with a blaster, whether he'd seen combat before—before grudgingly declaring *he'd* be the one to watch Bodhi's back.

Almost no one spoke to Jyn unless she spoke first. Saw had always been *above* his people, a symbol of the cause; now Jyn had been pushed into that role. With a pang, she realized how much she missed the camaraderie of Saw's cadre—not the people, not their bitterness and fanaticism, but the unspoken knowledge that they were bound together under one man's leadership.

She sat beside Baze and Chirrut as the shuttle descended. She had them now, but it wasn't quite the same.

She jumped when a hand tapped her shoulder and she turned to see a broad sniper looming over her. She tried to remember his name. *Sefla.*

"What is it?" she asked.

"Small problem with the troops," Sefla said.

Jyn waited.

"They like you, ma'am, but if you want to give a speech they'll have trouble *respecting* you. You're not military. You're not even Alliance."

"Not really my problem, is it?" Jyn said, more nonplussed than irritated.

"Hardly the right attitude, ma'am." Sefla arched his brow. "Morale is everyone's problem. So if Captain Andor won't do it, it falls to me as an Alliance SpecForce lieutenant to brevet you the rank of sergeant. Congratulations."

Sefla never smiled, but Chirrut was laughing silently.

"You're a cretin," Jyn said.

"Yes, Sergeant," Sefla replied, and walked back toward a cluster of Pathfinders.

Guess I'm giving a speech now, too, Jyn thought. She stood from her seat and began to pace. *Let them watch.*

A short while later Cassian clambered down the cockpit ladder. "We're landing," he murmured to her, and then called to the group, "We're coming in!"

A dozen soft conversations came to an immediate end. The soldiers rose, tightened the straps of their rifles, and secured their equipment for the final descent. After the clicking of metal and the rustling of leather stopped—all too swiftly for Jyn's tastes—their eyes turned to her.

She'd failed to rally the Alliance council. She wasn't much of a speaker. Fighting was all she knew.

Maybe this was her perfect audience.

She began, raising her voice above the rattle of the deck plating. "Saw Gerrera used to say, *One fighter with a sharp stick and nothing left to lose can take the day.*"

No one heckled her. No one asked questions. A few SpecForce officers nodded.

"They have no idea we're coming. They have no reason to expect us. If we can make it to the ground, we'll take the next chance. And the next. On and on until we win or the chances are spent.

"The Death Star plans are down there. Cassian, Kay-Tu, and I will find them. We'll *find* a way to find them."

There was no applause, either, yet the soldiers looked proud and ready.

She could have promised them their lives. She could have promised a great victory for the Alliance. But this was all she could offer, and she hoped it was enough.

Cassian stepped forward before anyone's attention could drift. "Melshi, Pao, Baze, Chirrut—you'll take main squad, move east and get wide of the ship. Find a position between here and the tower. Once you get to the best spot, light the place up. Make ten men feel like a hundred. And get those troopers away from us."

"What should I do?" The call came from Bodhi, climbing down from the cockpit and leaving K-2 behind.

"Keep the engine running," Cassian said. "You're our only way out of here."

Assuming we make it back, Jyn thought. She might have said it aloud, but she was sure they were all thinking it anyway.

CHAPTER 16

THE CARGO INSPECTION WENT AS well as Jyn could have hoped.

The shuttle hadn't been built to carry two dozen armed rebels laden with gear, let alone conceal them from a curious Imperial security team. But the inspection, Bodhi had assured them, was unavoidable. All they could do was try to take advantage of it.

So Jyn had secreted herself in the cockpit, squeezed in tight between Cassian's shoulder (smelling of blaster oil and Eadu's dirt) and the main console. She listened to the boarding ramp descend, heard booted feet against the metal deck and Bodhi making quick, awkward introductions in the main cabin. She listened to the murmurs of the inspection team. She listened for the sound of two dozen men and women crammed into cargo stores and crawl spaces like refugees.

"Hey, you're probably looking for a manifest . . ." Bodhi said, sounding less convincing all the time.

"That would be helpful." Another voice, curt and officious.

"It's just down here."

Jyn wrapped her fingers around her blaster's grip. She could spring out of the cockpit in one leap if she had to. Maybe even land at the base of the ladder without breaking her legs.

She heard the creak of a cargo hatch swinging open. There was one brief, muffled cry and then the sounds of multiple impacts against the deck. No shots fired. She scrambled forward, fumbled her way down the ladder in time to see Baze emerging from the cargo compartment with a terrifying smile.

Bodhi stood wide-eyed among the bodies of the inspection team.

"Off to a good start," Jyn said, as the rest of the rebels emerged.

Three minutes later, she had managed to fit a too-large Imperial security uniform over her clothes. The black chest plate looked too large on her, and the sleeves felt too long over her gloves, but it would have to suffice. She almost winced when she looked at Cassian, wearing an officer's suit and cap like they were perfectly tailored. Even the code cylinder in his pocket was at a regulation angle. "You've done this before," she murmured, and he ignored her. The rest of the soldiers were stowing the bodies and passing around stripped weapons and comlinks.

She checked her blaster one final time, strapped on her helmet, and looked to the boarding ramp. Melshi made what she took as a *ready* signal from a cluster of soldiers. She started to move toward Cassian and the exit before she felt a great shadow at her side. Baze, with a touch as light as a windblown leaf, touched her shoulder.

"Good luck, little sister," he said. He spoke with warmth and gravity, as if the words were a Jedha custom or an honor of the Guardians of the Whills.

Jyn didn't know. She didn't have to know. She smiled at him, searched for words and found none. She hoped he understood her gratitude.

Cassian waited for her at the ramp. Together, in the garb of the enemy, they stepped out onto Scarif.

. . .

Scarif was bright as a desert, bright as her cave was now. Jyn could taste salt water in the air. The warmth of the sun might have been unbearable under her black uniform if the breeze hadn't been in constant motion, swelling and ebbing as if jealous of the tides. She tried not to look at the shuttles thundering overhead, to keep her chin up and her eyes forward like a proper guard. She wasn't sure how well she managed the act; twice she had to slow her pace to allow Cassian, her "superior officer," to take the lead. K-2SO trailed them both, servos whirring with every step.

They marched down off the shuttle pad cramped with consoles and cargo crates and power stations. From there, they followed a short trail to an aboveground bunker linked to the repulsor rail system that would lead to the Citadel. Jyn blinked away the sunlight and a sudden, distant drowsiness.

"Sir!" As they reached the terminal, a guard tapped a button and the doors of a car slid open, admitting Cassian, Jyn, and K-2.

Stay focused, Jyn.

"Our odds of failure have gone up," K-2 said. "I have a bad feeling about—"

"Kay!" Cassian hissed.

"Quiet," Jyn added.

The doors closed in time to deny entry to a pair of stormtroopers. Jyn shook her head briskly and shifted her weight as the car hummed into motion.

"What?" K-2 asked.

Neither she nor Cassian answered. *Focus,* Jyn told herself again, even as she shifted her weight back and forth, found no outlet for either her nervous energy or the tension building in her mind. She thought of Baze's smile, of her *promotion* by Lieutenant Sefla, of what her comrades were preparing to do outside.

"What is it?" Cassian asked. His voice was low, and sun and shadows danced across his features as the car raced over the water. Jyn waved a hand dismissively, but he only asked again more sternly: "What is it?"

She twisted and peered through the window. The Citadel Tower was growing larger, dark against the shining sky. "Just—what I told them all back there. About what Saw Gerrera said?"

"What about it?" Cassian asked.

She tugged awkwardly at one glove's fingers. "We never fought like this with him. *I* never did. With Saw, missions were usually about hitting the Empire hard—hitting back for revenge, slowly bleeding them to death."

"And what we're doing now is different." Cassian was being careful, showing nothing of his thoughts.

"*Yes,*" Jyn said. "If we don't win this, people out there—" She waved at the unseen stars. "—don't just ignore it. We have to get those plans. I'm not sure I know how to fight to *accomplish* something."

All of it was true. None of it was what troubled Jyn most. None of it was what she wanted to hide from herself, now that she'd seen the truth.

"You're going to do fine," Cassian said. And he was trying, speaking with a gentleness and compassion Jyn had barely seen echoes of, but it wasn't the answer she needed.

She would fight to find the plans. She would trust Cassian and Chirrut and Baze and Bodhi and Melshi and all the others to push her down the course she needed to go. But if the mission began to go wrong, what then? If she lost them in the chaos . . .

She'd fought all her life. But even in Saw's cadre, she'd fought— more than anything, more than for vengeance or ferocity—for her own survival.

If she fell back on old instincts, what then? She could risk herself for a person. Wrestle an innocent girl out of the crossfire. But if she found herself alone, she didn't know if she could risk herself for the *cause.*

"We're slowing down," Cassian said.

Just focus, Jyn.

The railcar's hum changed in pitch and the dancing shadows relaxed their frenzy. "We need a map," Cassian went on. "This place is too big and we're too vulnerable to wander around looking for the vault."

K-2 swiveled his head but didn't look toward Cassian. "I'm sure there's one just lying about."

"You know what you have to do," Cassian answered.

Jyn frowned. Before she could ask what Cassian meant, the railcar doors were sliding open. They emerged into the Scarif Citadel, where the light that had permeated the outdoors was gone—replaced by rows of illumination strips embedded in dark metal walls. Corridors branched off from the rail station and officers, guards, and the occasional stormtrooper moved at an unhurried pace down the line.

Cassian was right. Without a map, they were helpless. Jyn tugged at her uniform, which felt more ill fitting than ever.

A security droid identical to K-2SO strolled past. Cassian nodded toward K-2 and they started a leisurely pursuit. Jyn forced herself not to reach for her weapon, reminded herself to stay calm. If they'd been detected, an alarm would have gone out. If the others had been detected, the whole complex would have been in a frenzy.

They tracked the droid down a long corridor. When it ducked into a terminal alcove lined with machinery, Cassian stationed himself against the wall to one side. Jyn took the other side and watched K-2 follow his twin.

With a single motion, K-2 reached out with a fist, ejected a retractable data spike from his wrist joint, and plunged it into the back of his twin's metal head. The second droid let out a garbled, electronic wail that lasted no more than half a second; then he dropped to his knees as K-2 stood over him, maintaining the connection.

"Do it fast," Cassian urged. He stepped in front of the alcove, still watching down the corridor, as if his body could block a view of the two towering droids. Jyn joined him, glancing between her end of the corridor and K-2.

The droid's head was swinging on his neck, back and forth like a weather vane. "Is he all right?" Jyn asked.

"KX-series droids are hardened against intrusion," Cassian said brusquely. "Getting past their programming is a challenge."

After nearly a minute, he asked, "Kay?"

K-2SO lifted his head and extracted his data spike from his twin.

"Our optimal route to the data vault places only eighty-nine storm-troopers in our path," he said. "We will make it one-third of the way before we are killed."

The second droid limply tumbled to the floor.

"All right," Jyn said. "Let's hope everyone's in position."

Baze Malbus neither knew nor trusted the rebel soldiers around him. He did not respect their loyalties. He could not rely upon their skills. He would fight alongside them because Jyn Erso had accepted them into her own revolution—not the revolution of the Alliance, but one that had risen from the ashes of the Holy City to bring retribution where resurrection was impossible.

He trusted Jyn's fury and her fire. Most of all—though he was loath to admit it—he trusted Jyn because of Chirrut Îmwe. Those whom Chirrut trusted, Baze could find a reason to trust as well.

Life was more convenient that way. Even Baze found eternal wariness exhausting.

"Go!" Bodhi cried from the cockpit of the cargo shuttle. "Now! You're clear!"

Together the soldiers poured onto the landing pad. Baze kept his cannon up and walked in Chirrut's shadow, letting the blind man choose their pace and sweep the ground with his staff. They followed the rebels off the platform and between the broad-leafed trees of the jungle, away from the eyes of stormtrooper patrols and starfighters.

Five soldiers had remained aboard the shuttle to protect the extraction point and Bodhi Rook. In another life, Baze might have prayed for the pilot; in this life, Baze knew that Bodhi would live or die according to skill and chance. More likely the latter than the former.

One of the rebels, a clean-shaven spotter, fell back to Baze's side. "Can he keep up?" he asked softly, nodding toward Chirrut.

Baze snorted and didn't bother turning toward the spotter. "Hide your trail better. Then he can keep up." He flicked a finger at the white sand and Chirrut's feet. Where Chirrut tapped at the ground with his staff, he flung the sand aside and half-covered the soldiers' tracks. Where the skirts of his robes trailed, they occluded what markings remained.

"*He* can hear you," Chirrut snapped.

The spotter nodded briskly. Chagrined, he offered Chirrut a crisp "Sorry, sir," and shuffled toward the fore. Baze noted that this time, the rebel took care to obscure his footprints.

"At least he didn't ask if you were a Jedi," Baze muttered, but Chirrut had begun chanting. *May the Force of others be with you.*

They wound their way deeper into the jungle, the vivid green canopy never thick enough to obscure the sun. As sand began to give way to richer soil, Baze knelt and, mid-stride, swept up a few pale grains between thumb and forefinger. He raised the pinch of sand to his nose; it smelled of sea salt and loam. He touched the grains to his tongue and spat them out.

Even the dirt tastes different, he thought. Dirt was all that was left of Jedha, but he did not think he would ever return there. Scarif— with its trees the gaudy emerald of cantina lights, with its tepid oceans and sand like crushed bones—was as much his home now as any- where.

The city is gone, old man. NiJedha is gone.

He reached an arm behind him, clasped the exhaust vent on his portable generator. In the warmth of Scarif, he would need to mind how he strained his cannon. It wouldn't do to quit shooting at the wrong moment.

The soldiers drew to a halt near a low hillock. Sergeant Melshi, who commanded the team, peered over the crest with a set of quad- nocs. Baze squinted through the sun and saw a squat Imperial struc- ture and two squads of stormtroopers across the way. "Barracks," he murmured, and Chirrut nodded in acknowledgment.

Melshi scrambled to the base of the hillock and signaled one of his subordinates. The second man walked among the rebels, briskly but deliberately handing out magnetized detonators. "This is as far as we get," Melshi said. "Fan out. One detonator per landing pad. You see a better target, take it, but there's no resupplying so pick your spots."

The rebel carrying the detonators held out one each to Baze and Chirrut. Baze shook his head, and the boy moved on. Melshi was still talking. "We want to draw them out, so keep moving once we start and don't let them pull back to the bunkers. I'll call the timing." He scanned the group and nodded sharply. "Go!"

The rebels scattered in ones, twos, and threes. Melshi looked to Baze and Chirrut. "You too good for demolitions duty?" His tone was good-humored but puzzled.

"Someone must keep your soldiers alive," Baze said. He smiled, showing teeth.

Melshi appeared unamused. "Well?" Baze asked, flapping a hand at Chirrut.

Chirrut's lips were moving. When he finished his chant (*The Force is with me, and I am with the Force . . .*), the Guardian strode after one pack of rebels. "We won't be long," Chirrut said, and looked back to cast a blind glance at Melshi.

As Chirrut followed the rebel soldiers, Baze followed Chirrut. Together, they hunted.

Among the stormtroopers who roamed the dirt paths and landing pads and bunkers were many dressed in specialized armor the color of rotting teeth. The uniform was evidently lightweight and flexible, appropriate to heat and to wading along the beaches. Vulnerable, Baze thought, to hard, swift strikes that broke legs and necks.

Chirrut downed the first two stormtroopers of the day, sweeping them off their feet before they could complete their patrol around a landing pad and catch a glimpse of the rebel spotter planting his detonator. Baze claimed another trooper soon after, bursting out of the vegetation to wrap his hands around a neck encased in a black bodysuit; he dug his fingers beneath the rim of the struggling storm-trooper's helmet as he dragged the man back between the trees and denied him air until the helmet tumbled off and Baze could slam his face against a rock. The stormtrooper did not move again.

They hunted in sync, Chirrut always prowling near the rebels and Baze always prowling near Chirrut. Baze did not limit his targets to those who might spot the blind man, but he kept Chirrut under observation nonetheless; where the Force would fail Chirrut, Baze would not.

His hands and arms quickly grew sore. Baze was strong, but he was aging, and he didn't have the luxury of using his cannon. He mopped his brow with a sleeve and took a swallow from his canteen as the rebels regrouped near Melshi, now closer to the barracks than ever. Chirrut crouched between trees a dozen meters away.

The soldiers looked anxious. They looked resolved. They watched the barracks and their surroundings, their rifles ready as they lay prone in the sand or pressed tight against trees for camouflage.

Maybe, Baze thought, he could trust them after all.

He heard Melshi's voice over his comlink. "Ready, ready. Standing by."

He listened to the hiss of sea foam spilling over sand and the far-away howl of shuttles.

Eventually, Cassian's response came over the comm:

"Light it up."

"Director Krennic, we are entering the Scarif shield gate. General Ramda has been informed of your arrival."

Orson Krennic grunted in acknowledgment and touched a fore-finger to his throat, worrying at the soreness and the bruising. Darth Vader's assault would take a day or more to heal; in the meantime, a lingering ache brought Krennic a reminder of the precariousness of his position.

He stood at a metaphorical cliff's edge, stamping his foot in an ef-fort to cause an avalanche. With Galen Erso's treachery undone, he would gain the allegiance of Vader. With Vader's backing, he would expose the incompetence of Tarkin—the revelation of rebel survivors from Jedha. With Tarkin humiliated, Krennic's command of the Death Star would be uncontested, and he would confer with the Em-peror himself as to how it might best be used.

Krennic would be, in every way that mattered, the most powerful and decorated man in the Empire.

Or he would fall from the cliff and bash his skull open on the rocks. And his Death Star would fall into the fumbling hands of *Wilhuff Tarkin*.

Tarkin, Erso, Vader—how had so many men conspired against him for so long?

"Beginning final descent now," the pilot's voice called.

Sulk like a child another day. Solve your Erso problem first.

He disembarked with his escort of death troopers, waved a brusque acknowledgment at the lieutenant who'd come to guide him off the Citadel's executive landing pad, and ignored the seductive caress of the warm Scarif air. Galen had possessed nearly unrestricted access to the Citadel; under the supervision of Imperial minders, yes, but Scarif's overseers lacked *rigor,* earning their assignments on the tropical world largely through cronyism. They trusted to the stormtrooper garrison, the planetary shield, and the Star Destroyers in orbit; they relied too much on the Citadel's automated security measures. The damage Galen could have done was considerable.

Krennic overtook his guide as he disembarked the turbolift and made for the Citadel command center. General Ramda and his people were waiting at attention as Krennic descended into the control pit. "Director," Ramda declared. "What brings you to Scarif?"

Krennic bristled at the voice, at the tone of a man who'd prepared a facility tour and an official dinner instead of foreseeing the crisis at hand. Ramda was another officer whose *incompetence* exceeded his vision.

"Galen Erso," Krennic snapped. "I want every dispatch, every transmission he's ever sent called up for inspection."

"I'll put three men on it immediately." Ramda hid his confusion poorly as Krennic brushed past him, heading for a console. "What are they looking for?"

Krennic stopped, pivoted, and stared at the general with curdled disgust. "I'm inspecting them *myself.* That's why I'm here."

"Every one?"

"Yes. *All* of them. Get started."

Maybe, Krennic thought, he'd managed to overestimate Ramda's competence. Maybe he'd accepted too much responsibility himself for Galen's treachery. Not that shifting the blame—no matter the justification—would mollify Vader.

He had a plan for the task ahead. He would start by checking any outsized transmissions. In all likelihood, Galen hadn't dared to broadcast complete files from the data vault—even Scarif's lax security should have detected that—but it was best to be sure. After that, Krennic could look for the names of anyone inside the Empire Galen might have drawn into a conspiracy; the Galen Krennic knew lacked the charisma to win allies and the guts to attempt blackmail, but the Galen Krennic knew wouldn't have abandoned his life's work in the first place.

He took a seat at a duty station by the windows as officers shuffled nervously behind him. Once he was through with the obvious possibilities, he'd need to start culling through messages by hand. He'd need to look for code words, for anything off kilter.

Galen knew too much, had *seen* too much. If he'd sent the rebels intelligence on Imperial defenses, on hyperspace routes, it could leave more than one planet vulnerable to a well-coordinated attack. If he'd authorized shipments of equipment or weaponry, he might have supplied his allies somehow. But if he'd sent information about the Death Star just a little at a time, "forgetting" to properly encrypt the data so that the Rebellion could eavesdrop—

—then what? What could the Rebel Alliance do? There was no defense against the battle station.

You'll never win.

The brief bass rumble that interrupted Krennic's thoughts seemed to him an irritation: another failure on the part of Ramda and his men to provide him with what he needed. But then another rumble followed, and others swiftly in sequence. Krennic snapped to a stand, stared out onto the Scarif landscape as smoke and fire rippled up from a dozen points out of the green.

The officers were yammering behind him. He heard no words, but recognized a shared tone of surprise and confusion. Were they truly so oblivious?

"Are we blind?" he shouted, spinning to face the command center and ignoring the roughness in his throat. "The rebels are *here!*"

He had the attention of the room. *Attention* was not what he required.

"Deploy the garrison!" he screamed. "Move!"

And they did move, at last, Ramda barking orders and his subordinates pulling up aerial maps and holograms. Ramda was ignorant, of course, of the enemy's true objective, but Krennic knew this was Galen's work. One more consequence of his sabotage, of his secret messages. Krennic cursed the man before seeking to put the news into context.

Rebels (almost certainly rebels) were attempting to reach the data vault. They were attempting to steal the schematics for the battle station.

Why? To build their own?

To search for a weakness.

There *was* no weakness.

Even the possibility was unacceptable.

And another thought crawled through the back of Krennic's brain—a thought that should not have frightened him, one that meant *nothing* at this juncture, had no implications for the reality on the ground, but which made his clenched fist tremble nonetheless.

The survivors of Jedha had struck on Eadu—and he had *seen* one of them, there on the platform as the bombs fell, though he could not remember his enemy's face. From Eadu, they had followed him to Scarif.

He vowed not to let them escape a third time.

CHAPTER 17

YAVIN 4 WAS A PRISON world. It seemed discourteous to say so aloud; Base One had given Mon Mothma a home, a shelter from an Empire that would have eagerly chased her into the wilds of the galaxy for the slimmest chance of executing her. But *leaving* Yavin was next to impossible for those same reasons. Mon's travels offworld were rare and short-lived, and they always ended back in her cell within the ziggurat.

She was chief of state of the Rebel Alliance and her power extended as far as the tree line of the jungle. She fought a fierce envy as the councilors she'd summoned piled into their starships, soared one by one into the bright-blue sky. They went to their homeworlds and their battlefields and their mobile headquarters, ready to wage war or flee or surrender, for the Alliance's deadlock remained unbroken, and Mon's speeches had not swayed them.

She watched Senator Pamlo's unmarked transport depart for Coruscant, where Pamlo would publicly decry the Death Star battle station before resigning her office and urging the Rebellion to disband.

Mon had extracted that *concession* during her eighty-three minutes of debate with Pamlo that morning. Maybe one day Mon would look back and admire Tynnra Pamlo's principles. But not today.

She turned back to the hangar, crossed the tarmac, and stepped into the shadows of the ziggurat. A steady trickle of councilors continued to their ships, apparently supervised by Davits Draven and Antoc Merrick.

Merrick was, by all accounts, an excellent pilot and a worthy commander of Blue Squadron. Seeing him with Draven, Mon had to resist the urge to ask: *Who are we assassinating now?* Instead she said, "Are the departures secure?"

There was no point worrying at wounds before they'd even scabbed over.

"Blue Squadron is ready to launch if anyone calls for assistance," Merrick said.

Draven grunted. "Everything's clean so far. At least the Imperials didn't follow anyone here." He glanced from side to side, nodded to an oblivious senator's aide, and lowered his voice. "Even so, I'd like to start scouting new headquarters. Too many people know about Base One, and we can't be sure how many of them will still be on our side tomorrow."

Just like that, Mon thought, *we're preparing for the breakup of the Alliance.*

"Do it," she said.

Merrick started to speak, but was interrupted by a shout from the rear of the hangar. "Senator! Senator Mothma!" One of the base privates was powering his way past a huddle of technicians and a C1-series astromech, racing toward her. Draven stepped out of their circle to intercept him, grasping his shoulder roughly as if he were ready to throw the man to the ground.

As if, Mon realized, Draven were protecting her from a would-be assassin. She wasn't sure whether to feel grateful or worried.

"Stop right there, Private," Draven said, low and stern.

The man stood stiff, practically shaking with nervous energy.

"Let him speak," Mon said.

"Intercepted Imperial transmission, ma'am," the private answered. "Rebels on Scarif."

Scarif? How was that possible?

But the answer was obvious. She saw it on Draven's face, too, and Merrick's.

While Mon had spent the night clutching like a miser at whatever pieces of the Alliance she might preserve, Jyn Erso had gone to risk everything she had.

She fixed the private with a sober look. "I need to speak to Admiral Raddus," she said.

"He's left already." The man was almost stammering. "He's in orbit aboard the *Profundity*. He's gone to fight."

"I see," she said, and slowly smiled. Merrick's expression was expectant; Draven's grave and resolved.

Perhaps she had given up hope too swiftly.

Less than ten minutes later, sirens were announcing the departure of Red, Blue, Green, and Gold Squadrons along with the U-wing transports. Raddus had already contacted all capital ships within range of Yavin or Scarif. Draven had brusquely warned Mon not to think of joining the mission, no matter how *inspirational* she thought she might be; but the warning hadn't been necessary. Mon understood her limits too well to get in the way.

Instead she reminded herself of her pride in the soldiers of the Alliance and watched pilots and infantry personnel and technicians scramble to their vessels. Anyone capable of contributing would find his or her abilities welcome in the coming battle.

As the last transports began to fill, she turned back to the corridors of the ziggurat and set out for the communications center. She had to step aside for a gold-plated protocol droid and an astromech unit hurrying toward the tarmac, and faintly overheard the former indignantly declare:

"Scarif? They're going to *Scarif*? Why does nobody ever tell me anything, Artoo . . . ?"

. . .

Grand Moff Wilhuff Tarkin made it a point not to dwell on the flamboyant ambitions of Orson Krennic. Over the course of more than a decade, the director had gone from a nuisance to a genuine threat and back again, all the while demanding far more attention than Tarkin was prepared to grant him. Krennic had been too useful to dispose of and too self-motivated to trust, but an admixture of neglect and rare, forceful reminders of Tarkin's authority had kept him largely on the outskirts of Tarkin's personal galaxy.

Nonetheless, as Tarkin stood on the overbridge of the Death Star and stared into the stars on the viewscreen, he took a moment to acknowledge the director's contributions. A project of such scale needed to be handled with both an eye for detail and an emphasis on implementation; and Krennic, despite his faults and obsessions, had made the Death Star *work*.

Tarkin had half expected every nonessential system on the battle station to burn out after the test on Jedha. Yet the Death Star remained intact, invulnerable—its full fury yet to be unleashed. It would be remarkable, Tarkin thought, to see if it could truly demolish a planet . . .

He laughed inwardly at his own childish eagerness. There was no hurry. The Death Star was a tool like any other, to be applied at the appropriate hour.

"Sir?" General Romodi had approached. Tarkin indicated his attentiveness with a cock of his head. "Scarif base—they're reporting a rebel ground incursion. Firefights around the Citadel."

Now, *that* was a surprise. Scarif was a hardened target, one Saw Gerrera might have struck while feeling particularly ambitious. If the Rebellion was hitting Scarif so soon after Gerrera's death, it was for a *reason*.

Possibilities flitted across Tarkin's mind. None of them alarmed him. Very little truly alarmed Tarkin anymore.

"A ground incursion," he said. "But no spaceborne support?"

"Not that Ramda's people mentioned."

Which suggested a last-gasp effort or a plan not yet fully implemented.

"I want to speak to Director Krennic," Tarkin said.

"He's *there,* sir," Romodi replied. "On Scarif."

The day was full of surprises.

Tarkin spoke with detached consideration, as much to himself as Romodi. "The original plans for this station are kept at the Citadel, are they not?"

"They are."

Along with other technical schematics for projects covered by the Tarkin Initiative. *It would be a special pity,* Tarkin thought, *to see War-Mantle and Stellarsphere set back.* But hardly a major blow to the galactic timetable, particularly with the Death Star finally online.

Best to suffer a minor loss to avoid a greater one. What the rebels could *do* with the technical schematics was limited, of course, but Tarkin had always been a man who preferred to elude the specter of risk.

"Prepare the jump to hyperspace," he said. "And inform Lord Vader."

Romodi hurried off, and the soft hum of the reactor rose gently in pitch as the lightspeed engines drained away power. Tarkin folded his hands together and observed a pair of TIE fighters on the viewscreen race toward one of the station's hangar bays.

He was curious to see the rebels in action. He was curious, too, what opportunities might present themselves. Just how many victories might be scored in one battle?

But Tarkin was a patient man. He would wait and see what Scarif provided.

SUPPLEMENTAL DATA: THE REBEL FLEET

[Document #MH2215 ("Short Notes on the History of the Rebel Alliance Navy"), from the personal files of Mon Mothma.]

The Clone Wars redefined interstellar conflict, forcing us to grapple with realities we'd blessedly forgotten after generations of peace. This was, perhaps, the very worst of the wars' crimes—they ushered in an age when mass bloodshed was no longer unthinkable, but rather an essential feature of military action.

I've argued that our rebel movement is not a response to the political question of the Clone Wars, and I continue to believe this; nonetheless, no one can claim that our military doctrine is not largely defined by the desire and need to *do things differently.* What worked in the Clone Wars cannot work again: The partnership of Jedi Knights and Kaminoan clone armies constituted a peerless weapon that no longer exists.

Consider a brigade of clone troopers served by a Jedi commander: Such a unit might penetrate a world's orbital defenses and seize control of the entire planet while taking (and inflicting!) minimal casualties. I do not mean to understate the role of naval warfare during the last conflict, nor to denigrate the sacrifices of starship pilots and crew who were lost, but what blockade could be thorough enough to keep out a handful of determined starfighters and a single clone drop ship? (Yes, such blockades existed, and in greater numbers toward the conflict's end, but their cost helped to fracture and bankrupt the nascent Separatist government.)

With the Clone Wars' end, the destruction of the Jedi Order, and the decommissioning of the Kaminoan cloning facilities, the self-proclaimed Emperor and his military advisers determined that the future of warfare was in large-scale naval weaponry—in a fleet of battleships and battle stations that could atomize any enemy, whether on a planet's surface or among the stars. They rebuilt a military not for precision strikes but for hammerblows; a military that could counter the interstellar movement of any mobile infantry that an uprising might field.

This was the vile genius of Emperor Palpatine's plan. He knew a rebellion like ours would have no difficulty assembling a vast army of ground troops from thousands of oppressed worlds. But his stormtroopers could curtail a local uprising's growth on any single world, and his fleets could decimate spaceborne troops during any attempted landing. No potential rebellion could dare eschew infantry altogether, but—lacking the elite support of Jedi or clones—the cost in lives would be abominable (see, for example, the affair of the Sixty-First Mobile Infantry at Ferrok Pax).

Thus, the importance of the rebel navy.

While the Empire constructed its behemoth Star Destroyers and its TIE fighter swarms, another fleet was forming in less mechanistic fashion. In the early years of what would become our Rebellion, there was little coordination among insurgent cells—yet each, on its own, understood the need to obtain starships for military strikes and transport. A retooled freighter here, augmented with illegal weapons salvaged from Separatist wrecks; a pirate corvette there, donated by a sympathetic underworld contact; a handful of starfighters, stolen in a daring raid on an Imperial base.

As insurgent factions in different sectors began to coordinate and share resources, new challenges arose. One TIE fighter is little different from another—its mechanisms and its pilots can be swapped with ease when repairs or injuries warrant. Not so with the variety of ships flying for the rebel cause. Staffing and maintaining a patchwork fleet is a task that under less expert leadership (I do not include myself!) would have, *should* have been impossible.

Rebel captains proposed a threefold solution to our challenge. First, an underground pipeline was to be established through which both smugglers and legitimate merchants would obtain and distribute badly needed starship parts. This distribution network would need to rival those of some of the Republic's larger corporations to operate effectively. The assistance of former Separatist advisers would ultimately prove invaluable.

Second, pilots would be encouraged to coordinate and learn from one another and to train on as many types of ships and simulators as possible. This would not only allow skilled pilots to be placed on new vessels should their personal spacecraft be destroyed, but also prove vital for multiship engagements. As Admiral Raddus puts it, "No one wants to fly in formation with a stranger."

Third, rebel leadership would expend whatever resources were required to obtain additional starfighter squadrons. These efforts would cost credits and lives, and the details must remain confidential for now. Nonetheless, our access to X-wing fighters in particular is testament to our success.

As our Rebellion gained visibility, new opportunities arose as well. The arrival of the Mon Calamari city-ships was a shocking (and perhaps, given our limited effectiveness against the occupation of Mon Cala, undeserved) boon, emphasizing the significance of winning the hearts of the galaxy's civilians above all else.

Over time, leaders like Raddus and General Merrick performed a startling feat, transforming what might have amounted to a pirate armada into a genuine fighting force. We've long since known that our pilots, crews, and commanders can easily match the skill and bravery of their Imperial counterparts; what remains to be tested is whether our vessels can engage in a full-scale fleet battle and triumph against a technologically superior opponent.

My hope is that such a test is never needed. But if the day does come, I believe we will emerge victorious.

CHAPTER 18

Bodhi Rook should have felt guilty. From inside the cockpit of shuttle SW-0608, he watched black smoke rise from half a dozen landing pads—the sort of smoke that spilled like blood from a crashed cargo ship or a burning speeder. He'd seen Saw Gerrera's rebels blow up installations before. He recognized himself in the black-clad figures that raced to extinguish fires or who took cover behind patrolling stormtroopers.

Bodhi had never thought of himself as a soldier or a killer. He should have felt guilty. But he'd picked a side when Galen Erso had told him of the crimes he was enabling. He'd felt his last doubts burn away in the fire that had consumed Jedha City.

"Troopers!" It was Corporal Tonc's voice, from down the cockpit ladder and outside the ship. "Troopers on the left!"

Bodhi heard boots ring against deck plating as the five rebel fighters who'd stayed with the shuttle hurried inside. Through the viewport he spotted a squad of stormtroopers racing across the landing pad, sprinting past cargo crates and control consoles. None of them gave the shuttle more than a glance.

For the moment, at least, Bodhi could keep hiding.

Tonc scrambled noisily up the cockpit ladder, the barrel of his shoulder-slung rifle striking each rung as he went. Bodhi tried to look confident, *tough* in the man's presence—Tonc had spent most of the flight to Scarif interrogating Bodhi before volunteering to guard the shuttle. Bodhi still wasn't sure what the corporal thought of him.

Tonc struck Bodhi with the flat of his hand, square between the shoulders. "How're we doing up here?" he growled.

Bodhi winced at the force of the blow. "Looks like they've grounded noncombat vessels, but overall they're ignoring the shuttles. I can't really tell what's going on . . ." He gestured vaguely at the viewport and the smoke. Occasionally he made out the crimson flash of a blaster bolt, but the trees obscured his view of the pads, bunkers, and barracks closer to the Citadel.

"What's going on is *fighting*," Tonc said. "That's the Pathfinders for you."

Bodhi was adjusting his instruments, head down over his console. But the admiration in Tonc's voice caught his attention. "I thought you were a Pathfinder?" he asked.

Tonc laughed. "I can't do half what those SpecForce guys do. But I heard Captain Andor needed volunteers, so I volunteered." His voice took on a gruffer quality as he added, "Still a better shot than *you*."

Bodhi didn't doubt that.

The comm crackled and a voice came through, urgent and angry. "Pad twelve! Close it down!"

Bodhi slapped his thighs in triumph. "I've found the main security channel. We can track their movements from here."

Tonc pursed his lips and nodded approvingly. The chatter was fast and overlapping: The Citadel demanded status reports and assessments of rebel troop numbers while stormtroopers called for emergency reinforcements. "We have rebels everywhere!" one voice called, and Bodhi couldn't help but smile.

"We just going to sit here and be smug? Or are you going to help out?" Tonc asked.

Bodhi bristled, though the words were more friendly than challenging. He reached for the comm controls again and bit his lip.

Baze and Chirrut were out there, probably shooting and getting shot at along with all the rebel soldiers. Cassian and Jyn and K-2 were inside the Citadel by now. If everything went well, even if everything went *perfectly*, not everyone would make it back alive.

They weren't his friends. They hadn't gone drinking with Bodhi after his crush on Bamayar had rejected him, or helped him reassemble his astromech after he'd stupidly taken the droid apart on a dare. But they had saved him from Saw Gerrera, *believed* him when Saw and his people hadn't. They'd never once put him in cuffs. They'd needed him on Eadu and never once pretended they hadn't.

They wanted to stop the Death Star.

They didn't deserve to be hurt.

Bodhi should have felt guilty.

You don't have to feel guilty.

He punched a button, lifted the link, and shouted into the open comm, "Pad two! This is pad two! We count forty rebel soldiers running west off pad two!"

Then he muted the comm and adjusted the settings with one shaking hand. He felt a rush of energy, terrifying and invigorating, as he passed the link to Tonc. "Tell them you're pinned down by rebels on pad five," he said.

Tonc grinned broadly and took the link. "Who needs SpecForce?" he asked. "We can do this all by ourselves."

For an instant Bodhi felt sure that was true. But he was glad not to be fighting alone.

Jyn's fears had begun to multiply. In the starkly revealing light of the cave in her mind, she seemed to find another with every moment that passed. Fear for her companions, and the danger they were in; fear for how she might fail or abandon them; fear of what the Death Star would do if not stopped; fear of failing to deliver the redemption her father sought.

It was fear that guided her hand to her blaster as she walked with

Cassian and K-2 down a Citadel subcorridor and saw thirty storm-troopers rush toward her in formation. It was fear that made her *eager* for a fight, eager to channel her dread into pitiless blows and the pain of bruised ribs.

Eadu and Jedha had given her numbing solace in the form of end-less marches and racking storms and sunlight gone cold. Scarif's comforts let her *think* too much. And when the stormtrooper pla-toon passed by without a glance, footsteps in sync as they made for the main entrance to the Citadel, she couldn't help but feel disap-pointed.

"Guess our distraction's working," Cassian murmured.

Jyn forced herself to look approving. "It was a good plan."

They hadn't heard from Melshi or the others since the detonators had gone off. The rebels were supposed to signal if they had anything Jyn or Cassian needed to know.

Unless, of course, they all died.

Stay focused, Jyn.

She tried to remember how she'd kept radio silent during runs for Saw; how she'd managed to wait back at base for comrades like Maia and Staven to return. But the vague, inchoate memories made her feel ill. And even then she hadn't needed those people the way she needed Bodhi and the Guardians and Cassian: to keep her on-task, to keep her from just *surviving*.

Stay focused and do your damn job.

"This way to the data vault," K-2 said.

They moved as swiftly as they could without drawing attention. The corridors emptied while they traveled, officers withdrawing to their stations and troopers racing for the perimeter. At last they reached a heavy blast door. "Inside," K-2 said. The door opened with-out a code.

The antechamber to the vault was as starkly appointed as the rest of the facility. A single squat lieutenant sat behind a console, guard-ing entry into a brightly illuminated tube ringed with devices Jyn didn't recognize.

"Can I help you?" the lieutenant asked.

"That won't be necessary," K-2 replied, and brought a metal fist down onto the man's skull. The lieutenant slumped onto the console as the droid maneuvered around him, shoving the unconscious body aside and plugging into a dataport.

Cassian rushed to drag the man out of view of the doorway. Jyn stood in the circular frame of the tube, blinking at the light and peering at the massive vault door at the far end. A long-forgotten recollection of a bad night in the crawl space of an Imperial treasury flashed in her mind; she could still feel the sparks burning on her cheeks, the calluses from four hours working a plasma cutter. Carving through the metal, she decided, wasn't an option.

"How does it open?" she called.

"Biometric identification. Lieutenant Putna should do." K-2 gestured absently at the body in Cassian's arms. "I must remain here."

"What for?" Cassian asked. Jyn repositioned herself to help grapple the unconscious lieutenant, lifting his legs as Cassian hoisted him beneath the shoulders.

"No data tape can be removed from the vault without authorization and assistance from this console," K-2 said. "In this way, any single would-be thief is denied success.

"In the event of a security breach," the droid added, "the screening tunnel can also be energized to wipe all data storage. I prefer to keep my memory intact."

Jyn craned her neck as Cassian led the way down the tube. The rings of equipment seemed no less threatening, even knowing they were designed to thwart electronics instead of people.

Cassian grunted at Jyn. She dropped the lieutenant's legs and Cassian rolled the man over, slapping his hand against the scanner in the vault door. For several seconds, nothing happened; then a short, low buzz indicated rejection of the scan.

Jyn swore to herself and felt her skin prickle with heat.

"It's not working," Cassian called.

K-2's voice came echoing through the tunnel: "*Right* hand."

"You're a terrible spy," Jyn hissed. She was surprised by her own intensity, the easy jibe laced with frustration.

Cassian ignored her and rearranged the body. The vault door chimed swiftly this time. Metal locks disengaged and a current of vibration ran through the floor.

Slowly—excruciatingly slowly—the door opened.

For the better part of five minutes, the rebels held the advantage. The stormtroopers who survived the initial detonations were stunned, deafened, blinded, injured by the blasts and thunder and shrapnel. They did not panic—they raced dutifully to their posts and clustered their shots in well-timed volleys—but they were scrambling to compensate for casualties before they had even spotted the enemy. They were easy to kill and easy to herd.

Baze took satisfaction in the cries of alarm and the tumbling of bodies as his companions caught Imperial squads in particle barrages; he took no less satisfaction each time Chirrut emerged from the shadows to send a stormtrooper sprawling, or when his own meticulous cannon shots burst through one suit of armor after the next.

Baze had heard once—he could not recall from whom—that the Jedi considered anger an abomination; a path to what they called the *dark side* of the Force. But the Guardians of the Whills were not Jedi; and Baze's anger was righteous, able to guide his shots where the Force would not.

And if anger had not sufficed to save the holy city? Then Baze would need to be twice as fierce on Scarif to give Jyn Erso the *distraction* she required.

Baze, Chirrut, and the rebels swarmed and regrouped, separated the squads of their enemies and picked off the reinforcements who arrived one by one. But soon the stormtroopers regained their strength and their reinforcements came by tens and twenties.

That was when the rebels began to die.

Baze did not know their names. He did not hear their wails over the endless reverberations of blaster bolts and the lower thrumming of his cannon. He left smoking bodies behind as he fell back. The fallen would not receive proper death rites, but Baze decided that if anyone lived through the day, he would honor the dead with his fellow survivors.

The air smelled like ashes. It was better than the tang of sea salt.

Squads of stormtroopers crept away from the barracks, forming a spearhead aimed at the hillock where the rebels were attempting to hold ground. Baze saw the opportunity when Melshi did—one brief chance to break the enemy—and as Melshi cried, "Forward!" Baze provided cover for the rebels to shatter the spearhead. An allied rocket blasted armored bodies through the air; then the moment was gone, and as one the rebels scampered into the cover of the jungle, allowing the stormtroopers to give chase.

In the relative shade of the trees, Baze's eyes spotted with streaks of color as blaster volleys flashed by. His back had begun to ache from the weight of his generator, and sweat plastered his beard to his chin. He did not stop moving until he realized, with a start, that he had not seen Chirrut in some moments.

He spat a curse, spun about, and fired at a stormtrooper over the head of a rebel half crawling through the underbrush. If he yelled for the blind man now, a dozen guns would be aimed his way. But if he'd *lost* Chirrut . . .

The smoke was everywhere. Trees burned as their trunks absorbed bolt after bolt. Baze stalked back the way he had come, concentrating his focus, narrowing his cone of vision as if sheer intensity would allow him to penetrate the haze.

"Baze! *Baze!*"

He heard Chirrut before he saw him. The blind man's robes were marred with soot and soil and his expression was wild with alarm, but he appeared uninjured. Baze felt a rush of fury and an equal rush of relief.

"What?" he snapped. "What is it?"

"Run," Chirrut said. "Run!"

With those words, as Chirrut grasped Baze by the arm and pulled him toward the shoreline, Baze's senses expanded again. He heard the heavy snapping of wood—not *burning* wood, not wood ravaged by a grenade, but the broad-leafed trees of the jungle being compressed beneath an unfathomable weight until they broke and burst.

He turned and saw the towering metal forms of Imperial walkers on the march. Their legs dwarfed the trees, and the laser cannons attached to their cockpits pumped ruin toward the scattering rebel soldiers. The stormtroopers had slowed their pursuit, staying out of the crossfire as they attempted to cut off the rebels' routes to escape.

The rebels had already begun to die. But death was not failure.

Failure lay in the shadow of the metal beasts.

Go, little sister, Baze thought. *Go!*

Dozens of vessels winked into existence against the shroud of space, filling the void as if some mythological deity had upturned a bottle of fresh stars over the heavens. Admiral Raddus—Raddus of Mon Cala, Raddus of the Floes, Raddus of the Clutch of Zadasurr and the Spear of Tryphar—knew many of the ships by their silhouettes: X-wing and Y-wing starfighters, U-wing and Gallofree transports, Dornean gunships and Hammerhead corvettes. All of them had served the Rebellion well.

It was a tremendous sight, unique in the history of the Rebellion. If the fleet had a vulnerability, it was that selfsame uniqueness: *We fight as siblings who have never known a shared home,* Raddus thought, *against an Empire that knows naught but tyrannical discipline.*

Raddus did not avert his gaze from the main display as he gestured to his comm officer. "Are all capital ships accounted for?"

"Yes, Admiral," came the answer in that rasping, *human* voice.

Raddus had yet to adjust to keeping aliens aboard his bridge, no matter how skilled; the *Profundity* had been built by Mon Calamari and only recently refitted for war by the Rebellion. With the refit had come unexpected diversity. "Very good. And General Merrick?"

The general's proud bellow came through the comm with a burst of static. "Ready to fight, Admiral—sending possible attack runs now." There was a brief pause before the voice continued, "This is Blue Leader. All squadron leaders, report in."

Raddus turned from the viewport to the tactical holodisplays, scanning the battlefield as the squadron leaders replied.

"Blue Leader, this is Gold Leader."

"Red Leader, standing by."

"Green Leader, standing by."

The *Profundity* had detected—and its crew or its allies had visually confirmed—two Star Destroyers, at least nine distinct TIE starfighter squadrons, and innumerable midsized vessels ranging from shuttles to patrol cruisers, all situated between the rebels and Scarif. Other enemy craft, as yet undetected, could have been hidden behind planets and moons or running dark on auxiliary power. On its own, the Imperial fleet would pose a formidable challenge—but not a dispiriting one.

Yet Scarif's planetary defenses were considerable. Draven's spies had reported an energy shield built to withstand massive bombardment, and the orbital gate station appeared to be festooned with turrets and starfighter hangars. Combined with the Imperial fleet, the battle would be—at the very least—memorable.

For all that, the decimation of the Alliance navy was the least of Raddus's concerns.

On Yavin 4, Jyn Erso had described a battle station capable of destroying whole worlds. Raddus had never known the Empire to be restrained in its use of weapons, and of all the planets in its grasp he could think of few as defiant as his own homeworld.

Mon Cala had resisted. Mon Cala had been punished. Mon Cala had, time and again, offered its warriors and resources to the Rebellion.

If the Rebellion failed to stop the Death Star, Mon Cala would be obliterated. For this reason—and for a hundred others—Raddus would fight as long as the *Profundity* endured.

General Ramda was a fool, and Krennic had already decided to have him tried and imprisoned for gross incompetence. Still, there was no one on Scarif whom Krennic trusted to replace him, and Krennic himself knew too little of the Citadel's vulnerabilities. So he allowed the general to race about the command center while Krennic seethed, listening to cries and reports from troopers in the field. Krennic was not, at heart, a military man; he believed that if a battle had to be waged, something had already gone wrong.

The enemy's numbers at first seemed impossibly strong—surely a product of confusion and disarray, but no less obfuscating for all that. Yet as the fighting proceeded, no breaches in the base's defenses were reported and the conflict remained at some distance from the Citadel Tower. Soon a lieutenant shouted triumphantly and declared that walkers had routed the rebels and pushed them to the shore.

Krennic had no words of praise for the officers of Scarif, but this was enough to dampen his ire. The data vault was pristine. The Citadel was safe. The Jedha survivors would be sifted as ashes from the sand.

Again, he tried to recall the face of his attacker on Eadu. Had it been a woman? Would he recognize her if the troopers cataloged the dead? He'd give the order to sort the bodies once the battle was over. And he would interrogate any captives himself—if they were Galen's revenge, he would learn the truth.

One of Ramda's aides signaled the general. "Transmission from Admiral Gorin," he called. Krennic watched Ramda hurry to a console and tap frantically at the screen. When Ramda approached Krennic, his jaw was set to defy a fresh terror.

"Sir," Ramda said, "part of the rebel fleet has arrived from hyperspace and amassed outside the shield. However, the admiral believes they are no threat to the planet—"

"They aren't trying to *take the planet*," Krennic snapped. He would have struck the man if he hadn't needed Ramda so. "Lock down the base. Lock down everything!" He was shouting full-bore into the general's face.

Ramda stood, his breath hitching but otherwise unaffected. "And close the shield?" he asked.

"Do it!" Krennic roared, and Ramda and his men scurried to act. When the orders had been given, Krennic lowered his voice but still heard himself quivering with fury. "Is there any way," he asked, "that the rebel fleet can break through the shield? *Think* before you answer."

"The shield gate itself," Ramda said with deliberate care, "is the only weak point. With massive amounts of firepower, an enemy could conceivably punch through the field contained by the ring. But Admiral Gorin is positioning his ships to prevent even that unlikely occurrence."

Krennic nodded briskly and waved Ramda off. He fought down his blinding rage and updated his reconstruction of the attack: A team of rebels had infiltrated the planet somehow in an attempt to penetrate the Citadel and steal the Death Star schematics. When the attack had gone poorly, the rebels had brought in their *fleet*—if not in its entirety, then in irreplaceable force—fighting a battle they couldn't possibly hope to win.

Was it an act of true desperation? Had some rebel commander decided that it was worth losing everything for even a *chance* at extracting the team seeking the plans?

There was logic in it, given certain premises. The Death Star was an existential threat to the Alliance. If the rebels believed—if Galen had *made* them believe—there was a weakness in the station, then they were taking the only conceivable path to avoid doom.

It hadn't occurred to Krennic that the rebels might sacrifice so many lives for such an unlikely gain. He'd known they were individually suicidal; a mass death wish was something new.

He slammed a fist onto the nearest console and ignored the frightened looks of the officers.

You must have told quite a story, Galen.

"This is Admiral Raddus. Red and Gold Squadrons, engage those two Star Destroyers. Blue Squadron, get to the surface before they close that gate!"

Merrick's answer crackled through the comm on the bridge of the *Profundity.* "Copy you, Admiral."

Raddus pressed his palms together and let his mouth hang open, allowing the thick, artificially humid air to condense inside his mouth and throat. Then he wet his lips and barked new orders to his crew. "I want one-third of the fleet each supporting Red and Gold Squadrons. That should force those Destroyers to engage. The remainder will protect our flank; when the Empire brings in reinforcements, I don't want our escape route cut off." It was an almost simplistic plan, cobbled together from skirmishes at Nexator and Carsanza, but there was no time to compose anything more elaborate; this was an opening gambit, not a strategy to win the day.

And improvisation had always been one of Raddus's talents.

"What about *Profundity,* Admiral?" the tactical officer called.

"We cover Blue Squadron," Raddus said, and jutted a finger at the viewport. "We target the shield gate."

The battle was joined, and chaos ensued.

Raddus moved his attention calmly, surely, between the tactical holodisplays and the viewport. The former revealed the state of the battlefield; the latter revealed its timbre. He saw the motes of light signifying Blue Squadron bearing toward the shield gate; and he saw the first wild emerald volleys unleashed by the Star Destroyers, spattering and rippling against the deflectors of rebel Hammerheads. He said nothing during the opening moments of violence—he trusted his gunners and his captains to swim as the tide demanded.

Barely aware of his own motions, he rose from his seat and crept toward the viewport as the shield gate came into full view. The iridescent flicker of energy outside the ring had begun to diminish as—like water in a river lock—the gate regulated the energy flow and permitted the gap in the shield to close. It would take only moments before the shield was fully reestablished.

A wave of Blue Squadron fighters and U-wing transports hurtled toward the closing gate, flashing through before entering Scarif's atmosphere. A second wave continued forward, and Raddus heard a panicked cry through the comm station: "Pull up!"

A single starfighter vanished in a burst of sparks and metal, battered into oblivion against the energy shield. The first Alliance loss of the battle.

Raddus turned back to the tactical displays.

Jyn Erso and her colleagues—*Rogue One*—had their ground support.

But delivering Blue Squadron had been the simple part. Now things would become more difficult.

The walkers stalked the rebels like hunting hounds, relentless and unafraid. Their blasts splintered trees and showered Baze with burning dirt and sand. They did far worse to the soldiers struck with any precision. A quick death, Baze thought, did not make a *good* death.

He emerged with Chirrut and the dozen rebel survivors onto the beach, racing along the shore as the mechanical grinding of walker legs drowned out the ragged gasps of his breathing, the beat of his boots on sand. A long trench ran near the water—built by the stormtroopers, he supposed, to help repel an invasion by sea—and one after the next the rebels leapt or swung inside. As if a mound of sand would stop the walkers for a fraction of an instant.

But then, if a fraction of an instant was all Baze had left to give Jyn Erso, it was better than no gift at all.

Besides, he had nowhere else to run.

He scrambled into the trench near Chirrut and didn't pause to glance toward the walkers before dropping his cannon and seizing a rocket launcher from a rebel who hastily passed the weapon his way. If he aimed well, he might be able to shatter one walker's cockpit—kill or expose the pilot, damage its controls, make the vehicle useless.

He would not have the time or the ammunition for a second shot. But he might earn the rebels a few instants more before the other walker buried them all.

He rose from the trench, turned to face the foremost walker—maybe fifty meters distant now, at the edge of the tree line. He set the launcher on his shoulder, lined up a shot while the rebels alongside him fired blasters uselessly. His body lurched as the rocket leapt forward, soaring toward the terrible machine.

The explosion nearly deafened him. Fire and smoke streamed from one side of the walker's cockpit, and the machine twisted its head away as if in pain. One of its temple-mounted cannons was a wreck. But Baze's aim had not been true. The walker was not disabled. It turned back toward the soldiers.

Death had chased Baze for a long time. He bared his teeth at it in defiance.

The burning walker targeted the trench. Before it could fire, the sky above Baze wailed and a shadow crossed the sea. Pulses of light hotter and faster than the rocket impacted the walker's cockpit and a second blast of fire tore the mechanical head asunder, sent sheets of smoking metal tumbling through the air and onto the beach. As the walker's body began to topple, its attacker sped above it and over the green of the jungle: an X-wing starfighter.

The Alliance had come to fight after all.

Baze's comrades were cheering, raising fists in the air and shouting in triumph. To his surprise, he heard himself laughing with them.

CHAPTER 19

THE DATA VAULT WAS UNLOCKED. Jyn wanted nothing more than to rush inside, to snatch the tape containing the Death Star's schematics, and race back to Bodhi and the shuttle. Every moment they delayed was another chance for the Imperials to catch them inside the Citadel; and out on the beaches and in the jungles, people were surely dying by now.

How many rebels were even left? How many stormtroopers could they hold off?

Would anyone have told her if Baze and Chirrut were gone?

Instead, Jyn was helping Cassian drag the unconscious lieutenant out of the screening tunnel and back to the antechamber. "In case there's another biometric lock on the console," Cassian had muttered. "I don't want Kay-Tu to have to unplug."

He was sweating under his officer's cap, and she'd seen him reach reflexively for his comlink more than once. He wanted to know what was happening outside as much as she did.

They dropped the body roughly by K-2, still linked to the console port. "I've accessed internal Citadel communications," the droid said. "The rebel fleet has arrived."

"What?" Jyn shook her head in confusion.

"Admiral Gorin has engaged them." The droid went on, as if reading from a list: "There's fighting on the beach, they've locked down the base, they've closed the shield gate, they've alerted—"

"Wait—what does that mean?" Jyn cut him off, trying to comprehend the implications, to sort positive from negative. *They've closed the shield gate?* "We're trapped?"

She looked to Cassian. His expression was grim, his mouth tight. It was answer enough for her.

She swore under her breath, a parade of every obscenity she'd ever heard uttered. She saw the walls of the cave closing in, darkness creeping at the edges of the bright hope that had brought her this far. She racked her brain for a plan, and found nothing—locked down or not, they could find a way out of the Citadel, but if they had no way off Scarif . . .

"We have to tell them we're down here," she spat. "We're close!"

"They wouldn't be here," Cassian said, "if they didn't know."

Jyn leaned in close enough to smell the cleaning chemicals on his Imperial uniform. "Last we saw those people, they didn't want to be here at all. I'm not giving them an excuse to leave, and if they've got a way to get us out I'd like to know."

Cassian held his ground, staring down at her until his lips finally twitched into something like a smile. His eyes remained hard and troubled. Jyn wasn't sure if he'd gotten worse at hiding things or if she was simply getting to know him too well.

She was ready to call him on it, to ask what he knew that she didn't, when K-2 interrupted. "We could transmit the plans to the rebel fleet. We'd have to get a signal out to tell them it's coming. It's the size of the data files. That's the problem. They'll never get through. Someone has to take the shield gate down."

Cassian brought his comlink up. "Bodhi. Bodhi, can you hear me?" The moment of reflection, of confusion was over—he was all tense action again. "Tell me you're out there. Bodhi!"

Be alive, Jyn thought. *All of you, be alive.*

"I'm here!" Bodhi's voice came through, rapid and short of breath. "We're standing by. They've started fighting—the base is on lockdown!"

"I know," Cassian said. "Listen to me! The rebel fleet is up there. You've got to get a message out." He squeezed his eyes shut, mouthed something to himself, and then spoke aloud again. "You've got to tell them they've got to blow a hole in the shield gate so we can transmit the plans—"

"I *can't*." Bodhi sounded aghast. "I'm not tied into the comm tower. *We're* not tied in—"

"Find a way." Cassian cut off his link and pocketed it. "Good enough?" he asked Jyn.

"Good enough," she agreed. Maybe it was and maybe it wasn't; but she tried to pretend the arrival of the fleet was good news. Their escape plan hadn't exactly been foolproof before, and if the Alliance couldn't punch through Scarif's shield, what hope did it have against a Death Star?

If nothing else, someone was finally on their side.

Cassian looked between the door to the antechamber and K-2. "Cover our backs," he told the droid, and started toward the screening tunnel.

Jyn pictured stormtroopers rushing inside and spotting the body of the unconscious lieutenant. Out of instinct more than reason, she pulled the sidearm she'd taken from the lieutenant out of her belt, checked its readings—fully charged, no stun setting, hard to work wrong—and held it grip-first toward K-2. "You'll need this," she said. "You wanted one, right?"

K-2 snatched the blaster with a disconcerting eagerness. His other hand remained plugged into the console as he turned the weapon about and placed a finger on the trigger. He kept the barrel pointed at the ceiling. "Your behavior, Jyn Erso, is continually unexpected."

I couldn't ask for a nicer compliment, she wanted to say. But she decided she could do without the inevitable correction.

"Jyn." Cassian stood framed in the entrance of the screening tunnel. "Come on."

She flashed a vicious grin at the droid and went to steal what she'd come for.

Bodhi hadn't cheered when the Alliance had arrived. He'd managed a sickly little smile for Tonc's sake, but he'd known immediately how the Empire would respond. By the time X-wings were blazing over the jungle and U-wings were delivering SpecForce troops to the beach, the shield gate had already closed.

There was no way off Scarif.

He didn't blame the Rebellion, but that gave Bodhi little solace. Maybe it was his fault for not suggesting an infiltration of the orbital gate station. Maybe he'd explained the planet's defenses poorly to Jyn and Cassian and the soldiers, hurrying through it all in the excitement of the flight to Scarif. Maybe he should've been *up there* instead of *down here*.

Or maybe Cassian was right, and they had to tell their new allies exactly what they needed. Somehow.

The technical details swam in Bodhi's mind as he climbed down the cockpit ladder. They were a distraction, a *welcome* distraction, from what he was about to do—though the sounds of distant explosions and blasterfire from outside and the angry shouts of Imperial troops from the comm were equally distracting and far less welcome. Tonc and the others were spread around the cabin with their weapons aimed at the boarding ramp, but they looked his way as he hurried to the equipment hold. "All right," Bodhi said. "Listen up." *Breathe deep and sound like a flight instructor.* "We're going to have to go out there."

He wasn't afraid the rebels would refuse. He was afraid they wouldn't *believe* him. And afraid of dying, of course. He knelt by the hold and started sorting gear, hoping for the best. He needed KS-12 cable, or anything L-series with a connection adapter. A signal booster, if he could find one. A multitool for the hookup . . .

"What're you doing?" Tonc asked.

Bodhi hauled a spool of cable out and grimaced at the weight. He set it aside and forced himself to face Tonc. "They closed the shield gate," he said. "We're stuck here." Tonc knew that much already, but it meant Bodhi could delay the rest a little longer. "But—the rebel fleet is pulling in. We just have to get a signal strong enough to get through to them and let them know we're trapped down here."

"Fine," Tonc said. "I won't complain about planning a rescue. But why do *you* need to go out there?"

The emphasis wasn't lost on Bodhi; he just ignored it. "For that?" he said. "To get a signal out, with the shield gate shut? We need to connect to the communications tower; that's the whole *point* of the thing, to let the Citadel keep talking to the rest of the Empire without opening the defenses." A deep breath. "Now, I can patch us in over here, out on the landing pad—" *If I'm not cut down in the crossfire, or crushed by a falling starfighter.* "—but you have to get on the radio, get one of the guys out there to find a master switch."

Tonc was staring at him, evidently torn between duty and bewilderment. He opened his mouth and Bodhi spoke over him, answering the question Tonc was least likely to ask. "You don't build a comm tower just anyone can access. There's mechanical, physical connections controlled by the switches, and the switches are like the data vault—totally off the computer network. I only know all this because—" But he realized the last time he'd thought of those days was in the lair of Bor Gullet, and he hurried on. "Get one of the soldiers, Baze or Chirrut, *someone,* to activate the connection between us and that comm tower. Otherwise, we're not going anywhere and that data tape stays on Scarif. Okay?"

Tonc stiffened, suddenly sure of himself. He glanced to the other rebels in the cabin, who offered curt nods of acknowledgment.

"Then go!" Bodhi cried. "Call them!"

Before anyone could answer he was pocketing the tools and heaving the spool over his shoulders, where it could be harnessed like a backpack. Shifting the weight awkwardly, Bodhi hurried to the boarding ramp and peered around the doorway onto the landing pad. He could hear Tonc behind him, talking through his comlink: "Melshi, listen up! You guys have to open up the line . . ."

He couldn't see blasterfire. But then, he couldn't see very far at all. The landing pad was cluttered with cargo crates and substations, and the shuttle's undercarriage blocked much of his view. He could smell so much smoke, like the whole jungle was burning.

The network console you need is only ten meters out. Maybe twenty. You run, you hook up the cable, you head back. Think of it like a race. You used to bet a lot on racing . . .

He wanted to ask Tonc to do it, but Tonc couldn't adjust the connector if something went wrong, wouldn't know how to run a diagnostic. And Tonc wasn't dressed like an Imperial pilot; that might buy Bodhi an extra minute or two.

He had to go. He'd risked his life before. Just never quite like this.

The Rebellion needed him. Jyn needed him. Her *father,* who'd set him on this path, needed him. He braced his legs and got ready to run.

"What does it look like?" Tonc called, and Bodhi's urgent determination was shattered. He straightened, looked back at Tonc in confusion.

Tonc was holding up his comlink. "The master switch!" he said. "What's it look like? Where is it?"

Bodhi tried not to choke on a laugh and stepped back inside, tugging at the straps of the cable spool. "Let me talk to Melshi," he said.

Apparently, he had a few more moments to dread his mission.

An X-wing pilot, dashed against the shield gate, was among the first to die above Scarif. But fatalities mounted rapidly after that, first one starfighter at a time and then by the dozen. Raddus watched, cold as the waters of his homeland, as a rebel gunship was reduced by turbolaser fire to a spreading globule of molten metal.

A great commander, Raddus believed, *felt* each loss among his people but did not act on it. Mon Mothma might have disagreed, but she was no soldier. General Merrick, too, might have disagreed, but he had led Blue Squadron through the gate to Scarif, and now starfighter command fell to Raddus as well.

"What's going on down there, Lieutenant?" Raddus called.

"Unknown, sir," came the reply. "The shield jams all communications."

Raddus swore to himself. Victory in Scarif's orbit meant nothing if Rogue One failed. "We've got to buy Erso and her team some time," he said. "Throw our weight at those Star Destroyers and let's start probing that shield."

If the Alliance was lucky, Erso had an exfiltration route already planned. If not, the burden was on Raddus. "Yes, sir!" he heard, and kept his eyes in their steady rotation between viewport and tactical displays.

A wing of Red Squadron fighters strafed the orbital gate station, maneuvering among clusters of sensor towers and laser turrets. The attack did little damage, but inflicting damage hadn't been the goal—the fighters had claimed the station gunners' attention, left a few turbolaser platforms in burning ruin, and given Gold Squadron's Y-wings the opportunity for a bombing run. The impacts of the Y-wings' proton torpedoes winked out the viewport even as the scanners revealed swarms of TIE fighters pouring from the station hangars.

The command ships were faring better against the Star Destroyers. Any single vessel in the rebel fleet compared poorly with the Empire's mighty warships, but Raddus—speaking only a word here and there—kept the Destroyers boxed in, unable to turn their full firepower on one target without exposing a flank to concentrated volleys. It was, in a sense, a delaying tactic, but delay defeat long enough, and a triumph might eventually find its way home.

"Sir!" The lieutenant again. "Enemy fighters coming in!"

Red and Gold Squadrons were busily engaged against the gate or the Destroyers. Pulling them back to defend the *Profundity* was no option worth considering.

"Withdraw to fifty thousand kilometers from the shield gate," Raddus said. "Stay in the TIE fighters' range but force them to stretch their line. If they don't think to regroup, the point-defense gunners can handle the bulk of them."

Even as he spoke, the *Profundity*'s shields coruscated with energy as cannon fire struck home. The ship rumbled and its generators strained. But it could hold.

Another X-wing blinked out of existence on the tactical display, then another. A rebel freighter, desperately evading TIE fire, skimmed the Scarif shield until its hull crumpled and its burning components rolled and bounced across the energy field. One of the Hammerheads, caught between the two Star Destroyers, momentarily lost its overtaxed deflectors and signaled for help as turbolasers left blackened, burning holes in its sides. Raddus observed the carnage patiently and waited for an opportunity to change the course of the battle; waited for an insight that he could apply with the precision of a knife.

He thought again about the dead, and how Mothma and Merrick might react. Maybe humans felt loss more keenly. They spawned so rarely and so few. His own grandchildren numbered in the dozens, and though he loved each he knew some would never come of age.

The death of individuals was no tragedy in battle. It was the death of hundreds that would haunt him.

He listened to cries of despair on the starfighters' frequency and an anguished scream as Red Five was torn apart. The *Profundity*'s shields flashed constantly now. The chatter among the bridge crewmembers was growing louder and more frantic.

"We're having no effect on the shield gate," the lieutenant said. "And we're sustaining heavy losses, Admiral."

"I'm aware," Raddus said. And he was, but the state of the battle had not changed. He had to assume Erso was still on the ground, still working to obtain the Death Star schematics that would reveal the weakness she'd promised.

He could not withdraw. He could expect no allied reinforcements. His fleet was crewed by the best officers the Rebellion could provide.

He waited for opportunity. For insight. For an error.

Then he saw it, and cried orders so swiftly it seemed to stun the crew. "All ships nearby, close to support the *Heartbound* and *Deviant*! Match current trajectories! Demand that Destroyer's attention!"

One of the Star Destroyers had allowed itself to be flanked on two sides while leaving its forward firing arc empty. Its weapons had been almost entirely diverted to port and starboard. Raddus was ready to shout another command, but Gold Squadron recognized the opening and he heard a voice on the comm: "Y-wings, on me! Path is clear!"

The bomber wing, barely out of its last attack run against the shield gate, altered course and powered directly toward the exposed front of the Destroyer. TIE fighters pursued, faster than the bombers but unprepared to pull away from their defense of the gate. The Destroyer itself recognized the danger, attempted to swing away and simultaneously bring its guns to bear, but far too late. The Y-wings converged and flew so close to the Imperial vessel that the tactical displays couldn't differentiate them from the Destroyer's mass.

"Ion torpedoes away," the wing leader declared. Raddus called up a visual and watched the Y-wings climb out of the attack, illuminated by bright electric bursts that crawled across the Destroyer's surface. Lightning silently ravaged Imperial deflector dishes and weapon emplacements. The glow of mighty ion engines went dark.

"They're down, sir!" the lieutenant called. "The Destroyer has lost power!"

"Press the attack," Raddus said, calm as ever. "Maintain fire against the remaining Destroyer, but divert available ships to the orbital station. Let's see how much the shield gate can take."

Now the state of the battle had changed. But time was still working against them. Sooner or later, Imperial reinforcements would come. Rebels would continue to die.

What are you doing, Rogue One?

Tonc had insisted on dispersing his troops around the landing pad. "If you get caught out there, we're not going to do any good guarding the shuttle. You say you need to talk to the fleet to get the data tape offworld? Fine. That means we protect you like we would the tape."

Bodhi had tried to argue, but he'd mumbled only a few words before Tonc's people had hurried out. "Wait for our signal," Tonc had said, gripping Bodhi tight by the shoulder. "When the way is clear, run fast as you can." Then he, too, had gone.

Now Bodhi adjusted the straps of the cable spool, looking out from the boarding ramp and listening to the thunder of starfighters overhead. A momentary fancy put him in a world where he'd scored higher, *much* higher at the Imperial flight academy; a world where he'd been assigned to TIE duty, and where he was the one shooting at invading X-wings on Scarif.

His mouth was dry and his heart was pounding. He wasn't a soldier.

One of the rebels gave a hand signal from across the landing pad. Bodhi ran.

Heat hit him like a wall—not just the heat of the sun, but the hot flecks carried by the smoke of the battle. The shuttle had filtered out the worst of it before; now Bodhi felt sweat dampen his flight suit, had to breathe openmouthed to draw in enough of the stinking air. Each impact of his boots on metal jostled the spool on his back, caused the straps to slip a little lower until he was fumbling to right them as he moved. He'd meant to keep his head down to avoid being spotted, but he couldn't stay low and manage the spool at the same time. He could only hope that no one but Tonc and the rebels was watching.

He turned a corner around a stack of cargo crates and crouched beside the network console. He didn't take the time to look around; he tugged the end of the cable in one hand, slammed it into place, and stayed in position only as long as it took for the console to register and accept the connection. After that, he spun about and charged back the way he'd come.

His legs were already sore, but each step became easier as the cable unspooled behind him. He was almost at the shuttle when he was suddenly jerked back; he nearly lost his balance, stumbled around, and saw that the spool had run out.

No. No, no, no. He'd checked the length beforehand. He'd been *careful.* Which meant the cable had snagged somewhere, probably on one of the cargo crates. He almost laughed. He saved the energy for the run.

With cable wriggling behind him, still attached to his back, he retraced his steps until he found the kink—as he'd expected, under the corner of a crate. He knelt to prize out the cable, intending to run it over the crate to give him the extra length he needed.

He didn't get the chance. "Hey, you!" an electronic voice called. Bodhi squeezed the cable tight in his hands. "Identify yourself!"

He unclenched his hands and let the cable drop. He stood slowly and faced the stormtrooper closest to him as others nearby observed. "I can explain—" he started, but he never got a chance to finish. Red blaster bolts flashed around him and the stormtroopers staggered and fell.

The stream of bolts didn't stop, however. Bodhi dropped to his knees and saw more troopers racing toward the landing pad, firing in the direction of Tonc and his men. He lifted the cable again and looked toward the shuttle. It seemed as far away as the Citadel or the stars.

The broad shaft of the data vault rose half a dozen stories inside the Citadel. In the center of the shaft stood multiple towers of stacked data banks, each bank aglow with dim red lights indicating the storage status of ten thousand cartridges. Each cartridge, in turn, contained enough data for a lifetime of perusal—scientific treatises and bureaucratic memoranda and schematics detailed to a microscopic level. Jyn hadn't known what to imagine when her father and Bodhi had talked about the data vault, but it hadn't been *this*—not a library too vast to comprehend, not a monument to Imperial atrocities grander than anything she'd ever encountered.

Every book Jyn's father had ever read to her, every history of every planet she'd ever visited, could have fit on one of those tapes. And every one of them held some dark secret of the Empire.

The vault shaft proper was divided from a control room by a broad glass viewport. Cassian suppressed his awe and his vertigo faster than Jyn and headed straight for the main console. Jyn shivered at the icy air, like a refrigeration unit or a morgue. She followed Cassian and tried to think of worse places to die.

"Schematics bank," K-2's voice announced through the console. "Data tower two."

"How do I *find* that?" Cassian asked.

"Searching," K-2 replied. "I can locate the tape, but you'll need the handles for extraction."

Handles? Jyn scanned the console, spotted a bewildering set of mechanical manipulators.

Cassian looked equally nonplussed. "What are we supposed to do with these?"

Jyn leaned over the console, propping herself with a knee and peering through the viewport into the upper reaches of the vault. Cassian doffed his officer's cap and tugged off his gloves before fumbling with the manipulators; once he began, Jyn spotted a mechanical arm rising rapidly through the tower, turning to one bank of tapes after the next. "Figure it out fast," she muttered, and slid back to the control room floor. "There's a whole fleet waiting on us."

"Schematics bank," Cassian muttered. "Data tower two."

Servos whined loudly and metal roared. Jyn turned in time to see the vault door clamp shut. The air seemed more frigid than before. K-2's voice came through the comm only faintly, as if he were speaking at a distance: "The rebels! They went . . . over there."

Jyn remembered the droid's awkward, unconvincing dissembling in the Holy Quarter on Jedha. *Damn.* Had the Imperials found them? If they were trapped now, everything happening outside would be for nothing . . .

"K-2?" Cassian grimaced, looking from the manipulator controls to the comm. "What's going on out there?"

The comm growled with indecipherable static. Jyn saw something new flash across Cassian's expression. He was afraid—not intellectually afraid, not afraid of failing the mission, but afraid for K-2.

Afraid for his friend.

"Keep moving the arm," she murmured, and searched the console for a readout. She tapped a key and found it: a registry of cartridges in each bank. "You fly, I'll navigate."

Cassian's grip visibly tensed as they heard a series of noises very much like blaster shots.

Was this *hope*? Facing fear after fear, for oneself and for friends and for the galaxy, all out of some desperate need to accomplish the impossible?

Maybe, Jyn thought, she'd been better off without it. *If you were alive, Papa, I'd have a lot to blame you for.*

"Hyperspace Tracking," she read off the screen as the arm whirred about the tower. "Navigational Systems, Deep Core Cartography—" The vault was arranged by subject, clearly; beyond that she hadn't a clue how to search. Maybe there was an index somewhere, but Saw Gerrera's training hadn't prepared her to serve as a data librarian.

"Two screens down," K-2's voice announced, as if he'd never stopped speaking. Cassian parted his lips and Jyn raised a hand, silenced him and urged him back to the controls. The catalog scrolled rapidly on her screen as the arm kept moving. "Structural Engineering," the droid said. "Open that!"

"Kay-Tu!" Cassian snapped. The arm stationed itself at a cartridge bank. "Tell me what's happening!"

Jyn's screen switched to a listing of tapes, once again organized in no fashion she could discern. Maybe they had identification tags she wasn't seeing. Or maybe it was yet another layer of security; hard to rob the vault if you couldn't find what you were looking for.

"My riot control protocols are now active," K-2 said. "But the situation is well in hand?"

Jyn winced at the self-conscious lie of a question. There was nothing she could do from the control room.

She spoke sternly, demanding Cassian's attention as she read from the screen. "Project code names: Stellarsphere. Mark Omega. Pax Aurora . . ." Were all of them weapons like the Death Star, designed for terror and genocide? Had her father known about the others? She couldn't afford to think about it—there were too many horrors down that road. "War-Mantle. Cluster-Prism. Black-Saber."

And she stopped.

The next name stood out with burning intensity, so obvious she might have found it by touch.

"What?" Cassian asked.

"Stardust," Jyn said. "It's that one."

"How do you know that?" Curiosity and urgency mixed in his voice, as if he wanted to say: *Be sure.*

Jyn was sure. "I know because it's me."

Cassian looked at her with astonishment. Then he turned back to the console, gripped the controls fiercely. "Kay, we need the file for Stardust!"

The comm was full of noise, inchoate and intermixed, like a war zone filtered through a downpour. No sound came through the solid vault door. The arm, already stationed at its proper data bank, maneuvered among the cartridges and reached out needfully. "Stardust," K-2 said, and Jyn heard *strain* in the droid's voice.

Cassian still clutched the handles. Jyn couldn't tell whether Cassian or K-2SO was performing the final maneuver. "That's it," she said. "You almost have it . . ."

The arm's manipulators closed around the cartridge and pulled.

Then the lights of the control room went out, leaving the console, Cassian, and Jyn illuminated only by the sinister red glow of the vault shaft through the viewport. The refrigerated air pricked at Jyn's skin, arousing gooseflesh down her arms and spine. The comm didn't stop its static shrieking—until a moment and an eternity later, it did.

"Kay!" Cassian screamed into the silence, hunched over the console.

Jyn stared up at the rigid arm clinging to its data cartridge high above. In the artificial midnight of the control room, the tower shaft seemed very much like a cave.

K-2SO's reprogramming by Cassian Andor had stripped the droid of certain ineffable qualities. He remembered, as if at a great distance, a sort of *conviction* that had come with serving the Galactic Empire.

He remembered, too, the pride and confidence that had come with fulfilling exactly the duties he was designed for—with knowing that every servomotor and every processing cycle contributed to enforcing his Imperial masters' edicts. Cassian had denied him that exquisite sense of *purpose* and replaced it with individuality. With individuality came doubt and cynicism: an awareness not only of the odds of success or failure but of those outcomes' repercussions.

Cassian had killed K-2SO (whose true designation was far longer and far grander, rich with meaning and history that described his factory of origin, the date and time of his initialization, and more) and brought him back both smaller and larger than he had been. K-2SO did not mourn for his old self, but there were times he grew wistful over what he had been.

When the first stormtroopers had entered the antechamber to the data vault, K-2SO had suppressed his hardcoded obedience instinct, forced himself to attempt deceit (to little effect, despite having watched Cassian lie masterfully time and again), and finally resorted to activating his enforcement protocols. He had severed his connection to the console while leaving the comm open, and—after eliminating his opponents through force and a superbly aimed blaster bolt—spent twenty-seven milliseconds considering whether to return to the console at all. K-2SO was not a data pilot. He was not an astromech unit. The joyful rush of utilizing long-neglected skills was, in its way, intoxicating.

He could have abandoned Cassian and Jyn to proceed with further enforcement. He chose not to.

During this initial skirmish, K-2SO also suffered damage to the carboplast-composite casing of his midsection. The blaster shot itself did not harm anything vital, but the heat of the burnt casing melted a length of interior wiring. He rerouted his functions and continued.

He had attempted to comfort Cassian when his master asked for an update. This particular dissemblance was, on reflection, a poor use of resources; it diverted K-2SO's attention from an increasingly variable combat situation as well as his attempt to locate the Death Star technical schematics. As additional stormtroopers entered the antechamber, K-2SO had deactivated his self-preservation warnings, maintained his connection to the console, and savored the pleasures of wielding a personal energy weapon.

At that time, he also took several additional blaster shots to nonvital sections of his chassis. Rerouting his functions was becoming more difficult.

After this, two equally unavoidable complications arose nearly simultaneously:

First, a stormtrooper (K-2SO identified her as TK-4012 but resisted the urge to download her Citadel personnel file) fired a blaster bolt that impacted just over four centimeters off K-2SO's programming port access door—a normally nonvital area through which K-2SO had rerouted multiple vital functions. The irony was not lost on him. He estimated he now had well over twelve seconds before a cascade failure resulted in his permanent deactivation.

Second, another stormtrooper (unidentified) fired a poorly aimed burst that delivered multiple particle bolts into the control console. Despite the Citadel's unusually redundant systems, K-2SO found himself unable to access various vault mechanisms.

With approximately twelve seconds until total shutdown, K-2SO considered his options while Cassian screamed his name.

He loosely projected eighty-nine ways to prolong his own existence (for periods ranging from point-eight milliseconds to forty-three days). Suspecting all of them would involve the capture or execution of Cassian Andor and Jyn Erso, he dismissed them without detailed study.

He reexamined his mission parameters and projected only two ways that Cassian and Jyn might retrieve their desired data cartridge and escape Scarif. Upon refinement, both appeared infinitesimally unlikely. K-2SO reexamined his parameters a second time (at a cost of several milliseconds) and deprioritized the survival of Cassian Andor and Jyn Erso.

He actively denied himself any opportunity to mourn or reflect. He chose to eschew further loose projections and estimations in favor of detailed simulations and hypotheticals.

He began with this premise: Cassian and Jyn now had the opportunity to manually recover the data cartridge.

With approximately nine seconds until total shutdown, K-2SO activated his vocoder assembly and spoke into the comm: *"Climb!"*

Retrieving the cartridge was *not* sufficient for mission success; the Death Star technical schematics needed to be relayed to rebel agents off Scarif.

This would be difficult so long as Cassian and Jyn were trapped. K-2SO had no way to free them.

He made internal inquiries. Could the data be transmitted to the Rebellion directly? The amount of data stored on a single cartridge was vast; secure transmission to Yavin 4 was out of the question under even ideal circumstances. These circumstances were *not* ideal, but a communications system was available.

"Climb the tower!" K-2SO said. He did not take conscious note of the blaster bolts blazing around him. *"Send the plans to the fleet!"*

Even the Citadel's communications tower could not transmit an entire data cartridge with the shield gate in place. But Cassian had already taken measures, through Bodhi Rook, to open the gate.

Had Cassian foreseen this scenario?

"If they open the shield gate—" K-2SO's protocol systems endowed his words with extreme emphasis. *"—you can broadcast from the tower!"*

With approximately three seconds until total shutdown, K-2SO listened to Cassian's voice cry his name one last time. Then, without regret, the droid turned his weapon on the console. The comm cut out. With the controls now reduced to a melted plastoid-metal compound, the stormtroopers would have considerable difficulty entering the vault.

With one second left until total shutdown, K-2SO chose to mentally simulate an impossible scenario in which Cassian Andor escaped alive.

The simulation pleased him.

SUPPLEMENTAL DATA: SUNSET PRAYER

[Document #JP0103 ("Sunset Prayer of the Guardians of the Whills"), recovered from the outskirts of NiJedha; provenance uncertain.]

> In darkness, cold.
> In light, cold.
> The old sun brings no heat.
> But there is heat in breath and life.
> In life, there is the Force.
> In the Force, there is life.
> And the Force is eternal.

CHAPTER 20

KRENNIC TRIED TO FOCUS ON Galen Erso's communications archive. He scrolled through endless memoranda and dispatches while General Ramda's men shouted updates and orders across the command center. There was nothing Krennic could do for the stormtroopers on the beach or for Admiral Gorin's fleet; nothing but dig for the truth of Galen's treachery among engineering personnel transfer requests and complaints about thermal exhaust ports.

Galen had set this in motion. If he had reached out to allies in the Rebellion, sent the traitorous pilot to contact those allies on Jedha, summoned those allies to Eadu, arranged for them to hound Krennic even after Galen was rotting in a mudhole of a mass grave . . .

Krennic stopped short. He remembered now, on the Eadu platform—a flash of dark hair and a face covered in ashes. He recalled the voice saying: *You'll never win.* But it was Lyra who spoke, not Galen.

"—unauthorized access at the data vault."

His attention left his console, snapped into crisp focus on one of Ramda's lieutenants. *"What?"*

"It's just come in, sir." The lieutenant's head twitched to one side, as if he were seeking support. No one came to his aid. "There's a security team already in place, but no details about the intruders. We're waiting for more now—"

Krennic shut out the man's nattering. The rebels were inside the Citadel. They were *inside the vault.* They were determined to steal the schematics, to find an imaginary weakness, no matter how many lives they lost. They were determined to *haunt* him on Galen's behalf.

And Ramda wasn't up to the task. The shield gate was shut and escape was surely impossible; yet too many impossibilities had already occurred for one day.

He hurled his words behind him as he marched toward the stairs. "Send my guard squadron to the battle! Two men with me!" There was someone in his way; he roughly shoved the body to one side, not bothering to identify the man's face. "And get that beach under control!"

He didn't wait for acknowledgment. As he emerged from the command center, two death troopers fell into step behind him and he thought of another day long before: another planetfall; another squad of troopers; and another danger to his life spawned by Galen. That day on Lah'mu had ended in victory, too.

Orson Krennic was going to war.

Tonc was dead. Bodhi hadn't seen it happen; he'd crouched low to shuffle half a pace forward along his sheltering wall of cargo crates, and when he'd looked up and across the landing pad he'd spied the soldier motionless on the ground. He fought down the urge to rush to Tonc's side, to yell for aid from the rebels who still survived; there was nothing he could do. People were dying all around. And the stormtroopers kept coming.

A blaster bolt crackled over Bodhi's head, close enough for him to feel the heat and smell the ozone of vaporized atmosphere. He

smoothed the cable on the ground with one hand and looked help-
lessly toward the shuttle.

"Bodhi? Are you there?" Bodhi snatched the comlink from his
pocket. Cassian's voice sounded hoarse. "Talk to me!"

"I'm here!" Bodhi said. "I'm here. I'm pinned down. I can't get to
the ship, I can't plug in!" He didn't mean to sound desperate, but what
was the point of lying? The situation was bad. It wasn't his *fault*, but
it was bad.

"You have to!" Bodhi had heard Cassian angry, heard him determined, but this was something new—almost pained. "We need the
fleet, Bodhi. You have to get a message out!"

"Are you okay?" A thought too awful to dwell on crossed Bodhi's
mind. "Is Jyn okay?"

"We're fine," Cassian snapped. For a moment Bodhi heard only
long, ragged breaths. Then Cassian seemed to steady. "We're changing tactics. We're not sure—we may not make it back for extraction,
but we can try to transmit the schematics from the comm tower."

Bodhi wanted to argue—what *exactly* did *we may not make it back*
mean? But Cassian kept talking. "That's a *lot* of information," Cassian
said, "and even the tower won't be able to push it through the shield
without data loss. Tell me I'm right about this, Bodhi!"

Bodhi forced himself to concentrate. Audio was one thing, but
sending a data cartridge through the shield would be like trying to
broadcast it across the galaxy. Too much data, too much interference.
"You're right," he said. "You're right."

"So you need to let the fleet know," Cassian said. "They need to get
in position to receive, because I doubt we'll get two shots. And they
need to hit that gate! If the shield's open, we can send the plans!"

"What about—" *What about you? What about Jyn?* But Cassian
sounded ready to crack under the strain, and Bodhi couldn't bring
himself to keep the man on the line. "All right," he wheezed. "I'll find
a way."

He roughly pocketed his link and looked toward the shuttle again.
The barrage of blasterfire wasn't stopping, wasn't even *slowing*. Tonc's
soldiers weren't winning. Maybe, Bodhi thought, if Baze and Chirrut

returned to the landing pad—but no. He'd already sent them to the master switch.

How long did he have before the pad was overrun?

Don't talk yourself out of it.

Just go!

His first stride almost sent him sprawling as he went from a crouch to a barreling run. He caught himself and kept going, listened to the cable hiss and writhe behind him as it trailed from the spool on his back, saw flash after flash of crimson scorch the air between him and the shuttle. A bolt struck the undercarriage of the vessel as he approached, dropped a burning spark between his forehead and his work goggles; he ignored the distraction and the pain and climbed the ramp, dashed across the cabin to a terminal. He fumbled at the spool with sweat-slick hands, wrested the cable free, and plugged it into the socket.

The terminal registered the connection. Bodhi screamed in triumph, ignoring the warning light that indicated the ship's computer couldn't find the comm tower. Baze and Chirrut and Melshi's team would get to the master switch *soon*. Bodhi would tell the fleet about their new strategy.

And when Cassian and Jyn were atop the tower, transmitting the tape? He'd swoop in and find them like he had on Eadu, and they'd all make for the open shield gate together.

That was the plan. That was *his* plan. He hoped Tonc would approve.

He hoped his comrades could work fast.

How long now, before the pad was overrun?

Cassian's hands were trembling, but his eyes were steady as he lowered his comlink. "Bodhi's working on the fleet. He'll get it done."

The vault control room remained dark save for the red glow of the shaft. The refrigerated air was heating rapidly and filling with a sharp, metallic stench; Jyn could hear the muffled hiss of plasma torches on the far side of the sealed vault door.

We may not make it back. She'd heard Cassian say the words to Bodhi, but not to her.

She craned her neck and looked up the shaft, up the center of the Citadel Tower. Her father's data tape was there. Somewhere, beyond the red glow, there was also a way out.

"Step back," she said, and gestured Cassian away from the viewport.

She drew her pistol, took steady aim with both hands, and fired into the glass. Jagged shards, melting and blackened, exploded onto the console and down into the vault shaft. They rang like wind chimes. Jyn stepped forward to study the broken pane, then began stripping off the helmet, bulky chestpiece, and heavy overclothes of her security uniform. She was long past the point of disguises, and she didn't need extra weight during a climb. Cassian followed her lead, pulling off his officer's jacket.

When she had stripped down to vest and pants, Jyn scanned the shaft for grips. Data cartridge extraction handles protruded at regular intervals, and the stacked data banks jutted with slender metal flanges. It wouldn't be an easy climb, but she decided against shedding her boots for extra traction—she remembered one very long night after leaving Saw that had ended in bloody soles, broken toenails, and a valuable lesson about proper footwear.

"Come on," she said. *Before it all closes in,* she nearly added. But Cassian didn't see the cave walls.

She mounted the console, bent her knees, and leapt across the gap to the nearest data tower. She caught a set of cartridge handles and scrambled to find footholds. After an instant, she felt the cartridges shaking under her hands and feared she might pull them loose; but it was only the vibration of the data banks themselves, rattling with the mechanisms that cooled and cataloged the tapes.

She climbed a meter, testing the force she could apply to the tapes and feeling out the distance between them. She looked down into the yawning darkness in time to see Cassian leap tentatively out of the control room. He, too, caught hold.

Jyn looked back up, fixed the retrieval arm in her sights, and began ascending in earnest.

She heard Cassian struggling behind her over the noise of recirculating air. She knew she should have said something more to him: *I'm sorry about Kay-Tu,* or *We might still get off Scarif,* or *We're going to finish this.* But she'd never been much good at commiseration or encouragement, and she'd spent so many words—on the Alliance councilors, on the rebel soldiers—in the past days. She didn't have the strength to spare for him; just the drive to haul herself up one row of cartridges at a time, drag herself away from the darkness and toward the hope of light.

She counted fifteen rows to the retrieval arm, then ten. She glimpsed a doorway in the shaft wall—secure maintenance access, she imagined—but she wrote it off as a means of escape. The Empire had to be watching. Five rows more. Her shoulders began to ache, and her wrists felt stiff from trying to grip the cartridges without yanking them free. The sounds of Cassian's climb were receding below, but she couldn't wait for him.

One row. Then she was perched beside the retrieval arm. It grasped the Stardust cartridge like a dead miser.

The cartridge was unlabeled, no different from any other. No different from the thousands surrounding her, except that her father had given his life to reveal it.

She wedged a boot against the stack for leverage, set a free hand on the handle of Mark Omega or Pax Aurora or Heartchopper or whatever ghastly thing the Empire's scientists had thought up, and tugged at Stardust in the hand of the machine. The frozen arm clung tight; then she jerked the tape away and the arm bobbed loosely in the air.

"I've got it!" she cried, and she did—she had it, she *had* it, and she squeezed it and brought it close enough to smell the metal over the cold, dry air. However else she'd failed, however many deaths (Saw, her father, the girl on Jedha, the *droid* who'd sacrificed himself) were her fault, she'd come this far. She was ready to shout obscenities at the universe, defiant imprecations against fate and the Force and the Empire.

Then her boot slipped and she scrambled, one-handed, to regain her holds. "Careful!" Cassian shouted from below, and she was grinning fiercely as she panted. "You okay?" he called.

She didn't answer. She was already climbing again, the cartridge safely hooked on her belt. The surge of triumphant, exultant energy faded as swiftly as it had come, leaving Jyn with only an urgent need to escape the dark. Her arms began to tremble with the strain of the ascent, her muscles recalling the agonizing climb up the landing platform on Eadu. Through the gloom she made out a warm, blinking light high above—an aperture at the top of the tower, pulsing open and closed, barely wide enough to cast shadows.

Close. So close.

Then she heard another shout beneath her. Fury mixed with alarm in Cassian's voice as he cried her name.

Jyn dropped a hand and twisted just in time for a flash of crimson to obscure her vision—to spark against the stack of data banks and leave a mass of melted polymer where her cartridge-handhold had been. Standing in the maintenance entrance were three figures out of a familiar nightmare: the man in white and his stormtroopers in black.

They had seemed impossible on Eadu, so much so she'd nearly forgotten them in the aftermath—written them off as an exaggeration, a trick of an exhausted mind wrapping a figment from her past around a sliver of reality. Now they'd returned to send her plummeting into madness.

The man in white looked up. She wanted to scream; instead she swallowed the sound, like she had when her mother died. She wanted to freeze, to hide inside herself and drop away from the data banks.

And if she did?

Stardust, the cartridge against her hip, would be buried in her cave along with her own remains.

She tore her gaze from the man in white and looked back up the shaft. Captivated by dream logic, knowing it was untrue, she thought: *If I make it to the light, I can escape forever.*

Climb!

Crimson burst around Jyn as she swung on the cartridges, trying to rotate herself to the far side of the data stack and find cover from her attackers. She caught a glimpse of Cassian attempting to do the same; but he was slower, and he'd drawn his own pistol, firing wildly at the doorway. One shot landed miraculously, sending a black-clad figure over the edge and into the depths. The fall dragged her further into reality—whatever they were, *whoever* the men in black and white were, they were people and not dreams. They could die, and so could she.

The Imperials targeted only Cassian now. He swung desperately toward cover as sparks spilled off metal all around him. Jyn started to call to him, but he cried out louder, "Keep going! Keep going!"

She reached a trembling hand toward her pistol. She could die. So could they.

She knew she had to climb.

The decision was taken from her. The second stormtrooper took a hit as a bolt flashed toward Cassian. Trooper and spy fell together; Jyn couldn't tell whether Cassian had been struck or if he'd simply lost his grip, but he plunged out of view without a scream or a word. She nearly loosed her clutching fingers, nearly followed him into the abyss, but a swell of vertigo shocked her out of her horror and impelled her to cling more tightly to the stack.

Cassian was dead, like so many others. So many taken by the man in white.

She had to escape.

Climb!

Scarif was burning. Dueling starfighters sent cannon fire and torn metal raining onto the beaches. The mountainous corpses of Imperial walkers bled smoke that shrouded whole swaths of jungle. Reinforcements delivered by rebel U-wings had replaced the fallen with new soldiers; and these were cut down in turn by newly arrived stormtroopers in black, men and women who moved with the sober calm of executioners, picking off their foes one by one.

Baze Malbus waded through the inferno in silence, untouched by fear or grief or particle bolts. He followed Melshi and Chirrut, trusting them to see to the mission, and guarded lives where he could. He snapped off swift, precise shots, downing too many stormtroopers to count.

He felt no responsibility for the allies he could not save. He had made no oaths, promised safety to no one. He failed to stop a storm-trooper from ambushing a dark-haired woman and leaving her dying in the shallow tide; he failed to drag a sniper his own age out of view of a strafing TIE fighter. He had spilled more blood in a day than he had thought possible, and though his generator hummed warningly and his muscles felt stiff as dried leather, he was ready to fight on. He would endure through the night if need be, if that was what Jyn Erso required.

And if the mission failed? If there was redemption to be found through killing, he had surely already found it. But he would fight on nonetheless.

Melshi's tattered platoon was running toward the Citadel on its quest for Bodhi's "master switch." Just within the outer perimeter, Melshi promised, was a bunker complex containing what they sought. Baze did not know *why* the switch was important—something about the rebel fleet—but as he hurried beside his comrades on the beach, he grimly marveled that the fate of planets might be altered by such a trivial thing.

A U-wing was toppling from the sky. It hit sand a stone's throw ahead of the rebels, sending a shock wave along the ground and plowing a deep trench. Mud and fire splashed as metal ruptured and wailed. As the rebels approached, a salvo of blaster bolts tore through the wreckage and the flames; through gaps in the burning metal, Baze spotted more of the black-clad stormtroopers closing in. He loosed a barrage of cannon fire that did little good—the stormtroop-ers crept low to the ground, eliminating their targets slowly and cer-tainly as Melshi waved his people frantically toward the bunker complex.

The soldiers sprinted away from the water and the wreckage, ex-posed and vulnerable. One rebel fell, then another. Chirrut leapt be-tween the troopers' bolts as if their passing pushed him aside, but his fortune was not others' fortune. Baze vaulted over more than one corpse, turned back to spray cannon blasts at the troopers, then raced into the shadow of the Citadel Tower. He saw Melshi attempt to haul an ally to safety and take a bolt to the side for his troubles; stinking badly of melted fabric and burnt flesh, Melshi hobbled with Baze into the relative shelter of the squat bunker.

Only four warriors remained. Chirrut stood near the front of the spartan bunker with Baze, panting and leaning lightly on his staff. A broad sniper—someone had called him Sefla—took potshots at the troopers through the bunker's narrow embrasures as the enemy formed a perimeter. Melshi struggled to stay upright in the far corner.

There might have been other survivors scattered across the battlefield. Or Baze, Chirrut, Sefla, and Melshi might have been the last.

An urgent voice issued from Melshi's comlink: "Melshi, come in, please! Anybody out there! Rogue One! Rogue One! Anybody!"

Chirrut raised his ornate lightbow, firing at the stormtroopers as they forced Sefla down and into cover. The stormtroopers adjusted and targeted Chirrut; Baze replaced Chirrut, as Chirrut had replaced Sefla, who now prepared to replace Baze. Together, Baze thought, they could hold off the Imperials for several minutes. Likely no longer.

"They've got the plans." The comm spoke with Bodhi's voice, mixing triumph and terror. "I'm tied in at my end, but I can't hold out forever. We lost Tonc . . ."

The troopers had established a broad circle around the bunker and the adjoining equipment—consoles and charging stations and signal relays. Baze snarled in satisfaction—*she has the plans!*—as he fired a shot that took a man off his feet, then jerked back his head as his foes returned a volley.

"Rogue One! Can anyone hear me out there? I've got my end tied in, I need an open line—"

"Hang on!" Melshi gasped, and tossed his comlink to the ground before beckoning to Baze. He stank of death. Baze crossed to his side and let Chirrut and Sefla take up the slaying work.

"Be quick," Baze said.

Melshi nodded, his eyes wide and glittering. "The master switch," he said. "It's out there, at that console." He raised a trembling finger and pointed into the kill zone.

The workstation was ten meters away. Far beyond reach.

Before anyone could react, Sefla was out of the bunker, dashing toward the console, pumping arms and legs as sweat dripped down his back. He moved with brisk, brave certainty. He died in an instant, cut down by a dozen particle bolts, accomplishing nothing.

Baze looked back to Melshi. He had slumped to the ground beside his comlink.

Maybe it would have been better, Baze thought, *to be killed by the walkers.* To die cowering in sight of an unachievable victory was a humiliation.

Maybe death always was.

Baze raised his cannon. Perhaps there were other survivors. Perhaps if he downed enough troopers, reinforcements might reach Bodhi's master switch. A final slaughter was all he could offer Jyn Erso and the dead of Jedha; all he could offer to torment the Empire one last time.

But before Baze could fire, Chirrut rose from the bunker and stepped into sunlight.

Chirrut Îmwe felt the warmth of an alien star on his skin and a sea breeze pawing at his robes. The heel of his staff dug into hard-packed sand. Beneath the odors of conflagration and death was the perfume of jungle flowers and the sweet stink of dirt beetles. Beyond the electric snap of blaster bolts he heard a high-pitched chittering—the noise of a beast he had never encountered. To this cacophony, he added his voice:

"I am one with the Force and the Force is with me."

Whatever Chirrut had become in his life—and without the temple he could not truly be a Guardian of the Whills; without joy and frivolity he could not be a clown and jokester among sober peers; without the Holy City he could not be a protector of his beloved world—whatever he *was,* he was not a warrior at heart, and the events of the day had eroded his spirit. While Baze, his brother and ward, had embraced his role with vicious resolve, Chirrut had fought and run and killed because fighting and running and killing were necessary.

Now they were necessary no longer, and he was glad.

"I am one with the Force," he said again, "and the Force is with me." The words echoed inside him. *I am one with the Force and the Force is with me.*

Baze yelled his name from the bunker. Chirrut did not stop.

He felt hot bolts whip past him, heard leather gloves squeeze metal triggers, and turned his body as if shouldering his way through a crowd. He tapped the heel of his staff, feeling his way toward the console by the traces of buried cables. He listened for telltale echoes, where the noise of the battle resounded off terminals and equipment.

He did all this without thinking. The art of zama-shiwo, the inward eye of the outward hand, attuned his breathing and heartbeat to his chant. It was his chant that guided his motions, controlled his pace as he strode forward. *I am one with the Force and the Force is with me.*

"Chirrut!" Baze called. "Come back!"

Baze was terrified. Chirrut was not. In the instant before he'd risen from the bunker, he'd questioned his own wisdom: How might he separate the will of the Force from *his* will, *his* ego, demanding action where action was unneeded? But there was no doubt in his heart now. The Force expressed itself through simplicity, and all it asked of him was to walk.

I am one with the Force and the Force is with me.

His staff rapped metal. The side of a console. The chant guided him to its front and he glided his fingers across buttons and readouts. He touched a broad, hinged handle recessed in the console: a *master switch,* if ever there'd been one. A particle bolt reverberated centimeters from Chirrut's left ear as he urged the switch forward and felt it lock into place.

I am one with the Force and the Force is with me.

He smiled softly and thought of Bodhi, the strange pilot who smelled of Jedha beneath his Imperial suit.

Chirrut's chant was faltering now. With the switch activated, his path had become obscured. He listened to the storm of blasterfire and heard Baze's voice again: "Chirrut! Come here!" So he turned toward Baze and the bunker and began retracing his steps. The rhythm of his breath was off, and the thousand noises and odors and sensations all about him failed to coalesce; each tugged at him, insisted on his exclusive attention.

Then there was only one noise: a terrible thunder like the world splitting open. He was driven forward as pain flashed through his old bones and every injury he'd ever suffered ignited. Somehow, as Chirrut impacted the dirt and rolled to one side, he was aware of Baze shouting his name again.

He couldn't feel his staff. He couldn't feel his *hand,* except for a terrible throbbing and its numb weight at the end of his arm. But the art of zama-shiwo had much to say about controlling pain, and Chirrut permitted his blood to spill without experiencing suffering. The violence inflicted upon his body troubled him less than the violence he had inflicted upon others.

He was dying, of course.

He felt Baze's heavy, familiar tread pound the ground, smelled his brother's sweat as he leaned close. He wanted to say, *Baze! My eyes—I can't see!* but Baze Malbus had always needed comfort more than humor.

"Chirrut," Baze murmured. "Don't go. Don't go. I'm here . . ."

He wondered for a moment how Baze had crossed the battlefield to reach him. But of course the Force had reunited them before the end.

Baze's callused fingers rubbed life into the back of Chirrut's hand. "It's okay," Chirrut said. "It's okay. Look for the Force and you will always find me."

He tried to smile, but he was no longer sure he could.

The words of the chant echoed in Chirrut Îmwe's heart once more before he died:

I am one with the Force and the Force is with me.

· · ·

The stormtroopers were closing around the cargo shuttle. Bodhi could tell because, not infrequently, a particle bolt would blaze up the boarding ramp and impact the interior bulkhead, raining sparks onto the floor. Bodhi didn't know how many of Tonc's people were still alive, fighting desperately to hold their foes back; nor did he know whether, at any moment, someone might sever the cable snaking up the ramp to the communications console.

He was almost out of time, and all he could think was: *I'm sorry, everyone. Sorry for promising what I couldn't deliver. Sorry for not coming up with a better plan.*

He'd tried. That counted for something, didn't it?

When the console readouts updated to indicate a connection between the ship and the Scarif communications tower, he wanted to weep with joy.

Instead, he hunched over the unit, adjusted his frequencies, and prayed someone would hear him. "Okay, okay," he began. "This is Rogue One calling the rebel fleet!"

He heard only the soft hiss of static in reply.

They didn't even know he was trying to reach them. They were fighting for their lives, and he was broadcasting aimlessly—as if some bridge officer was going to notice and pick up mid-battle.

"This is Rogue One, calling any Alliance ships that can hear me!" He fought back the tremor in his voice. "Is there anybody up there? This is Rogue One!"

I did my part, he told himself. *I got a signal out. I'm sorry if no one was listening . . .*

He thought of Jyn, of Cassian, of Baze and Chirrut and Tonc. He wondered if any of them would be capable of forgiving his failures.

Galen had forgiven him, at least. Galen had understood the need for forgiveness better than anyone.

"This is Rogue One!" Specks of spittle dotted the console. He wiped them away with a sleeve. "Come in! Over!"

"This is Admiral Raddus aboard the *Profundity*!" The comm came to life with a roar. "Rogue One, we hear you!"

Bodhi uttered a laugh that might have been mistaken for a sob. "We have the plans!" he said—and maybe that was a lie, he couldn't know for *sure,* but he was too desperate to care. "They found the Death Star plans. They have to transmit them from the communications tower!"

He heard voices in the background—bridge officers, maybe, debating how to respond. Bodhi powered through. "You have to get in position, get ready to receive. And you have to take down the shield gate. It's the only way to get through!"

For an achingly long time, there was no answer.

"Copy you, Rogue One," the voice finally said. "We'll get it done." Then, directed not to Bodhi but to someone else on the bridge: "Call in a Hammerhead corvette. I have an idea."

The signal went dead. It didn't matter to Bodhi; he'd said what he needed to say.

The blasterfire outside had stopped. The silence was almost peaceful. Hands trembling, Bodhi straightened behind the console and glanced from the boarding ramp to the cockpit ladder. He thought of his plan to take off, to fly through the gauntlet of TIEs to rescue Jyn and Cassian from the communications tower. He thought of the strain he'd heard in Cassian's voice, and of his last signal to Melshi— the one that had gone unanswered.

If he didn't have the chance . . . he'd done enough. It was okay.

"This is for you, Galen," he said, and started for the ladder.

Bodhi Rook heard the ring of metal once, twice, in the cabin, and then the soft clatter of something rolling across the deck. He turned in time to glimpse the detonator. He heard nothing as the cabin flared impossibly bright.

Like a pilot should, he died with his ship.

Baze Malbus cradled the last true Guardian of the Whills in his arms and answered Chirrut's dying words. "The Force is with me," Baze said. "And I am one with the Force."

A flare rose in the distance. Something was burning on landing pad nine. In all likelihood, Bodhi Rook, too, was gone.

Gone before he had ever sent his message? Gone, and rendering Chirrut's sacrifice pointless?

Once again, the Empire had stolen meaning from Baze. He might have screamed if not for the man he held.

"The Force is with me," he repeated. "And I am with the Force."

Did he believe the words? Did it matter? Had it *ever* mattered?

The stormtroopers' perimeter was intact. They'd momentarily drawn back after murdering Chirrut, away from the smoke of the explosion; now they were closing again, sweeping their rifle scopes toward Baze. Their actions seemed interminably slow—as if time had become Baze's tormentor, so that he might suffer the anguish of a lifetime in a second.

He spoke the words, and in them he found not comfort but conviction—or the memory of conviction, as if the words were a key to the forgotten faith of his youth. The unlocked memory strangled him, wracking and intense. He knew again the significance of the Force in every breath and action, knew all he had forsaken in years past; saw the vast gulf between the Guardian he had been and the man he was now, and wept in his heart for both. He gently laid the body down and raised his cannon, identified a trooper who was tensing to fire; he sent an energy blast through the trooper's chest and sent him reeling into sand and dirt. As the rest of the squad returned a fusillade, Baze squeezed his trigger, held it and let his generator scream and his weapon writhe and buck. He alternated swift bursts and raging, aimless streams with precision killings. He advanced on the men and women who had taken his past, his home, his friend, his hope, his faith; but he did not stray far from Chirrut.

He had nowhere to go. He would not leave Chirrut now.

He recognized a pain he had felt before—the hot, half-numb agony of a blaster bolt, his nerves obliterated at the epicenter of the wound and screaming around the corona. He fell to his knees and forced himself to rise again. His body was caked in ash and sweat and he stank of burning hair, and he embraced the nightmare, raged with shot after shot until he had surely slain a hundred or a thousand stormtroopers.

It was not enough. It could never be enough to restore Chirrut or the years he'd lost.

Baze saw a dying trooper fumble for a grenade and lob it in his direction. The grenade would land short of its target; but Baze could barely stumble forward, let alone run for cover. He wrenched himself about, craned his neck to see Chirrut one last time.

When death had come for him in the shadow of the walker, he had faced it with defiance. Now there was grief.

There was no fear.

Baze Malbus died in pain, but it did not last long.

Rogue One was alive. Jyn Erso had the Death Star's schematics, and in those schematics was the chance to save the Alliance. A chance to save Mon Cala. There was no price Admiral Raddus would refuse to pay to see that chance realized.

With the disabling of one Star Destroyer, the tide of battle above Scarif had turned. Yet while the advantage belonged to the Alliance fleet, bombardment of the orbital gate station uncovered no weakness in either the field or the station itself. A prolonged siege might result in victory, but Raddus didn't doubt enemy reinforcements were en route; massive firepower might break the gate open, but the Alliance's fiercest warships lacked the catastrophic might of the Empire's.

In silently articulating the dilemma, the solution had become apparent to Raddus. He had laid out his plan to his officers and they had not questioned him. But even to Raddus's tastes, the price was high.

He had chosen the Hammerhead *Lightmaker* and its captain, Kado Oquoné, to implement his vision. Oquoné's ship had been badly damaged after being flanked by the twin Destroyers, and had since withdrawn from the field of fire to guard the line of retreat. For these reasons it would serve Raddus's purpose.

"Are you prepared, Captain?" He spoke to Oquoné from the bridge of the *Profundity,* his eyes fixed on his tactical display.

"Nonessential personnel have evacuated," Oquoné replied. "It's

just me, a skeleton crew, and a handful of droids. Course is locked."
His voice did not tremble. Raddus gave him credit for that; when he'd
explained his intent, Oquoné had reacted angrily—yet only for an
instant. Since that moment, the captain had been nothing but resolved.

"Then begin," Raddus said. The comm went silent. The *Lightmaker*'s engines pulsed as the great vessel turned—first away from the
battle, then back in a wide arc, adjusting its trajectory by fractions of
a meter as it went. Raddus had not demanded that Oquoné and his
chosen few remain aboard, but such precise work was best left with
organics instead of droids alone. Oquoné knew it as well as Raddus.

The swarm of Alliance starfighters around the second, surviving
Star Destroyer formed a loose cordon, locking the vessel in place as
larger rebel ships disengaged. These actions would leave both fighters
and command ships vulnerable to TIE counterattacks, but Raddus
had deemed that price acceptable as well.

The *Lightmaker* picked up speed as it approached the fray, pulled
by Scarif's gravity as it pushed with its engines toward the disabled
Destroyer. The second Star Destroyer seemed to realize what was
happening, but much too late; caged by Red and Gold Squadron
fighters, it could go nowhere in time to escape its fate.

Raddus watched the *Lightmaker* descend like a spear into the mass
of the disabled behemoth. Metal sheared and crumpled, and Raddus
feared for a moment that Oquoné's velocity had been too great—that
the *Lightmaker* would be dashed to nothingness and the most delicate part of the plan, still to come, had failed. Yet the Destroyer absorbed the impact and began to tumble away, its frame marred but
intact.

He spotted the motes of escape pods against the stars. He did not
dare hope that they had come from the *Lightmaker*.

The disabled Star Destroyer drifted toward its caged twin. Oquoné's
course had been set with precision. As the Alliance starfighters broke
away, the two Destroyers collided. Both ships flared with destructive
power, and both tumbled more swiftly as Scarif's gravity gripped
them. Locked together by cataclysmic devastation, their entwined

wreckage plummeted toward the inner ring of the orbital gate station.

Where the Star Destroyers struck the energy field, the shield shimmered and radiated and finally broke, dissipating like foam on the crest of a wave.

"Get us into geostationary orbit above the Citadel, now!" Raddus cried. "All fighters move to defend the *Profundity*. We *must* be in position to receive that transmission!"

The TIE fighters would concentrate on his flagship once the Empire recognized his intent. But in truth, he didn't need to hold out long. The shield gate would regenerate swiftly enough; Rogue One's window of opportunity to transmit would be narrow, and if it closed there would be no other.

Silently, Raddus pledged to name his great-grandchildren after Oquoné and the crew of the *Lightmaker*. Then he clasped his hands together to await word from Jyn Erso.

CHAPTER 21

CASSIAN WAS DEAD—ALONG WITH how many others, Jyn didn't know. The man in white who had been there for the worst moments of her life was present again. The darkness enveloped her, broken by the thousand red eyes of the data cartridges. Her arms trembled violently every time she pulled herself higher, as if ready to wrench loose from their sockets.

But she could see light above her.

Climb!

Her gloves were soaked in sweat turned cold by the data vault's refrigeration. Wedging her boots into narrow footholds over and over had left her toes numb from compression. The cartridge on her belt felt heavy enough to drag her down below the crust of Scarif.

She could see the pulsing aperture in the ceiling clearly now. A series of vents opened and shut in sequence, suctioning the warmest air from the tower. It seemed to buoy her as it wafted free.

Climb!

She caught glimpses of blue sky. She was at the top of the data stack, close enough to the first vent to put her arm through. She pictured herself making the attempt and being crushed and bloodied and broken by the pulsing door. For a single despairing moment, she couldn't bear the thought of another climb. Then the moment passed and she counted *one, two, three,* to time the movements of the vents.

Liana Hallik and Tanith and Kestrel—old names, old lives—had done braver, bolder things than this. Jyn Erso could, too.

She scrambled through a vent, leapt to the next; climbed and waited. Resting was as agonizing as motion. While she paused between apertures, counting seconds, her muscles begged for momentum or eternal stillness—not a tortuous stop-and-go. *One, two, three, go! Wait, two, three* . . . She barely noticed the air turn from frigid to warm, the balmy humidity moistening her lips and throat. *One, two, three, go!* Then there was nowhere for her to climb and she was sprawled on metal plating, the surface uncomfortably *hot* in the sunlight as she crawled forward.

She was out of the data vault. Out of the dark.

She lacked the strength to feel triumphant. She forced herself to stand, fumbled at her blaster as she searched for stormtroopers, for black-clad killers or the man in white. But she was alone atop the tower, on a broad platform in the shadow of an enormous antenna dish. Her knees knocked as she surveyed the bright sky, dense with white clouds that met the sea at the horizon.

The serenity was marred by the scream of starfighters, cannons blazing in fiery red and sickly green as rebel pursued Imperial and Imperial pursued rebel. The smell of ashes rose from somewhere far below.

Yet she was alone.

You don't have long, she told herself, and coaxed her body into motion.

She spotted a control panel built into the outer railing across from a turbolift and hobbled over to it, trying to kick life back into her legs. She didn't recognize the layout—it looked like a comm terminal, but there was no audio input and a dozen toggles she didn't recognize.

She found a slot for a data cartridge, however; half disbelieving, she probed it with her fingers before loading the Stardust tape.

The screen flashed with options and technical jargon. An authoritative, electronic voice repeated sternly: "Reset antenna alignment."

She swore and slammed a fist against the panel. She wanted to kick K-2SO for sending her here, kick him until the droid fell to pieces; and immediately, she felt sick with guilt at the image. Back aching, she leaned in to examine the screen.

She wasn't even sure what she was looking for. Had K-2SO configured the dish to send to the fleet? Had Bodhi, if he'd made contact? Was the shield down, so the antenna had to be reset in response? She didn't know, and the panel didn't tell her. But images flashed on the screen indicating another control unit off a catwalk extending from the tower platform.

Fine. We'll reset the antenna alignment.

She wasn't going to be the woman who doomed the Alliance because she couldn't figure out a damn comm panel.

Clutching her blaster tight, she made her way to the catwalk and spotted the cylindrical control unit rising at the far end. The wind sent her swaying as she stepped onto the plank, and the guardrails looked much too low to do any good. She hurried to the unit, found a dial, and turned it awkwardly between her fingers, one way and then the next, until the voice announced again: "Dish aligning."

She heard servos grind and turned to see the great antenna dish in motion. It rose and adjusted until it pointed straight overhead. "Dish aligned," the voice said. "Ready to transmit."

Please be right.

She started back along the catwalk. The shriek of a TIE fighter rose on the wind, but at first she ignored it. Then the vessel itself swept into view, descending toward the platform with its great cockpit eye fixed on her. She froze, unsure whether to run or to drop to the catwalk in the hope of hiding.

She ran, and the fighter's cannons pulsed.

Emerald light and fire stained her vision. The catwalk undulated like a flag in the wind, then dropped away altogether. The sound of ripping metal filled her ears as shrapnel tore at her legs and sleeves. Her face felt like it was aflame. She reached out desperately, felt her fingers close around *something*—the remnants of a guardrail or the underside of the twisted and dangling plank—and she screamed a breathless, silent scream as the muscles in her overtaxed shoulders seemed to tear.

The broken catwalk swung haltingly in the wind. Jyn clung as tight as she could and tried to slither upward as her sight began to return. Through a smeared and smoky filter she made out the blackened edge of the platform, barely an arm's length away.

Climb!

There were no data cartridge handles this time. No convenient footholds. The burning and sunbaked metal felt blisteringly hot against Jyn's body. She dragged herself upward a centimeter, a millimeter at a time, as the wind tried to prize her fingers free. She was close enough to touch the rim of the platform when she felt a shadow pass over her. She raised her eyes from the catwalk and saw a smudge against the blue sky that she tried to blink away.

Her eyes stung as ash mixed with tears, but the smudge only grew clearer. A perfect gray sphere hung high above the planet, its surface etched with lines like circuitry.

She hadn't *seen* it on Jedha. Not really, not in the state she'd been. But she recognized it anyway, knew it with her subconscious mind, and felt no surprise.

The Death Star had come to Scarif.

The deck shuddered lovingly as the battle station dropped out of lightspeed. Dozens of objects flashed onto the overbridge's tactical displays—Imperial and rebel vessels in conflict throughout the system—and Wilhuff Tarkin made his assessment after seconds of perusal.

The Empire was losing over Scarif, but that was about to change.

Duty officers called out status reports for their assigned sections of the Death Star. The hyperspace journey had gone smoothly and the station was ready for war. Its gunners and fighter pilots were at full alert; more Imperial ships were on their way.

"Sir, shall I begin targeting their fleet?"

There was proud enthusiasm in General Romodi's voice. Tarkin looked to the old warhorse, then shook his head. It might be amusing—even illuminating—to test the station's capabilities against a rebel armada, but now was not the day to toy with the enemy. Director Krennic, General Ramda, and Admiral Gorin had all failed to solve the problem at hand, granting the rebels opportunity after opportunity to seize the schematics from the Citadel.

At last report, the data vault itself had been breached. It was a show of incompetence so great that Tarkin was almost curious to know how Krennic might explain it away.

Almost curious.

No. Best to start fresh—to eliminate the threat of the rebels, however slight, and clear away the deadwood of the Imperial military.

"Lord Vader will handle the fleet," Tarkin said. "The plans must not be allowed to leave Scarif, at any cost."

Romodi understood. "Yes, sir," he replied, and began calling orders to his aides.

Tarkin looked to the viewscreen and to Scarif: an ocean-drenched sphere of islands rich with rare metals, useful as a construction outpost and research incubator away from the Senate's prying eyes. But Tarkin would not miss it. Over the years, too many officers had treated it as a place for unofficial retirement; a tropical paradise where they could neglect their duty in comfort. The loss of the Citadel and the planetary shield would be a pity—but no more than that.

"Single reactor ignition," Tarkin said. "You may fire when ready."

Orson Krennic turned his pistol over in his left hand, tracing the ridges of the grip through his glove. He rarely ever drew the weapon— his custom DT-29, maintained with exquisite care over the years— but he had chosen it for the brutal force it delivered in a single shot. It was a killing tool, meant to end a foe at close quarters.

The circumstances in the vault had negated its effectiveness. Even his death troopers had been unable to fell the woman. Her accomplice didn't concern him—the man was a stranger, and a dead one at that—but the woman . . .

She'd *looked* at him.

From her perch among the data cartridges, with wide eyes full of mockery and hatred, she'd *looked* at Krennic. The same woman who had come for him on Eadu; who had, he did not doubt, received Galen Erso's message on Jedha and escaped the destruction of the Holy City. She had recognized him, and he now felt with wrenching certainty that he had seen her long before her infiltration of the research facility.

He could not say when or where. But he knew.

Whoever she was, Galen had selected her to be his vengeance from beyond the grave—turned her into *his* weapon. Krennic wanted to scream at Erso, to rage at the injustice of a dead man placing fresh obstacles in his path. *You were a hypocrite and a coward in life. There is no changing that now!*

But exorcising Galen would require more than words. So Krennic rode the maintenance turbolift to the top of the communications tower, where he might put an end to the man's last act of sabotage.

As it approached the top, the lift shuddered violently and its lights went dim. Krennic nearly dropped his pistol as he set a palm against the wall for balance. The carriage had halted. Once it steadied, he raised a fist to strike the door before thinking better of the choice. He did not know how precarious his situation was.

He activated the control panel comlink and adjusted its settings. "General!" he snapped. "What's going on at the top of the tower?"

He heard multiple voices murmur in swift consultation before one of Ramda's lieutenants finally answered. "Minor damage from the aerial battle, Director. Do you require assistance—?"

"I've already signaled my security team," Krennic growled. He regretted sending so much of his detail to the battlefield, but the deed was done; and he'd chosen not to wait for them outside the data vault. "Get me full power to the lift immediately."

Even if his foe had retrieved the DS-1 technical schematics, she would surely be unable to beam them to a ship in orbit. There was *nothing* she could do. Yet Krennic found little consolation in that thought.

"At once, sir. Also, we haven't received an update from Admiral Gorin—" Krennic snarled and prepared to close the link; before he could, Ramda broke in: "Visual confirmation! The Death Star has entered orbit—the rebel fleet is doomed!"

Heat rose up Krennic's face. *His* Death Star had been commandeered? But if it had come to assist against the rebels, Ramda was right—nothing the Alliance could field could possibly stand against the battle station.

If it had come to assist. An alternative crossed Krennic's brain that he did not wish to contemplate. As the lights flickered on, he severed the link and reactivated the lift. The carriage hummed into motion then quickly jolted to a stop.

He gripped his pistol and squared his shoulders. The Death Star's presence was one more reason to put a halt to Galen's interference.

He stepped out onto the platform to kill the last of the Jedha survivors, and silenced Lyra's inexplicable taunting inside his head:

You'll never win.

Clinging to the ruined catwalk, Jyn stared at the planet killer lodged in the bright sky.

Cassian was dead. K-2SO was gone. Bodhi and Chirrut and Baze might have been alive, but it was hard to imagine anyone surviving the war zone she saw below the tower. No one had called her comlink for a long while. If she wasn't the last of the men and women who'd come from Yavin 4, she suspected she was close to it.

She'd done better than most; it would take the Empire a whole battle station to end her.

With ragged, whimpering breaths, she shimmied up the last stretch of the catwalk. She wrapped her legs tight around metal to steady herself, then raised one gloved hand and slapped the rim of the platform, working sore and half-numb fingers until she located a grip. She mirrored the motion with her other arm and forced torn muscles to pull her weight up, *up* and over the edge, until she was on her knees on steady ground and quivering from the effort.

When she looked at the sky again, the Death Star was still there.

Kill me, you bastard, she thought, *because there's nothing I can do to stop you.*

Maybe her mission to Scarif had been doomed from the start; maybe she'd even known it; but the Death Star made it impossible to pretend.

She had been afraid of losing her way. Afraid that fearing for her allies would distract her. Afraid that losing her allies would regress her to the *survivor* she'd been all her life, ready to abandon everything she'd come to Scarif for. Now surviving wasn't an option and no one was left as a distraction. Her fears had been laughably naïve. Nauseated and racked with pain, she took greedy gulps of air and waited to see what would come.

By the time she felt she could move again, the Death Star still hadn't killed her.

She realized nothing had changed. *Nothing.*

The *thing* that had brought her to Scarif—not her father, not her comrades, not some impulse buried below the cave, but the monstrosity that killed and killed and killed until every little girl and pilgrim and mother in the galaxy was dead—was staring down at her, as real as ever.

Her mission was the same. She just had less time to finish.

She propped herself on one leg and rose to a stand. The platform sputtered with flame where the TIE's cannons had struck, and ashes wafted in dense clouds between Jyn and the control panel. She took a tottering step and lurched to a stop as a silhouette appeared in the smoke.

A man in a cape. The man in white.

Not now. Not now!

The Death Star was, for all its apocalyptic might, a *comprehensible* threat—a machine built by her father to kill planets. The man in white was a nightmare, an impossible creature that had followed her across her life.

She reached for her blaster, but she'd dropped the weapon off the catwalk. It was somewhere in pieces at the base of the tower.

The man in white was alone. He held a pistol in one black-gloved hand and aimed steadily at Jyn's chest. Eyes the same color as the ash that drifted around him fixed on her with a strange mixture of rage and bafflement. Jyn parted her lips, unable to speak, barely able to keep from shaking in terror or fury or both.

"Who *are* you?" he asked.

He had ruined her father and killed her mother and killed Cassian. He had stolen her home and forced her into the arms of Saw Gerrera. He had whittled her with a knife out of a block of flesh. She almost screamed, *How can you ask that?*

But as the words penetrated and the implications heated her skin, she met those wild eyes. His breathing was haggard, and not merely from the smoke.

"*Who are you?*" he repeated. His hand twitched. The blaster barrel jerked up to point at Jyn's collar.

He was *afraid*.

He was not the *Empire*—not every moment of oppression and indignity and torment she had ever suffered. He was an *Imperial*, a petty, spiteful, scared little man who'd forgotten his own atrocities.

And he didn't know her at all.

She decided to make him remember.

"You know who I am," she said, and though her body felt brittle her voice was steady. "I'm Jyn Erso. Daughter of Galen and Lyra."

She couldn't remember ever saying that before, let alone with pride.

The man in white stared. "The child," he finally said.

"The child," Jyn agreed. She tried to shrug; the agony in her shoulders kept her from lifting them.

He straightened his firing arm. She couldn't rush him, couldn't possibly close the distance and disarm him; not in her condition, not without a delay or a distraction. Panic and wild indignation rose inside her at the prospect of *this man*—diminished or not—bringing about her ultimate failure, but she tamped it down. If she could control her fear, she could control his, too.

"You've lost," she told him.

If she could keep him from shooting, her opportunity might come. And if he *was* going to kill her—if she couldn't claw his face or punch him in the gut or put a blaster to his skull; if he stopped her mission, loosed the Death Star on the galaxy—she would damn well make him never forget her again.

"Oh, I have, have I?" the man in white asked, unctuous and cruel. He didn't lower his weapon; he didn't shoot, either.

"My father's revenge," Jyn said. She resisted the urge to sneer. Her voice came out proud and defiant. "He built a flaw in the Death Star. He put a fuse in the middle of your machine and I've just told the entire galaxy how to light it."

The man in white scowled. His head twitched toward the great communications dish.

This is your chance. Go! Go!

But her legs wouldn't move. If she leapt at him now she'd sprawl on the platform utterly defeated.

"The shield is up," the man in white snarled. He was burying his fear, his fear of *her*, beneath patronizing disdain and venom. "Your signal will never reach the rebel base."

Maybe he was right. But he couldn't *know*. "Your shield is—"

He cut her off, enraptured by his own words. "I've lost nothing but time. You, on the other hand, will die with the Rebellion."

He checked his aim. Jyn prepared a desperate lunge; she wouldn't die, *refused* to die holding still. If he caught her in the side, maybe she could stop him, crawl the rest of the way to the control panel and transmit with her last breath . . .

She planned it, fantasized it. Yet when the blast came, she wasn't ready.

She heard the electric echo of the bolt rip the air.

She saw the man in white drop to his knees and fall prone, his expression nothing short of astonished. A black hole was burned in the fabric of his ivory cape.

Like that, her nightmare was over.

Behind the man in white, stepping out of the smoke, came a bloody and limping Cassian Andor. He looked like a man who'd fallen twelve stories and clawed his way back to the top. He looked as beautiful as anyone Jyn had ever known, but she couldn't spare a moment to even shout his name.

Instead she ran. Somehow she ran, thinking through the motion of each leg and certain she would slip on the platform; certain, too, she would scrabble up again and *keep* running. She tried to draw a lungful of air and found her mouth and nostrils raked by burning cinders. She heard a distant rumble, an explosion from a faraway battle, and pushed on. Soon her hands were on the control panel, fumbling as she looked to the screen in incomprehension. She forced herself to slow, to focus.

She pulled the broadcast lever.

She watched the screen flash. She couldn't read it through the haze, but she heard the voice: "Transmitting."

Her breath came in racked, tearless sobs of relief and elation. She had to grip the panel to keep from falling as vertigo stronger than anything she'd suffered in her climbs overtook her. She wanted to shout, but she lacked the strength. She wanted to laugh at the heavens, at the fleet and the Death Star, but she lacked the strength for that, too. Instead she turned to Cassian, who still waited in the smoke.

She stumbled to him, smiling like a child, and did not speak.

CHAPTER 22

"Admiral! Receiving a transmission from Scarif!"

The *Profundity* trembled under the onslaught of TIE fighters. Its shields burst, re-formed, and burst again as emerald volleys struck. Three decks had already been forced to evacuate due to radiation leakage. But the *Profundity* endured where other vessels had been torn apart; in geostationary orbit above the Scarif Citadel, it was the center of a storm of molten metal and rent ships.

The Death Star had not turned its weapons against the rebel fleet, but it carried enough fighter squadrons to swiftly achieve battlefield supremacy. Admiral Raddus was not prone to awe or terror, yet he had not imagined the scale of the horror he faced.

Thus, he knew wonder at the words of his comm officer.

"Confirm!" Raddus snapped, and hid his need as best he could.

"Checking the data," came the reply. "We have the plans!"

"She did it," Raddus hissed. The deck lurched and he caught his balance, barely noticed. He watched his displays and began issuing orders to reconfigure the fleet.

"The battle station, sir," his lieutenant called. "Massive energy buildup—"

Raddus cut his man off with a gesture. Jyn Erso had made the station's power clear on Yavin 4. Stopping it over Scarif was a task for nobler fools than he.

"Rogue One—may the Force be with you," he said. Then he straightened and inhaled a mouthful of humid air. "All ships," he cried, "prepare for jump to hyperspace!"

He made a show of confidence for his people. But he saw the tactical display flicker and register a new vessel entering the system.

A third Star Destroyer had finally arrived.

In a haze of smoke like thunderheads, Orson Krennic searched his memories for a time before he had met Galen Erso.

He thought back to Eadu, to the squeal of wet boots on metal and his attempts to commiserate with the scientist in the early days after Lyra's death; his efforts to soothe Galen regarding the fate of his daughter and to remind him of the magnificence of the work.

He thought back further, to Coruscant, where he'd been inspired to pluck Galen out of obscurity for "Project Celestial Power." He thought to the games he'd been forced to play, knowing Lyra's provincial interests would distract Galen from his focus.

Back still further, to the Futures Program, when he'd drawn Galen into his circle and recognized with wonder—not *jealousy*, but unadulterated *wonder*—the galaxy-changing potential of the man's genius.

And before then?

He could follow Galen Erso's thread through his life. He could see the full extent of the tragedy, the waste of effort on a wasted man. But what about *before*? He sought refuge in his childhood, tried to recall an Orson whose hopes had not yet been cast in shadow . . .

Instead he heard a peal of thunder, and he raised his chin and left his memories and saw that the thunder was the roar of fire atop the Scarif comm tower. His body was full of pain.

He found he could move his limbs if he ignored their weight. He dragged himself forward—for what purpose, he wasn't entirely sure. Survival? The work?

The child!

He gasped thin, whistling gasps as he tried to rise, failed, crawled forward a few more meters. He looked for the child—for Jyn Erso—but she was gone. He raised himself higher, rolled back his eyes until his skull hurt, and recognized the penumbra of the Death Star in the sky.

It was Wilhuff Tarkin who had commandeered his battle station. Tarkin alone would have the arrogance. Tarkin alone would have the *spite* to loom over Scarif and threaten the wellspring of all his own triumphs.

The Death Star's focusing dish glittered with emerald light. Krennic's fury built in key with the station's energies and sought purpose, an outlet, a *target*. But Krennic's body was ruined. His enemies were far from him. He had no one to command and no one to master, no one to sway into sharing his vision for the future or the Empire or his personal aggrandizement.

My father's revenge.

Krennic was doomed, then, though it galled him to admit it. Yet while he might die at Tarkin's hands, he would die in the fires of *his* creation. The Death Star would endure. He licked blood and spittle from his lips and imagined world after world consumed by his station's power. Even the Emperor would not leave such a mark on the galaxy. The Death Star, *his* Death Star, would alter star systems and civilizations, be remembered a thousand generations after Tarkin had been erased from history.

And while Tarkin *did* live? He would know that every victory he eked out would be due to Krennic's work. He would fumble his way through battle after battle, not truly understanding the weapon he wielded, until his arrogance destroyed him.

He built a flaw in the Death Star.

The focusing dish glowed brighter.

Krennic squeezed his eyes shut and used the last glimmerings of his mind to see the station as it was meant to be seen: to stand on the overbridge of his behemoth creation; listen to the reactor's muffled roar turn to a shriek; feel the tremors in the deck plating turn violent as the kyber core exerted its strength. Jyn Erso had given her life to steal the Death Star schematics, but those schematics were etched in his heart.

You'll never win.

He would die not on Scarif, but inside the Death Star.

And as he envisioned the cataclysmic energies building within the vast station, he saw it—a detail he had overlooked and forgotten, some trivial adjustment of Galen's: a single exhaust port leading from a narrow trench down and down, down kilometers of blackness, past conduits and hatches and radiation plating, down and down—

—and into the main reactor.

The primary weapon of the Death Star battle station fired.

Orson Krennic, advanced weapons research director and father of the Death Star, died alone on Scarif, screaming in fury at Galen Erso, at Jyn Erso, at Wilhuff Tarkin, and at all the galaxy.

The last time Cassian had hurt so bad, K-2SO had carried him to a safe house and along the way enumerated his every injury, thoroughly assessed the likelihoods of infection and permanent nerve damage. It had been the droid's way of showing he cared—or at least the droid's way of showing he was invested in his master's fate.

K-2SO hadn't been there for Cassian at the top of the Citadel communications tower. But Jyn had turned to him from the control panel looking like the last survivor of a war, and she'd smiled in a way he'd never seen before. It hadn't been a smile predicated on anticipation or courage, or one touched by sadness or doubt; just a smile so ordinary it seemed to change Jyn from a hero out of myth into a woman he might have known and understood.

He hadn't known her, didn't know her, of course. There wasn't the time.

She'd half stumbled to his side and gingerly wrapped an arm

around him, led him toward the maintenance turbolift. He'd tried not to show the extent of his pain (standing still was bad; moving was worse) but had given up after a moment or two, leaning heavily on her. Somehow she'd carried his weight.

"Do you think," he'd asked, "anybody's listening?"

He hadn't been able to raise an arm, to point skyward after her transmission, but she'd seemed to understand.

"I do," she'd said, soft and—to his ears—earnest. "Someone's out there."

And she'd brought him into the turbolift and supported him as he leaned against the metal wall. He was there now, one arm draped around Jyn, feeling her impossibly frail and human form.

He didn't know whether she was right. Didn't know whether, in fact, someone really *was* out there or if the Empire had seized victory. As he turned the question over in his mind, he was surprised to realize he wasn't worried about the answer.

Maybe it was his injuries. Hurt and exhaustion narrowed his reality, made it difficult to envision anything outside his sight line. When he thought about the people he cared about, the people who would have to carry on the fight against the Empire and the Death Star (the ones who hadn't volunteered to come to Scarif), he could picture no one; and that couldn't be right. Could it?

The more he thought about it, though, the less he believed the fog in his brain explained his lack of worry.

He'd told Jyn: *We've done terrible things on behalf of the Rebellion.* Some he remembered now—Tivik, who'd made all this possible and been rewarded with death—but most, to Cassian's shame, he couldn't bring to mind. He'd bartered his ideals and the lives of others away, one by one, to find a victory that would make it all worthwhile. Yet as he watched the pulsing lights of the turbolift he felt keenly that neither victory nor defeat would change the *terrible things* in his past. Jyn couldn't give him what he'd come for.

That was the crux of it, really.

Because he'd given her what she needed, and he'd done the mission *right,* and he found that was enough.

She believed someone was out there. Maybe it was even true.

He *did* want it to be true. With all his heart, he did.

Her faith carried him with her.

He didn't say any of it. He didn't want to disturb the silence as they rested against each other, hurting and relaxed, listening to the hum of machinery and the distant billowing of fires. He stowed thoughts of old missions and thoughts of the future away; decided to focus on what he could see and hear and smell for the last moments of his life on Scarif.

When Cassian Andor died, he would be ready, and he would be content.

The Citadel had evacuated. Its officers and troops had panicked once they'd realized the Death Star's purpose. Jyn didn't know that for sure, but it would explain why she and Cassian encountered no one on their departure from the tower, heard only distant shouts and the rumble of shuttles. If the shield gate was open, a few Imperials might possibly make it offworld before the end.

She tried her comlink, just to see if anyone answered. No one did, which was as she'd expected.

Even if there were shuttles left, she knew she wouldn't make it to a landing pad in time. Every step was an effort, and Cassian's grip was growing weaker. His strides faltered. She kept propping him up. But he was warm, and his breathing was regular, and it felt good to have *life* close to her. It wasn't at all like cradling Galen, who'd seemed apt to wash away in the rain as he died.

Without anywhere better to go, she led them toward the beach.

There had been beaches on Lah'mu, protected by jagged boulders that had—to a child, at least—seemed like mighty cliffs. She'd sent Stormy on harrowing adventures there, recounted them at night to her mother. Scarif's placid waters and white sands seemed a pale imitation of Lah'mu's grandeur, but they would have to do.

They passed the body of a rebel soldier along the tree line. Jyn positioned herself in Cassian's way so he wouldn't have to see.

When they reached the beach itself, Cassian struggled with his footing in the sand. He dropped to both knees and Jyn crouched beside him. They'd gone far enough, she decided; a breeze was clearing the air of ash and smoke, and they could no longer hear shouting.

For an instant, Jyn looked up, expecting against reason to see the glimmering of the rebel fleet among the stars. But of course she couldn't see anything—the sky was blue and bright, and the only artificial construct in sight was the battle station. In all likelihood, the rebels had already fled, setting course away from Scarif the moment they'd received her transmission.

Instead she looked to Cassian.

"I'm glad you came," she said.

When the words finally touched him, he gently smiled and took her hand. She entwined her fingers with his so that they didn't drop away.

The Death Star was pulsing with emerald light. Jyn tried not to tense. She wasn't afraid of what would happen, but she didn't want to suffer. Somehow she found herself closer to Cassian than before. Her breathing matched his, or his matched hers, deep and steady.

The Death Star flared too bright to watch and a tremor went through the beach. The placid waves rolled higher, spraying flecks of warm seawater over Jyn's cheeks like tears. An unfathomable rumble echoed ten or a thousand kilometers away.

"Your father would be proud of you," Cassian said, so soft Jyn barely heard. She thought it was true, even though it wasn't why she'd come to Scarif—not entirely, not *really.*

It was good to hear aloud, from the lips of someone close.

The rumbling overwhelmed all other sound. Jyn tightened her grip on Cassian, and he found the strength to hold her. The world grew brighter, emerald at first and then a clean, purifying white. In Jyn's mind, the cave below the broken hatch was illuminated with the strength of a sun, and then the walls turned to dust and there was no longer a cave but only her spirit and heart and everything she had ever been: the daughter of Galen and Lyra and Saw, the angry fighter and the shattered prisoner and the champion and the friend.

Soon all those things, too, burned away, and Jyn Erso—finally at peace—became one with the Force.

EPILOGUE

THE IMPERIAL STAR DESTROYER *DEVASTATOR* cut through an ocean of ships and trailed a wake of burning gases and crackling particles. The light of Scarif reflected dully on the vessel's hull as it swung into the planet's gravity well, coursing toward the damaged Mon Calamari cruiser positioned above the Citadel.

Darth Vader observed the chaos surrounding the *Devastator* and reordered it behind the red glow of his mask. He recognized the maneuvers of fighter squadrons on both sides, identified pilots who broke from their formations to better or worse effect. He saw the battle in microcosm and macrocosm, was instinctively *aware* of how each shot could contribute to ultimate victory or defeat.

Yet only the cruiser concerned him. He made a single stroke of his hand as the enemy came into firing range.

The ensuing echoes of turbolasers were garbled static in his helmet. Streams of energy poured from the *Devastator* toward its foe, illuminating the darkness like lightning. Starfighters—friend and foe—caught between the two massive ships suffered instant obliteration. The cruiser's shields shimmered with iridescence then vanished in a flash. Fires flared along its port side as hull plating shattered or melted and venting oxygen combusted.

"The rebel flagship is disabled, my lord," the *Devastator*'s captain reported crisply at Vader's side. Darth Vader did not turn to him as he spoke. "But it has received transmissions from the surface."

Vader stared at the burning ship. There was death at play, suffering and fear, yes—and something entirely different. Something that repelled his withered, agonized flesh.

"Prepare a boarding party," he said.

"Yes, my lord."

The destruction of the Citadel—the lancing of Scarif with the Death Star's superlaser, the evaporation of a sea and the disintegration of archipelagos—sent a tremor through Vader's shuttle as Vader and his squad rode to the flagship. Vader felt fear then, too, vast and powerful and purer than that which emanated from the cruiser. When his vessel reached the flagship and his stormtroopers burned their way through the hull, he started toward the rebel bridge and then pivoted.

Perhaps instinct guided him. Perhaps something more. It did not occur to him to wonder. He sent his troops to continue on his prior path and moved on alone.

The corridor lights flickered while alarms blared. Trapped in the blood-red chamber of his helmet, Vader was troubled by neither. He attuned himself to emanations of panic and desperation and followed their trail. When he encountered rebels reaching for their blasters or dashing to seal blast doors, he drew his weapon and cut them down with unhurried strokes of his crimson blade.

The voice of a stormtrooper spoke to him through his comlink. "A data tape was recorded on the bridge just before we boarded. No sign of it here."

Vader did not answer, but he bolstered his pace.

He wound through the cruiser leaving corpses behind him. He found his prey at last in a corridor thick with rebels backed against a security door. As particle bolts shot toward him, he watched a data tape pass between desperate soldiers. He knocked the bolts aside with his blade, tore a blaster from one foe with a might that defied nature and gravity, and marched on. He delivered killing stroke after killing stroke, awakened and relentless.

The security door opened a mere crack and rebel hands shoved the tape through. Vader reached through life and matter and air and by will alone he *pulled.* He fueled his will with rage and fear and need. It was enough to tear the rebel from the door and drop him at Vader's feet.

But it was not enough to claim the tape.

He grasped the rebel sprawled before him by the throat, lifted him and stared at him through bloody lenses. "Where," Vader demanded, "are they taking it?"

The reply was a strangled whisper. "Away from here," the rebel said. "Away from you."

Vader clenched his gloved hand until the man's neck snapped. Then he tossed the body aside. He activated his comlink and barked to his stormtroopers, *"Find their escape vessel."*

The prospect of failure crept over his skin like fire. The supremacy of the Death Star could not be jeopardized. The total obliteration of the Rebellion remained possible; that it was in question at all was unthinkable.

Darth Vader chased his quarry, seeking solace in the final triumph of the Emperor.

The *Tantive IV* wasn't ready to fly, let alone fight. It had been the subject of frantic repairs during the lightspeed voyage from Yavin to Scarif, secure in the hangar of the *Profundity* where it had lain, stubbornly malingering, since its last mission. Even after its host vessel had arrived in-system and joined the battle against the Imperial armada, Captain Raymus Antilles and his engineers and droids had worked desperately to make the corvette spaceworthy—to seal the leak in its hyperdrive motivator and clean the buildup in its exhaust ports. Admiral Raddus had made the situation clear: Every ship in the fleet had a part to play.

Raymus loved his ship. He'd nearly lost it once. For the Rebel Alliance, he would risk losing it again.

But the battle over Scarif had ended before the *Tantive IV* could join the fray. Just as the corvette's reactor had come to life, the *Profundity* had screamed with punctured metal lungs. The *Tantive IV* had rocked in the hangar bay, nearly dislodging the boarding ramps clamped to its air locks. Instead of ordering it to flee its burning host, Raymus had called for his crew to prepare for takeoff and then departed his own vessel. Under flickering emergency lights, breathing air thick with smoke and poison, Raymus had waved Raddus's crew aboard the corvette, hauled friends and strangers alike to safety.

He'd recognized one of Raddus's technical chiefs—a middle-aged woman who lurched into his arms. Her face was burned, but she pressed a data tape into Raymus's hand and pulled away. "We got what we came for," the woman said. "You need to go. Admiral's orders."

He wanted to argue. Instead, he made sure the burned woman boarded the *Tantive IV*. Then he turned his back on the brave rebels who remained on the *Profundity* and made for the bridge.

The *Tantive IV* wasn't ready to fly, but it *flew*. It emerged from the burning wreck of the cruiser and sped away from Scarif. For a blessed few seconds it moved swiftly, confidently through space. Then the ship rocked again and echoed with thunder and sparks. From his station on the bridge, Raymus could smell circuits melting.

"Star Destroyer closing!" called the officer at the tactical console. Raymus didn't recognize the face—one of Raddus's men.

He erased the fear from his own expression. "Get us into hyperspace," he said. "Make sure you secure the air lock. And prepare the escape pods."

The *Tantive IV* might jump out of the system, but it was hurt and it would be pursued. Best not to take chances.

He saw a figure in white robes near the bridge entrance and turned the tape over in his hand. He approached the woman and said, his tone respectful, "Your Highness. The transmission we received . . ."

The woman looked toward him. He'd seen her face many times before, knew it well. She was *young,* seemed younger every day, even as her responsibilities grew and grew.

He held out his hand. Childlike fingers took the data tape.

"What is it they've sent us?" he asked.

Princess Leia Organa looked at him as if he'd placed another burden on her shoulders—another responsibility to add to a count of thousands—and she was proud to bear it.

"Hope," she said.

Raymus believed her.

SUPPLEMENTAL DATA: IN MEMORIAM

[Document #MS8619 ("Unpublished Reflections on Jyn Erso"), from the personal files of Mon Mothma (via the Hextrophon Collection).]

I regret to say I only met Jyn twice. To claim I knew her well would be an insult to the young woman whose fervor captivated so many. Conversely, to speak only of her effect on our movement—to recount yet again the rallying of the Rebellion and our transformation from a wary coalition into a unified nation—would be both redundant *and* insulting.

So put no stock in my words. I can tell you of those two meetings and what I saw in her—or what, looking back, I *remember* seeing in her, which may be far removed from the truth. You may find more of a weary ex-senator than Jyn Erso in all this.

Jyn was in chains when we met before Operation Fracture. I'd seen her file and chosen her for the mission for reasons I wish I could be proud of. I expected to meet a troubled girl who had been failed by the Alliance in a hundred different ways: failed by Saw, failed by those of us who *knew* Saw, failed when she went out on her own, and failed by our inability to save her father or mother. I expected she could be persuaded (by which I suppose I meant *manipulated*) into helping us, and that in doing so we might help her, too.

But the woman I met at Base One could not be manipulated. There are a very few people whose will and ferocity are so great that they pull other people in their wake. I've known some who cultivated that talent as politicians and generals, for good or ill. Jyn, I think, never knew the effect she had on others—never realized the intensity of her own humanity or the presence she brought to a room. She was, as expected, troubled and quarrelsome; she was also impossible to ignore or forget.

In her short life, she had seen relentless hardship and become hard herself. But her fire shone bright.

If our first meeting was brief, our second was even briefer. We exchanged a handful of private words when she briefed Alliance High Command on the threat of the Death Star, and the woman I met then was far different from the one we'd chained. Was she at peace? I don't believe so. But she held herself with a newfound certainty.

It's become fashionable in some quarters to claim Jyn Erso went to Scarif intending to die a martyr—that she realized she had lost everything and chose her path by its inevitable end. I will dispute this claim until my own dying days. I think Jyn fully recognized who she was and sought a way to channel her best and worst impulses, her darkest moments and her brightest, toward a cause worthy of her true incandescence.

In a kinder universe, she would have walked away from Scarif. I cannot imagine who she would have become, but I think she would have been extraordinary.

I am grateful I knew her, no matter how short the time.

ABOUT THE AUTHOR

ALEXANDER MARSH FREED is the author of *Star Wars: Battlefront: Twilight Company,* as well as many short stories, comic books, and videogames. Born near Philadelphia, he endeavors to bring the city's dour charm with him to his current home of Austin, Texas.